I0737955

Breaking
the
Glass Slipper

Across Time & Space series

The Eternity Stone
Mountain of Glass
Desert of Fire
Desert of Ice
The Hidden Door
Whiter Than Snow

Fairytale Memoirs series
The Mostly Forgotten Memoirs of Rose Red
Viola Sends Her Regrets
Gifted

Standalone books
Breaking the Glass Slipper
Unshakeable
Tyger

For information on new and upcoming books,
go to **mmarinanbooks.com**

Breaking the Glass Slipper

M. Marinan

First published in New Zealand in 2018
by Silversmith Publishing

This is a work of fiction. The names, characters, events and localities, except those in the public domain, are fictitious, and any resemblance to actual persons, living or dead, is purely coincidental.

Text © M. Marinan 2018
Cover art illustrations © M. Marinan 2018
The moral right of the author and illustrator has been asserted

A catalogue record for this book is available from the National Library of New Zealand

ISBN 978-0-473-43501-1

All rights reserved. No part of this publication may be reproduced, stored in a retrieval system, or transmitted, in any form or by any means, electronic, mechanical, photocopying, recording or otherwise, without the prior written permission of the publishers. The only exception is brief quotations for the purpose of printed reviews.

This book is sold subject to the condition that it shall not, by way of trade or otherwise, be lent, re-sold, hired out or otherwise circulated without the publisher's prior consent in any form of binding or cover other than that in which it is published and without similar condition including this condition being imposed on the subsequent purchaser.

For Grandad, who loved to tell stories.

*Inspired by Charles Perrault's Cendrillon,
and the works of Brothers Grimm.*

*Also thanks to Kate, Jen, Grace and
Anne-Marie for your input and support.*

 Contents

Prologue   1
1. Hopeful   3
2. Grumpy   21
3. Sleepy   39
4. Curious   60
5. Audacious   78
6. Contrite   91
7. Perturbed   105
8. Baffled   121
9. Wretched   141
10. Distant   154
11. Startled   170
12. Determined   188
13. Excited   212
14. Weary   233
15. Triumphant   254

Afterword   263
The Eternity Stone   265
excerpt

 # Prologue

**Real News 10 July 2097 AD 'The Sweetheart Saga'
VR/RA interview attempt one (transcript)**

Interviewer: *The Sweetheart Saga. We've all heard of it: intrigue and high-stakes crime in one of the world's most famous luxury resorts. You've followed our series of interviews, and today we're finally visiting the home of the famous – or should I say infamous – Valentina Redwell, who you'd all know to be a central player in the drama. (Taps on doorbell, waits for door scanner. Door opens.)*

Valentina: *Yes? Who are you?*

Interviewer: *Hi Valentina, I'm Ambrose Martin from Real-*

Valentina: *No thank you.*

(Door slams shut. Interviewer looks momentarily stunned.)

Interviewer: *Same to you, (CENSORED). (Turns towards camera) Um…that wasn't live, was it guys?
Pause.*

Interviewer: *(face red) Oh…chestnuts.*

1 Hopeful

'Wow! What a looker!' – From an interview with Ralph K

Real News 2 March 2097 AD
Six-star resort set to reopen amid high expectations

In the shallow waters of picturesque Silver Bay, a six-star resort has undergone a Cinderella-like transformation after fire damage last year.

"Sweetheart Island will be more than just a luxury retreat," the project's co-owner John Carver tells us. "It'll be a one-of-a-kind opportunity to experience your fantasy in the most beautifully designed environment that this hemisphere has to offer."

Now while the reclusive billionaire might be excused for being biased — this project has been underway for the last fifteen years in some shape or form — one can't argue with the cost. It's estimated that twenty billion credits went into the transformation of this sparsely populated island: rebuilding the hotel that closely resembles a castle, and with an entire village of boutique shops and charming cottages to round out the fantasy. But then when one considers the locals…

"A full half of them are AI," Mr Carver tells us proudly, "created just for the set, and programmed to act out various characters as needs require. This is revolutionary technology, and I dare any customers to tell the difference between the AI and the human staff."

But with a week's accommodation costing six months of this journalist's wages, it's safe to say that only the ultra-rich and fanciful will ever face that particular-

…and the text cut off. I tapped at the bottom of the touchscreen inset in the coffee table in front of me, trying to pull more of the article into view, but the screen flickered then changed back to the same drinks menu all the other touchscreens showed.

"Chestnuts," I muttered. "I was enjoying that."

But I'd learned something new, and I studied the gleaming hotel foyer with fresh eyes. A fantasy-themed resort, hmm? Kingsley hadn't mentioned that, and I couldn't see it myself. Everything was…white. White, shining, and beautiful. Not a hint of destruction from the fire that the article had mentioned. I'd have to ask him about it…if he ever got here.

Forgetting the article, I looked up again towards the huge panes of weather-sensitive glass that made up the entryway of the White Hotel. It was late afternoon, the low sun dimming the glass to a soft pink. I could still see all the way from my secluded alcove off the side of the large foyer, right out to where the hotel guests came and went: bright patches of colour in the pristine white surroundings. Staff moved about too, unobtrusive and emotionless in matching white uniforms. No Kingsley.

I reached for my cinnamon latte, found it was cold, then set it back on the table with a grimace. I ordered another through the touchscreen menu, then leaned back into the comfortable couch, tapping my fingers impatiently on my knee. The large ruby on my ring finger perfectly matched the scarlet of my sundress, and at the sight of it a little burst of happiness fluttered through my belly. Engaged – again – but this time would be better than the last. Kingsley was better than the others. *I'd* be better, I vowed. I'd be selfless and charming and flawlessly beautiful as long as age allowed me to be, and he'd not regret a thing.

Just then a message flashed on my silver wristpiece. *Hello, Fairest. I'm sorry I'm late. I can't wait to see you again, but I was held up a little. I have a surprise for you…*

I smiled to myself and reread the message. Didn't he know that all I wanted was his undying affection? But gold – or chocolate

– wouldn't hurt either.

Just then, there was the sound of female laughter from the alcove next to mine. It was separated from me by an ornate white screen that blocked the view, but didn't do a thing for noise. I smiled in response to their happiness: I was happy too, so the whole world should be.

The hushed whispers came through the screen, and then a woman said more loudly, "I know, right? Her dress is *so* trashy! I know this is going to be a themed hotel, but what does she think she's trying to be? An escort droid?"

Ouch. My smile faltered at the thought of whichever poor girl these women were verbally tearing apart. Being compared to a robotic streetwalker was never flattering. I tried to distract myself by checking my lipstick in a small, handheld mirror, but I couldn't block out their conversation.

"She's clearly had work done," a different female voice continued. "No one has a figure like that naturally. And her colouring – hasn't she heard of tanner? Fish belly-white skin went out of fashion centuries ago!"

My own pale reflection frowned back at me from the mirror. Surely they didn't mean me? Sure, I had a nice figure. Nature had been kind to me, and I'd done what I could to keep in shape. Not that it was hard when I was only twenty-one… And not everyone had to be tanned, right?

"Aren't natural blondes supposed to be pale?" a new, male voice cut in, sounding a little defensive. "I don't know what you ladies are talking about. I thought she looked very nice."

"You would!" the first woman retorted, and there was another burst of feminine laughter. This time it sounded distinctly mocking.

"But what I don't get," the second woman said in a low voice, "is why she hasn't had that mole removed. Lord, it must be the size of a pea! Can you imagine seeing that thing staring back at you all day? It makes me shudder!"

This time they were definitely talking about me. I snapped the mirror shut on my horrified reflection, complete with blonde hair, careful makeup, and a small, dark spot beside my nose.

"Beauty mark," I said under my breath, feeling my face heat with embarrassment. "Not mole." And it was flat, too; not at all pea-like. Kingsley had called it distinctive. *He* clearly didn't mind it.

"Your cinnamon latte, Miss Redwell?"

I jumped a little, feeling as though I'd been caught eavesdropping. A blandly handsome server stood before me, dressed in the hotel's compulsory white, and holding a tray with a tall, steaming silver glass. He smiled at me pleasantly.

Oh, it was only an android server, and it wouldn't judge me for eavesdropping, or for having a mole. AI didn't do anything that it wasn't programmed to. I sighed, scrubbing a hand over my flushed cheeks. "On the table, thanks."

BOOM.

Just as the server set the drink in front of me, a loud, sudden noise sounded from outside the hotel. It reminded me of an explosion from a movie, or perhaps a gunshot, and I gasped, throwing a hand to my chest then rising to my feet. I could hear a burst of startled chatter from the next alcove too, and I looked around anxiously. I couldn't *see* anything wrong, not even through those big glass walls.

But the server continued as though nothing had happened, removing my old, cold drink and then moving as if to leave, and I set my arm on its sleeve. It looked back at me with polite curiosity – all programmed, of course. Being entirely robotic, androids were never curious about anything. Apparently not even suspicious explosions.

"What was that?" I asked it quietly, hearing the urgency in my tone. "That noise."

"What noise, Miss Redwell?"

"That loud booming noise," I snapped, a little agitated. "Don't tell me I imagined it. Check your communications. Is there any kind of danger?"

The server just stared at me; its perfectly-shaped blue eyes unblinking.

The silence stretched on long enough that I was tempted to panic. Then I realised the issue. Privacy breach – perhaps it thought it couldn't tell me, since I was a guest. "You know I'm Valentina Redwell," I told it impatiently. "I'm going to marry the hotel's owner, Kingsley White, in two days. You should know that already too. Soon enough I'll co-own everything, so you *can* answer my question."

There was a brief silence where the server must have been checking back with the main intelligence hub, then it replied, "There is no danger, Miss Redwell. The sound was just a car backfiring."

I frowned. "What's that?"

There was another silence, and I sighed. It didn't matter what 'backfiring' was, because clearly there was no danger or the server would have said. That was the thing about AI – it couldn't lie. It couldn't pass for human either, I thought with some humour, even if it could be more flawlessly gorgeous than even the most beautiful human (and without moles, too). The android servers that kept the White Hotel running were a perfect example. They'd smile and say the right things (as long as the question wasn't too hard), but they didn't eat, and they didn't drink. They also had no sense of humour, nor of subtlety.

"Never mind," I said finally. "But it's actually Mrs Redwell. I'm a widow."

"Yes, Mrs Redwell."

I sighed. Even coming from an android's mouth, completely with unmoving tongue, that name sounded wrong. "Strike that. Call me Ms, will you? Mrs makes me feel like someone's mother, and I'm way too young for that. Besides, I hate people asking about my first marriage, it's embarrassing. Not that it's any of their business…"

I petered into silence, realising I was babbling to what was essentially a toaster. It was those stupid people in the next alcove, I decided, who had shaken my confidence. "You're not even alive," I told the android with some humour. "You may as well call me 'Your Supreme Highness'. It won't make a difference to you either way."

"Yes, Your Supreme Highness."

I snickered to myself, now feeling a little better. I was so easily amused. "Thank you. You can go."

"Yes, Your Supreme Highness."

The server left, and I sipped slowly at my latte, trying to regain my sense of composure. The volume had dropped in the next alcove; perhaps the guests had overheard my conversation and realised that if they could hear me, then vice versa. And Kingsley was still late…

I looked up again towards the front of the hotel, and saw through its glass panels a familiar vehicle pulling up at the entrance. It was a white limousine, and that could only belong to one person.

My heart skipped in joy and anxiety, and I quickly pulled out the hand mirror again from my small purse. Teeth check: all clear. Hair: good enough. Mole…still there.

"Chestnuts to that," I muttered under my breath, replacing the mirror in the purse. "It's a beauty mark." But in my excitement I fumbled and dropped the thing on the floor. I bent down to pick it up, and spotted something odd stuck underneath the table top. It was the size of an old coin, round and metallic grey, but it was otherwise completely plain. I tapped at it curiously, and it came off into my palm, like it had been waiting there for someone to collect.

I scolded myself for being fanciful and tried to stick the thing back under the table top. But whatever had held it there was gone, and it just fell back into my hand. Finally I stuffed it into my purse along with the mirror, then promptly forgot about it. I had more important things to think about – Kingsley was here!

Deep breath. Here we go…

I rose to my feet and strolled towards the entryway, ignoring what felt like burning stares from the neighbouring alcove. I returned the possibly-android doorman's polite nod, then stepped out into the sunlight.

Well, tried to step. I stumbled on my high heels, falling forward and almost smacking my face on the marble bannister leading from the doorway. But I caught myself at the last moment, my hand on the pillar, and my nose an inch away from being bloodied on the white rock. Awkward, but at least the blood would have matched my dress.

I took a moment to check if anyone had noticed, but didn't see anyone pointing and laughing. "We'll call that a win," I told myself, straightening my shoulders. "Be graceful, Valentina." Or if I couldn't manage that, at least I could be careful.

Up ahead the limousine had parked outside the carved marble steps at the front of the hotel. White-clad servers were moving to empty it of its baggage, and the vehicle's occupant stood on the tiled footpath. He was tall and strong and handsome, the sun gilding his greying dark hair as he bent down in conversation with some brightly-dressed shrimp of a village girl. But with the harshness of the late afternoon light, he looked nearly old enough to be her father…and mine.

Had he looked that old the last time I'd seen him? I found myself wrinkling my nose, and carefully made my face relax back into a welcoming smile as I moved down the long flight of polished steps. He *was* thirty-six, I reminded myself. Or was it thirty-eight? But then even Prince Charming had to age sometime.

Aside from the sizeable age gap, he was perfect. Kind, generous, adoring, rich…very rich. Best of all, he had no baggage. One long-dead wife, no children. I crossed my fingers. Third time lucky.

I paused at the bottom of the stairs, trying to look both genuinely happy and flawless (no easy task, even having practised it in the mirror!) and waited for him to notice me. But five seconds ticked by, then ten. My eye started to twitch from the strain of holding the expression…and he still hadn't looked up from his conversation with that same girl.

I dropped the smile, studying her with irritation. Her conversation must be scintillating, because she wasn't much to look at. Small and thin, with skin powdered chalky white, ink black hair, and heavy eye makeup that made her light blue eyes look washed out. I would have mistaken her for one of those retro goth girls if not for the cheerful yellow sundress and fire engine-red lipstick.

Damn. Except for the fact that my dress was red rather than yellow, we were dressed almost identically.

I took a step closer, a mere arm's length away from the two, and coughed gently, now feeling a little foolish.

Kingsley didn't budge, but the not-goth girl saw me. "Oh Daddy," she said in a breathy, high voice. "I think someone's trying to get your attention."

Daddy. I instinctively recoiled at both her tone and her use of the word. I hadn't known my own father, but I hated it when girls called a man 'Daddy' unless he was actually their parent. The strongly negative emotion startled me. I really wasn't myself today, I mused, since I was usually a calm, difficult-to-upset sort of person. Being upset was…upsetting. I'd have to try harder to control myself. Besides, in a minute the girl would be gone. Problem solved.

My fiancé finally turned to face me, his handsome face creasing into an expression of delight. "Fairest!" he exclaimed. "Look at you all in red, like a rose in snow. How beautiful you are." He leaned in to kiss me and I let him, feeling much more cheerful than I had a second earlier. This affection, this adoration, was why I was trying again. How could things go wrong with a sweetheart like this?

"Of course I'm beautiful," I told him dryly, pleased he'd noticed the contrast of my red gown against the white surroundings of the hotel. I'd chosen the dress carefully, wanting to make the best impression possible after our three week separation. "That's why you're marrying me."

Kingsley laughed as though it was a joke. "Silly Fairest. I'm marrying you because I love you, and I can't live without you."

Love, infatuation; did it really matter? Either way, we'd make it work. He linked his arm through mine, although made no move towards the hotel.

"Fairest?" the girl chirped in her too-high voice, looking from me to Kingsley, then back again. A lock of her ink-black hair fell into her eye, and she tucked it behind one ear with a thin white hand. "That's an interesting name. Why are *you* marrying Kingsley White, Fairest?"

I felt my eye twitch again. I decided in that moment that if the girl was working at the hotel, she'd have to stay far, far away from me. "I'm sorry, we haven't been introduced," I told her politely, "and that's a rather personal question for a stranger to ask."

The girl's mouth curved into a slight smile. "A stranger, is it?"

"Yes," I dragged out. "That's when you don't know someone, so you act more carefully around them. You don't ask intrusive questions, for a start."

Tired of the conversation, I turned back to Kingsley, only to see him break into a rumble of laughter. The girl joined in; hers chiming and as high-pitched as her voice.

"That's funny," she said, moving to rest her hand on Kingsley's other arm. "Daddy, you didn't tell me how funny she was."

He just stood there, smiling in his usual, good-natured way, and didn't say a word. I tightened my hand where it rested on his arm, my knuckles showing white through my already pale skin. A spiral of dread was moving through me. He hadn't corrected her... He hadn't told her to use his real name. "Who is this person, Kingsley?"

He stepped away from the two of us, holding both our arms and turning us so the girl and I faced each other. She looked up at me and her small mouth curved into a smile that didn't reach those pale eyes. It was like she knew the punchline to a joke that I hadn't realised was being told.

But on Kingsley's face I saw what looked like genuine affection as he looked first at me, then fixed his gaze on the girl's smug little face. "Fairest, I'm so happy to finally introduce you to my daughter Snow."

My daughter Snow. I froze, those three words echoing over and over in my head but still not making sense. My hand fell loose in Kingsley's grip.

He didn't seem to notice, continuing, "I said I had a surprise, and here it is! I know that once you spend some time together, you'll love each other just as I love both of you." He beamed. "Snow, say hello to your new stepmother Valentina."

No. *No!* I couldn't move, and I could only stare in shock and horror at this person who should never have existed. This was *not* a good surprise. It felt like opening a jewellery box to find it full of spiders instead.

But the horrible, unwanted, slightly-gothic little parasite clearly didn't feel the same way. Her painted face broke into a wide smile, revealing the smudged lipstick on her small white teeth. "Val!" she crowed, throwing her arms around my waist in a tight hug. "We're going to be best friends!"

Blurgh.

I threw up my cinnamon latte all over the back of her cheerful yellow sundress.

Thirty seconds later I was striding high speed towards the bathroom in the hall off the hotel foyer, my hand over my mouth to prevent a repeat incident. I felt more than just sick: I felt betrayed. How could this have happened? How could Kingsley have a *daughter*, and a grown one at that? Even a cubic zirconia would have been better than this!

"Fairest!" I heard him call from behind me, but I ignored him, moving through the nearest door and slamming a hand against the lock mechanism. The door smoothly slid shut behind me, and I headed straight for the toilet, giving up the rest of the latte and what sparse lunch I'd managed to get down earlier. I waited a few seconds after my stomach emptied, eyes closed and breath ragged, until the nausea receded. As it did, the memory of what had just happened flooded in. Snow-freaking-White's arms around my waist; my cinnamon latte second-hand on the back of her sundress. Had I really done that, and in *public*? How mortifying.

And what kind of name was Snow White? She sounded like a villain from one of those old children's stories I hated so much. A princess, perhaps, with a heart cold as ice. Maybe that explained Sweetheart Island's new, unnecessary fantasy theme. Maybe Kingsley was just buying in to please his not-so-little girl.

Suddenly angry, I stomped over to the nearby sink. I rinsed out my mouth with cold water until it didn't taste so disgusting, then rested my hands against the sink's smooth resin edges and stared into the mirror. I didn't *look* like I'd been sick. My blonde hair fell in flawless waves around my shoulders, my skin was perfect except for a spot of pink in the centre of each cheek, and my reflection's apple-green eyes stared back at me, wide and perhaps a little wounded.

There was a knock at the bathroom door. "Fairest?" Kingsley called through, his tone hesitant. "May I come in?"

My reflection's expression changed from wounded to angry in an instant, and I turned for the door, tapping the lock mechanism again. The door slid open and there he was in the secluded hall, his expression anxious. "Are you ill? Can I get you anything?"

"What you can get me," I snapped, "is an explanation for why you sprung this…this *person* on me without a word of warning! Why didn't you tell me about her, Kingsley? You said you were a childless widower!"

He blinked once, twice as if bewildered. "But…I thought you'd be happy. You're nearly the same age, and she needs someone to look up to…"

"I could care less about what she needs! And I am *not* happy! I'm very, very unhappy! This was not-" I choked a little, feeling the back of my throat burn. I wouldn't cry. I wouldn't bear that humiliation on top of everything else. "This is not a good surprise!" I finished in a hoarse whisper.

Kingsley's hands were outstretched towards me, his expression still bewildered. "I'm sorry to have upset you, Fairest, but I'm sure I never said I was childless. I had her when I was twenty – I've been a father for practically my whole adult life!"

"You certainly never said you had a child, either! I would have remembered! I would have-" I paused, considering my next words. Would I have refused to marry him, fearing a repeat of the Walter Green fiasco? I didn't know. All I knew was that my dream of a perfect marriage had just been flushed down the toilet along with the remnants of that latte. "I might have answered differently when you asked me to marry you."

His face fell. "But why?"

My lips tightened, and I saw over his suited shoulder a brown-haired young man in some kind of Arabian costume, staring at the two of us with wide eyes. I glared at him until he hastily vanished from sight, then lowered my voice to reply. "Children don't like me, Kingsley."

"Snow's not a child. She's practically a woman, or so she assures me." He said it with a hopeful, jovial tone as though I'd laugh and forget all my anger.

I didn't. And while I hated the way I'd reacted, I couldn't just make the feeling go away. *Calm, Valentina.* "Most women don't like me either, and Snow won't be any different," I said flatly. "You said it yourself, she's only a few years younger than me! I can't be her stepmother. I don't *want* to be a stepmother."

"Then be more of a stepsister," he suggested.

I raised an eyebrow. "What, and braid each other's hair? I'm marrying you, Kingsley, and it would be…creepy to treat her as a sister." I didn't want to even see her again, and my intense, sudden reaction seemed to twist my insides. How could my moods change so fast? "Besides, after my last relationship…I don't want to go through that again." The feeling of being out of place, the constant battle for affections. The change from excited expectation to resentment and then hatred – on both sides.

Kingsley blinked again, then his dark eyebrows furrowed into a concerned bow. "You won't. It won't. Snow is a darling, and I *know* you'll love her as I do if you give her a chance. And how can she fail to love you when you're so very lovable?" He reached for my hand and I let him take it, softened a little by those last few words. "I see now that we should have talked about this, and I'm sorry I didn't tell you. But won't you forgive me, Fairest?" He pulled me towards him, resting his hands on my waist. "Come, let's get something to eat, and we'll talk this through."

I sighed, resisting the urge to pull away from him, then finally nodded. The initial shock was fading, and while I was still deeply unhappy about his 'surprise', I could see how this would play out. It wasn't like I could get him to disown the girl, so I'd have to work with him. "Let's go to the ground floor restaurant," I said, forcing my tone to be cheerful. *Make it work, Valentina.* "I've ordered something special, and this surprise I know you'll like."

He let out a short laugh, good humour restored. "A fancy meal, is it? Right-o, Fairest. Let's go, shall we? I've told Snow to meet us there."

Chestnuts. "Sorry, I've only ordered enough for two," I told him. "And it really is a *romantic* meal. Can't she eat separately?"

Kingsley laughed again – a sound that was beginning to annoy me – and squeezed my hand with his much warmer one. "Why would she do that?"

"Because children should be seen and not heard?"

Now he guffawed. "Good joke, Fairest. I'll have to tell her that one."

My lips tightened, but I didn't speak again.

As we came out from the hall into the foyer I saw that same young man in costume sitting on one of the plush couches nearby, partially hidden by a white latticed screen. He stared at the two of us as we walked by, his eyes wide and mouth a little open. No, that wasn't right. He was staring at *me.*

Perhaps earlier he'd been admiring rather than eavesdropping, I realised. Women might criticize my colouring or my, ahem, *beauty mark*, but men tended not to be so fussy. But I didn't want to encourage that kind of behaviour, so I lifted my chin and walked on towards the restaurant as if he didn't exist. It was a shame I couldn't do the same about Snow White.

As we walked, something caught my eye through one of the large glass windows. It displayed a view of the left side of the hotel, complete with fantastical white turrets. And at the top of one of those turrets, out of a tiny window very high in the air, was what looked like a long rope. It was golden brown and moved slightly in the wind, and it almost looked like…well, a plait of hair. But who would have hair that long? "Do you see that, Kingsley?"

"What's that, Fairest?" He looked at me with what seemed like amiable disinterest.

I turned back towards the window, but the rope-plait was gone. "Oh. Never mind."

"Righto."

Nope, definitely disinterested. I pushed aside the prick of annoyance at his lack of curiosity, then focused on something much more important as we entered the restaurant. "I really don't think we can extend this meal for three," I told him again. "Perhaps we could have starters with…um, Snow, and then just the two of us could have that dinner?"

"Oh, it won't be any trouble for us to make it stretch," Kingsley replied heartily, lifting his free hand in a brief wave to the approaching server. "Three for dinner, lad, and make it quick. This girl's got an empty stomach."

I frowned. Yes, I'd just been sick, but it didn't mean I wanted to eat right away. "I'm not hungry, darling. Perhaps we could wait?"

He smiled at me, patting my hand as if oblivious to my mood. "Just starters for you, then? Snow and I will have that meal. What have you ordered?"

"Gold-dusted Kobe beef heart with white truffle and Matsutake mushroom compote," the server answered for me, extending a hand to lead us towards our table. "A side of caviar-encrusted salade de florette, and to finish, saffron-apple tart with pearlized crème Anglaise."

I'd chosen the most expensive dishes on the menu, knowing that a man like Kingsley was used to the best of everything, even though I wasn't sure what half that stuff even was. I gave him a tight smile, and he beamed back. "That sounds delicious, Fairest. Are you sure you don't want to eat yet?"

"I do want to eat," I began, but just then we reached our outdoor table. It was as beautiful and secluded as I'd requested, the rose-covered trellis that extended all the way around this side of the hotel separating it from the main dining area. An elaborate, crystalline candelabra sat in the centre of the table, and two servers stood nearby; one with wine ready to pour, and the other with a cart layered with silver domes. It was perfect, except for the black-haired girl sitting at that table.

She'd managed to change her dress in the last few minutes, I noted, and her pale face creased into a smile as we approached. "Daddy! Val!"

Strike that. I'd be lucky if I didn't throw up all over her again. "No," I said to Kingsley, and my voice sounded hoarse to my own ears. "I don't think I could eat a bite."

"This apple tart is delish," Snow said some time later through a mouthful of orangeish pastry. "And it's so sweet the way it's shaped like a heart. I love hearts, and I love apples. Don't you love apples, Val?"

I cringed, resting my forehead on my clenched fist, my elbow propped on the empty table in front of me. Yes, it was heart-shaped because it was meant to be a *romantic dinner for two.* TWO. "As I said the last six times, I prefer to be called Valentina. And no, I can't say I love apples. They're a rather ordinary fruit, in my opinion, although perhaps the saffron improves them."

She swallowed, then took another bite and carried on talking just as she had through the entire meal. "Shame you weren't up to eating, Val. I think you might have liked this."

Oh, *help.* Would it be justifiable homicide if I smothered her in that plate of pearlized crème Anglaise?

Probably not. *Be nice, Valentina.* "Mm."

Maybe I could just wear earplugs whenever she was in the house, I fantasized. Maybe I could just lace her food with laxative, so she couldn't leave the bathroom. Maybe I could arrange for her to go on an extended holiday…

My almost-stepdaughter/sister *Snow White*, I thought with an unwanted pang of dislike, and suddenly something clicked in my head. I knew that name, but I could swear I'd never heard of this girl before today. "Snow White," I mused aloud. "That's familiar. Are you named after someone famous?"

She looked up at me, her eyes wide. "Er…yes, I am. A

princess, actually."

I frowned. That didn't seem quite right. "Really?"

"Of course. Snow White, the fairytale princess. You must've heard of her."

Fairytale…? Oh, she meant fictional, I realised a moment later, and barely stopped myself from rolling my eyes. "Maybe. I'm not fond of children's stories." I hadn't read one in many years, but from the little I remembered, I'd found them trite and irritating.

Snow laughed as if I'd made a joke, swatting her rolled-up napkin at my arm in what she likely thought was a playful fashion. "Well, *Father* loves fairytales. Didn't you know that? That's why he and Mother named me Snow White. It's almost as if they knew I'd be so pale!"

"Ha ha," I said dutifully, kindly not mentioning her heavy use of chalky foundation. I glanced at Kingsley, but he was still focused on his own heart-shaped saffron-apple tart, unheeding that his daughter was one bad joke away from a pie in the face. I had guessed right – no one was called Snow White. No one except this girl here, and some storybook character. "And I didn't know that, but it would explain the fantasy theme for the resort." No doubt Kingsley had been in full support, and that didn't please me.

But he didn't even look up, although Snow looked shocked for a moment. "Fantasy theme?"

I shrugged, bemused by her reaction. "You know, for the resort. I read an article…" I frowned, trying to remember the exact wording. "Or perhaps I misread it."

Snow was watching me with narrowed eyes, but the expression lasted only a moment before her sugar-sweet countenance was back in place. "Well, you might be right," she said lightly. "Sweetheart Island is so beautiful, it practically is a fantasy location, and who knows what new ideas the owners have come up with while I was away? But as for fairytales – who could dislike a fantasy with a moral, and magic, and a beautiful girl?"

Me. I could dislike them. In fiction, it seemed like the good people rarely suffered. Or if they did, it was just for long enough to be 'rewarded' with a happy ending, never again to struggle or feel pain. Real life was hard enough, without having to compare it to an impossible ideal.

"They're really not my thing," I said dismissively, trying to be polite. "And isn't it getting late for you? You must have had a long day." *Please, please go away, so Kingsley and I can have an actual conversation...*

"Of course not. It's only seven o'clock." She narrowed her eyes at me – possibly the first genuine emotion she'd shown all night. "I'd almost think you were trying to get rid of me, Val."

"It's Valentina, please!" I snapped, suddenly losing my temper again. I turned to Kingsley beseechingly. "Can you please get your daughter to use my real name?"

He looked up blankly from his dessert dish. "Sorry Fairest, what was that?"

"I was just telling how you love fairytales," Snow cut in. "*Val* here didn't know that."

Oh, yes. I caught the emphasis on that word. No one, *no one* could be stupid enough to misunderstand what I'd asked. For all of her smiles, Snow didn't want me anymore than I wanted her. Fair enough. If I had my own way, she'd be shipped off to Antarctica, never to be seen again.

"I'm sure there's a lot I don't know about you," I told him through gritted teeth. "But enough private dinners, and I'm sure we can fix that gap. As for me, I never had any interest in children's stories."

"Ah, yes," Kingsley enthused as if I hadn't even spoken. He, at least, had swallowed his food before speaking. "Fairytales. Tell us the story of Snow White, Snow. It's my favourite."

Seriously!? I let out a sharp breath from my nostrils, but Kingsley turned back to his dessert, oblivious to my distress.

Snow smirked at me. *She'd* noticed. "Great! So it goes like this. Once upon a time there was a beautiful princess called Snow White. She was called that because of her white skin and black hair-"

I abruptly pushed away my chair from the table, rising to my feet. Both Whites turned to look at me in surprise. "Excuse me," I bit out. "I find I'm rather unwell after all."

Kingsley finally showed some concern. "Shall I get someone to walk you to your cottage?"

"You're not going to go with me?" I'd requested an isolated room at the edge of the hotel grounds rather than in the main building, and it was barely a two minute stroll from where we stood.

He looked down at his dessert, then back up at me. "Oh. Would you like me to?"

"Not anymore," I snapped, feeling the back of my eyes burn with unshed tears. "Goodnight."

2 Grumpy

'I figured she was just naturally bad-tempered. What else could it be?' — From an interview with Jessie C

Without waiting for Kingsley's response, I turned and strode away, out of the restaurant and down the mosaiced paths that led around the edge of the hotel. Then through the maze of climbing roses, and down the short path that led to my secluded little cottage. The sun had gone down and it was a clouded night, the sort that would be pitch black except for the hanging lights dotted around the hotel and cottage. My little cottage, which was painted clean white and accented with climbing white roses in the day, now looked grey and foreboding. I paused near the front door, turning back to look at the hotel itself for a moment. From this distance it looked like the castle it was advertised as, with its towers and crenellations lit up from hundreds of glowing globes.

Bloody children's stories. Bloody Snow White. Bloody *Kingsley,* I thought furiously, turning away and stomping the last few steps to the cottage doorway. I slapped a hand onto the lock-pad, then again when I didn't hear the distinctive 'click' of the lock disengaging. Stupid bloody *lock.* Didn't anything work in this place?

Just then the front door slid open, and I saw the light was already on inside. Had I left it that way? But then I heard sounds from inside the cottage, just out of my sight. Hushed whispers, a man's low laugh…

I froze in place, horrified as I realised I might have gone to the wrong cottage. There were seven of them, after all. But then I double-checked the brass name plate over the door, and it still read 'Fairest' just as I'd specially requested when I'd arrived three days earlier. The plate had originally read 'Grumpy' – whatever *that* meant – and none of the other cottage names were any more appealing.

This was my cottage, and there was someone inside.

I paused, debating what to do, then pressed the small red bead on my silver bracelet that linked directly to my personal assistant, Jorge. A mere moment later I heard his gravelly voice in my earpiece. "Yes, Your Supreme Highness?"

I froze. "What?"

"I understand you wish to be referred to as Your-"

"This isn't the time for jokes, Jorge!" I cut in urgently, realising he must have heard it from the androids somehow. Strange, because he didn't usually have a sense of humour. "Call me Ms Redwell, like normal. Please, I need your assistance immediately at my cottage. Be discreet."

"Always, Ms Redwell."

The call ended, and I carefully picked up the metal sculpture adorning the side of the entryway. It was supposed to look like an old-fashioned umbrella in a stand, and when I'd first arrived here the hotel's servers had proudly told me it was solid copper, plated with platinum. Now I held it I strongly doubted that it was more than a hollow shell, but even so its slight weight was comforting.

I stepped inside the cottage, lifting my chin in preparation of what might be in there. Robbers…vandals…someone with really, really bad sense of direction …

No. None of the above. What I saw was a red-trousered backside sticking out through the inner doorway that led to the main part of the cottage. I studied it for a moment, noting that it was both male and well-built, and also unfamiliar. I.e. no matter how nicely built, this backside didn't belong in my cottage. A moment later whoever-it-was straightened up, showing a white-shirted back and a head of black hair. He seemed to be carrying something. "Watch it!" I heard him say to someone out of sight inside the cottage. "If you knock anything over, I'm not cleaning it up."

I quietly lifted the metal umbrella, pressing its tip against the man's lower back. "Hold it right there!" I ordered.

The man froze, then he turned his head awkwardly to see me. He was young, I noted, and had a neatly trimmed black beard. "Who's that?"

"The person who's staying in this cottage, that's who," I snapped back. "Who are *you*?"

"Is she here?" I heard another male voice say from inside the room. "Is it her?"

The dark-haired man rolled his eyes, then he stepped away from me, into the room, and dropped whatever he was holding. It looked like one end of a rolled-up carpet. "Yes, it's her. Have a look for yourself."

Feeling less threatened now, I stepped forward so I could see inside the room. Holding the other end of the same carpet was a boy – or a young man, really. He was about my age, and wore the same white shirt and red trousers as the other man, but his outfit was topped with a black vest. He had deeply tanned skin and dark brown hair tied at the back of his neck, and he was staring at me with his mouth open. Again.

I put the sculpture down next to the doorway, then set my hands on my hips. This didn't feel like a burglary anymore, although I didn't know what else it was supposed to be. "What exactly are you two doing?"

"Delivering your carpet," the bearded man said, just as – *thunk*. The brown-haired boy dropped his end of the carpet. It hit the edge of a small coffee table, flipping it sideways and sending its contents spinning across the room to smash against the nearby wall. Glass and red wine went spraying everywhere, soaking into the white carpet, and for a few moments we all just stared at each other.

"I am so, so sorry," the boy began to say, but I'd realised what had been broken.

"No no no no no no!" I cried, rushing over to the scene of destruction. My heels crunched on the broken glass but I ignored it, crouching to gently pick up a large piece of the bottle. The label was wine-soaked and dull with age, but still readable. *Chateau de la Reine-Rouge.*

The one and only.

"Oh, noooo," I breathed. This, on top of everything else today? I rocked back on my heels, lifting a fist to my mouth as tears pricked my eyes. The one thing they could have broken here today, and it had to be the one thing that was irreplaceable.

"It's OK," the boy was saying softly. He'd come to crouch beside me. "We'll get the servers to clean it up, just as good as new. We'll get you some new wine, or even a new cottage if you want one…"

I shook my head dully. "There's nothing you can do."

"What is it, a red? If it's a valuable one, then our insurance can cover it-"

I turned to him sharply. He was leaning in too close, and while I could only see concern on his face, it just made me angry now. "Who are you again?"

"Um…" The boy moved back, his expression sheepish. "We're from Ali's Exotic Jars 'n Carpets, down in the village. We were supposed to deliver the carpet while you were at dinner. It was a gift from Mr White."

A gift from Kingsley. What a nice thought, and how horribly it had backfired.

I waited, and he added, "I'm Caleb. That's Jafeer, behind you."

Jafeer was leaning against the wall, his arms folded in front of his chest. He was rather good looking in spite of the beard, I noted, but his customer service skills were terrible. He smirked at me, and my eyes narrowed.

"As you see," I said evenly, "I came back early from my dinner. And if your insurance covers the ninety thousand credits that bottle cost, that's very nice for you-"

"Ninety k," Jafeer cut in with an impressed whistle. "What is it, liquid gold?"

"…but it won't fix the real problem," I continued, ignoring him. "That bottle was Chateau de la Reine-Rouge, and it was bottled in 1996. It was the only one left in the world. More importantly, it's all I have left of my late husband." I paused, and we all looked down at the widening patch of red. "All I had left."

I'd sold off all the other bottles when James had died, both to pay his debts and to support myself. But I'd kept this one. He'd been so very proud of it...

I stood abruptly. Caleb stood with me, but I lifted a hand, palm outwards, keeping his concern at a distance. "I'm going out," I said brusquely, even as I turned towards the door. "Call the servers to clean this up, or don't. I don't care. I don't expect to see any of you again."

"But the wine," Caleb was saying.

It wasn't fixable, and I felt like crying. I just shook my head, and as I left the cottage I heard Jafeer say, "Nice one, *Caleb*," but then I was out of earshot.

Stupid boys. Stupid *me*. Had I really left that bottle on the coffee table? It didn't matter, because now it was gone.

Just outside the cottage I almost bumped into a familiar figure. A grizzled ex-redhead in his early sixties, Jorge was wearing his standard subdued black and had blended into the background as usual. I tended not to notice him until I needed him. "Oh. Jorge. I called you, didn't I?"

"Yes, Ms Redwell. How can I help?"

I paused, turning to look back at the still open cottage door. Through it I could hear the sounds of conversation, or perhaps an argument. The two delivery guys didn't seem to like each other much. Then I thought of the shattered wine bottle, and my eyes burned. I tightened my lips. "Apparently I have a new carpet. Please find somewhere nice for it. Please also place an insurance claim for a 1996 bottle of Chateau de la Reine-Rouge, and see that the stained area in the living room is covered or replaced within the hour."

True to character, Jorge barely flinched. He, out of everyone in the world, knew what that bottle had meant to me. I watched his face, waited for some kind of sympathy or condolence or *anything,* but he simply nodded. "Yes, Ms Redwell."

I sighed, suddenly feeling weary. I'd known Jorge for over two years, longer than anyone else currently in my life. I trusted him more than anyone else too. But we weren't friends, because our conversations consisted of me giving orders, him agreeing to carry them out. (Except for that one, odd joke earlier.) And if we weren't friends, then I didn't *have* any friends.

"That'll be all, Jorge."

He nodded politely and headed for the cottage door. I went in the opposite direction, heading up the low hill behind the hotel. The path disappeared, and I wound my way through the forest of scattered pines, panting slightly from the exertion and silently cursing my choice of footwear. Four-inch heels were perfect for sitting at dinner; but here they sank into the dirt with every step.

Finally I reached the summit and sat down in the grass. In this darkness I could just make out the shape of what might be a greenhouse just down the hill, although it appeared to have a tower of sorts attached to it. Past that were the lights of the White Hotel, unmissable as always, then a winding road down to Sweetheart Village, marked by the same glowing globes that characterised the hotel. It was pretty, and when I'd arrived here three days earlier to start planning my wedding I'd had great hopes for this place. I'd imagined my position as Kingsley's wife; adored and admired by him and by everyone around me; safe and comfortable and *happy.*

Snow had stuck a pin in that dream-bubble, and as for Kingsley? His behaviour today had been so, so disappointing. He hadn't warned me about Snow, and he hadn't even noticed how upset I was. It didn't bode well for our future.

That last thought upset me even more. I hadn't been myself today. I'd been so moody, swinging from normal to fury to tears within moments. I was *never* like that. I was calm, and I didn't get angry easily, no matter what the challenges. Oh, and there'd been challenges, alright.

It's Snow's fault, I thought suddenly. *If she hadn't been here, the day would have been perfect.*

A moment later I let out a snort of disbelief. Where had that idea come from? "Don't be stupid, Valentina," I scolded myself. "It was a bad day from before that car backfired." Whatever 'backfiring' was. I made a mental note to ask Jorge.

I slipped my shoes off and tucked myself into a ball, wrapping my arms around my bent legs and resting my chin on my knees. The lights of the town didn't change, but a tiny yellow light flickered to my left, offshore. Once, twice, then sporadically over the next few minutes. A boat, I figured, or some idiot who'd left a contact device on Sweetheart Island's uninhabited sibling, Little Sweetheart. More fool them.

Several minutes went by, and I found my mind wandering. Back to the wine, and back to Caleb's face. He seemed so familiar for some reason. Not his colouring, but maybe his features? But then he had regular features, so probably looked like a thousand other blandly handsome youths. He'd never be mistaken for AI, though. He had enough tiny imperfections to make it clear he was human, and besides, he was far too animated.

But what was with those *outfits…*?

I remembered a moment later that the whole island was probably being reinvented in some kind of fantasy theme, and that Ali's Jars 'n Carpets would fit right in. Clumsy Caleb was almost certainly a character actor, just like the kind those nasty women had discussed earlier today. I hoped he didn't lose his job because of the accident with the wine. Really, it had been just as much that Jafeer's fault, because he'd dropped his end of the carpet first. But then I had sneaked in and given them a fright…

Chestnuts, my head was just buzzing today, I mused. My thoughts were so chaotic I could almost hear them aloud.

Right then I realised that I *could* hear something, and it wasn't my thoughts. It was the faint sound of voices, and it seemed to be coming from my purse. Curious, I tipped it out into my lap. A few seconds later I'd narrowed it down to that odd metal coin-thing I'd found stuck under the table in the foyer. I lifted it to my ear, trying to make sense of it. The voices were so quiet I could barely make out the words.

"...*the island...second ship...quickly.*"

Was it a radio? I'd never seen one this size before. "Volume up," I told it, just as I would any other entertainment device.

The voices went silent. Chestnuts.

"Hello?" I tried. "On. Turn on."

There was a silence, then a voice said through the coin-thing, "*Who is this?*"

I froze. Not a radio, then. "Who is *this?*"

"*I asked first.*"

Good point, but it didn't mean I was going to answer. This could be *anyone*, and I didn't fancy being someone else's joke for the next day. *'You'll never guess who was chatting on our comm. unit. Thought it was a radio.'* No thanks. But there *was* someone who I didn't mind making look silly… "Snow White," I replied finally. "Now who's this?"

There was the sound of muffled chatter, then the coin-thing suddenly went silent. "Hello?"

But after several minutes when it became clear that no one was going to respond, I gave up. I put the thing back in my pocket, deciding I'd waited here long enough. A breeze was picking up, and even though the night wasn't cold, my hands and feet were growing chilled. My circulation wasn't good, and my fingers were always the first to feel it.

I took my time returning to the cottage. The outer light was on, and there was someone sitting on the ornate bench next to the entryway. A moment later I realised it was Caleb. He stood when he saw me approach.

"Valentina. Are you alright?"

I stopped at a distance. "It's Ms Redwell. And I'd be better if I could go to bed. Alone." It didn't seem like Kingsley had come to make any scraping apologies for his insensitivity, and he'd have been the only person I would have spoken with.

Caleb's cheeks reddened a little. "Sorry, Ms Redwell. I know you'd like me to go, and I will, but I just had to apologise. It was incredibly careless of me to knock over that wine, and I will do anything I can to make it up."

I sighed. Compared to Kingsley and my exes, Caleb seemed so…young. But he also seemed sincere, so that was a point in his favour. "It was an accident. I'm claiming insurance, and really, there's nothing you can do to fix it."

"But it was your husband's," he persisted, even as I walked past him to the door. "It clearly mattered to you. I can't just brush it off."

"What are you going to do?" I snapped, raising my hand to the lock-pad. "Offer to work it off for the next ten years of your life?"

I'd meant it as a joke, but he barely hesitated. "Alright then."

"You've got to be kidding."

"Not for the whole next ten years," Caleb quickly corrected. "But while you're here on the island, I can help you. Do things for you. Whatever you need."

I turned to stare at him. He looked entirely sincere, and again I couldn't shake that sense of familiarity. "Have we met before?"

His jaw dropped, and his eyes widened a little. "Do we look like we have?"

"I don't know," I retorted. "But I'm getting married in two days. Even if I didn't already have Jorge, I don't think it's a good idea to have a vaguely familiar-looking boy following me around, staring at me and knocking things over."

There was a silence. "I've been on the island a couple of days," he said finally, his eyes flickering to my left cheek, where the beauty mark was. "I've noticed you, and I thought you might have noticed me. I don't make a habit of staring, or of knocking things over. And I wouldn't hit on you! I know you're…er, taken. Even if Mr White is much, much older."

Maybe that was it, that I'd just seen him around the island. But the last thing he'd said had pricked my pride. "What does Mr White's age have to do with anything?"

Caleb's mouth curled in an awkward smile. "He's coming up forty, and you're about twenty, and well…"

"Well what?"

There was a long silence. "Surely you don't find him attractive," he replied finally.

I stared at him, the implications of that bold statement slowly making sense. Kingsley was older than me, so Caleb couldn't see how I'd find him attractive. And if I wasn't marrying Kingsley because I found him attractive, then – in the mind of a boy like this – why would I be marrying him? He *was* very rich…

My lips tightened. Clearly *Caleb* didn't have trouble both finding me attractive…and thinking I was a gold-digger. "Thank you," I said flatly. "That'll be all." Then I stepped in through the doorway and pressed the lock-pad.

"But wait, there's-"

The door closed, and I headed into the main room, then slumped onto the nearest couch. I felt as weary as if I'd run a marathon. The room had returned to its usual spotless self, except for the new, ornate carpet now on the floor. Its red, black and white design curved out from a large rose centrepiece: especially fitting considering how I'd chosen to dress today, but I couldn't see a card.

Finally I spotted a faintly glowing notepad on the same coffee table where I'd briefly kept my Chateau de la Reine-Rouge. It was next to what looked like an almost finished glass of red wine – which was definitely *not* mine. I picked up the notepad curiously and read its typed-in message.

Valentina: Again, so sorry for breaking that bottle, and I swear I'll make it up to you.

Caleb, and clearly he'd written this before our 'Ms Redwell' conversation. I rolled my eyes, but kept reading.

I managed to salvage a little wine from the base piece of the bottle. It's not much, but it's definitely clean, since I ran it through the kitchen strainer. It's yours if you want it, although it smells kind of funny. I think it'll taste like vinegar.

- Caleb

Of *course* it smelled funny, I thought wryly. All wine did, but ancient wine smelled even funnier. The boy had probably never tasted a decent glass before. Unlike me, who'd been married to the wine connoisseur/rich kid James Redwell for a whole eight months before it went belly-up. Still, I was strangely touched by the gesture, and I studied the half-centimetre of red liquid with pleasure.

But before I tasted my last drop of precious wine, I had one more thing to do. I reached for the phone receiver next to the chair, and the call-screen on the wall came alight. "Karey Godmother."

A moment later the screen flickered and the wall became a video, showing an attractive woman in her fifties; her slim figure neatly clad in a fitted pink skirt and matching jacket. The silver streaks in her neat dark chignon and the small pair of glasses perched on her nose were the only things that hinted at her true age. If the wedding planner had been fifteen years younger, or had a less reserved manner, she would have been a total babe. For some reason that made me nervous. "How may I help you, Ms Redwell?"

"You can tell me about Snow White, please. You've been the events coordinator for the hotel for how long, five years?"

"Eight," she corrected.

"Eight. Then you'd know her well enough to answer this question. Has there ever been a time where Kingsley has shown interest in a woman, but has been put off by his daughter?"

She looked away from the viewing screen, frowning a little. "I'm sure I don't know about my employer's personal details, ma'am."

"There's no one else at my end to overhear," I told her, "and I need to know what to expect. The wedding is planned for two days, and I was not expecting *this*."

Karey didn't ask me to elaborate. Instead she replied carefully, "If you're afraid that Snow will cause trouble between you and Kingsley, I'll say I think it's very unlikely. As long as she knows that her father's affection for her is secure, then she'll quickly grow accustomed to the change."

"But *I* still need to get accustomed to the change," I muttered.

"Pardon?"

"Nothing." I sighed. "Is there anything you think I should know? About Snow, about her preferences?"

Karey paused thoughtfully. "She might like to be a bridesmaid. I know you weren't planning to have one, but perhaps that would help make her feel a part of things."

"Fine. Do I need to do anything about that?"

"Not at all. Leave it to me."

Because that was her job, after all. I ended the call then leaned back into my chair, swirling the last of my priceless wine in its oversized glass, and thinking of my planned wedding to Kingsley. I imagined him there at the altar, in front of a cheering crowd, watching me with adoration…and with his daughter off to the side, watching with open dislike. I imagined the reception, all themed in white with splashes of red – that was my request – and then after the reception we'd finally consummate our relationship…

I found my lips were downturned with distaste, and that didn't make sense. When we'd met at the resort a month earlier, Kingsley had been so dashing, so handsome: I hadn't even noticed his age. But today, he'd seemed so different from my memories. So much older. Maybe it had just been the light…?

Surely you don't find him attractive, Caleb had said, as if there was no question of my answer.

My lips tightened. I took a sip of wine then let it sit in my mouth, considering the flavour. Ten seconds later I was spitting it in the sink, then tipping the rest of the glass after it. Caleb had been right; it did taste like vinegar.

The next morning I woke up with my mind a blank. I didn't know where I was, or even *who* I was. But then as normal, a few seconds later the memories came trickling in. Sweetheart Island, Kingsley, the wedding. Some guy in Arabian costume. Oh fiery chestnuts, *Snow White*.

I'd hit my head very hard when I was sixteen, and it had left permanent fuzzy spots in my memory as well as a sizeable scar hidden in my hairline. I rarely told anyone about it, and the memory blanks were always worst in the mornings, or when I felt particularly stressed. I would deal with the issue by lying quietly in one place, trying not to think about anything, until I felt more like myself. Then I'd take myself to my bathroom mirror just as I did now, and stand there, staring at my reflection until the world felt safer. Better.

"You're beautiful," I told my reflection. "You're special. You're the one and only Valentina, and you *will* be happy."

But the pale girl in the mirror just stared at me sadly, her eyes seeming too green, her hair too blonde, her skin too white. The mole to the left of her nose was the only hint of familiarity, and finally I turned away, cursing quietly to myself. I compensated for my unease by dressing in one of my more glamorous velvet dresses, finishing the outfit with heavy emerald studs and a slash of deep pink lipstick, and went back to the mirror, my best smile already in place.

But now my reflection looked gaudy and unfamiliar and heavily made up. Not me, whoever *me* was. I wiped off most of the lipstick, mussed up my hair a little, then decided I still looked like a tart. That was the problem.

So up went the neckline a little, and the emerald studs were swapped for slightly smaller diamond ones. But I still didn't like my reflection in the mirror, and eventually I decided it was less to do with my looks and more to do with how I was feeling.

Stupid Snow White. Why did she have to exist? But Kingsley would get upset if I did something about that, so I'd have to put up with her.

Ha, ha.

I headed out towards the hotel proper, making sure to lock the door behind me this time. The building and surroundings looked even more beautiful by day as they did by night, and I studied it as I walked through with a dispassionate eye. The fabulous rose gardens and outdoor restaurant? They'd be mine once I married

Kingsley. The koi-filled streams, low bridges and ornately carved garden sculptures? They'd be mine too. The enormous shining foyer with its blandly beautiful android servers and three-storey-high ceiling, impressive enough to hold a ball in? Mine, mine, mine.

And you'll be happy? An inner voice asked quietly. *Just like with James and Walter?*

James and Walter didn't own hotels, I told that inner voice. And Kingsley's so much better than they were. It wasn't at all the same.

Hmm. And you know Kingsley so very, very well, do you?

I thought of that week we'd spent together a mere month ago, where he'd swept me off my feet and proposed, and I'd accepted, full of hope and expectation. It all felt fuzzy and distant, my memories still seeming as if they might belong to someone else, but I remembered that much.

A week? The voice scoffed. It sounded a bit like Caleb. *You can't know someone in a week. You'll just live out the same situation over and over-*

"Shut up!"

The android server behind the front desk looked up at me, her pleasant features curved in polite uncertainty. Her name tag read 'Rhonda'. "May I help you, Ms Redwell?"

I blinked, realising I'd spoken aloud, and that I couldn't really recall why I'd come in here in the first place. "Uh…good morning. Do I have a meeting planned for today?"

The server glanced down at a screen in front of her briefly. "Yes, Ms Redwell. You're meeting Mr White and Karey Godmother in his fourth-floor suite in ten minutes."

Yes, that was right. We'd agreed to that yesterday, before Kingsley had arrived. "Um…thank you, Rhonda."

"You're welcome, Ms Redwell."

I nodded politely, then turned away and headed towards the elevators. I was always grateful for the non-judgemental nature of AI. I might have been acting like a fruitcake, but she – it – hadn't commented.

I should have stayed in bed longer, I mused glumly on my way up. I could have claimed a headache, and no doubt it was the stress and shock of yesterday making me feel so out of sorts. But when I reached the penthouse and saw who was waiting there for me with Kingsley, I knew it wasn't the stress. It was one particular person.

"Val!" Snow cooed, stepping forward with arms outstretched. "Are you feeling better?"

Ugh. I tried to sidestep the hug, but I was moving too slowly and she got me around the side before I managed to push her away. At least this time my stomach was empty. "It's Valentina, Snowball. And no, not really."

"Fairest." Kingsley stepped forward, his handsome face creased in concern, and leaned in to give me a kiss of greeting.

I had to steel myself not to cringe away, and when he lingered I pushed him away too, forcing a sweet smile. Had his cheeks always been so scratchy, his lips so wet? "Not in front of the child, please."

"Of course." He beamed at me, seeming oblivious to my involuntary distaste. "I see you got your beauty sleep."

"I don't need beauty sleep," I replied with a quick smile. "I'm always beautiful."

"And so you are."

There was a brief, awkward pause, which Snow filled by brightly saying, "Father says I'm always beautiful, too. He says I look like Mother, who was the most beautiful woman he'd ever seen."

I raised my eyebrows in disbelief – doting fathers would say any kind of drivel, wouldn't they? – but Kingsley just smiled, his gaze becoming soft and a little sad. "Indeed she was, and taken too soon."

Snow let out a deep sigh and patted his arm reassuringly. He turned and smiled at her, and they held the gaze for a long moment. I just watched, a little stunned and perhaps even a little jealous. After a few long seconds, feeling quite reminiscent of yesterday's meeting, I coughed. "Aren't we missing someone?"

My voice came out sharply, and Kingsley finally looked away from his daughter. "Ah. Karey, of course. I told her to meet us down in the second parlour."

"Shall we go down there, then?"

"Oh, no, no," he replied lightly. "We're quite comfortable up here, aren't we Snow? I'll go down and fetch her. You two girls can get to know each other while I'm gone."

Snow and I silently watched as he left the room, and once the door had slid shut after him, I said, "You know, he could have just messaged her."

Snow turned to look at me, her gaze flicking over me in a far less friendly fashion than before. "My father likes to do things the old-fashioned way. It's one of the best things about him."

"Is it?" I said dryly. "So he uses a chamber pot and rides in a horse-drawn carriage, does he?"

She just gave me a blank look, and then her eyes narrowed as she got the joke. "Well, it's hardly as if *you* know him. You only met him a month ago."

"I did." I took a deep breath, studying her right back. Today she wore a similar bright sundress to yesterday's, this one a bright pinkish-purple with tiny capped sleeves. Her red mouth was pinched into an unhappy pout, and her black-lined eyes were flicking over my velvet gown with suspicion and judgement – or so it looked to me. "Shall we take a moment to be honest, Snow?"

"I'm always honest."

Now that made me smile; a real smile.

"What? I am!"

"Good," I said simply, not bothering to challenge her on the lie. "Then we can talk. You don't like me, do you Snow?"

She folded her thin arms in front of her chest. "I don't know what you're talking about. I like everyone, especially you, Val. We're going to be best friends."

I echoed her gesture, mirroring her from a few feet away. "Not if you keep talking to me so disrespectfully. I might be only a little older than you, but if I'm going to marry your father we need to treat each other with basic kindness. You call me Valentina, and

I…" I paused. *I wouldn't football-kick her across the room if she called me Val again?*

"You'll tell Daddy about what happened to your last two relationships?" Snow's tone was sickly sweet, but her words made me go cold.

"Excuse me?"

"A dead husband and a dead fiancé in less than two years. That's unfortunate, isn't it."

"What are you insinuating?" I asked in a low tone. "Kingsley knows I'm a widow. He knew that from the start."

"Hmm." Snow pouted, her eyes lighting up with malice as she moved to perch on the nearby couch. "But everyone doesn't know that your husband dropped dead in mysterious circumstances-"

"James Redwell had a brain aneurysm! It was a genetic fault!"

She raised her voice. "…And your second fiancé Walter Green died of a heart attack a week before the wedding. Poor, poor Valentina. The former waitress, not even twenty-one, and left with a fortune each time. You didn't even have to *marry* Walter to get his! Why, it's no wonder their families call you a black widow."

I was shaking with fury, and I had to slump back into one of the couches behind me to keep from stumbling on my high heels. Now the real Snow was coming out to play, and she was *nasty*. I hadn't imagined her earlier malice, and suddenly I didn't feel so bad about my intense dislike for the girl.

"You've been looking me up, I see," I said, and was pleased to hear my voice was as smooth and even as if I'd been ordering coffee. "And I also see you've heard the worst of the gossip. I thought I'd left that behind when I moved cities. I suppose you're going to tell your precious Daddy, are you? Warn him that if he marries me his days are surely numbered?"

Snow leaned back on the couch, her small mouth curving in a catlike smile. "I already did, and he didn't believe it. He said you'd never hurt a fly, and that I should ignore such foolish rumours."

I sagged with relief. He knew, and he didn't believe it. Wonderful, wonderful Kingsley. "But you haven't ignored them, have you?"

She shrugged her small shoulders casually. "I'm sure that if you really were a murderer you'd have been brought to justice by now. Good always wins out."

Idiot. "Sure it does," I said sarcastically, ignoring her tittering laugh. "But this is what I need to know. Are you going to cause trouble, Snow? Or can we coexist for Kingsley's sake?"

"Of course we can coexist," Snow replied, and her voice was syrupy sweet. "You make Daddy happy, and who am I to get in the way? As long as you understand one thing."

"And what is that?"

"It doesn't matter what you do to him or for him, or how sexy or beautiful you think you are, or how many compliments he gives you. I'm his daughter, and I will *always* come first."

Had I thought she was nasty? I upgraded that to psychotic. But I didn't know what I would have said in reply, because the doors slid open and we had company.

3 Sleepy

Kingsley had found Karey Godmother, but perhaps the doors had slid open a little too fast. She was leaning close into him, whispering something in his ear, and for a moment before she looked up and saw us, I'd have sworn I saw malice in her expression. His was just blank. But that must have just been me projecting my feelings, because a moment later he was smiling at Snow and I, and Karey was standing a respectful distance away, once again the consummate professional in her pink matching suit and skirt.

"There we are," she said with a smile. "The whole wedding party in one room."

Wedding party? I recalled a moment later that I'd said Snow could be a bridesmaid, and stifled a groan. I stood abruptly, moving towards Kingsley as an excuse to get out of Snow's immediate vicinity. But she was faster than me. She leapt up from the couch, running across the room and reaching him before I did; slipping her arm though his and cooing up at him. "Daddy! You're back!"

"Good grief," I muttered in disgust. "It's been five minutes!"

Kingsley just set his hand on hers, moving forward into the room with his usual genial expression. "Made friends, have we

Fairest? Talking about lipsticks and fashion, no doubt, as girls do."

I didn't answer.

Karey's eyes flicked from me to Snow then back again, then she smiled at me politely. "The bridal party, Ms Redwell. I have some suggestions for how Snow can fit in as your maid of honour."

"No," I blurted out.

"Pardon?"

I shook my head. "I've changed my mind. No bridal party. No bridesmaids – definitely no maid of honour. Just Kingsley and I, that'll be enough."

Over Karey's shoulder I saw Snow's jaw drop in disappointment, and she turned to tug at Kingsley's arm. "Oh Daddy, did you hear that? Val wants me out of the wedding!" Her face twisted in an odd expression, eyebrows furrowing over her nose, eyes scrunching up. "Oh Daddy, I know it's your special day, but I *do* so want to be a part of it."

She was trying to cry, I realised belatedly, and failing miserably at it.

'Daddy' wasn't so observant. "Of course you can be part of it," he assured her. He turned to me. "Snow will still be a part of the wedding, won't she? A flower girl or something?"

"Actually, flower girls are traditionally very young," Karey pointed out. I silently blessed her. "Snow could just be a bridesmaid, as we'd discussed? Since you're wearing a non-traditional red and white gown, Valentina, she could wear something subtle and neutral – pale yellow, perhaps?"

"Or white!" Snow piped up. Her 'tears' had vanished completely. "People always say I look lovely in white."

All three of them looked at me expectantly, and I felt my hands begin to shake again. I clenched them into fists, feeling a headache come over the back of my head, squeezing my temples. Over my dead body was Snow wearing white at *my* wedding.

"Fairest?" Kingsley said after a few moments when I didn't answer. "What do you think?"

"I think…" I forced a breath in, trying to push away the fuzziness that threatened at the edge of my vision. No, no, not now! I let out a deep breath. "I think I can't talk about this now. I have a headache."

"Oh, poor Val!" Snow pouted in mock sympathy. "Not again."

"You should go and have a long lie down," Kingsley said reassuringly from where he stood at Snow's side. "You told me migraines can hit you so hard you lose patches of memory."

"Of course I know that!" I snapped at him. "It's my bloody migraine, isn't it?"

His dark eyebrows lifted in surprise, and Snow put one hand over her mouth, not quite hiding a smile.

That was it. "Sorry. I have to go." I turned and headed for the door, stepping around father and daughter without another word.

As the doors slid shut behind me I heard Karey call, "I'll just sort this out and then message you, shall I?"

I waved a hand dismissively, not caring, and ran for the stairs.

I made it back to the cottage without incident, turning the lights down to dim the moment I was inside, and lurched towards my bathroom. I kept my medicine in the small black leather chest where I kept my makeup, but the now-crushing pain in my head meant I fumbled to open it, to get past the top level. Frustrated, I pushed at the release button a few times, and the chest split in half.

And I mean split in half. Instead of just lifting up the top level to reveal my migraine medication and a few others, the top half of the chest had swung up and over to reveal a small compartment in its base. It was padded with black velvet, and a series of tiny, unlabelled bottles were arranged in neatly cut sections in the padding. I stared at them blankly for a few moments, waiting for a flash of recognition, but they still seemed completely unfamiliar.

They must have already been in the chest when I bought it, I decided. I slammed the lid shut, then tried again. This time the draws opened perfectly. I pulled out my migraine injector, set it against my temple, and clicked. There was a brief flash of pain, then the crushing pressure around my temples began to recede. I dropped the injector, stumbled over to my bed and lay down with the blankets over my head.

Ting ting ting. Ting ting ting. Ting ting ting…

I blinked muzzily. My vision was filled with grey, and that annoying sound was repeating over and over. Where was I? Ugh, there was something in my mouth…

A moment later I remembered, and pushed the blankets off my face. The light in the cottage was still dimmed, and someone was waiting at the front door, hence the doorbell.

I felt bruised, exhausted; but at least my headache was gone. It would probably be Kingsley coming to see if I was well. I felt a pang of anger shoot through me at the thought of him, and of the kind concern he'd no doubt show. It wasn't enough to make up for the horror of a stepdaughter he was about to inflict on me. Now sharp hatred filled me at the thought of Snow, and my stomach roiled in distaste. I didn't think I'd *ever* felt so strongly negative about someone. I was supposed to be calm, and tolerant, and sociable…but not with Snow White.

Here's the problem, I imagined myself saying to Kingsley. *I hate your daughter so much that she literally makes me vomit. How can we fix this?*

I didn't have the answer.

But it wasn't Kingsley at the door after all. It was a tanned, good-looking guy in Arabian costume, and his expression brightened when I opened the door. "Val- uh, Ms Redwell! You were out the last time I came, so I came back. And here you are."

I blinked at him. "Um…here I am. And you're here because…?"

His face fell. "The bottle of wine, and you were very upset…"

A moment later the pieces clicked into place in my memory, and I scrubbed a hand over my tired face. "Ah. The Chateau de la Reine-Rouge. And you're Caleb, of Jafeer's Jars and Carpets, come to make amends during work time."

"It's Ali's Jars, actually. And Ali doesn't mind. I've got the morning off."

I studied him curiously. Last night still felt like an embarrassing, upsetting blur, but I was beginning to remember him more clearly. Funny, I still couldn't shake the feeling he was familiar… "Is Ali a relative?"

Caleb looked sheepish. "I'm actually Ali. It's a stage- I mean, it's my name while I'm at the shop. I just forgot to use it when we met last night."

A stage name, he'd been about to say. "You're an actor," I said in dawning understanding. "Or are you a shop boy?"

"A shop *man*, excuse me." He grinned. "I'm both, but you're not supposed to know about the acting part."

"Oh? Why is that?"

Caleb floundered a little. "Er…because the experience is supposed to be so authentic, I suppose."

I rolled my eyes. "Oh, come on. My grasp of history isn't that great, but even I know that a French patisserie shouldn't sit next door to a Persian carpet store." His eyebrows shot up, and I continued, "But I can't believe you would choose to give up your time off like this. What exactly do you think I'd have you do?"

He shrugged. "Clean your cottage?"

"It's spotless," I countered. "The servers come in twice a day and clean everything except my personal items. Are you going to offer to polish my shoes?"

His nose wrinkled. "Do you want me to, Ms Redwell?"

"Not particularly." I studied him. He didn't look inclined to leave, and perhaps I was a bit bored…or lonely. "Call me Valentina, will you? We've been talking for long enough. And unless you've changed your mind, I suppose I'll have to find you something to do."

I looked back inside the cottage, but as I'd said, it was spotless. Outside was just about the same. In fact, the only part of the grounds that wasn't perfectly tended was up the hill, in the small pine forest that covered a chunk of the island. "I've just thought of something. Let me put some shoes on."

Five minutes later we were tramping back up that same path

I'd walked last night. It was prettier in the daylight, and we hadn't been walking long before I saw a familiar structure up ahead. The greenhouse was *not* prettier by daylight. It was overgrown and covered in enough grime that even its single tall tower didn't reflect the sunlight. If I hadn't been looking for it, I might have missed it.

Caleb didn't seem to notice. His long strides easily kept pace with my shorter ones – even my lowest heels weren't that easy to walk in – and I'd seen him watching me out of the corner of my eye.

"So how was the wine?" he asked suddenly. "Did you try it?"

I let out a startled laugh. "Yes, I tried it, and I tipped it out. I think it was better in the bottle."

Caleb didn't look surprised. "So it was your husband's, right? That's an unusual inheritance."

"His father made a fortune in property," I replied as we drew up to the greenhouse. "And collected wine. James wanted to do the same thing, and that bottle was the first of his own collection. After he died, it was the only one I kept."

There was a silence, and when I turned to look at Caleb, he had an odd expression on his face. It vanished as he met my eyes. "Did you love him?"

"No, I married him for his money, just like I will Kingsley," I replied sarcastically. "Of course I loved him! Right up until I found out that he'd been cheating on me. I would have divorced him if he hadn't dropped dead, while in another girl's bed. Kind of hard to keep the lovin' feeling in a situation like that."

"Oh."

"And hard as it may be to believe," I continued coolly as I spotted the doorway, "I choose my partners based on how much I *like* them, not how rich they are. It just so happens I've chosen badly in the past."

I was pleased to see that the greenhouse was even filthier close-up. With the conversation we were having, I was thinking that was a good thing. Let Caleb scrub all day. He'd deserve it.

The doorway was partially covered in trailing greenery. I

pulled it away, locating a faded old lock-pad. That was a problem, I thought, because that would be keyed to someone else's print. But I pressed my thumb against it anyway, and a moment later the door clicked open. "Huh." What were the chances of that?

Inside, the greenhouse was dark and dingy, filled with the scent of moss and earth. It appeared empty except for a few pots, and just across from the doorway was another door, leading into a staircase. I turned back to Caleb. "Aren't you coming in?"

He was standing a few feet away, his hands in loose fists at his sides. "I wasn't calling you a gold-digger."

Ah, he was still stuck in what I'd said thirty seconds ago. I raised an eyebrow. "You asked me if I loved my husband. And last night, you suggested that I couldn't possibly find Kingsley attractive, and we're getting married tomorrow. So what were you calling me?"

He paused. "OK, maybe I was. But I shouldn't have. That was really rude."

"Yes, it was," I replied evenly. "James' friends used to call me the same thing, because I wasn't raised wealthy like they were. They were wrong too. And if you thought I was so calculated in choosing Kingsley, why are you still here? Do you think I'll want to take a lover on the side, and you want to be first in line?"

Caleb's jaw dropped. "What? No!"

I set a hand on my hip. "Really. Then why are you here, Caleb? Do you truly want to spend your days off cleaning this place? Because that's what I'll get you to do. You won't spend time with *me*."

He looked up at the greenhouse, his nose wrinkling, and his mouth curving in a crooked smile. "I do feel bad about the wine bottle thing. Really."

"But…?"

"But I was also trying to spend some time with you," he admitted. "Not because I want a relationship! Or even a hook-up," he said quickly when I would have spoken. "It's because… well, you look like someone I used to know."

My eyebrows shot up again. I hadn't expected *that*. "Seriously?"

Caleb shrugged a shoulder, looking a little embarrassed. "She had dark hair and brown eyes, but apart from that, you're a dead ringer. She even had the…you know. The mole." He tapped at the space next to his nose. "I wanted to see if it was all in my head, or if you really do look like her."

"It's a beauty mark," I said automatically. I was absolutely stunned. Out of all the reasons why he could have fixated on me – alright, only two: looks or guilt – I hadn't seen this coming. "So you're seriously following me around because I *look* like someone you used to know."

"Yeah, basically. Sorry."

"Who is it? This girl who looks like me."

Caleb looked uncomfortable. "My girlfriend."

I sighed heavily. That made it even worse! "You know I'm not her, right?"

"Trust me," he agreed forcefully. "You're nothing like her. Besides, she died six months ago."

Oh. I didn't know if that made it better or not. It was definitely sadder.

In the silence he said, "So are we going in or not?"

I turned and went further into the greenhouse, heading straight up the narrow staircase. The steps were concrete and worn, but seemed sturdy enough, and his footsteps echoed behind mine as we ascended.

"I'm not interested in dating again," he said from behind me. "But I find you interesting, and not just because you look like her. And your husband died too, so you'd understand. I thought we could be friends."

Friends? I gave him a startled glance over my shoulder as I finally reached the top of the staircase, but didn't answer. We came out into a small, square tower room. The sun struggled to make its way through the thick layers of grime, and the whole room was bathed in dull green. Lovely.

How, I wondered, had this place got so bad when everything else was spotless?

There was a stunned silence while Caleb took in the magnitude of the filth, then his eyes lit up. "Hey, here's a window!" He pushed at the stiff joints, finally forcing it open, then stuck his head outside. "Rapunzel, Rapunzel, let down your hair…" he sang, then turned to grin at me.

I was bemused. He'd just told me something terrible, and now he was acting like a kid. Was he sad or not, and how was I supposed to react? "Isn't a rapunzel a type of pastry?"

"What? No! It's a…*she's* a fairytale character. Haven't you heard-"

"Ugh. Say no more," I cut in. "See, we can't be friends, Caleb. Because even if I look like your…" *Deceased?* "…girlfriend, I can't stand children's stories, particular the sappy fairytale kind. And besides…" I felt the corner of my lips curve in a mischievous smile. "I brought you up here for a reason. This'll make a lovely sunroom once it's cleaned. I was going to get some servers onto it, but if you're so keen to help, you can do it."

Caleb looked around again at the dense green mildew on the glass, his dark eyebrows lowering over his eyes. Then he looked at me again and shrugged. "Sure."

"Really?!"

"But only if you'll have a drink with me tonight."

I scowled. "I'll get the servers onto it."

"Oh, come on," he coaxed. "Just a drink and conversation. I'm not that bad."

He wasn't bad at all; that was the problem. In fact, he was growing on me far too much in such a short space of time. It was like we *had* met before…

And then he moved, and the sun hit his face just so, and something clicked in my memory.

"James," I said abruptly. "You look like him."

Caleb's eyes widened, and another almost eager, hard-to-read expression came over his face. "I look like your ex-husband? What a coincidence."

"Not exactly like," I corrected. "Just enough that it's been bugging me ever since I first met you. He was fairer, and maybe not as lean, but there was something in the way he smiled that reminded me so much…” I petered into silence as I realised I was babbling again. Caleb was watching me with *something* in his own expression, and confused, I felt my cheeks flush pink. “Right, what a coincidence. Or maybe we both just have incredibly ordinary features, and we actually look like everyone.”

“Must be.” Caleb smiled again, but this time it looked a little forced, and his eyes were still fixed on my face. His gaze flicked to my beauty mark…

I turned away, floundering, and took a step towards the stairs. “That’s it, then. Do whatever you can, and we’ll call it even. I’ll get the servers to finish the rest.”

I left as fast as I could, determined not to think about Caleb anymore, or about James, or about Caleb’s dead girlfriend with a mole next to her nose. I had enough to worry about, what with my fiancé turning out to have a daughter who was overly attached to him, and who I’d have happily pushed into a lake if there was one handy.

Was that normal, that kind of affection between father and daughter? I didn’t know, my own father having vanished somewhere in my early childhood, and any other knowledge just coming from media. A face floated vaguely in my imagination: kind, bearded, loving – what an ideal father might look like. A moment later I realised that looked quite a bit like Kingsley, and recoiled in distaste at the connection I’d made.

“He’s my fiancé,” I said aloud to the empty forest, picking up my pace. “I’m going to marry him tomorrow, and we’re going to be very happy.”

But it felt like I was playing a role, and I couldn’t even remember why I’d made that decision in the first place. Perhaps I should have stayed in bed this morning. “I need to clear my head,” I muttered desolately.

I paused halfway down the hill, tapping at my silver bracelet. *Feeling better*, I wrote to Kingsley. *Are you free for lunch?* I needed to remind myself of what we had, of why I cared for him.

A few minutes passed before the answer came. *Just having brunch with Snow. Will you join us, Fairest?*

My jaw tightened, and I began breathing heavily through my nose. Even seeing her name in writing seemed to spark that same, almost unreasonable fury in me. Was she really that awful, I wondered, or was it just with me?

No thank you, I responded with restraint. *I would love to spend some time together, just the two of us. When will you be free today?*

At dinner. 5 pm at the ground floor restaurant?

Perfect, I messaged back. *See you then*. I paused, then made myself add, *Darling*.

I waited for him to respond something like 'I await your presence with bated breath', or even, 'Lots of love', but there was just silence.

Finally I lowered my wrist and stomped my way back down to the hotel gardens. If I headed one way I'd pass the outdoor restaurant, and I couldn't stand the idea of seeing either Kingsley *or* Snow right now. So I headed the other way, down the path beside the grain fields at the back of the hotel. I didn't know whose idea those were – I'd never seen anyone harvesting, and so the area was good for nothing but hiding bugs – but it was peaceful, and usually deserted.

But today I heard voices: the sounds of men arguing and of metal ringing against hard earth. Perhaps gardeners? Construction? Kingsley hadn't mentioned any changes to the hotel, but then we'd not had a real conversation since he'd arrived.

I turned a corner and then I saw them. There were four men just off the path, practically in the grain field, shovels in hands. One was holding a large piece of paper that could have been a map or some building plans. They were all young, ranging from skinny and longhaired to bespectacled to one who was muscular enough to be a body builder. They all looked up as I walked past, openly staring. I lifted my chin and acted as if I didn't notice they were there, and I'd just passed them when I heard one say, "There's one. You want to check her out?"

One what, exactly?

I heard laughter, and I clenched my fists, fighting back the anxiety that rushed over me, and steeling myself to show no reaction as I picked up my pace. *Please don't follow me. Don't talk to me. Don't touch me…*

But I heard no pursuing footsteps, and the laughter became distant as I reached the more public paths that led down the east side of the hotel. *Phew.* Had I overreacted? I glanced back over my shoulder reflexively and saw they were all staring after me. One, a tall, dark-haired guy, gave me a little wave and a smirking grin. I scowled at him then turned away, stomping a little in my heels until finally I'd made it around the corner and out of sight.

They were just being jerks, I thought angrily, even if they hadn't caused any real harm. I'd have to say something to Kingsley once I saw him this evening. We couldn't have contractors hanging around the hotel, acting so unprofessionally and disrespectfully. We had *guests* here, and if those men couldn't behave themselves, they could get lost.

Calm and easy-going, Valentina?

I told the thought to bog off. Yes, I was grumpier than I ever remembered being – and I was starting not to care. Even so, I decided I wouldn't be walking out here alone again. The path merged into the hotel carpark, and I headed down the short road that led towards the village. I knew it would be populated and would hopefully provide some distraction from my foul mood. Along the way I passed dwellings of various sizes. A couple of cottages with actual thatched roofs and bright, well-maintained flower gardens; several larger homes set back from the street with large trees casting shade over their grassy lawns; buildings that could be described as mansions.

Some were just amusing. There was a cottage that had an odd shape reminding me of an old boot. The sign out the front read 'Old Abby's Childcare', but there were no children in sight. Perhaps it was the off-season. Still, something rang familiar about the scene. "An old woman who lived in a shoe," I murmured to myself, then shrugged, moving on. Maybe that was something else I'd forgotten due to my head injury.

The next house was enormous, set far behind high iron gates. It was also covered in climbing roses over one side; covered to the point where I wondered how anyone could even get inside the barely-visible door. I could see the jagged thorns even from here! There was also a rather hideous statue in the front yard. It looked like a cross between a very tall man and a hunch-backed warthog. How *beastly*. Ugh.

The next house was equally as enormous, although far more attractive. Through its gate I could see a long driveway, its length marked with small, straight-trunked trees with their foliage trimmed into perfect spheres, and at the other end a three-storey neo-Georgian mansion covered in creeping ivy. The elegant brass plate next to the gate read 'Charmant'. I studied it curiously for a moment, vaguely recalling some gossip about the wealthy family that had this as their holiday home. A happily married couple, their son, and a dragon of a grandmother, if rumour was true.

But if this was for holidays, I'd have loved to see where they really lived. It must look like a palace.

Just then the distant front door slid open and a blond male figure stepped into sight. His classic good looks and sunglasses were visible even from this distance, and I quietly moved back behind the wall before he saw me. Now I remembered. Daniel Charmant was the son, and was spoken about by some of the local girls with awe. A playboy, I'd concluded, and had someone mentioned something about an unusual taste for women's shoes? Either on him or on the woman, I didn't know.

I set back towards the village, wondering absently how the long-term residents like the Charmants and the small business owners running the local shops felt about the island's 'renovations'. Now I'd read the article, I could see that almost every shop had bought into the fantasy theme, if quasi-medieval counted as fantasy. Wooden storefronts with shutters and flower-boxes, hanging wooden signs with hand-painted text, with the island's few cars barred from access to the town's very centre by quaint wooden barriers in the cobblestone streets.

Perhaps those barriers were a mistake, because today, like the other days I'd visited, there were very few people around. Come to think of it, the hotel hadn't been very busy either, as the nasty women in the alcove yesterday were the last guests I remembered seeing. Maybe the fantasy idea was a desperate attempt to bring more business onto this somewhat isolated island.

I detoured into the nearest café, ordering a meal, then sat in a secluded alcove at the very back. There was a touchscreen inset in this table, just like at the White Hotel, and I made a point of scrolling through the articles. Most of them were in line with the island's theme. Not very interesting, but I still managed to kill some time as I ate.

I finished my meal, then checked my wristpiece as I left the café. It was only one pm. "Chestnuts!" I muttered. "This better not be an indication of what my life here will be like." Because so far, Sweetheart Island was *boring*.

Just then I saw a familiar dark-haired figure in a purple sundress, her back to me as she looked into a store window. Snow, and she hadn't seen me. Suppressing my gag reflex, I quickly stepped through the nearest doorway.

I found myself inside a dimly lit shop full of jars and vases. They ranged from cup-sized to chest-high, and several dozen simply enormous ones were lined up all along the length of the shop, each big enough to fit a person inside. The floor and walls were mosaiced in blue, white and red, and the far side of the room was filled with carpets in every colour, either rolled up in piles or stacked against the wall or in a couple of cases, hanging. I looked around in interest. It felt like I'd stepped into ancient Baghdad, except for the clean, slightly chemical smell instead of the scent of dust and spices I imagined a place like this ought to have.

I spotted the merchant across the room, recognising him immediately. Chestnuts. "I swear I'm not following you," I blurted out.

Caleb's eyebrows shot up, and his lips curved in a crooked smile. "Are you sure? I know I'm fascinating. Entrancing, even."

I rolled my eyes, now amused as well as embarrassed. "And no issues with self esteem, I see. I suppose the greenhouse is no longer green?"

"Hmm… Not quite." He shrugged, and the tassel from his little round hat fell into his eye. He flipped it back but it promptly fell over his face again, so he took off the hat with a grin. "There was nothing to clean with, and then I had to come to work anyway. I've just started."

"You really don't have-" I began, but then I saw Snow out of the corner of my eye, walking into sight right outside the shop. She paused to look at something in the window, and I reacted instinctively, dropping into a crouch behind a couple of large clay jars. "Don't tell her I'm here!" I hissed at Caleb.

His eyebrows shot up but he didn't respond, and a moment later I heard the jingle of the old-fashioned doorbell as someone stepped inside.

Caleb moved past me out of sight, then I heard him say, "Welcome to Ali Baba's, madam! Home of fine quality carpets and jars. How may I help you today?"

"Not with carpets or jars, that's for sure," Snow replied with a sniff. "I thought I saw someone in here. Another customer."

There was a short silence. "We've been known to have other customers, madam, but at this moment you have my full attention."

"Oh." Snow's tone was rife with disappointment. "Unless you're a fascinating conversationalist, which I doubt, then I don't want your full attention. That'll be all."

I heard receding footsteps, then the jingle of the bell once more as she left. A few seconds later Caleb stepped into view. He walked past me to the front counter, reaching over as if to press something, then turned and grinned at me. "She's gone, and I've locked the door. You can come out."

But my headache had come back with the very sound of her voice, and I just sat there for a moment, my head in my hands. "A moment, please."

He walked over, then crouched down beside me. "Are you sick?"

"Just a headache," I managed to say. "I've had a few of those lately."

"I have something that can help you. Can you come with me?"

I nodded, waving away his offered arm as I got to my feet, then followed him past the counter and through a beaded curtain. Out the back was a small kitchenette with a couple of worn-looking couches surrounding a small coffee table. Through another doorway I could see the edge of a bed. I sat down on one of the couches, blinking in the brighter light, and feeling my headache recede with every passing second. Still, I took the basic painkiller he offered. His hands brushed mine briefly as I did so, and his brow furrowed in confusion. "Your hands are like ice. Can I get you a hot drink?"

I shook my head, checking the medicine was familiar then tossing it down. "Bad circulation. They're always like that."

"Oh. Isn't that uncomfortable?"

I shrugged. "I'm used to it. And thank you, by the way. Will you get in trouble for locking up in the middle of the day?"

"You're welcome, and only if anyone notices." He disappeared out the door back into the shop, reappearing a moment later. "There. I'll have to go out if there are any more customers, but no one needs to know you're here."

I gave him a tight-lipped nod, one hand pressed against my temple. "Thank you."

"Ah…can I get you tea anyway? Coffee?"

"Whatever you're having."

Two minutes later Caleb set a steaming cup on the table in front of me. My headache had receded almost as fast as it had arrived, and I took the cup gratefully. "Coffee?"

"With milk and sugar. I didn't think to ask-"

"That's fine," I said, meaning it. "Coffee's disgusting without milk anyway."

He gave me another unreadable glance, but sat down beside me. "How's your head?"

"Better, but the headaches seem to be connected to Snow White." I let out a bark of unamused laughter. "Have you met her before today?"

"Can't say I have. She seems…" He paused. "…nice."

I shot him a narrow-eyed glare, one eyebrow raised. "Sure. And you and Jafeer are best friends, right?"

"Mm. We're actually cousins."

I studied him with new curiosity, trying to see the resemblance. Both were handsome, with a similar tall, lanky build, and the sort of skin that tanned well. I couldn't really recall Jafeer's face all that well, but then we'd only met very briefly. If they were family, then it might explain how they'd been so comfortable arguing. Relatives didn't tend to hold back. "How did you both end up working here?"

"Well, Jafeer knew someone here already, and he knew I was looking for work. Artificial intelligence can't run the island alone, of course, even though I think that's the final goal. So here I am."

"Really, they want AI to run the island?" I queried in disbelief. "That's a big ask. Android servers are great, but they're so literal. They misunderstand things all the time. I would have thought it would be decades before there'd be good enough technology to manage even a single restaurant."

"Not servers," Caleb said. His eyes skidded away from mine. "More advanced AI."

"Like what?"

"Oh, it doesn't matter."

"You've said it now," I persisted. "What kind of AI exists now, and is better than servers? I really want to know."

"Oh…you know." He coughed. "Cyborgs."

I frowned, confused. "I thought a cyborg was just a robot that looked like a human. Isn't that what a server is too?"

"Yes…" Caleb allowed. "But servers are only robotic. If AI had human components too, then it would be something else. We might call it a cyborg."

I screwed up my nose, imagining metal and wiring hidden beneath blood and muscle. Yuck. "If its body was flesh, but its brain robotic, then it would be AI," I said, thinking aloud. "But if its brain was human, and only parts of its body robotic, then surely it would just be a human with prosthetics."

He was watching me carefully again, and his eyes flicked to my mole. "But what if it was both, and what if it was made in a lab, not born?"

I considered the question. "I don't know," I said finally. "I would think it's our will that makes us human. The ability to make our own choices, rather than just act out some programming. But it's all hypothetical, isn't it? That kind of AI doesn't exist yet."

Caleb didn't answer.

"It doesn't," I persisted, smiling. "Unless you've got something to tell me…?"

He finally smiled back. "No, Valentina," he replied dramatically. "I am not a cyborg. Are you disappointed?"

"Not at all. I prefer my men with real flesh and blood," I joked. Then I realised what I'd said, and felt my face heat. Caleb wasn't my man; Kingsley was. "I mean…doesn't everyone?"

His smile hadn't reached his eyes, I saw. "It makes for a warmer hug. But flesh and blood is so easily damaged."

He seemed to be saying more than just those words, and I didn't understand. I set the coffee cup back down on the table. "How did your girlfriend die?" I asked.

"Car accident. The auto-driver failed."

And flesh and blood had failed too, by the sound of things. "I'm sorry," I said sincerely. The words seemed so weak, so pointless, but they were all I had.

Caleb sighed heavily. "Me too. And thank you." He rose to his feet. "I'd better go back into the shop again. You can stay here, if you like."

I stood abruptly. "Thanks, but I should be going too. I suppose I'll see you around. I'll be living here for some time, unless Kingsley wants to move."

"So you're still marrying him?"

"I'm supposed to be," I replied. But even I knew that wasn't an answer. "I'd better go," I said again.

Thirty seconds later I was back on the cobblestoned main street, and I *still* had time to kill. I didn't want to be alone with my thoughts, so I detoured into a nearby clothing boutique. There were racks and racks of beautiful cocktail and full-length gowns, suits, furs, and accessories. The shop was almost empty except for an attractive man browsing in the far corner. He checked me out as I came in, and I checked him out right back, only far more discreetly.

It was Jafeer, Caleb's cousin, I realised a moment later. He really was the quintessential tall, dark and handsome, though his neatly trimmed beard gave him an element of sleaziness that I thought he probably deserved, based on the way he watched me.

"Good morning Ms Redwell," the shop girl greeted me cheerfully. She was short and curvy, with just enough asymmetry to her features to show she was an actual human being rather than an android server. "You'd be wanting a dress for the bachelor auction, I presume?"

A local girl, I decided, as she didn't look to be playing any part except that of a salesperson. She knew who *I* was, though. That seemed to be happening a lot around here. "What auction?"

"It's this afternoon at the White Hotel, three pm. It happens every year."

"I'm engaged," I demurred. "I really oughtn't to go."

"But all the ladies go, Ms Redwell, and all you do is bid for a meal or an outing with some lucky lad. All the proceeds go to charity, and Mr White is a big supporter. He was up for auction himself last year."

I checked the time on my wristpiece. As expected, there was no hurry. Funny to think I was supposed to be getting married tomorrow afternoon, but I didn't have to sort out any details. Good old Karey – Kingsley was getting his money's worth with her. "Why not?" I said to the shop girl. "Show me something that'll make me look amazing." If I was going to be bored, frustrated and confused, then at least I could look good.

Her eyes brightened, and a few minutes later I was in the changing rooms, half a dozen beautiful gowns waiting for me to try them on. I'd just slipped into the first, a skin-tight gold cocktail dress, when I heard Snow's voice outside the stall.

"This sky-blue velvet looks pretty, doesn't it?" she chirped. "Or is the green silk nicer?"

I froze in dismay. Argh, she was like a bad smell! I just couldn't get rid of her.

"Both of them would look gorgeous, I'd bet," the shop girl gushed. "But then that's not hard with a face like yours."

I made a face in the stall's mirror, one that was definitely not gorgeous. While salespeople needed to earn a living like anyone else, their compliments had to at least be believable.

Snow clearly was more credulous, because she giggled. "Oh, you're too kind."

"No, I mean it," the ship girl persisted. "You've got to be one of the prettiest girls I've ever seen. I mean, ever."

I snorted. Talk about bullsh-

"Oh, but my father's fiancée is prettier than me," Snow countered with a high laugh. "He even calls her 'Fairest'."

The shop girl knew I was in here, didn't she? But her voice dropped low – although I could still hear it – and she whispered, "That's a matter of opinion, isn't it? But skin-tight clothes and high heels don't make the beauty. That comes from inside."

Ouch. A wave of embarrassment and anger washed through me, and I lifted my chin. I pushed aside the curtain and stepped out of the stall into the central area with its many mirrors. Snow and the shop girl both turned to look at me with wide eyes.

"This gown is rather tight," I said crisply, "but I think with the right pair of high heels it'll be just beautiful. Although that's only my opinion. Does it come in other colours?"

"Ahh…" the girl stammered. "Dark blue and red also."

"I'll try them both. You know my size." The girl disappeared into the shop, and I turned to Snow. "If you're stupid enough to believe the words of someone who's paid to admire you, then that's on you," I told her, "but I don't appreciate you using me as comparison."

She lifted her chin. "Are you really so sure she was flattering me? Maybe *you're* not as beautiful as you think you are, *Val.* Or maybe there are other types of beauty besides yours."

I sighed. "And how beautiful do I think I am, Snow?"

She shrugged a shoulder. "You insist on being called 'Fairest'. You keep telling Father how gorgeous you are. What do you think?"

I stared at her for a moment. I could hear my heartbeat pounding in my head, and in that moment I felt nothing but cold disdain for her. "Do you see that dark-haired guy out there in the store? The handsome one."

She glanced briefly into the shop. "That's Jafeer. He works in the village. What about him?"

"Is he watching us?"

She preened a little. "Yes."

"Now I'm going to walk over to the counter and buy this dress, because it looks good and because I can't be bothered being in here any longer. And you watch him, and see if he looks at you or at me." I bared my teeth at her, enjoying the sight of her tightened lips and darting eyes, then took a step away. "You might be rich, and you might fake sweetness, but if this is a beauty contest then I know who'll win."

He watched me. Of course he watched me; I could see him out of the corner of my eye as I made my way to the counter where the shop girl waited. And the whole time that I was sashaying across the shop, I was thinking, *what am I trying to prove?*

"Sorry, Ms Redwell, I'll just get you those gowns," the girl said, not meeting my eye.

"Don't bother," I told her flatly. "I'll wear this one out, and you can charge it to my account. My dress is in the stall. Please send that to the hotel."

"Yes, Ms Redwell."

I slipped my jacket over the gown, knowing I was ridiculously overdressed but not caring, and left the shop. I glanced at Jafeer as I did so, meeting his dark eyes. He winked.

Point proven. Snow: zero. Valentina: one.

But then why did I feel so foolish?

4 Curious

Out on the cobblestone street I was regretting my dramatic exit. Not just because I'd acted like a snooty diva, but because the gold dress was tight all the way to my knees. Combined with my heels, it was really affecting my balance.

I stopped to sit on a nearby bench, slipped off the heels and was debating whether to walk back barefoot when Mr Tall, Dark and Handsome himself stepped out of the shop. His eyes met mine, and he made a beeline towards me.

"I noticed you noticing me," he said with a smooth grin, rocking back on his heels with his hands in his pockets. "And if looking good was a crime, in that dress you'd be guilty as charged."

In spite of my irritation I huffed out a short laugh. "Do you practice terrible pick-up lines?"

"It's not terrible if it works. Is it working?"

I tapped the red button on my wristpiece twice – my signal for Jorge to come get me now. "If by working you mean making me want to overlook my fiancé, then no. It's not. And don't you owe me an apology?"

"Do I?"

"The Chateau de la Reine-Rouge," I told him. "Ninety

thousand credits. Remember?"

He blinked at me. "That was Ali."

"Riiight. Either way-" *I wouldn't touch you with a ten-foot pole*, I might have said, but then we had company.

"Val!" Snow sounded short of breath, like she'd had to run out of the shop, but this time I didn't mind the interruption. "Won't you introduce me to your friend?"

I stood, noticing a familiar black car pull up in the gap between buildings. Jorge must have been waiting for me. "Now why would I do that when you already know who he is?"

She didn't even blush. "Yes, but we haven't been *introduced*."

"Snow White, meet Jafeer. I don't know his last name, but he's trying to convince me to cheat on your father."

Jafeer made a protesting noise, but Snow's eyes lit up. "Are you going to?"

I rolled my eyes, grabbing my shoes by the heels. "If I was going to I'd hardly tell you, would I? And no. Now if you'll excuse me…"

I began to walk towards the car, my speed still hampered by the tight gown, and Snow ran to catch up, her breath coming in short huffs as she drew alongside me. "I got the blue dress instead of the green," she announced. "It makes my eyes look like sapphires."

"How nice for you. Why are you following me?"

"I thought we could walk back to the hotel together. After all, tomorrow we become family."

Ugh. At that reminder I felt my stomach roil again, and a headache threatened at the edge of my temples. It must have been stress.

"Or perhaps you're feeling unwell again," Snow said in the silence, an edge to her voice. "That seems to happen a lot."

Just around you, Snow. Just around you.

Up ahead Jorge held the car door open, and I picked up my pace to leave Snow behind. I could hear her puffing – for such a young girl she really was unfit – and I slid into the back seat, pulling the door shut and locking it, then sliding down the window slightly. Snow came to a halt outside the car, her expression uncertain as she studied the closed doors. "Are you going to let me in?"

"Sorry, I can't walk in this outfit," I told her sweetly, "but a strong girl like you? I'm sure you'd enjoy the exercise and the fresh air back to the hotel. Bye." I clicked the *shut* button again and the window slid closed. "Go, Jorge."

The car pulled away, juddering a little on the cobbled road, and I glanced back over my shoulder for just a moment. Snow stood there alone, looking small and a little forlorn as she watched us drive away. I felt a pang of guilt, which only served to make me angry – and then guiltier because I was swallowed up in this dark, intense hatred. I didn't want to feel this way, and I didn't think I'd disliked anyone so much, ever. Except maybe my exes, right before they'd died...

"She can't decide if she wants to be my best friend or my worst enemy," I said irritably. "But she's only managing the latter."

"Pardon, Ms Redwell?"

"Just thinking aloud, Jorge."

"Very good, Ms Redwell."

Back at the hotel I decided to stay in the gold dress, although I changed into more comfortable shoes. The preparations for the auction were taking place in the second ballroom, which was on the other side of the hotel from my cottage. Gold balloons and decorations had been arranged around the hotel foyer and ballroom, and I studied them with some amusement. Without meaning to I'd matched myself perfectly to the decor.

Karey Godmother stood on the other side of the room, in conversation with a trio of servers. She spotted me from a distance, then walked over with a polite smile. "Ms Redwell. The auction doesn't start for an hour."

"I know. I was looking for Kingsley. I'd like to talk to him, please."

"I'm afraid he's out at the moment, but I can take a message, if you like?"

I sighed, running a hand through my hair. He'd told me he was busy, but I'd hoped to see him anyway. I felt…off. Miserable, and partly because of the way I always seemed to behave around Snow. It was like I couldn't help myself. "Never mind. I'll see him at dinner."

"Is there anything I can help with?"

Just then something else came to mind. "Karey, is Kingsley having work done at the back of the hotel?"

"Work?" she echoed. "What do you mean?"

"Earlier today there were some men out there with shovels and what looked like a paper map or plans. They were digging behind the hotel, and they looked at me very impolitely."

"I'm sorry to hear that," Karey said, a note of *something* in her voice. Amusement? I shot a glance at her, but her expression was as professional as always. "But I think I know who they might be. Have you heard of a pirate named Blackbeard?"

I shrugged a shoulder nonchalantly. The name sounded familiar, although as with a lot of things I couldn't place its origin. Myth, history – who knew? "Of course."

"Well, rumour has it that he buried a fabulous treasure here four centuries ago, and that it's still somewhere on Sweetheart Island. Some say that it's even inside the hotel itself, which is why about once a year we have to deal with people traipsing around with maps and shovels looking for the thing. It is nonsense, of course."

"You mean there's a rumour of actual treasure here?" I said in disbelief. "Not just setting up a treasure hunt for future guests who want to play out some foolish fantasy?"

Karey suddenly made a choking noise that turned into a cough. "Uh…well, I wouldn't dismiss the idea of a treasure hunt being arranged as part of the resort makeover, as it would reduce the unsanctioned visitors-"

"So that's what those men were doing. Setting up a treasure hunt with Kingsley's permission?"

"No, I don't believe it was anything official-"

"Then they're trespassing on White land," I cut in. "If they're looking for real treasure, then they're extra foolish. This building can't be more than eighty years old. And even if there *was* treasure, it'd belong to the owners of the land, not some rude fools with shovels."

"Indeed, Ms Redwell."

"Good. You'll call security then, and see to having them sent off hotel land immediately?"

"Oh, no!" Karey exclaimed suddenly, and I turned to look at her in surprise. She flushed, lowering her voice. "I mean, I can sort that out quietly and quickly, without any unnecessary physical force. I am the events coordinator for the entire island, of course, so I do have a record of who comes and goes. I can fix the issue, if you'll just give me a description?"

I thought back to what they'd looked like, but it was hard to remember except the vaguest details. "One big burly one, I think, and one young with long brown hair, and one had glasses…and one with dark hair, perhaps? I can't remember any more than that."

Karey dutifully noted down the details, then asked, "If that's all, might I carry on with my duties?"

Duties which included organising my wedding, as well as today's function. "Of course. Thank you."

She trotted off to do whatever she did, and I perched myself in another of those alcoves that the hotel abounded with, watching the flurry of activity around me. The servers in their perfectly white uniforms moved about in synchronised haste, interspersed with the occasional local hired for the occasion. Those always stood out: they also wore white, but they were animated with worry or humour or concentration, and their grooming was less than perfect.

I smoothed a hand over my hair reflexively. It was rarely messy. In fact, it was almost always beautiful, or so I'd been told. And if I couldn't go by what other people told me, then how *could* I know if I was lovely or not?

Who cares? That quiet inner voice whispered. *Find someone who actually likes* you, *not just your looks.*

Shut up, inner voice, I told it, but with less force than last time. I didn't know where those thoughts were coming from – regurgitated from something I'd seen or read somewhere, no doubt – but they weren't helping the situation. I was supposed to be marrying Kingsley tomorrow, and things were hard enough without this inner conflict.

Supposed to be?

That was the plan, yes! He adored me. Fine, maybe not as much as I'd thought he did, and he wasn't the man I'd remembered from that one week at that other resort. But if I didn't marry him, what would I do with my life?

Anything at all. You're rich.

Rich enough to go off to another resort where I'd meet another besotted rich man. A younger one, maybe, without any children this time. Or maybe I'd turn down the men – but I'd still be alone.

The inner voice was quiet in response to that thought, because I'd found something that had stumped even it. And that was the real choice, I realised. I wasn't choosing Kingsley or not-Kingsley, as though he was the key to my future happiness. I was choosing Valentina-and-someone, or Valentina-all-alone, and that choice was much, much harder.

An image of Caleb flashed to mind, and I staunchly pushed it away. I didn't know what to make of him either. But even if there'd been no Kingsley, I definitely wasn't going to take up with someone who was so clearly confused, and so clearly grieving for someone who resembled me.

Finally guests for the auction began to trickle in, so I quickly redid my lipstick, smoothed my hair, then found a seat at the very back. Around me other women chattered as they took their seats, and I tuned out the hum of voices and music, still pondering my options. The wedding dress hanging in the cottage. The cake that was even now being made. Kingsley's terrible disappointment if I changed my mind. My solitary future without him, stretching out ahead of me, empty of anyone except myself. So lonely…

Think happy thoughts, Valentina! Desperate to distract myself, I searched my purse for the coin-thing from the other day, the one that was either a radio or a weird sort of communication device. But I couldn't find it anywhere, and I finally had to conclude I'd lost it. "Chestnuts." It hadn't been much, but at least it had been a challenge trying to figure out what the thing was.

Just then two words stood out amongst the chatter. "Snow White!"

Again. Double chestnuts! A pang of irritation and guilt shot through me. I put my head down, pretending to fiddle with my wristpiece, but I couldn't tune out that conversation.

"Oh, you look just *stunning*," a high female voice was announcing somewhere to my right. "That shade of blue makes your eyes look like sapphires. Doesn't she look stunning, Darla?"

"Lovely. Just lovely," a slightly deeper female voice agreed. "Just like your beautiful mother. A real beauty, not like some these days."

Who could say that and really mean it? Irresistibly curious, I finally looked up to see Snow standing in the aisle near where I was sitting, surrounded by a gaggle of women. She was wearing the sky-blue velvet dress, and when her eyes met mine, her lips curved into a triumphant smile. "Excuse me ladies," she said gaily, "I've just seen someone I know." A moment later she was skipping along towards me, and she plunked herself into the seat next to mine. "Hi, *Val.*"

"Snow," I said through gritted teeth. "I see you made it."

"I called my own car. It was too far to walk, and it wasn't kind of you to leave me in the village."

She was right about the last part. *Sorry,* I tried to say, but I couldn't spit out such a blatant lie. Instead I found myself saying, "Perhaps you'll want a seat closer to the front."

"No. Why would I want to do that?"

"I don't intend to bid," I persisted. Guilt and dislike had fought briefly, and dislike had won. "But no doubt you'll want to buy yourself a date?"

"I don't need to buy a date, Val. True love will find me." My eyebrows shot up, and a moment later she added, "Besides, I'd almost think you were trying to get rid of me."

Then she'd be almost right. Thankfully at that moment the auctioneer's voice boomed out over our conversation, and Snow's attention was finally diverted. "This is my first auction," she told me, her eyes fixed on the temporary stage up ahead with clear excitement. "I was too young to attend the others."

The auctioneer was a large-boned, jovial woman who was dwarfed by the enormous image on the screen behind her. I tuned out as she greeted us then introduced the first of the 'bachelors', a bespectacled guy whose hunched shoulders indicated he'd rather be anywhere except there. The screen listed him as 'George Tailor, tailor, offering a picnic lunch on Little Sweetheart Island'.

Heh, his name and his occupation were the same. But funny or not, someone made the winning bid, and he flushed in relief as he was allowed to flee the stage.

This was for charity, I reminded myself, and these men had probably paid for their own prizes. I watched with little interest as the auction continued; half a dozen males of various ages and appearances offering their company along with a meal, or a game, or a drink…

The screen changed to read 'Daniel Charmant, longtime Sweetheart Island resident', and my attention was pricked. Finally, someone I recognised. There was a slight cheer from some of the audience as he sauntered onto the stage. He looked good, I'd admit it: white tuxedo, sun-streaked blond hair, sunglasses that he pushed back onto his head as he reached the podium and began his brief introductory speech.

"Ooh, look at him," Snow breathed from beside me. "What do you think, Val?"

"Valentina," I corrected automatically. "And I think he's very pleased with himself, but all he's offering is a shopping trip and a coffee. He probably wants someone to carry his bags."

"*I'd* carry his bags," came a wistful voice from beside me. I looked up to see a redhaired girl in a white server's uniform, staring up at the stage with the kind of desire I usually reserved for shoes or diamonds. She saw me looking and flushed a little.

"Sorry."

I shrugged a shoulder, then turned back to the stage where the opening bid had been called. It quickly escalated to a figure that impressed even me, the winning bid being made by a bejewelled woman in her forties who shook her fists in happiness when she won.

Out of the corner of my eye I saw Snow, her hands clenched on her lap as she watched the stage eagerly. "You didn't bid," I said in surprise.

She shrugged. "He's not for me."

That was an interesting way of saying he was a bad bet. In that case, he 'wasn't for me' either.

But then the next bachelor was called onto the stage, and Snow sat bolt upright, her eyes wide and mouth open. "That's him," she hissed. I looked at her in surprise and she added, her tone a lot sweeter, "That's the one!"

'Tarquin Prince,' the big screen read. 'Longtime Sweetheart Islander and son of PrinceInc's CEO – offering a candlelit dinner for two'. It showed a close up of Tarquin's face: big, baby-blue eyes with black lashes, swept back dark hair, perfect cheekbones and a slight cleft in his chin. A beautiful boy, but with those smooth cheeks and slim figure he couldn't be more than seventeen or eighteen. Barring Snow and I, most of the women in here were old enough to be his mother.

He looked out at the audience and even from here I saw his eyes widen and his throat move in a 'gulp' as though he'd heard Snow's words all the way across the room. I smiled.

But then the auctioneer called the opening bid. A couple of girls up ahead raised their hands, but Snow leapt to her feet, calling a number triple what the previous had been. I waited for the auctioneer to correct her, to explain that wasn't how bidding worked, but instead the woman shrugged. "Can anyone beat that?" Three silent seconds ticked by, and then Snow had won. She finally sat down, visibly vibrating with excitement.

"Did you see him meet my eyes?" she breathed. "He's perfect."

And rich too, by the sound of it. I wondered how he'd respond to Snow's enthusiasm.

The last few bachelors were auctioned off, and then came the crowd of women moving towards the food here at the back of the room or going forward to meet their 'prizes'. I sat back, watching the meetings with interest. Some looking shy, some grinning as if they'd known each other already, and some clearly awkward. I saw Daniel Charmant smile down at the woman who'd bid for him, only to stagger back as she launched herself at him and planted a kiss on his lips.

I laughed to myself at his horrified reaction, which he quickly covered by another white, slightly less confident smile. Perhaps a public shopping trip was a good idea – as long as he didn't let her corner him in the changing rooms.

But then I saw Snow. She stood in the crowd at the front of the room, the overhead lights giving her inky hair a slight halo, staring up at the approaching Tarquin with that same wide-eyed, eager expression. I smirked again, thinking of how horrified he must also be, but then I saw his own face. Any anxiety he'd shown on stage was now gone, and he was staring back at her with a similar expression. It looked like awe.

No, it must be horror, I told myself. But then he leaned down and took her hand, then laid a soft kiss on her knuckles before saying something I couldn't hear from this distance. She simpered and looked away briefly before glancing back at him; his eyes hadn't moved from her.

I leaned back in my chair, one eyebrow raised and arms folded. I knew all about instant attraction – I'd had it with James and my first boyfriend before I learned how to control it – but I wouldn't believe it had happened to these two. Snow was cute at best, not the sort who made boys swoon. She just wasn't, and I wasn't being mean or spiteful by thinking that.

Was I?

But then Snow took Tarquin by the hand and led him over to me, her lips fixed in a gleaming smile. "Val, have you met Tarquin? We're going to have our special lunch tomorrow, right before your wedding."

"It's Valentina, Snowball. And no, I haven't met him."

The boy, who'd been staring down at Snow with what was to me an inexplicably fascinated expression, finally looked away, flicking his eyes over me quickly before returning to Snow's face. "A pleasure to meet you, Val."

"Valentina," I repeated, irritation seeping into my tone. "So, you're a longtime island resident, are you?"

"More or less," he agreed politely. Then to Snow he said, "I just can't believe we've never met before today. It feels like fate."

I stood, which brought me level with him in my high heels, and studied his face suspiciously. He was a bit short but very handsome, but then so were a lot of the men on the island – and many of the handsome ones were androids. It was only his clear anxiety on stage which made me think otherwise, and which made his behaviour now so incomprehensible. He wasn't looking at *me*. Not at all. Why?

"Rather than fate, I'd suggest it was Daddy's fortune enabling her to make that bid," I said. "Now Tarquin…did you hear about the fire at the circus?"

He turned, blinking those big blue eyes at me, his perfect brow furrowed. "Pardon?"

"It was in tents."

I'd delivered the line deadpan, and there were a few seconds of silence before he let out a short, awkward laugh. "Ah ha ha. Good joke."

Snow was watching me with narrowed eyes, but I still wasn't convinced. I leaned over and grabbed a glass of wine from a passing server, holding it out to him. "Here, have a sip. Kingsley only provides the finest reds."

Tarquin stepped back, still holding Snow's hand, and didn't take the glass. "Um…I don't really drink, but thank you for offering."

Hmm. I took a step forward, following him. "Stick out your tongue," I ordered.

His eyes bulged, and Snow let out an irritated huff. "Oh Val, stop trying to see if he's an android! He's a person, and he likes *me*. Haven't you heard of love at first sight?"

Tarquin's confusion cleared, and now he laughed, a real-sounding one. "But of course I'm not an android. Why would you think that?"

"Your inexplicable and sudden display of favour for Snow. Why else?"

He blinked again. "But it's not inexplicable. Not at all." He turned back to Snow, gazing warmly down into her pale little face. "I knew her as soon as I saw her. She's the most beautiful girl I've ever seen."

Snap. The fine stem of the wine glass broke in my hand, sending a flood of crimson down my pale gold gown. We all stared at the broken glass for a moment. Snow tittered.

"If you'll excuse me," I said with dignity. "I do believe that's my cue to leave."

I went to the nearest bathroom, trying to see if the gown was salvageable. It just looked worse in the large mirror, like I'd been stabbed…or had committed murder. I rested my hands on either side of the vanity, staring at my reflection in the mirror. I looked attractive, except for the wine stain. That was an objective opinion, right? OK, so I looked a little cranky, but that was understandable considering the chaos that had been my life over these last few days. Before that too, if I was honest.

I remembered those compliments Snow had received from the women before the auction started, and then that lavishly stupid compliment from the shop girl. They'd all said – or at least implied – that Snow was prettier than I was.

Even if I had a mole instead of a beauty mark, that was impossible. But then why had Tarquin reacted to her the way he had?

You had a head injury. What if it damaged more than just your memory?

Oh, *fiery chestnuts.* Was it possible that Snow *was* prettier than I was, and there was something wrong with me so I just couldn't see it? I turned abruptly away from the mirror, leaning back on the vanity. I was shaking with panic and fury. She *couldn't* be prettier than me. Because if she was – and she wasn't! – then she'd be better than me. She'd win, and then who would I be? Just another made-up girl in a too-tight dress, going through disaster relationship after disaster relationship in search of something that probably didn't exist…

"Valentina, you're being ridiculous," I told myself, trying to breathe evenly. "You're better than this."

An image flashed into my mind: Snow surrounded by adoring crowds, Kingsley at her side, the spotlight on her smug little face. And me, in the background. In the dark, ignored.

Alone.

Never, I vowed. I would *never* let it happen.

I guessed I wasn't better than this after all.

Just then one of the stall doors behind me slid open, and a redhaired girl in a plain white suit came out, moving to wash her hands in the vanity beside me. About my age, her stooped posture and averted eyes detracted somewhat from her classically attractive figure. I watched her morosely. Perhaps I only thought her attractive because she shared my basic features – tall, slim curves, even features. Perhaps I mistook glamour for true beauty, and other people saw what I didn't see.

The girl's eyes met mine, and she smiled politely, then moved to leave. "Excuse me."

"Wait." The girl turned, and I finally recognised her. "You're the server from the auction. The one who'd be happy to carry Daniel Charmant's bags."

She flushed pink under her freckles. "It was just a silly comment. I'd appreciate it if you didn't pass that on."

I shrugged a shoulder. "No offence, but I couldn't care less about your affection for Sweetheart Island's biggest playboy. I-"

"He's not a playboy!" she burst out. "He's just popular and outgoing, and hasn't met the right girl yet! You don't need to talk about him that way!"

I stared at her, and her shoulders hunched, head down as she realised what she'd done. "I'm sorry, Ms Redwell. I won't…I was just upset about the auction."

"Valentina," I corrected, unoffended. "And who are you?"

"Cindy Rayla. I work at the French restaurant in the village, except when there are events like this."

"Cindy." I'd meant to ask her a question, but now I was curious. "You live here full time?"

"Yes, Valentina. With my stepmother Melaina Weatherwax." Her lip curled. "She's the one who won Daniel in the auction."

Hmm, interesting that the stepmother wore jewels while the stepdaughter served drinks…and both wanted the same man. "I assume you've met Snow White. What do you think of her?"

Cindy shrugged a shoulder, appearing relieved that the questions were no longer so personal. "She's nice, I suppose. I've never really spoken to her. We move in different circles."

Rich girl, poor girl. I'd been both. "And do you consider her beautiful?"

"Beautiful? Of course."

"Of course?" I echoed in dismay.

"Mm. She has a lovely face and figure. Petite…just about perfect." She shrugged again, now looking confused rather than upset. "Is that all you wanted?"

I waved a hand at her dismissively, stunned into silence by her words. Snow, perfect? She didn't look a thing like me.

So what did that make me?

When I came out of the bathroom Snow was waiting outside, her small hands clasped in front of her tiny waist, a beatific expression on her face. "There you are!" she chirped. "But your dress is still a mess!"

I shrugged, uncaring. I couldn't have fixed it anyway. "Where's Tarquin?"

"He went to get me a drink. Isn't he just perfect?" I didn't answer.

"I'll be having dinner with him," she continued, "and then we can spend the whole evening together. Oh, it's like a dream! I'd ask him to be my date to the wedding, except he has to go away for a while, off the island." She sighed dramatically and clasped her hands together in front of her chest. "How can I bear to be away from him for so long?"

"I don't know," I said numbly. "I daresay you'll manage it. Excuse me."

I left as quickly as my tight gown would allow me to, heading down one of the quieter halls usually used by staff – a shortcut to the cottage. I didn't want to talk to anyone or even have to smile at anyone. I felt confused and angry and just *upset,* like I had from the moment I'd met Snow.

Stupid girl. This was all her fault.

But thinking angry thoughts meant I wasn't paying attention to where I was going, because I found myself in an unfamiliar hall. It was narrow and plain, without the decorations the guest halls usually had. Up ahead I could see what looked like a kitchen dining area – a functional, plain one unlike anything else I'd seen in the hotel. I'd gone right into the staff quarters.

I walked inside, searching for an exit to the rose gardens that even now I could see through the kitchen windows, but there was no door in sight. Not very fire safe, was it? But now I'd have to retrace my steps.

Just then I heard the clicking of heels on the hall floor; someone was coming. I froze in place.

A pink-clad figure trotted into sight, heading straight for the pantry opposite where I stood. It was Karey Godmother, and she didn't seem to have seen me. She tapped the lock-pad beside the pantry door, then leaned in and said, "Open Sesame."

The door slid open to reveal a lit-up room, and in the few seconds as she stepped inside I caught a glimpse of many shelves full of...everything. There was an ornate mirror, a sparkly blue dress hanging on the closest wall, and what might have been an old brass lamp of some kind. But then the door closed, and I was once again alone.

What an odd place for a storage room. But then they could hardly keep it in the guest areas, could they? I shrugged, then turned back the way I'd come.

This time I made it to the cottage without incident. I changed out of the gold dress, balling it up and tossing it in the washing basket. I really ought to get Jorge to have it cleaned before the stain set, but at this moment I didn't care if the wine ruined it. I walked barefoot to the walk-in closet in my bedroom, studying the array of clothes available. They were all the same kind, I realised; whether they were long or short, they were all either low-cut or tight, tight, tight. Even the wedding dress currently hanging off the main closet door was the same. Its fabric was fine and stretchy, and it had a slit up to the thigh to enable me to walk – and to show off my legs. The racks of shoes were also all similar; mostly strappy with high, high heels. The ones I'd worn to the auction were my lowest.

What had the shop girl said? *Skin-tight clothes and high heels don't make the beauty. That comes from inside.*

That was a nice thought, but no one really believed that, I thought dismissively. Even Caleb had seemed happy enough with my 'outside', even when he'd thought I was marrying Kingsley for his money. And I'd always, *always* been told I was beautiful when I was wearing those high heels and skin-tight clothes. No one had ever complimented my looks when I had messy hair and wore sweat pants. Had I *ever* worn sweat pants?

But still I found myself brushing past the hangers of tight dresses, looking for something else. Something plainer.

Then at the back of the closet I found two hangers I hadn't noticed before. One held a one-piece suit in browns and oranges; twenty years out of date and ugly to boot. The other held a dress that reminded me of something a gypsy would wear, and a long, hairy black thing hooked on the back. A wig.

Why on earth would such things be in *my* closet? I didn't remember putting them there, and I certainly wouldn't be caught dead wearing them. A moment later I realised that I hadn't unpacked my clothing. Jorge had, and that those two outfits must have already been in here.

I pulled out the gypsy dress, studying it with curled lip as if further observation would improve its looks. It didn't, but something else was revealed. Something brown and long and oddly-shaped, propped up in the very corner of the closet. I pulled it out, realising what it was once I saw the whole thing. An antique wooden air rifle, highly polished and almost beautiful in its simplicity. There was a small cloth bag hooked around its barrel, and I could feel the little pellets inside.

"I'll have to speak to Jorge about clearing out rooms properly before I stay in them," I said aloud, but my interest had been piqued.

I slipped on a new dress then sat down on the bed, examining the rifle. Something about it felt familiar, which in my experience meant I'd seen one before, but had just forgotten. Damn that head injury.

I stroked one hand over the smooth wood then gave the barrel a hard knock. It folded forward, exposing the empty chamber, and I tipped the wasp-shaped pellets out into my hand, feeling like I was reliving some forgotten moment. Scenes flashed into my mind: large hands on mine, showing me where to grip the rifle; the shock of the blast and the slight jolt of the recoil on my shoulder; tiny holes in the centre of the distant target; a smiling male face, fuzzy in my memory but recognisable.

James. He'd taught me how to shoot at some point, probably at the start when he was still trying to impress me. Obviously the lessons hadn't continued, or I would have remembered before now.

I methodically loaded a pellet into the rifle, snapping its barrel back into place and holding it to my shoulder. I looked down the sight, focusing on a metal figurine across the room, then pulled the trigger.

Ping. The figurine skidded off the shelf to land on the floor, and I set the rifle down with a smile of satisfaction. Now, if James had died from a gunshot wound, perhaps I would be a genuine suspect in his death. But you couldn't fake a brain aneurysm. They were practically an act of God – and James had deserved what he got.

Just then another scene flashed into my mind: my gloved

hands on a tiny bottle, carefully opening the lid; James' smug expression, that dimple in his cheek…

I blinked. James didn't have a dimple; Caleb did. He must have made more of an impression than I'd realised if he was blurring together with James in my memory. But the bottle… I remembered that other compartment in my makeup chest. Perhaps they belonged to me after all.

Damn you, head injury. It was times like this when having memory gaps made me feel crazy.

"Shh, she might be home!" A quiet voice cut in through the silence, coming from outside my window. Male, not too old. Unfamiliar.

"She's not home, it's dinner time," a second male voice responded. "She'll be out with, er…"

"King White," a young voice said. A boy. "The old man."

"Kingsley White, idiot," a different male voice scolded. This one was colder than the others, emotionless. "If you want to blend in here on the island, you've got to know everyone's names."

"Sorry."

"Ah, forget them," a new voice said. "Just do your job, and I'll do mine, alright? Now get on with it. She might be out now, but she won't be all day."

I'd sat silently through the whole conversation, but now I perked up. I knew that last voice – it was Mr Tall, Dark and Handsome from the village. Jafeer. And what was the bet that he wasn't delivering a carpet this time?

I clenched my fists, my jaw tight. Who else was outside my cottage, and what were they doing that they needed me to be away? I tapped the red button on my wristpiece. Then I waited until the sound of footsteps faded, picked up the rifle and went to the door.

5 Audacious

'She scares the c**p out of me.' – from an interview with Jake P

I propped the air rifle beside the door, just within arm's reach, and opened the door. Standing in the entryway, hands in his pockets, was Jafeer. He jolted in surprise when he saw me, then plastered a smile on his now clean-shaven face. "Oh hey. I wondered if you were home."

"Ringing the doorbell is an excellent way to find out," I said in my coldest voice. Inside I was burning with anger. "What are you doing here?"

He didn't blink. "I thought I'd come pay you a visit, finish our earlier conversation."

Liar. I folded my arms. "Go on then."

"Ah…so, do you come here often?"

Seriously? I stared at him for one long moment. I wanted to shut the door in his face, to call security, but I also wanted to know what he and the others were doing here. And something about his clean-shaven face was tugging at my memory. What had I forgotten? "You really are the king of dreadful pick-up lines," I said conversationally. "But with looks like yours, I expect most girls choose to find it endearing."

Jafeer dipped his head in what was clearly false humility, spreading his hands out in front of him. "Aw, thanks. I-"

"I knew a boy like that once," I interrupted, reaching silently for where the rifle stood beside the doorframe. "He was my first boyfriend."

He grinned, raising an eyebrow. "Good memories?"

"Not particularly. He was absolutely gorgeous, but he wouldn't take no for an answer."

Jafeer smirked. "So you do think I'm gorgeous, do you?"

"Mm. But don't you want to know what happened to him?" I asked, closing my fingers around the rifle's barrel. "The boy who couldn't take no for an answer?"

"Alright," he asked, shrugging his shoulders. "What happened to him?"

"He died," I answered, swinging out the rifle and pointing it at him. "It was a tragedy, the obituary said, but I wasn't sad at all."

He reared back, hands held out in front of him defensively. "Whoa…easy! You don't need to shoot me!"

"Apparently I do," I snapped. "Because otherwise you wouldn't think you can show up here with your friends, acting like some kind of spy! I want to know their names and what they're doing here. All of them, *now*."

"What friends? I don't know what-"

I stepped forward, shoving the barrel right into his chest. I was so furious, I felt almost out of control. "*Now!*"

"We're nobody, really! Just four of us, looking around the area for something…something that was lost. We didn't mean to cause any trouble!"

My lips tightened. "You're one of the treasure hunters. I didn't recognise you earlier because of your stupid fake beard!" That was why he now looked familiar – he'd been the dark haired one who'd waved to me this morning. Karey hadn't dealt with them as she'd promised. "Is Caleb one of you?"

"What? No!"

That sounded sincere enough. I relaxed a little, but didn't lower the rifle. "The others. What are their names?"

"Ah…Hercules, Sinbad, and Aladdin. That's all."

"Who's who?"

"Um…Hercules is muscly, Sinbad wears glasses, Aladdin is the youngest…"

"Are they actors or guests?"

"What do you mean?" he hedged. "We all live here."

"If you want to blend in here on the island, you've got to know everyone's names," I mimicked in a sing-song voice. "Someone said that just five minutes ago, so I know they're not real residents. You might be an actor, but what are the others? Actors, paying guests, or trespassers?"

Jafeer's mouth opened then closed again, and he took a step backwards, grabbing hold of the rifle's barrel. "I bet this thing isn't even loaded, *Valentina*. And how do you know about the actors?"

I narrowed my eyes, jerking the rifle away with a snarl before raising it back to my shoulder. Jafeer stumbled backwards then caught himself, clearly deciding it wasn't worth the effort, then turned and sprinted out of sight.

I went inside and locked the door again, putting down the weapon once more. I was trembling, and I didn't know if it was fear or fury – they felt the same to me. But then I heard the voices on the *other* side of the cottage, coming through the tiny vents in the bathroom wall…

"I'm telling you, she hates me," Jafeer was saying. He sounded quite shaken. "As a distraction, that one sucked."

"What, you didn't get any ice-queen nooky," someone else said sarcastically. "Poor you."

"She was asking questions, wanted to know who you all were," Jafeer continued. "I didn't expect her to even notice!"

"What did you tell her?" another voice came, the cold one. "Did you give our names?"

"Not the real ones."

"Good."

So they *were* fake names. I knew it. Those other names – they didn't sound right. Just then I heard the unmistakeable sound of shovels tapping against the hard ground.

"Are you crazy?" the young voice said, echoing my thoughts. "She's just in there, and Jay said she has a gun."

Jay? Did they mean 'J' for Jafeer?

"She told me that she killed some guy with it," Jafeer added.

"She looks crazy enough to do it, too."

Actually, I hadn't said that at all. The boy who couldn't take no for an answer *had* died, but he'd fallen off a cliff.

"I doubt it was loaded," the cold voice said. "It's probably ornamental. Now here is where the map said we should look, so get moving. Time's a wasting."

"That stupid map's messing us around," Jafeer said bitterly. "But we should leave this for later. She's crazy!"

"She's a free agent," the cold voice countered. "She's won't kill, but otherwise she does what she wants. It's a fluid game, and she's just made it more interesting."

The way they talked about me was so strange, so impersonal, and it just made me feel angrier. And that mention of a map... If there was real treasure, I thought grimly, then it wouldn't be theirs.

Calm, Valentina. Don't lose your temper-

Too late. I stepped out of the front door, still barefoot and again holding the newly loaded rifle, and walked around the cottage until I saw the treasure hunters. They were about fifteen feet away, standing in a loose huddle in the space between my cottage and the forest, and the one with glasses was holding an ancient-looking paper that had to be the aforementioned map. They all looked up at me with varying expressions of surprise.

"I'm so glad I've made your lives more interesting," I said icily, moving the rifle into practised position: the stock at my shoulder, my head tilted so I could see through the sights. "Drop the map."

The burly one – who must be 'Hercules' – glared at me with little, squinty eyes, his tight t-shirt outlining his overdeveloped muscles. "I bet that thing isn't even loaded," he sneered. "You'd be better off hitting us with it."

"If I have to," I agreed. Then I aimed the rifle and with perfect accuracy shot the map out of the bespectacled one's hands. The men all jumped back, dropping their shovels even as I smoothly reloaded. "Surprise, it's loaded. Now be so kind as to tell me what you're looking for before I shoot you all in the kneecaps."

"It's just a rumour," the young one babbled, his eyes bulging wide. He must be 'Aladdin'. "We're just looking! We're not doing any harm, I promise."

"Shut up," Hercules hissed at him, but I ignored him.

"You all need to give up on this treasure hunting idea, or at least conduct it off the grounds of the hotel. You have no right to be here, and if you remain, I'll make you very, very sorry. That's a promise."

The men were all standing stiffly, clearly tense, but the bespectacled one lifted his hands, palms out in a conciliatory manner. Jafeer had called him Sinbad. "Valentina, we can make this worth your while. We can do the work, but share the proceeds with you."

"It's Ms Redwell to you. And I will never work with any of you. I don't like the way you look at me, or the way you talk to me, or your complete lack of respect for boundaries. So you should go now, or I'll start deciding who to shoot."

"The map," Hercules muttered to Sinbad. It still lay on the ground between me and them, where Sinbad had dropped it.

"Leave it," I ordered. My tone was confident and cold, but inside my heart had begun to pound. If they didn't listen, what would I do? I might have stepped into something I couldn't control. "Now *go*."

Aladdin was already backing away, Jafeer close behind, but Sinbad smiled. "She's only got one shot at a time," I heard him whisper to Hercules, and then as if they'd rehearsed it, both ran forward. I shot at Hercules, he was the bigger target, but I must have missed because within seconds he'd reached me and tackled me to the ground, sending the rifle flying. I didn't know what he'd planned but the moment I felt his weight on me I panicked, thrashing around frantically.

Filled with fear-fuelled energy, I threw him off and grabbed for the first thing that my hand touched – the handle of the shovel. It felt as light as aluminium foil but I swung it anyway, hitting him in the ribs with all of my strength.

Crack. I swung the shovel around again, this time hitting him on the shoulder and knocking him backwards, away from the map.

Sinbad lunged for me but I swung again, blade sideways this time and he jumped back barely in time to avoid having something vital cut off. I might have shrieked something like, 'I'll take off your head!' but I was so angry that the whole scene felt like a blur.

But then Sinbad had backed away enough that I found the rifle again, and loaded it…

They ran, unsurprisingly. All of them, even Hercules who was limping rather than running, and I shot at them as they left. I was aiming for Jafeer's backside, but he proved to be a fast runner and shock made me slow.

They disappeared from sight around the side of the hotel, and I didn't pursue. I stood there, my face twisted in a painful snarl, and the rifle still gripped tightly in my hands. The sun was out, shining through the trees, and in spite of the gunshots no one had come to see what had happened.

Had that really happened? I would doubt it if not for the map and the shovels still at my feet. I wasn't a violent person. I just wasn't! That whole scene had felt so surreal, like I'd switched into a previously hidden, alternate personality – an angry one. I was still vibrating with the aftershock of that fierce rage and hatred that I hadn't known I was capable of, and I could feel the adrenaline coursing through my veins and my face contorted into a grimace. The back of my throat burned, and my eyes pricked with tears.

"Ms Redwell."

I jolted, spinning around and aiming the rifle, but it was only Jorge. I lowered it, letting out a heavy sigh. "Careful. You could have lost an eye."

"Is there anything you require, Ms Redwell?"

I looked at the rifle, then at his placid expression. Did nothing shock him? "I…uh…I want my things moved from the cottage to the hotel immediately – the best suite available. I will also need these shovels to be disposed of, and then I want you to send out security to find those four treasure hunters and make it very clear to them that they're not to come back." I paused. "If that doesn't work, you are to go yourself, and use whatever persuasion necessary."

"Yes, Ms Redwell. Is there anything else?"

I sighed again. "No, thank you." I'd better not make things any worse.

"Yes, Ms Redwell."

Jorge left, and I just stood there for another few moments, rifle still in hand. He was the ex-military one. I should have waited for him, I realised, rather than charging out there on my own and turning into some sort of crazy person.

Too late. I huffed out a heavy breath, then retrieved the map before it blew away. I'd gone to a lot of trouble to get the thing. It was made of strong, very thin paper, and it showed what looked to be Sweetheart Island, but scattered with an assortment of pen marks and symbols. There was no 'x' marking the spot, not like treasure maps from the movies.

I could have a go at treasure hunting myself. But technically this was a stolen map, even if I did have the right to be on White land. I might just hang onto it for a while, then pull it out when I was sure the treasure hunters were well and truly gone. But for now, the map needed to be hidden somewhere that they'd never find it, somewhere away from me. Somewhere that no one would ever, ever look…

I quickly detoured back into the cottage, shoving the rifle under the low bed then tossing the bag of pellets after it. Then I took the map, folded it carefully and slipped it inside my sleeve, and headed down into the village. In the farthest inside corner of Ali Baba's store I found a large statue of a dog creature with hollowed out nostrils. It was vaguely Egyptian in appearance, and I supposed the holes must have been a clever way to avoid the clay cracking when it was fired, but chestnuts, it was hideous. Surely no one would buy it – which made it perfect. After a surreptitious check no one was looking I shoved the map into the nostril and tapped it so that it fell inside the statue's hollow body. Good luck finding it there, treasure hunters.

"Good afternoon…Valentina! Hi again."

"Caleb! Hi." I stepped back, feeling as though I'd been caught doing something wrong. "I was, um, wondering if there were any more of these dog statues."

"That's the only one we have in stock, but we can order you another if you want it?" He looked unconvinced.

"Don't bother," I said lightly. "I didn't like it that much anyway."

"Valentina," he said, studying my face intently. "Are you feeling alright?"

"Um…yes."

"Really? Your eyes look a little red. I can get you some more painkiller if you like."

"No, that's OK." I paused. "And I'm not stalking you."

"I didn't think you were." But the edge of his lip curled into a smile. "Do you need another drink?"

"No, thank you," I replied politely, feeling my cheeks heat again. "But maybe you can answer a question for me."

"Anything."

"Do you know three men calling themselves Sinbad, Aladdin and Hercules? They're friends of Jafeer's."

Caleb's eyes widened. "Ah…I've met one or two of them. Why?"

"Because I shot a couple of them just now."

His eyes just about bugged out of his head. "You *shot…* who?"

"Just with an air rifle," I explained. "They're not dead." Then to my horror I felt my face crumple, and I turned away blindly.

I felt his hand on my shoulder, large and warm. "Don't go," he said gently. "Tell me what happened."

"I don't know why I'd tell you anything," I said. "We hardly know each other."

"Perhaps you just need a listening ear," he replied lightly, "and I don't mind providing it. So, these treasure hunters. What did they do to provoke you into shooting them?"

I brightened a little at his wording. They *had* provoked me, but not everyone might see it that way. I told him about walking past them earlier and feeling scared by how they'd looked at me, then about how I'd tried to have them evicted, unsuccessfully it seemed. Then about how they'd started digging right outside my cottage, and they'd spoken about me so strangely before I'd confronted them…

"And then when the big one knocked me down, I hit him with a shovel," I finished. "They ran away after that." I didn't mention that I'd taken their map and hidden it in this very shop. He might be a little less sympathetic if he knew those details. "Do you think I'm going to be arrested?"

Caleb shook his head, eyebrows raised in amazement. "Um… no."

"Really?!"

"If it was self-defence," he said carefully, "then you'll be fine. Maybe. I hope they weren't badly injured, because with your background…"

I froze, staring up at him. "What about my background?"

His mouth opened, then closed again awkwardly. "Ah… you're a widow…"

"Yes," I agreed slowly. "I told you that already. What does that have to do with anything?"

There was another long pause where his eyebrows furrowed. He was clearly unhappy. Finally he answered, "There's a rumour going around that your exes died under suspicious circumstances."

Exes, not ex. Clearly someone had been telling tales. "Did that rumour come from Snow White? Because she accused me of the exact same thing earlier today. It's not true, of course. Walter had a heart attack, and James had a brain aneurysm." I'd said it so many times that it came out by rote.

"Walter?"

I ducked my head. "My other fiancé. He died a week before the wedding last year."

"I see." But Caleb didn't sound surprised that James hadn't been my one-and-only, and I didn't like that. "Well, I don't remember who was spreading the rumour, but of course you didn't kill them. I'm sure you'd never kill anybody." His tone was light, almost careless, but I couldn't tell if he was sincere.

"I just told you I shot some men today, so why would you be so sure about that?"

He smiled, that dimple appearing in one cheek. "Because I like you, and I don't want to believe something so terrible of you. Besides, surely the coroner would have checked the bodies for foul play, especially after the second time."

"Exactly! And they did confirm natural causes, but the families were angry at me because of the money I'd been left. They'd never liked me, especially not Walter's children and siblings. Although…" My voice became very small. "I *am* the common factor. Maybe I'm just bad luck."

"Or maybe you've just had bad luck," he countered, then grinned. "Although if it happens again, maybe you can reconsider that idea."

I wrapped my arms around myself, shaken. "It's not going to happen again."

"Because you're not going to marry Kingsley White tomorrow? Or because he's a very healthy sort?"

"Because…" *Was* I going to marry him tomorrow? "…because life wouldn't be so cruel as to widow me yet again," I said instead.

Caleb had been watching me intently, but at that he glanced away, his smile disappearing. But then he knew how cruel life could be, didn't he? "You don't sound that thrilled about it. Do you really want to marry him?"

"Haven't we already had this conversation?"

"Yes, and it ended with you getting angry with me." I could hear the smile in his voice. "I'd rather if this one ended differently."

"Maybe you shouldn't ask the same question and expect a different answer," I said tartly.

"And you're avoiding the question. And maybe you've changed your mind, so you'll give a different answer. Valentina, do you *want* to marry Kingsley White?"

I sighed; a long, heavy sigh that seemed to take all my energy with it. "Yesterday morning I would have answered yes, absolutely. But everything's so different now. It's been so hard here on Sweetheart Island these last couple of days, and Kingsley isn't the person I thought he was.""So you're not going to marry him?" He looked hopeful, and I almost laughed.

"Oh Caleb, if I didn't, then what would I do instead? Besides, it's so close to the wedding…"

He shrugged. "People change their minds, and better to do it now than afterwards when you're married and dissatisfied. Go on, give everyone a shock. Change your mind."

"You make it sound so easy." I thought about it, if I did just decide not to marry Kingsley, and what that would lead to. "Ha, if I did then Snow would be ecstatic." My voice came out bitter, although I tried to make a joke about it. "We can't have that."

"What, so you would sacrifice your own happiness just to spite some silly girl?" He looked sceptical. "That's making her a lot more important than she needs to be. It makes you sound jealous."

"I'm not jealous of her!" I snapped. "She's jealous of me!"

Caleb's voice softened. "And I can see why. But don't waste your energy on her, Valentina. It's really not worth it."

When he put it like that, it sounded so obvious. "Are you speaking from experience?" I asked lightly. "Have you ever been with someone whose family hated you?"

There was a pause, and he looked away. "Ruby's family liked me, and she was my only serious girlfriend. So the answer is no."

So her name was Ruby; the girl who looked a bit like me. "Do you still see them? The family?"

He sighed. "Once in a while, and we're friendly, but all we have to talk about is what we've lost. It doesn't make for good conversation."

If I'd thought the previous silences had been awkward, then this one was far more so. Caleb wasn't like me with my dead exes, trying to forget they ever existed. He was mourning. But I cut across the silence, suddenly ashamed of my clumsy questioning. "I suppose we have something in common, then."

"It appears we do," he replied softly. He didn't seem at all offended by my misstep, instead still looking at me intently, perhaps even with affection. "That's why I don't want you to step into another bad marriage. I want you to have what I had; a life with someone who cares for you."

I shook my head and looked away. "Kingsley cares for me. But it's not enough. I think I've got terrible taste in men."

"So choose differently."

"I keep trying," I said softly, "but it all turns out the same anyway. Maybe it's *me* who's broken." I turned to look at him and he was sitting right next to me on the couch, close enough I could see his eyes were warm brown all the way through, with only a few gold flecks spiralling around the pupils. "How do you fix something like that?"

"One decision at a time, Valentina. Do what you wouldn't have done before."

"OK," I agreed, and I found myself glancing down at his lips. They were well-shaped and full, and his angular jaw was smooth and tanned. Suddenly he seemed unbearably attractive – so unlike Kingsley – and I found myself leaning in a little, until our lips almost touched...

And then he jerked back as if he was scalded.

Mortified, I pulled away. "I beg your pardon, Caleb. I forgot you aren't interested in me." Or maybe it was that I was engaged, even though he seemed to be trying so hard to change that.

"It's not that," he contested, pointing toward somewhere under my chin. "It's...you've got something on your neck."

"What?" I touched where he was pointing, the area just below my ear, and felt around until I found what appeared to be a wiry hair, barely half a centimetre long but impossible to miss. "Oh." Now that was even more embarrassing. Had he really had to point it out? I turned away and surreptitiously gave it a sharp pull, but was rewarded with an intense pain in the neck. Literally.

"I don't think that's a hair," he said, turning away as if he couldn't meet my eyes. "You should probably leave it be."

"Right." I stumbled to my feet, the moment well and truly ruined. "Well, thank you for the conversation, again," I said briskly. "I'll see you around." Then I left as quickly as I reasonably could, feeling grateful that my pale cheeks rarely showed a blush. If they had, now I would be beet red.

I detoured into the nearest public bathroom, where I checked the 'hair'. It was clear and almost invisible, but too thick; like a normal body hair that had overgrown in both volume and length. I tugged at it again tentatively. "Ow!" It was stuck right in there.

"Of course it's a hair," I said aloud to my reflection. "What else is it going to be?" But clearly it wasn't going to be plucked with just my fingers. I resolved to remove it as soon as I got back to the hotel.

But then I thought of how Caleb had jerked away from me; of how I would have *kissed* him, and my reflection's face crumpled.

It wasn't enough that I'd forgotten why I'd agreed to marry Kingsley, or that I felt the most intense hatred for his silly, vapid daughter, worse than anything I think I'd ever felt. It wasn't enough that I'd become consumed with rage and had shot at – *shot!* – some men today, and stolen something from them, and had probably broken half a dozen laws.

No, I had to try to cheat on my adoring, much-older fiancé, the very day before the wedding.

6 Contrite

'It seemed like she was two different people.' – Caleb D

"Ms Redwell?"

I looked down at my wristpiece in surprise, but the red bead was unlit. The voice was coming from outside the bathroom door. "Jorge?" My voice was hoarse with tears. "What's the matter?"

"You've been in there for some time, Ms Redwell. Are you ill?"

I was sitting on the closed toilet lid, just as I had been for the last fifteen or twenty minutes. "Just a minute."

I got up and washed my face, forcing a smile in the mirror. It didn't work, and even the stupid mole – *beauty mark!* – looked horrible. I closed my eyes, then resolutely turned away from the mirror and let myself out of the bathroom. "I'm not sick," I told Jorge. "I just got distracted. How did you know I was here?"

"You're meeting Mr White in ten minutes, Ms Redwell. You'll need a lift back to the hotel."

That didn't answer the question, but I shrugged dully. "Oh. Thanks."

I followed him to the car, which was parked almost exactly where I'd abandoned Snow earlier today. I remembered the lost, forlorn expression on her face, and again felt a mix of guilt over leaving her, and anger that she was…well, *her.*

We began to drive in silence as always, and finally I had to speak.

"Jorge…"

"Yes, Ms Redwell?"

"I shot some men today."

There was a silence, and I continued, "They were trespassing on White land, but it's not even mine yet. And I shot at them with an air rifle. I think I hit one of them, so I might be arrested for assault."

Jorge was silent.

Just like I had earlier with Caleb, I continued, "And I was going to cheat on Kingsley, but then I had…well, I stopped."

The silence dragged on. Then finally he said, "Yes, Ms Redwell."

Really?

"Don't you think there's something wrong with that?" I cried. "I probably broke the law with the first one, and I broke an ethical law with the second. I almost cheated on my fiancé!"

There was another long, painful silence. The kind where I would have loved a pat on the shoulder, or a 'there there, you're not a monster'. But just as always, he didn't move, and he didn't touch me. Then I realised he had never touched me, not once in the years that I'd known him. In fact, no one ever touched me unless I invited them to. Not for affection, not for comfort.

Finally he replied, "I don't understand the question."

I leaned forward to where he sat in the front section of the car, looking him in his glass-clear blue eyes. "You know me. You've known me for a long time, and you've seen my worst. You weren't even surprised by what I just told you. Do you think I'm awful?" I looked at him, begging to hear an honest answer. "Unlovable?"

His face was blank and emotionless, and it was a long moment before he answered. "No."

I waited for him to say more, but he just stared at me with that curiously neutral expression, as if his brain had gone into overload and he just didn't know what to say.

"Will there be anything else, Ms Redwell?"

My shoulders slumped. "No, Jorge, there won't be."

We arrived at the hotel and I made my way towards the restaurant dragging each step, my mind buzzing. How did someone like Snow make friends everywhere she went, when I only seemed to make enemies? I could put most women's attitudes down to jealousy, but children didn't like me either, and what did they have to be jealous of? Even the men who 'adored' me didn't keep loving me. James lost interest after the wedding…then died – and Walter chose his children over me *before* the wedding…then died.

It *did* sound bad when I thought of it like that, and most people didn't even know about my first boyfriend.

James died of a brain aneurysm and Walter died of a heart attack, I reminded myself. I knew this, just like I knew what year it was, or who the major world leaders were. But when I tried to visualise that time when I'd found out about their deaths, to think about how I'd felt, my mind was filled with fog. I only remembered snatches of information: *Walter died in the pool, his children around him. James died in someone else's bedroom, the night after we'd had an argument…*

And then me, wearing a black veil and dramatic red lipstick, standing stoically to hear the will read. The angry faces of his family, the names they called me. *Bitch. Murderer. Gold digger.*

If I'd made friends with them back when I'd first married James, then they wouldn't have hated me, I realised. They might have even sympathised with my loss.

The revelation was as shocking as the sun dawning in the middle of the night. Snow might just know something I didn't about the basics of being friendly. Or *looking* friendly anyway, since in private she'd been utterly malicious this morning. Even if she made friends better than I did, I still didn't have to like her.

I arrived at the restaurant just on the dot of 5 pm, and was shown to a private, beautifully arranged table. The same one as last night's, in fact. The other chair was empty, and I entertained myself by reading through the menu while I waited for Kingsley. We were going to have a proper talk, I told myself, and I'd remember why I liked him so much. I *would*. And then I'd get my head back together, and everything would be just fine…

But ten minutes ticked by, and then twenty, and I was still alone. I'd chosen my meal five times over, and my sense of humour had gone from minimal to nothing.

Then finally Kingsley wandered into sight, wearing a neat grey suit and with an amiable expression on his face. "Fairest! There you are, and looking as lovely as ever."

"Five o' clock, just like we agreed." My tone was a little acerbic, because the compliment didn't make up for his lateness and lack of apology. "Were you held up?"

"What? Oh, I was just talking to Snow. She was all excited about her date with that Prince lad, Tarkers. I'm sure you won't mind that I invited them to join us."

Tarkers? "Yes, I do mind," I snapped. I closed my eyes briefly, letting out a long, calming breath. "It's very important to me that we take the time to know each other, Kingsley. That means time alone, and *before* the wedding." My tone softened. "Surely you see what I mean?"

"Of course." He sat down across from me, setting his hand over mine. His was warm, just as Caleb's had been, but it didn't send the same butterflies fluttering through my stomach. "Remember that week we spent together at the beach resort, just you and I? I saw you across the room, and I thought, *that's the most beautiful girl I've ever seen. I must know her name.* And here we are."

I smiled a little, but I still felt awkward. My own memories of that week were vague, damaged by my ongoing memory loss. I only remembered the feelings: the excitement of the new relationship, of him offering me the ring I still wore on my fourth finger. Had I really felt so very attracted to him back then? Now I didn't feel even a hint of it.

"Thank you," I said politely, withdrawing my hand to fidget with my silverware. Anything as a distraction. "So…you were working this afternoon. What did you do?"

"I worked at the hotel," Kingsley told me, his eyes still fixed on my face. "In the office. Business things, you know."

"Yes, I would hope so." I smiled again. I didn't seem to have anything else to say. "Maybe I can take on a role at the hotel. I'm sure there's a lot to do."

"Oh, no, not at all. What I don't do, Karey does, and the opposite. And the servers, of course. They run the whole place. It's fairytale themed, you know. Do you like fairytales?"

My eyebrows shot up in disbelief. "But Kingsley, I told you yesterday-"

"Val! Val!" A familiar, shrill voice cut across our conversation. I looked up to see Snow flouncing her way across the restaurant, her small hands in tight fists at her side. She looked very upset, and also like she was *enjoying* being upset.

But then perhaps I was projecting my own dislike. And what did it say about our dinner so far, that the interruption almost felt like a good thing?

"Good evening, Snow," I said politely, feeling one eye begin to twitch. "No Tarkers?"

"It's Tar-*quin*," she snapped. "And how could you do it? How could you, Val?"

I turned to look at Kingsley, but he was reading the menu, unbothered by the drama unfolding. I sighed. "What did I do this time?"

"You purposely ruined my date with my soul mate, the one who I'm meant to be with!" Snow threw her hands up to cover her face, her shoulders shaking as though with tears.

She was faking. She had to be.

"Snow, what are you talking about?!"

She looked up at me, and while her expression was twisted in anguish, her eyes were dry. "Don't pretend you don't know! Why do you hate me so much?"

"Don't pretend *you* don't know," I snapped back. "Now what on earth are you talking about?" I turned to Kingsley. "Do you have any idea?"

He looked up from the menu, his eyes widening. "Sorry Fairest, what was that?"

I huffed out a disbelieving sigh. Had he really missed the

whole conversation? In my peripheral vision I could see some of the restaurant tables were occupied, and we had the guests' attention. My cheeks warmed, and I hunched a little into my chair. "Whatever you've got to say, Snow, can you say it more quietly?"

She pouted, and a moment later ran around the table to Kingsley, throwing her arms around him and burying her face in his chest. "Oh, Daddy!" she sobbed. "I know you love Val, and I know that you'll marry her tomorrow. But she's hurt me so badly!"

"There there," he soothed, then finally looked up at me.

I sighed, then shook my head. "Beats me."

Snow's head snapped up, and she glared at me. "I'm talking about my candlelit dinner with Tarquin Prince! The one that you called and cancelled for me, saying that I was sick. And Tarquin believed you!" She turned back to sob into Kingsley's cashmere-clad shoulder.

I sighed again, but this time it was in relief. "I definitely didn't call anybody, and I really don't know what you're talking about. Tarquin must have made a mistake." Or changed his mind about wanting to date Snow. I didn't blame him.

"Oh, he did!" she said vehemently. "He made the mistake of taking your word for it, rather than asking me directly. And then when I finally called him to ask where he was…he told me his time was up and he had to go…"

"What, commit suicide?"

"No!" she snapped. "He had to go *away*. We won't be able to see each other for *ages* now. At least three days, and it's all your fault!"

"Now now dearest, if Valentina says that she didn't call him, then I'm sure she must be telling the truth," Kingsley said placatingly. "Why would she lie about that? What we have here is a misunderstanding. I'm very sorry that you missed your date, but there will be other ones. You and Fairest will always be family, though, and you need to get on."

Snow sniffed. "Of course, Daddy," she said sweetly, her eyes still wide and woeful. "I'm sure that if Val says it was a misunderstanding, then it was. She wouldn't lie to my face." But she turned and shot me another narrow-eyed glare.

I blinked at the two of them for a few moments, feeling as though I was in a farce. And that was it, I decided. No more confusion. I knew exactly what I wanted to do…and not to do. "Why don't we go and talk about this in your suite, Kingsley?" I asked carefully, my voice shaking a little. I felt like I could break into laughter or tears at any moment. "I have something I'd like to say privately."

"Of course."

But his arm remained around Snow, and she didn't budge, and finally I sighed. "She may as well come too."

The lift up to the fifth floor was silent, and once we were finally inside the White suite, I took a deep breath and turned to Kingsley. Whew, this was harder than I expected, with the way he was looking at me so expectantly, so amiably.

"Fairest?"

"This isn't going to work," I blurted out.

He blinked at me. "What isn't going to work?"

"You and I," I corrected. "Us. *We're* not going to work. I can't marry you." I quickly slipped off the ruby engagement ring, holding it out to him. "I'm sorry."

"But…but…*why*?"

"We barely know each other, Kingsley, and you don't know me beyond that you like the way I look. I don't know you either! I liked how you made me feel – but that was before I came here, and realised what your life is really like. It doesn't have room for me, not in the way I expected it to." I put the ring in his hand, then folded his fingers over it. "You wouldn't make me happy, Kingsley, and I…I wouldn't make you happy either. Not in the long run."

He stared down at his closed fist, brow furrowed. "But *why*?"

Seriously? "I just told you why. We're not a good match."

"She means it's me," Snow burst out, speaking for the first time since we'd arrived in the room. "She's saying I got between the two of you, that you love me too much."

"Well, that's some of it," I agreed, disgruntled.

But she carried on, clutching at Kingsley's shoulder. "Oh Daddy, I'm so sorry! The last thing I want is to interfere with your happiness, even in the most unintentional way!"

I let out a startled laugh and she turned to me, her eyes wide and expression beseeching. "Oh, Valentina, I know we have our differences, but don't let them come between you and my father! I *know* you're meant for each other."

Snow was half kneeling before me now, in a pose I'd only ever seen on Shakespearean actors, and I took a couple of large steps back. Farce? Try circus. "I would have thought you'd be happy, Snow. You and I have clashed from the start, and now you'll have Daddy all to yourself."

"But *why?*" Kingsley said again. He took a step towards me, hands outstretched in a similar way to Snow, but his expression looked sincere. "I love you, Fairest. We *must* marry tomorrow."

I shook off his clutching hand, my sympathy rapidly dissolving. "You don't love me. You just think I'm attractive, and that's not enough basis for a marriage." Besides, it didn't go both ways.

"But we *must* marry tomorrow!"

Meanwhile Snow was pleading, "Please, Valentina, have pity on this poor wretch who adores you so! Forgive him!" Clearly she had no trouble remembering my name when it suited her.

"Enough!" I shouted, throwing my hands into the air and quickly retreating towards the door. "Have some dignity, both of you! It's over, and I'll be gone by tomorrow!" I turned and left the room, heading quickly down the hall towards the second lift. I was shaken. I had known it could be hard, but I hadn't expected *that*.

I'd just reached the lift when Snow caught up to me. She stepped in front of the lift door, preventing me from moving through, and set her hands on her hips. "You're not seriously jilting him. This is just a ploy for attention."

I tried to step around her, but she just moved to block me. "*Not* a ploy for attention, Snowball, just making my first wise decision in this whole mess. Now move."

"You want him to come after you, don't you? To publicly choose you instead of me. Because there is no way you could not marry my father."

"I don't want him!" I shouted. "I never did! He's too old, and I hate when he kisses me! I hate you even more, but at least you've done us the favour of getting in the way before the marriage took place. Now go AWAY!"

I grabbed her by the shoulders, forcibly moving her aside. She was light, and I could feel her bones easily even in that brief grip. Beauty, my arse. I waved my hand in front of the lift sensor, but it wasn't working. The doors weren't opening. "Stupid thing," I muttered, slapping at the sensor square. "Open!"

Behind me Snow was muttering something, and her voice became higher and higher pitched. "Breaking the glass slipper. *Breaking the glass slipper!*"

That made no sense. I gave her a single disgusted glare, then turned and headed for the stairs. Behind me I could still hear her screaming that same phrase. Then, "KAREY!"

I'd reached the second flight of stairs when I remembered my belongings had been moved into the hotel. My new suite was just down the hall from Kingsley's. I stopped, letting out a heavy sigh, then tapped at my wristpiece. "Jorge, I want my belongings packed as soon as possible. And find me somewhere else to stay for tonight. We're leaving the island tomorrow."

I waited for his usual brief response, but there was only silence.

"Jorge?"

Huh. It must be broken, damn it, and I'd have to do it the old-fashioned way – use the phone in my suite. I waited a moment then retraced my steps, hoping the Whites would be nowhere in sight, but when I reached the hall they were both there along with Karey. Snow was hopping with rage, gesticulating widely as she spoke to the events coordinator, while Kingsley stood silently in the background. His handsome face was creased with anxiety, and he held his closed fists in front of him, almost in the position where I'd left him.

I stopped at the doorway, trying to take a step backwards, but Snow had already seen me. "There she is!" she cried, pointing dramatically. "Get her!"

Karey closed her eyes briefly as if praying for patience, and then turned and smiled at me. "Ms Redwell. I understand there's a problem with the wedding. What can I do to help?"

"You can call off the caterers, for starters," I replied flatly. "Because the wedding won't be going ahead. This is not me having a temper tantrum, or a ploy for attention, or whatever Snow's likely told you. I have decided not to marry Kingsley, and I won't change my mind."

"See?" Snow cried, but Karey set a hand on her arm. "Perhaps you'd like to take a moment to calm yourself, dear. I'll have refreshments sent to your suite."

"But-"

"Please," Karey said, and her tone brooked no arguments. Snow fell silent, taking a step back towards the suite, but didn't leave. "Ms Redwell, perhaps we could speak privately?"

I sighed, shrugging. "Sure, as long as those two don't come."

She led me down the hall to a sitting room at the far end of the hotel, one with a less than beautiful view of the carpark. That would be why I hadn't seen it before. She closed the door behind her, then sat down on one of the couches. I sat too. I didn't particularly trust her, or even want to talk, but boy was I tired. "I suppose you want to know why the change of heart."

"I'm sure you have your reasons. What I wanted to ask was about your head injury."

The question so shocked me that I didn't speak for a few moments. Then finally I stumbled out, "What do you know about that?"

Karey shrugged an elegant pink-clad shoulder. "It's on your medical records, of course, and it's public knowledge that your boyfriend at the time died in the same fall that caused your injury. It's hotel policy to research any new guests – to ensure everyone's safety, of course – and I noted that rather interesting detail."

I clenched my fists where they lay in my lap. "Yes, I fell off a cliff when I was sixteen and hit my head. It makes no difference to today."

"Hmm. Except for the gaps in your memory,"

Oh fiery chestnuts, how did she know about those?!

"…and the irritability and the sudden rages…"

Were they so obvious? How had *she* known about them?

"And the feelings of disconnection. Oh, and the hallucinations."

"There are no hallucinations," I burst out. "Fine, I've been grumpy, and I've lost my temper a couple of times, and yes, I've always had missing memory. But I haven't hallucinated! Why would you think I had? And how did you know about the rest?"

She gave a sympathetic smile. "They're common effects from the type of injury you had, and they can last for years. Some of the implants that are supposed to help can cause unexpected side effects, such as being unable to interpret others' motivations or expressions. They can even make the sufferer imagine things entirely. One of my uncles had something similar happen, so I'm quite familiar with the possible outcomes, especially in situations of upheaval."

"Oh." I frowned, looking down at my hands. "Things have been difficult since…since Kingsley and Snow arrived. And I haven't felt my best, that's for sure. But I'm not crazy! I haven't imagined anything."

Karey was staring to the left of my jaw, and I reached up to feel that same stiff hair under my ear.

"Well," she said gently, "one of the servers reported that you'd heard a car backfiring yesterday, and that you'd reacted very badly, as though it was an explosion or a gunshot."

I'd forgotten about that. "It was a reasonable reaction," I argued. "I'm sure I wasn't the only one who didn't know it was a car, um, backfiring." Whatever that was. "That's hardly a sign of hallucinations, Karey!"

"Mm. Perhaps you're right, but I did hear a report of you chasing four guests around the back of the hotel earlier today.

They said you were holding a broom, and making 'bang bang' noises."

A cold chill ran down my spine. "What are you talking about?"

"Those four men that you mentioned to me earlier. I had them checked out, and they're all here legitimately. But I also saw the report from the medic today. They say they were attacked by a very angry blonde girl in an evening gown, and that she stole their equipment and hit one of them with a shovel before they managed to escape."

"That's absolute rubbish," I exploded. "They were talking about me! They were digging right outside my cottage, and when I told them to leave one of them knocked me down. I really thought they were going to hurt me. Besides, *you* should have got rid of them!"

"I ascertained that they had permission to be here, and that they weren't a threat," Karey replied calmly. "I'm sorry that you saw that differently. But the broom, Valentina? Or do you still think it was a rifle?"

My lips tightened and for a moment I didn't answer, not wanting to incriminate myself. "It *was* a rifle, an antique wooden air rifle that I found in the cottage. I just used it to chase them off, that's all." Then I argued more passionately: "You can't really believe I was waving around a *broom*!"

"Why would all four men make that assertion when the presence of a weapon would be easy to prove? We found no weapon in or around your cottage. And how would you know how to fire a rifle, Valentina? Who would have taught you?"

I clenched my fists, remembering the fuzzy images that had suggested James had taught me. It couldn't have been my imagination, because that would be *crazy* – which was far worse than the way they'd intruded into my space by checking my cottage. "I put the rifle under the bed," I said, and my voice cracked. "We can go find it."

"We checked under the bed, Valentina. There was no weapon." Karey's face was a picture of sympathy, and she came to sit beside me. "I'm so sorry. The last thing I want to do is upset you. But can't you see that something is out of place, and I'm not just talking about that wire from your skull implant. Will you come and see a doctor, please?"

I touched the hair again. Come to think of it, it did feel more like a wire. Had I had a skull implant? I knew they'd done all sorts of things to fix my head after that fall, and I hated the idea that they'd left me less than physically perfect. "The cottage first," I said, but my voice was smaller and less defensive.

"Of course. Will you contact Jorge on your wristpiece? We can get him to escort you."

"I suppose so, if it's working now." I bent down, tapping at the silver band, and this time the red light flashed. "Jorge," I began, but then I felt a small prick on my neck.

I turned to see Karey holding an injector, her face still creased in sympathy. "I'm sorry, Valentina. It's just a little something to relax you until the doctor gets here."

I tried to slap at her, but my hands were too heavy. *You had no right to do that* came out as "Youuoohdooo…"

She stood quickly, stepping away. "It's been hard, hasn't it? But it will all be better in the morning."

I couldn't move. I blinked, and the light around me became grey.

Blink.

Blink.

. . . . . .

White ceiling. White walls. Something soft under me and a weight over me, and my mind a blank. I closed my eyes again, the light shining pink through my eyelids, and waited.

I'm Valentina. I'm in bed. Sweetheart Island.

Why was I on an island?

Oh, that was right. Kingsley. I was here because of Kingsley White. A few moments later the memories trickled in: the argument, handing back the ring, shouting at Snow in the hallway. My, what an eventful day I'd had.

I scrunched my eyes tightly shut, then opened them again,

staring at the ceiling with its perfectly smooth surface. The scent of roses tickled my nose. I wasn't in the cottage, I realised, and a moment later remembered. I'd changed rooms because of the treasure hunters.

Grr. I slammed one fist down on the bed beside me and hit something hard. Something *not* the bed. I opened my eyes, turned sideways, and saw the man on the bed next to me. He wore a white tuxedo and his face was turned away, but I recognised his full head of greying hair immediately.

Kingsley.

I screamed.

7 Perturbed

'Dead as a doornail. That's the technical term.'
– from an informal conversation with an attending medic

I leapt out of bed, jostling Kingsley as I did so, but he didn't budge from where he lay. I realised I was wearing a silky red nightgown – *not* the last thing I remembered wearing – and that the suite was decorated with red. There were paper hearts hanging from the ceiling, rose petals on the floor. On the nearby nightstand was an enormous bouquet of red roses, next to an open bottle of wine. Two crystal glasses held dregs of red liquid. An image flashed into my mind: my pale fingers holding the bottle, filling the glasses. The feeling of triumph…

I walked over to the bouquet, checking the attached card. 'Congratulations Mr and Mrs White!' it read.

No. No. No no no no no…

"Kingsley!" I shouted. "Wake up!"

He didn't move. Not an inch, not even the slight rise and fall of his chest as he breathed, and a feeling of dread crept over me. I walked around to the other side of the bed so I could see his face. His eyes were shut as though sleeping, but his face was white, ashy. I reached with trembling fingers to check his pulse, but I already knew what I'd find.

Dead. Kingsley was dead.

I stepped away from the bed, stumbling backwards until I hit the wall, my hands pressed up hard against the textured paper.

"How can this have happened?!"

Ding. "Room service!"

I just stood there, and about ten seconds later the bell dinged again. "Room service!" came the young male voice in exactly the same tone. One of the hotel's many android servers, no doubt.

Finally I moved towards the door, giving the bed a wide berth, and leaned down to the speaker. "Um…I've got a slight problem."

"You'd like to delay the breakfast, Mrs White?"

Mrs White. Mrs White. What had I missed? "Skip breakfast," I replied hoarsely. "Call a medic."

"Yes, Mrs White."

I collapsed into a chair near the door, my arms wrapped tightly around myself, and I was still there when the medics arrived. Everything seemed blurry and distant: the medics checking me, checking Kingsley, asking me questions that I didn't know how to answer.

What happened?

I don't know.

Just describe what you remember. When did you notice he'd stopped breathing?

Just now. I don't remember anything *before that.*

But you were just married, the medic persisted. *Did he show any unusual symptoms last night?*

"I don't know!" I cried again, and realised I was screaming. I had the attention of both medics. "I don't know anything! I don't know how I got here!"

They exchanged glances, and one of them ran a scanner over Kingsley's chest. "Scan indicates he died of a heart attack," he murmured to the other one. "Likely eight or nine hours ago. Not long after midnight."

I'd spent the night with a dead man.

But how had this happened? *How?*

I huddled back into the chair, my blurry gaze fixed on the wall in front of me – anything except Kingsley – and a moment later in came Snow. She ran past me over to the bed, wailing "Daddy,

Daddy!" and as she collapsed over his prone figure I had to close my eyes.

A moment later someone put their arm around my shoulder and led me out to the living room. They sat me on a couch, put a cup of something hot into my hands and left me there, the chaos continuing around me with people streaming back and forth – Snow, Karey, the medics, servers…

I sniffed at the drink. It was a cinnamon latte. My favourite, but I didn't even have the strength to sip at it. My eyes pricked and a tear streamed down to drip off my chin *plop* into the cup. I set it on the small table next to me.

Out of the corner of my eye I saw a white clad figure approach. "Have you finished with that, ma'am?"

I didn't answer, and after a few moments of standing there the server just took the cup, gave me a neat little bow, and left. I'd only caught the barest glimpse of his face – yet another blandly handsome creation, except for the thick black moustache that someone had seen fit to attach. Blue eyes, dark hair, almost pretty features…

Suddenly alert, I bolted upright then ran out into the hall after the server. But he was nowhere to be seen, and I caught the attention of another android server, a blonde female version. "May I help you, Mrs White?"

The other one had called me 'ma'am'. "Start by not calling me Mrs White," I replied. My voice was hoarse. "Who was that other server, the dark haired one who took my drink?"

"I don't know, ma'am," the server replied pleasantly. "Would you like me to find out?"

"Yes. And where is Jorge?" I'd seen everyone else except him.

"He's speaking with the lawyers, ma'am. Would you like me to contact him for you?"

"Lawyers?" My heart skipped a beat. "Why is he speaking with lawyers?"

"To administer Mr White's will, ma'am. Would you like me to contact him for you?"

"Tell him to meet me in my suite."

I hurried back to my room down the hall. It looked just as I'd left it, and I quickly changed into actual clothing: anything except that too-sexy red nightgown. It seemed I'd been wearing it all night while Kingsley was dead beside me.

Dead.

%#@*!!!!

I'd married him.

%#@*!!!!!

I'd been widowed for a second time.

%#@*, %#@*, %#@*!!!!!!!!!!!!!!!!!

I paced anxiously back and forth in front of the suite door, my arms still tightly wrapped around myself as if that would stop the shaking. It didn't. "How could I have lost so much memory?" I whispered in disbelief. The last thing I remembered was speaking with Karey, and she'd *sedated* me…

I must have reacted to whatever she'd given me. I'd *never* been like this. *Never*. Not even after the original injury.

Just then the doorbell *tinged*. "Mrs White? It's Jorge."

"Don't call me that!" I shouted at the speaker. I scrunched my eyes shut, rubbing a hand over my brow. It wasn't his fault. "Come in, will you?"

Jorge stepped inside and waited, his hands neatly folded over his waist. "Ma'am, you asked for me?"

I paused mid-pace, turning to stare at him. "Yes I asked for you! One moment I was calling off the wedding, and the next I'm a widow! What on earth *happened*?"

He blinked. "I wasn't aware you had called off the wedding at any point, ma'am. I'd be unable to enlighten you on that."

No, Karey had been there. Karey and Kingsley and Snow… "Then tell me about the rest of it. Whatever you know."

"Mr White suffered a fatal heart attack last night around midnight, and was declared dead at nine-fifteen this morning. I understood you were there, and that you called the medics-"

"Please, Jorge!" I took a deep breath, carefully controlling my voice. I was *not* going to lose it. "I mean, what happened after I spoke with Karey yester- the day before the wedding? She sedated me, damn her, and I can't remember anything else!" I said the last in a hoarse, panicked whisper. "I didn't give her permission to sedate me!"

Jorge was silent a moment. "By all accounts you were very agitated, ma'am," he replied evenly. "Perhaps your memory of events isn't clear. I've seen the medical report, and the medic states there was a loose wire in one of your implants and that it may have affected you mentally."

"Mentally?" I whispered. "Which implant? *Did* it affect my memory?"

"You'd need to read the report yourself, ma'am. I can request it for you if needed."

"Yes, please." I closed my eyes briefly, taking a deep breath and letting it out again. "And then what happened?"

"You spent about three hours having it fixed, then you went straight to bed. When you awoke you seemed your usual self. You had breakfast with Mr White and Snow, then spent the afternoon preparing for the wedding-"

"So I *did* marry him?!"

"Of course, ma'am. Precisely as planned."

"Oh, *no*." I put my face in my hands. What had Kingsley promised me to make me change my mind? I'd been so very set against marrying him. It still seemed impossible that I'd actually gone through with it. "Did anything unusual happen during the wedding? Was I acting strange at all?"

"Not at all, ma'am. Everything went to plan."

I slumped into the nearest chair. If I'd been clearly upset then it might explain the missing memories, since that had happened before. But if I'd just been acting normally...

"You'll be gratified to hear that with the changing of Mr White's will, you will gain a small annuity along with full control of the hotel and assets," Jorge continued. "Although of course the hotel will revert to Miss White's control once she turns twenty, as she retains legal ownership."

I nodded numbly. He'd willed everything to Snow. Why was I surprised? "And me. Am I being investigated?"

"For what, ma'am?"

"For Kingsley's death. Because I've had two dead husbands, and a dead fiancé, in less than three years. You've got to admit that looks bad."

Jorge blinked. "There is no evidence of foul play, ma'am. It isn't uncommon for older men to suffer heart failure during heightened physical activity."

Heightened physical activity. I shuddered. But as for 'no evidence of foul play'? It didn't explain why I'd been in bed in my nightgown with Kingsley still in his tuxedo, why I'd slept through the whole night, and why I actually didn't have any sign of that kind of activity on *me*. And then there was everything that had happened with Snow and Karey on the night before the wedding, the last things I remembered… It was all a bit blurry, but a few odd details stood out.

"One more thing, Jorge."

"Yes, ma'am?"

"When we spoke outside the cottage yest- two days ago, and I told you to move my things into the hotel, I was holding something. What was it?"

His brow furrowed. "I believe it was a broom, ma'am. It was left in the cottage when your things were moved. I assumed you had no intention of keeping it."

A broom.

Oh, *no*.

I was silent for a long moment, and Jorge finally asked, "Will there be anything else, ma'am? I'm to assist with preparing for the funeral tomorrow."

So soon. Dead one day, in the ground the next. I shook my head, and a moment later I heard him leave.

I sat for a long time in that chair, in that silent room. Alone. The new widow, I thought with some self-pity, and not a visitor in sight. But then perhaps everyone knew I was damaged, or perhaps it was like the other times already. Bad Luck Valentina strikes again; a heart attack on the wedding night. But what a way to go! I ought to be more upset, I thought numbly. And I was upset, but mostly I felt distant, disconnected from it all. Probably the shock, I decided; not just from Kingsley's death, but from the wedding too.

Had that *really* happened? I had no memory of it; only a big blank patch and a whole lot of confusion. I closed my eyes and a faint image popped into my mind: *red roses against white skin.* My bouquet.

Ah, so there *was* something there. I sat quietly, breathing in the same way I did when I woke in the mornings with a blank mind, and the new memories came in smatterings, shards of images: *Kingsley's smile. Snow in blue…well-wishers. Our hands on the knife, slicing into the red velvet cake. Two gold bands on my ring finger…*

The ring. I looked down at my hand, but my fingers were bare of both the engagement ring and any wedding ring. I hadn't worn Walter's or James' after their deaths, as even seeing them on my hand reminded me of my loss. My failure. I kept them all in a section of my precious makeup chest, out of sight but not out of mind.

I stood and went to the bathroom. The chest was there on the wide marble vanity just where I'd seen it last, and I popped it open, ignoring my dishevelled reflection in the large mirror. In the top level was the usual assortment of brushes, palettes and creams, like an artist's supply of materials. I lifted that away, and in the second level was an array of medications, including my migraine injector. I found the small black velvet purse that held my rejected rings, opened it and tipped its contents out into my hand.

Five – two for each husband, one for Walter.

I'd put Kingsley's rings away even before he was declared dead.

Suddenly a memory popped into my head, fresh and clear. *Me, standing in this very place. Two glasses of red wine next to the sink. I open my makeup chest; revealing the bottom level with its tiny bottles…*

Ooh. A clue. I dropped the rings back into the chest, then reached for the chest again with trembling hands, feeling around until I sprang that hidden catch.

And there they were. Half a dozen tiny bottles or jars, none bigger than my thumb, each fitting into its perfectly carved section so that they wouldn't rattle when the chest was moved. Only one was slightly out of place; a little black one with a silver lid. Something gleamed wetly around its neck as though it had been used recently. I touched the glass, turning it slightly so I could read the label. The text was tiny and faded, but I could make out a few words: POISON! DO NOT CONSUME!

Weird. Why would *that* be in here?

But then another scene came to mind. *Steady hands tipping one, two, three drops into the nearest wineglass, then lifting the other to my mouth, leaving a red mark on its rim. That's* mine. *Don't mix them up. I stare solemnly at my reflected self: scarlet nightgown, hollow green eyes. He deserves it, I say. Goodbye, Kingsley.*

Huh. I froze in place with my hand on the bottle, then slowly withdrew it.

Goodbye, Kingsley. That sounded…not good. In fact, it sounded quite incriminating. Rather like having bottles of poison hidden in your personal belongings was also incriminating. I carefully closed the chest lid on the bottles as if I could also make that last memory disappear.

Memory? I meant *imagination*, because if that was a memory then I was…

"Just because I have a blank patch doesn't mean I did something wrong," I firmly told my reflection in the mirror. "I'm not a killer!"

Except for that thought I'd just had, and except for the bottles themselves, and except for my history of prematurely deceased exes. I'd been suffering memory loss for years now, and the idea that I was doing…bad…things when in those blanks, well, that was just *crazy*.

As crazy as chasing someone with a broom-rifle? As crazy as getting jealously enraged with a stupid teenager? As crazy as forgetting huge chunks of your life?

Hmm. My reflection just stared back at me, wide eyed, makeup-free and tousled, but didn't provide any answers.

The cottage.

Two minutes later I was briskly walking through the lower halls of the hotel, heading for outside. I dodged a couple of startled servers, then dashed through the nearest door, heading for the cottage. *Grumpy*, the plaque once again read, but I ignored it and pressed against the lock-pad. "Open!"

It flashed red; this was no longer my room. But wasn't I in charge of the hotel now? "Override," I told the lock, pressing my thumb against it and holding it there. "Administrator instruction."

The lock flashed green and I heard it disengage. I was in.

I went straight to the bedroom, crouching down to see under the low bed. All I could make out in the shadow was a long shape, and I reached in with one arm, grabbing hold of the hard surface. Wood. I pulled it out, barely breathing, and my heart sank.

It was a broom. And as I looked at it, as I held it, the memories came flooding in.

I sat on the bedroom floor, my back against the bed and my legs stretched out in front of me, the incriminating broom on the other side of the room where I'd thrown it. In my mind's eye the same pictures played over and over like a broken film reel. Me, opening those tiny bottles and dripping their contents onto James's travel pillow; into Walter's 'best dad ever' coffee mug; into Kingsley's wine glass. *They deserve it*, the memory-me had said to my hollow-eyed reflection, but I still didn't believe it.

Was that *really* me? Was I the person who blanked out, went homicidal, and then conveniently forgot about it? It couldn't be. I was sane. I was sound, and organised, and determined…

…Except for the lapse with the broom, of course. I turned to stare at it where it lay. "You," I told it, "do not look like a rifle very much at all."

Had I slipped so very far from reality in my moments of 'stress'?

Here and now I knew that James had deserved a slap in the face and to lose half his wealth in a nasty divorce, not death at a young age. Walter had deserved to have an embarrassing public break-up – maybe – not to die suddenly in front of his young children. And Kingsley… Kingsley should have floundered about after I'd left him, been comforted by his horrible daughter, then eventually realised he was better off without a too-young, high maintenance second wife. But instead he was lying in the morgue.

If those horrible thought-images (don't say memories!) were correct, then it turned out you *could* cause a heart attack; you just needed the right ingredients. Poison, and a heightened heart rate…

You'd never hurt anyone, Caleb had said with such certainty. *They'd have figured it out after the second death.*

He was right; they should have figured it out. And there was no way, no *way* that murder would be overlooked a third time. And whatever affection he thought he had for me? That would be gone if this turned out to be true.

I felt like I'd shrivelled up inside, like I'd found a fatal, festering wound where I'd thought I'd been healthy. *Here's the thing,* I imagined myself saying to the police. *When I get upset, I get homicidal. Possibly. Then I forget the whole thing…but then I might be imagining this too. Would you like to test these substances I've just found in my personal belongings?*

Perhaps not. But I couldn't make a decision. I couldn't decide how I felt about it, or what to think. I couldn't move. I just stared at the wall on the other side of the room, blinking occasionally.

Blink.

So tired.

Blink.

Sooo confused.

Blink…

I woke up with my face pressed against the side of the bed, my mouth open and feeling like the inside was coated with tar. Daylight streamed through the cottage's windows and my head was pounding as if someone was rhythmically hitting me with a small mallet. Chestnuts, I was hungry, but I couldn't have slept for long since it was still light out.

I pushed myself to my feet, kicked the broom back under the bed, and headed back to the hotel. I'd have something to eat, I decided, then a shower, then I probably ought to – I don't know, apologise to Snow or something. At best, I'd killed her father with too much lovin'. At worst, I'd poisoned him in a moment of insanity. Both options were equally distasteful. And I still had to confront Karey about that damned sedative…

My wristpiece flashed red and I tapped it. "What?"

"Ma'am?" It was Jorge's voice. "Do you require assistance? The funeral began ten minutes ago."

I stared blankly at the silver band. "No, it's not until tomorrow."

There was a pause. "The funeral is today, ma'am. It started ten minutes ago."

Ah, *chestnuts*. "You told me it was tomorrow! You said you were helping to organise it!"

"Yes, ma'am. And a day has passed since we last spoke." He paused. "I concluded you wished for privacy in your grief. Was I mistaken?"

"I…no. Never mind, I'm coming now."

"Yes, ma'am."

When I arrived at the hotel proper, an usher directed me towards the second ballroom. It was a real woman, a young, plain one obviously assigned to this role for the occasion, and her eyes flickered over my day-old red gown with what looked like judgement. I ignored her, slipping in through a side door and hoping no one would notice.

A hundred unhappy faces stared at me from a sea of black. I'd come in at the front of the room, right next to the funeral and the celebrant. Although there was nothing to celebrate, if you asked me. Kingsley was dead in that casket. I blanched and slipped into the nearest empty seat, resolving to sit silently and unnoticed throughout the service.

"As I was saying, Kingsley White was a well-loved man," the celebrant announced. "He leaves behind a legacy of kindness and generosity, both of which are clearly seen in his beautiful daughter,

Snow." There was a hum of agreement from the audience. "And of course, his new wife and now widow, Valentina." There was dead silence, broken by someone coughing quietly. "If anyone wishes to say a few words in honour of the dear departed, they may do so now."

In the front pew just ahead of me, a small figure shot to their feet. "I'll speak, sir. I know my father would have wanted it."

Snow made her way to the front of the room. Her black hair was loose, hanging down her back and disappearing into the darkness of her dress. She looked rather pretty, I admitted grudgingly, and was rewarded with a sharp pain in the head for it.

Snow looked out at the room with wide, imploring eyes. Her cheeks shone with tears, and she took a deep, shuddering breath then began to speak. Around me the audience seemed to sigh in unison, and I looked around to see a few sympathetic faces. One woman in a black veiled hat caught my eye and gave me a narrow-eyed scowl. I took my time turning to face forward again, but inside I was shaken.

It was almost like they knew the thing that I *might* have done, and hated me for it. I hadn't realised that I cared so very much what people thought, but I did. I wanted to be admired, even if not loved. But even strange, lovely Caleb wouldn't have a kind word for me if that was the truth, and if it came out…

I didn't take in a single word that Snow spoke. Instead I turned to where the coffin sat, lid down, with an enormous display of black lilies draped over it. Just like the rest of the ballroom, the flowers had undertaken a colour shift.

Finally the service was over. I didn't move from where I sat, instead remaining quietly in my place just like I had for the last two funerals. I was largely ignored, which suited me just fine, and I watched the crowds filing past the coffin and then paying their respects to the bereaved. Snow stood by the coffin, being smiled at and embraced by all manner of people. It seemed like the whole island had turned out, but then Kingsley *was* popular, wasn't he? I'd thought I'd adored him too right up until I'd had to share him with Snow.

"I'm so sorry for your loss."

Yeah, it was the same old thing over and over. I probably ought to go stand with Snow, what with being the unwilling new widow, but I couldn't face it. I wouldn't have known how to respond. *Me too; I wish it wasn't* my *loss; It's possible that I killed him?*

In my peripheral vision I saw someone standing close to my left; a blurry mass of dark grey. "Mrs White, are you alright?"

I jolted to attention, looking up. "Don't call me- oh. Caleb."

"Uh, it's *Ali*, at least here. And sorry, Valentina. I wasn't sure if you were still…" He made a vague gesture with his hands. "You haven't been yourself these last couple of days."

I blinked at him. "Haven't I? What did I do?"

"You didn't do anything," he replied with an awkward laugh. "It's just that we haven't spoken since before your wedding. I thought I might have offended you."

Why, was on the tip of my tongue, then I remembered. The almost kiss; the hair/wire. "Oh." It seemed so unimportant after everything that had happened since.

He shifted in place. "So, if you're not annoyed with me, then I wanted you to know that I'm here for you if you need someone to talk to."

"Oh," I said again, feeling on the edge of tears. "Thank you." I meant that sincerely, because I was so desperate for a kind face right now. I knew that out of everyone here, he'd listen to me. I wouldn't tell him about the maybe-memories, though. And even though I felt oddly like I'd betrayed *Caleb* by marrying Kingsley, maybe if he'd been at the wedding then he could fill in what I'd missed.

Just then I saw someone over his shoulder. Someone in white, hovering at the side of the crowded room. A young server with a thick black moustache…

I stood abruptly. "Excuse me." Caleb moved back wordlessly, and I said, "I'll come to your shop straight after this, if you'll be there?"

"Ah…sure." He looked startled but pleased, and I nodded at him before moving away, heading towards that server. I'd seen him across the room yesterday morning after he'd taken my drink, and I'd been too slow to catch his attention. But now he stood in the doorway, an empty silver tray in his hands, and his blue eyes fixed on something else. I followed his line of sight… Snow.

I knew it, I thought grimly. The moustache was no disguise, and the little liar hadn't left the island at all.

But his attention was so fixed on Snow that I'd reached his side without him even noticing. I stepped in front of him, my hands on my hips, blocking his view. "Hello Tarquin. Missed the ferry back to the mainland, I see."

Tarquin jumped in place with a squeak, then dropped the tray and sprinted away down the hall before it had even stopped clanging on the ground.

"Tarquin!" I huffed out a sigh, then took off after him as fast as my heels would allow. But I lost him on a corner, and eventually found myself in that same staff kitchen from a few days earlier. It was empty except for a large bowl of fruit on the central island.

Forget Tarquin. Food!

I sat on one of the high stools and was halfway through my third plum when I heard the faint sound of shuffling footsteps. In my peripheral vision a pale figure moved towards the door, so without looking up I said, "Fine, run off again like a coward. It's all you've done these last few days anyway."

The figure froze, but didn't speak.

"Yes, I mean *you*." I gestured towards him, still facing my rather large breakfast. "Who else?"

"I'm not a coward." I turned at the sound of Tarquin's voice, and he added, "I'm just trying to figure some stuff out. It's got nothing to do with you."

Figure stuff out. I could understand that. "Except for the whole lying to Snow about the date thing, and blaming it on me. Things are bad enough between us without you adding that little treat in."

Tarquin shuffled in place, looking down at his feet. "I didn't think you'd care."

"Surprise, I do." I shrugged a shoulder, sighing. "What with

Kingsley dying suddenly and me forget- uh, all the rest, I probably shouldn't care. But I do. So what was it? You were put off by Snow's interest in you and regretted your initial kindness?"

"No!" he burst out. "Not at all! She's...she's *amazing*. If anything I was overwhelmed by my feelings."

"Oh, please. Pull the other one."

"No," he insisted. "I really mean it. I can't explain what happened when we first met, but it was...it was something else. I felt like I was drawn to her with- with a super magnet, and all I could think about was how perfect she was. Even when I had to go, I couldn't think of anything else."

His blue eyes darted to his left, to a plain door set into the wall, and I remembered that I'd seen Karey go through that door into what had looked like a props cupboard. Had I really forgotten about all the actors on the island? I smiled in relief – it *finally* all made sense.

I nodded towards the door, lowering my voice. "I get it. You've got to say the right thing because you're in trouble if anyone overhears anything else. But I'm not going to tell, and the game hasn't started yet. The article said it doesn't start until next month."

Tarquin's jaw dropped, revealing perfect white teeth. "What game?"

I narrowed my eyes, leaning back. "You know, the fairytale game. This whole island fully switching into tacky fantasy theme, in case you've missed Snow talking about it, or haven't heard the news. But if you keep looking at that hidden room then you must know something."

Suddenly his whole manner changed. No longer sheepish, he leaned forward and set his hands on the bench top, eyes bulging and tone hoarse. "You too? You know about the room?"

"Yeeesss..."

He closed his eyes briefly. "Oh, thank heaven. I thought I was going mad, what with waking up in there and having all those memories of leaving, but no time had even passed! How does that work, I ask you? And forget all the stuff with Snow." He leaned forward even further, his face almost meeting mine. "Who put in the catheter? Do you know, because I'd bloody well like to!"

I blinked at him and we just stared at each for a few long seconds. "Catheter?"

Tarquin stood abruptly, stepping away. "Uh oh. I shouldn't have told you that. I just thought…"

"That I'd know something about missing memories? Why, do you have a head injury?"

"Extra memories," he corrected, but he didn't run. Instead he watched me, eyes wide and beseeching. "No head injury. But please don't tell anyone what I just told you. Something is wrong here, and I'm still trying to figure it out myself."

I closed my eyes, debating whether to trust him; whether to be relieved or scared by what he was saying. But then I opened them again and took a deep breath. "I won't tell anyone, because I know something about thinking I'm going mad. The last thing I remember is being sedated – without permission, mind you – and then I woke up to find I'd been married and widowed all in one go. I *slept* for the last twenty-four hours and almost missed the funeral." I shook my head in disgust. "Sweetheart Island's been a disaster from beginning to end. I probably should lay charges about the sedation thing, but it still hasn't completely worn off, and I've got some other things to figure out." Like had those murder-images been real, and the rifle/broom. Oh chestnuts, the broom.

"But you were at the wedding. I saw you there!"

"One would expect so," I said with grim humour. "But I still don't remember it."

Tarquin glanced again towards that door. "I don't understand any of this. But if only I could get back inside that room, maybe some of this would make sense."

"You don't know how to get in?"

He shook his head. "I can't get into my house, either. That's why I've been dressed like this. The servers can go anywhere."

Hmm. I very carefully got up from my seat and walked over to that door, then leaned down towards the lock. "Open sesame."

8 Baffled

'What the...?' – from an informally recorded
conversation with Ezra B

The door slid open to reveal the same cluttered room I'd seen earlier. I turned to Tarquin with a triumphant smile. "I saw Karey do it the day of the auction, but I didn't know if it would work for just anyone."

I walked inside, looking around curiously, and he followed me in. I heard the door close behind him. "I just pressed the button to get out last time," he told me. "Oh look, there's the bed I was on!" I followed his pointed finger to the long racks at the side of the room, and screwed up my nose. "Looks more like a shelf to me, though I suppose they could pass as bunk beds." For very thin, unloved children. "What's this on the top bunk?" It was a big brown bag large enough to hide a body. I prodded at the catch and it sprung open, revealing a pale face: eyes and mouth half open and expressionless.

We both screamed.

"A dead body!" Tarquin cried, but I noticed something else.

"Possibly not. Look at the mouth. I can't see a real tongue, can you?"

He scrunched up his face in distaste, but stepped up beside me to look closer. "Hey, you're right. I reckon it's an android server."

I let out a sigh of relief, dusting my hands on my dress. "That's alright, then. I suppose this is storage for all sorts of things, and

121

the server must need fixing."

"Valentina, *I* was on that shelf too. But I'm not an android, and I don't need fixing!" He opened his mouth, sticking out his tongue belligerently. "See?"

I tightened my lips, looking around the room. That was the only similar figure, but coming in here hadn't answered any questions, it had just created new ones. "I know you're not an android. Your reaction to Snow just made me wonder, that's all."

"Maybe I was programmed."

I turned to stare at him in shock. "What?"

He clasped his hands in front of him nervously, but his gaze was steady on my face. "What if I was programmed? You're right, that kind of reaction was weird. It was out of character. I know it was, but I couldn't help myself, just like I couldn't help my immediate distrust of you."

"Hey, that's not fair! What did I do?"

"That's exactly it! You didn't do anything. I just saw you, and I thought, *that's a bad girl*. And it was hard for me to shake that reaction."

"So that's why you kept running away from me." Even through what must have been leftover sedative, I still felt hurt at that revelation. *A bad girl*. And he didn't even know about my missing memories…or the extra, homicidal ones. I frowned. "As much as I hate to admit it, you might have a point. Something weird is happening here. If someone was messing with our heads…" I shook mine. "No. No, I can't accept that, because when would they have done it?"

"You said you were sedated, and you hardly remember the wedding."

"Yes, but I was acting weird *before* that." I frowned again. "Or so I was told. Up 'til then I thought it was everyone else who was acting weird. Kingsley, Snow. If it wasn't for the broom…" … then I would truly have thought something had been done to me while I was sedated. It made a horrible kind of sense – or it could be absolutely insane.

"Broom?"

I sighed. "A long embarrassing story that I'd rather not go into yet." I moved away from the android-bag towards the opposite shelf, my attention fixed on a very shiny pair of shoes. "Hey, look at these. Shiny." High heeled and with dozens of enormous plastic diamonds sewn all over the fine fabric, they would certainly catch attention if my feet had been small enough to fit in them. They looked a good two sizes too small for me. I gave one a light tap with my nail. *Clink.* "They're glass."

Tarquin frowned, thinking furiously. "I should know that. Something about that is familiar."

I shrugged a shoulder, replacing the shoes on their shelf. "Some old story, probably. Who cares."

Next to the shoes was a small tin. It was sealed shut and had a picture of glossy fruit and vegetables on the front. The text read: *PHOTOGRAPHER'S PRODUCE WAX. Will make any food look delicious. Lasts for hours.* Under the text was a red and black skull and crossbones symbol, and smaller text reading: *HIGHLY TOXIC. DO NOT CONSUME!*

I rolled my eyes. There was a recipe for disaster. How simple it would be for someone to pick up a shiny apple or plum like those on the table outside, just like I had.

Snow loves apples. An image of her in a coffin popped into my mind: face purple and eyes bulging. An unattractive death would be the worst sort for someone like her. *It would be so easy...*

My hand trembled on the tin and I carefully pulled it away, wiping my fingers on my dress again. *No*, I told myself firmly. It didn't matter where the thoughts were coming from – me, or something else. I was absolutely *not* going to think like that.

"Cool, a wooden gun," Tarquin enthused beside me. "I wonder if it's loaded?"

BANG.

I turned slowly to where he stood, weapon in hand and eyes bugging. "It just hit the ceiling," he said. "Sorry."

But I could only stare at the same air rifle from the cottage – the one that Karey had told me was imaginary. "Let me see that!" I grabbed it out of his hands, running my fingers over it and checking every angle. I even snapped it open, checking the firing chamber was now empty. It was – the pellet had dented the ceiling – but there was no doubt it was the same rifle. I swore under my breath; a curse of both anger and relief. "Did you find the pellets? They're in a little brown bag."

Tarquin shook his head, wide-eyed. "What's going on?"

"Someone's trying to make me think I'm insane, that's what's going on." I checked then double checked all the shelves, even under them, but couldn't see the pellets anywhere. I'd left them under the bed along with the rifle…

"I have to go," I said, handing the rifle back to Tarquin. "Replace this where you found it, and let's get out of here. No one must know we were here, especially not Karey Godmother. Is that clear?"

"Uh…yeah. Why? Do you think she's got something to do with all this?" He sounded excited by the last idea.

"Very likely, but even if she doesn't, she's not trustworthy. She forcibly sedated me with something so strong that I lost almost two days of my life. I woke up married and widowed all in one go."

"Ooh." Tarquin's expression became thoughtful. "I get it. This must be some kind of secret conspiracy where innocents are abducted and programmed, right here on little Sweetheart Island."

I paused. It sounded stupid when he put it like that, and I found it hard to imagine the reserved, professional Karey involved in anything so sinister. It was much easier to see the treasure hunters as villains – ones whose arses I would be kicking as soon as possible – and to blame them for misleading her. Except for the sedation thing, of course. "For what purpose?"

He shrugged, setting down the rifle in one corner. "Scientific research. I don't know."

"It's possible, I suppose. Unlikely, but we don't have a better explanation in the meantime." I zipped the android back into its bag, then moved towards the door. "When are you supposed to be back on the island?"

"Tomorrow."

"Then stay undercover until then. Don't tell anyone we've spoken, no matter what happens, alright?"

"Alright," he agreed timidly. "What are you going to do?"

I paused, hand on the door-release button. "I haven't decided yet, but I know where to start."

We left the room just as we'd found it. Outside, the kitchen and halls were as abandoned as they'd been before, and Tarquin disappeared back into wherever it was servers went. I felt a moment of guilt at my decision not to return to the wake, then dismissed it. Poor Kingsley was dead, so he couldn't be offended. And Snow? The further I kept away from her, the better. And there was one other person who'd given me misinformation… one who should have known better.

I tapped my wrist. "Jorge, I'm going to the cottage. Meet me there in ten minutes."

"Yes, ma'am."

I took my usual path through the ground floor restaurant, and I'd just reached the edge of the rose gardens when a familiar voice called my name. "Val!"

There she was, sitting at one of the tables to my right. I briefly closed my eyes, then picked up my pace. *Not now, Snow.*

"Valentina! I know you can hear me."

Oh. Talking to her was the last thing I wanted to do… but her father was dead, and it might be because of me. I had to at least pretend kindness. I stopped in the middle of the rose gardens, far enough from the restaurant for some privacy. "Snow. Hi."

She finally caught up, her pale cheeks pink with exertion. "Where have you been? Everyone's saying you went off with a waiter."

"I hadn't had breakfast."

Snow stared at me incredulously, and I amended, "I needed to be alone. It's the shock of it all, you know. Marrying Kingsley and losing him in a day."

Her expression changed in a moment. "Ah, poor Daddy. The doctors tell me he likely didn't suffer."

I thought of that image of me dripping poison into Kingsley's wine glass and wondered how much truth was in it. "Er…yes. Now if you'll excuse me-"

"But you can't go now!" Snow slipped her arm through the crook of my elbow, looking up at me with wide blue eyes. "You can't leave me all alone! Daddy's gone now, and you're my only family now, Val. We need to stick together."

My eye twitched and I quickly stepped away from her. "No, I really think we don't. I'm very sorry for your loss, but-"

"But you should come for lunch," she cut in. "We can spend some time together, really get to know each other. Maybe I can give you some beauty tips."

My eye twitched again. "Beauty tips?"

"Of course. I did have such lovely compliments today, but I noticed you weren't looking your best."

Eeeeeeeeeehhh. A vivid image slipped into my head of me slapping Snow on her stupid bereaved mouth, right here and now. *Control, Valentina.* My mouth twisted into a grimace, and I sucked in a deep breath to shout at her, but then another thought occurred. "Snow, what does 'breaking the glass slipper' mean?"

Her jaw dropped. "What?"

"You said it the night before the wedding, when I'd just broken up with Kingsley. You said it repeatedly, in fact."

"Noooo…I didn't. I did not say that."

Of course you did, I almost said, but then spotted another figure behind her. Jorge, most likely on his way to meet me at the cottage so I could grill him about the 'broom'. "Jorge! Over here!"

But he was already approaching us. I picked up my skirt, quickly striding over to him and lowering my voice. "Postpone that meeting. I need you to get rid of Snow quickly. She's driving me mad."

"Get rid of her, ma'am?"

"Get her out of my sight, I mean! She's always following me, needling me." I blinked, remembering the context of the morning. "It's the recent loss, no doubt, but I fear I'll do something drastic. I don't want to see her again, is that clear?"

Jorge barely blinked. "Yes, ma'am."

Snow had caught up. "Oh, hello Jorge. What's going on?"

"We're just going to have a little chat," I heard him say. Out of the corner of my eye I saw him take her by the elbow and steer her in the other direction. How very Jorge-like. I'd say I trusted him completely…except for how he told me I'd been holding a broom, not a rifle. That was why we needed to have our private conversation. Either he'd give me a decent answer, or I would need to hire a new assistant.

I quickly made my way to the cottage, unhampered this time, and overrode the commands once more to get inside. I went straight to the bedroom, crouched down on all fours and pulled out the broom, throwing it aside. Then I flattened my face right against the floor, squinting against the darkness.

There it was. A little dark shape almost hidden against one of the bed legs. A few moments later, with the help of the broom handle, I'd retrieved the bag of pellets. I tipped them out into my hand, counting them. Six, which allowed for the ones I'd shot at the treasure hunters, and the one lodged in the secret room's ceiling.

Ah, but there'd been one more. I crossed the room to the mantelpiece and found the metal figurine I'd taken a test shot at. On its backside, the side facing away from the room, was a small dent – the sort left by an air rifle pellet. I found the pellet itself tucked into the crease between wall and thick carpet.

Chasing after them with a broom, shouting 'bang bang'. Who would try such a ridiculous lie unless they were sure they'd never be caught out? But it hadn't even been hard to disprove. Ha, probably a car hadn't 'backfired' that day either. Perhaps it *had* been an explosion, and it had just been covered up. But for what purpose?

I put the pellets inside my jacket pocket, then ordered a full breakfast to be brought to the cottage, along with one of my favourite non-alcoholic drinks. I didn't think I could see a glass of wine again without thinking of that image of me and the tiny bottle. After brief consideration I added a second drink to the order. I didn't know what Jorge usually drank, but for the coming conversation I wanted him to be relaxed.

The lunch arrived quickly and I devoured it, but managed to hold off touching my drink. Then finally, a good hour after I'd sent Jorge off to remove Snow, he arrived.

I waved at the other seat across the small table. "Take a seat. Have a drink."

He sat, pulling the glass towards him, but didn't taste it. "What do you require, ma'am?"

I took a sip from my own glass. Some of the chill had faded, and it was just perfect. "Information. How did it go with Snow?"

"She won't be bothering you again, ma'am."

"Good." I hoped he hadn't upset her too much, but if she stayed away from me it would be worth it. "You don't like your drink?"

"I'm not thirsty, ma'am."

"Oh. Well, perhaps you can answer another question." And here was the difficult one. "When I spoke to you yesterday I asked whether you'd seen me holding something the day before. You said I had a broom. Why?"

Jorge's expression didn't change. "Because you were holding a broom, ma'am."

"You saw me with a broom," I echoed. "Really."

"Yes, ma'am."

Huh. No signs of guilt, no confusion. Not what I'd expected. If I hadn't seen the evidence myself, I might have doubted based on his certainty. His hands hadn't moved on the glass, and his expression hadn't changed. He'd barely blinked, and he hadn't questioned why I'd been asking, which was a normal thing to do. In fact he never questioned anything. He was just so, so trustworthy, which was why this was all so very strange…

…just like the thoughts in my head.

I closed my eyes briefly, embarrassed by my suspicions. "It's all very silly," I said in a joking tone. "Please forgive me, Jorge. I'm sure in a few days we'll think this is all very funny."

"Yes, ma'am."

But he wasn't laughing. His expression barely changed, just

like an android.

Then a thought occurred. I couldn't remember seeing him ever display strong emotion. I couldn't remember the last time I'd seen him eat or drink…

"Jorge," I said very carefully, watching his face, "what's my stepdaughter's name?"

"Snow, ma'am." His mouth shaped the words efficiently, his neutral expression never changed, but I knew what I didn't see.

A moving tongue.

For a moment I couldn't breathe, and my hands tightened so much on my glass that I heard it crack. Oh, *help*. Someone had replaced Jorge with an android.

"Is there anything else you require, ma'am?"

Oh, oh, *help*. When had he started talking like that? Why had I not *noticed* until now? "No! No, that…that'll be all."

I waited frozen in my seat as he rose and finally left, and the moment he was gone I let out a whimper. *That* was why 'Jorge' had told me he'd seen a broom rather than a rifle, and along with Karey's lies, had given me a few hours of thinking I was insane. Because androids were fully robotic and fully programmable, infinitely more so than a human, and someone had programmed him to answer that way. Not him, *it*.

And *that* was why he'd called me 'Your Supreme Highness' the other day, I realised in horror. Not because he'd suddenly gained a sense of humour, but because the local androids were all connected to the same central computer system that held all customer information, including any updates on how customers wanted to be addressed. Jorge – *fake* Jorge – was clearly also connected.

Why why why why why why *meeee*? Why had I been targeted like this? And where was the real Jorge? I must be the worst employer ever to not even *notice*! I never looked at him, that was the problem. As long as he did what I wanted, I was OK. He may as well have always been an android with the way I'd treated him.

This little cottage had felt like a sanctuary of sorts, but no longer. Now its very isolation felt sinister and threatening. I quickly left the cottage for the village, my thoughts racing. Who was controlling this place? Who was doing this? The manner of Kingsley's death along with my missing memories had always been so shocking and ridiculous that I didn't know what to make of it. The homicidal thoughts even more so, never mind that unexpected wire in my neck.

But now I knew that they'd taken Jorge – whoever 'they' was – I couldn't trust those thoughts, thank God. If I didn't remember seeing those little bottles before a couple of days ago, then it was because they *hadn't* been there, I realised. Someone was messing with my head, taking advantage of my injury. Kingsley was dead – there had to be a reason for that.

I'd been framed, with no one but me knowing of my 'guilt'. Yet.

My heart was racing and my head pounding when I finally reached the little village. It looked the same as it had in the days prior, the blue sky adding to the picturesque effect. The streets were empty, but I went straight into Ali Baba's. The store was also empty, but I headed for the back room, almost running over Caleb as he appeared in the doorway, a cloth in his hands. "Whoa! Valentina, hi. You said you'd come straight after the funeral, so I thought you'd changed your mind."

I clenched and unclenched my fists in agitation, feeling myself shaking. "Oh Caleb, something terrible has happened!"

His eyes widened in alarm, and he came forward to take my hands. "What happened? Did someone hurt you?"

I opened my mouth to answer, felt my lip tremble, and then burst into tears.

Caleb made comforting sounds, put his arm around me and led me out the back. Somehow I found myself sitting down on that same couch again, him sitting right next to me, and then my tears faded into sniffles and I spilled out the whole story. I told him about trying to break up with Kingsley, about Snow's odd reaction, about missing my wedding and Kingsley's funeral, about catching Karey in a terrible lie.

"And I've had these thoughts about time I missed, horrible thoughts, but I don't think they're mine. They can't be! And then today…" I took a deep, sobbing breath. "Today I found out that my assistant Jorge has been replaced with an android."

"An android?" Caleb echoed. He sounded stunned. "Are you sure?"

"Oh, I'm sure. No sense of humour, doesn't eat or drink, and his tongue doesn't move when he talks! I feel so guilty for not noticing before now, but then I've been so busy, and if he was only taken when he arrived on the island…" I shrugged, sniffing. "It makes sense, though I wish I'd seen it earlier. But whoever programmed him must have killed Kingsley too, probably because he found out about what was going on."

"Killed Kingsley."

Heavens, he was like a parrot. "Yes! It makes perfect sense. Someone has been taking advantage of my memory blanks; has made them worse in fact. I'm sure Karey must be behind some of it but I still haven't figured out why." I turned to him. "Do you have any memory blanks or unexplained thoughts? Has anything weird happened since you arrived on the island?"

Caleb's mouth opened and closed like a fish out of water. "Uh…no. I don't think so. Not any weirder than you'd expect from a fantasy-themed island resort."

"That's because *you're* a volunteer actor," I muttered. "Unlike me, who made the stupid choice to come here for Kingsley. Did you know they tried to make me think I killed him? Ha! And for a little while I almost believed it. Almost." We sat in silence for a moment, and I thought again of Kingsley. A pang of sadness shot through me. "I didn't want to marry him. Not in the end. But he sure didn't deserve to die like that."

"Hey." I felt Caleb's hand cupping the side of my face, and his thumb stroked across my wet cheek. "It's not so bad."

"How can it not be bad?" I exclaimed, staring at him incredulously. "Caleb, a man is *dead*, and someone's been messing with people's minds. Except for mass murder, that's about as bad as it can get."

His hand fell away and his mouth opened and closed again, expression twisted in anxiety, as though he wanted to say something or wasn't sure what to say. "Valentina…what if Kingsley *wasn't* dead?"

I stared at him, right into those warm brown eyes that I was so inclined to trust. I couldn't see any insincerity or mockery. "How can he not be? I was there when the medics declared him dead. I saw his body."

He leaned in and his voice dropped very low. "What I'm about to say will get me in big trouble, so I need you to swear you won't tell anyone. Not a soul."

My eyes widened. "I swear."

"Kingsley is a-"

"Stop!" The sharp male voice cut across our conversation and I jolted in surprise, almost knocking heads with Caleb. Jafeer stood there in front of us, his arms folded over his chest, and his expression seriously unimpressed.

"Jay," Caleb said guiltily. "I was just-"

"I know what you were doing," he drawled. "I was in the kitchen listening the whole time. Are you insane? You'll ruin everything, and we'll be out on our arses." He turned to me, making a mocking bow. "My apologies, *Mrs White,* but you'll need to leave now."

I scowled, irritated as always by his behaviour, and I leaned back into the couch. "I'm not going until Caleb finishes what he was going to say."

Caleb's face was twisted with guilt, but his lips straightened into a thin line. He stood. "It's not fair, Jay. You know what they're doing here."

"Fair or not fair doesn't matter," Jafeer shot back. "We do our job, we get paid. Now you've got thirty seconds before I'm calling breaking the glass slipper. *I'm* staying, even if you're too stupid to make the right choice."

"Breaking the glass slipper?" I echoed. I was scared now, but curious. "That's a code phrase, isn't it? For doing something that's out of character?"

Both of them turned to stare at me: Caleb with shock, Jafeer with glittering eyes. "She shouldn't know that."

"No, but she's been doing a lot of things she shouldn't do," Caleb told him quietly. "Don't call it, please. Not yet. She might know something else. Something helpful."

I stood too. I didn't like people towering over me. "Why shouldn't I know that? Because I've in been sucked into some kind of terrible game? I see you've played a part in it, Jafeer or Jay or whatever your name is, and I swear that once I get to the police, I'll be telling them exactly what you've done."

He sneered. "Really? And what exactly have I done?"

My lips tightened. I didn't know, but I was determined to find out. I looked at Caleb beseechingly. "Go on. What were you going to tell me? You *know* how important this is to me. It could be life or death. Do you know what happened to Jorge?"

Caleb's face twisted in uncertainty, and he turned to Jafeer, who raised both hands defensively. "Don't look at me. If you want piss off Karey some more, then do it. I won't get involved."

Just like Jafeer had said, *If you break something, I won't clean it up,* once upon a time. It was only three nights earlier, but it felt like far, far longer.

"Well?" I persisted.

"Jorge?" Caleb replied softly. "Jorge is the same as he always was. An android."

"Don't be ridiculous," I retorted with a scoff of disgust. "I've known the man for years, and as I said before, I *know* androids. What happened to him?"

"Nothing happened to him," he said again. "Do you remember what I said to you the other day about cyborgs? About the goal being for Sweetheart Island to be run by highly realistic AI?"

"Yes…but that was hypothetical. No one has that kind of technology for a true human-robot mix." There was a long silence, and I persisted, "They don't! Do they?"

Caleb looked at his feet. As for Jafeer, he was looking between the two of us with definite amusement, the unkind sort.

"Oh, spit it out," Jafeer said finally, rolling his eyes. "Tell the poor girl the whole truth, won't you? It seems like you've told her everything else, and it's not like it will matter in the end."

"What do you mean, it won't matter in the end?" I cried. I turned back to Caleb. "What is it you're not telling me?"

His hands clenched and loosened at his sides, but he still didn't look up at me. "It's the cyborgs, Valentina. They're not hypothetical. They're real, flesh and blood and metal. They're programmable, and they run the island."

"But…" I frowned. "Karey runs the island. Her and Kingsley, who ran the hotel. Are you saying…" I looked between the two men intently. "…that they are…artificial intelligence?"

Caleb's eyes widened, but next to him Jafeer scoffed in disgust. "Use your brain, girl. Take a look in the mirror. That's your thing, isn't it?"

"Excuse me?" I cried.

"*You* are a cyborg," Jafeer continued. "You, first and foremost."

There were two long seconds of silence, then I exploded. "What!? Don't be *ludicrous*! Give me the truth."

"It is the truth." Jafeer had paled a little under his tan, and his dark eyes were glittering, but remained intent on mine. "You are a cyborg; a blend of human and robot parts. And a rather brilliant one, as we've all been surprised to see. I'd say better than the original, but that's not a popular opinion."

"Jay," Caleb hissed, but Jafeer ignored him.

"Every last detail of how to live your life, anything that you remember from before the island – it never happened. They were implanted memories. Anything that happened since…" He spread his hands, palms outstretched. "That's your life, darling. Less than a week."

"Chestnuts," I retorted impatiently. "You're one of the ones who spread the story that I'd been running around shooting at people with a broom. A broom! And you expect me to believe this now?"

He grinned a little. "A broom, eh? I always thought that

wouldn't hold up, but Sinbad insisted. Mil- er, *Hercules* was pissed about it though. He's still recovering from the wounds."

So I had hit one of them. It didn't make me feel any better.

"And by the way," Jafeer continued, still grinning. "Chestnuts isn't a real swear word."

I just stared at him for a moment. "Yes it is. People say it all the time."

"No one except you says it," he countered. "It's because there'll be children on the island eventually. They want to keep you from getting too scary. I'd say they failed."

Out of everything he'd said, that was probably the stupidest. I shook my head, then stepped away towards the door. "If you won't give me the truth," I said slowly, "I'll find it somewhere else."

"Wait."

I turned to see Caleb facing me, hands loose by his sides, face pale. "You're Valentina, but you don't know your birth surname. You never had one. You never knew your father. Your mother was poor and neglectful and dated a series of different men throughout your childhood. You don't remember their names, but you remember that they were dirty and brutish and made your mother miserable. You swore to be different."

I froze in place, feeling the blood leave my face. That was true…and private. "Who told you that?"

Caleb just shook his head. "At sixteen you dated a rich boy. You fell in love, slept with him, wanted forever with him. But then he tried to break up with you in a scenic spot on a clifftop, said you weren't good enough. You were so upset that you pushed him off the cliff, then jumped yourself. And when you recovered and found he was dead, you swore you'd never let yourself be used and abandoned again. Next time you'd insist on marriage."

"That's a lie," I whispered hoarsely even as images of that horrible time rushed to mind. The boy's face – what was his name? I didn't know – and my hands, pushing against his chest. Watching his arms pinwheel in the air, then watching him disappear over the edge. Throwing myself after him… And now I was crying again. "That was an accident. Those were just nightmares. How could you know that?"

"He's memorized the guidebook, clearly," Jafeer said, his eyebrows raised. "Are you done, Cal?"

But Caleb was still watching me, his expression so very sombre, so very sad. "You were working as a waitress in a casino when you met James Redwell. He was charming and rich, and you married him. But then he betrayed you too. So you poisoned him, and he died before you could divorce. Is that how it happened, Valentina? Because that's what the programming says."

I didn't answer.

"Walter Green. An older family man, not so handsome or charming, but very taken with your looks. He even had his will rewritten before your marriage, but when he saw how much his children hated you, he tried to break it off. So you poisoned him too. And Kingsley White-"

"Enough!" I cried. Tears were streaming down my face, and I was shaking from head to toe. "Those are lies! Those are what everyone says, but I don't *remember*. I'm not a murderer!"

"No, you're not," he agreed quietly. "You've never committed a crime. Never done much of anything, actually, except break the mould. You weren't supposed to know about the themed resort."

"Then people shouldn't talk about it, and there shouldn't have been articles just lying around," I said sarcastically, "Because even this 'cyborg' can read." But inside I was terrified. Terrified it was true – terrified that it wasn't. "You're going to have to prove all of this."

"I can prove it," Jafeer said cheerfully. I stared at him with loathing. "I'll show you the advertising video."

Caleb just shrugged helplessly as if saying 'go ahead'.

So I just watched in silence as Jafeer – or Jay – walked over to the nearby wall where a large grey panel sat. The televiewer. He tapped the control panel, then said, "Show me True Fantasies."

The screen came to colourful life, and music began to play as a stylised image of Sweetheart Island appeared. Text scrolled across the screen reading, *True Fantasies'*, then a rich, smooth woman's voice began to speak. "The largest, most realistic set in history is prepared to fulfil your every fantastic desire. Live out someone else's life – whether real or imagined. There are over five hundred characters that you can choose from, from Snow White or Aladdin to historical figures like Napoleon or Shakespeare."

Stylised images of the characters came onto the screen as those names were spoken, including a vaguely familiar picture of a sweet-faced brunette as they said Snow White.

The voice continued, "Located on the beautiful, recently upgraded Sweetheart Island resort, True Fantasies is unlike any other of its kind in that there are no human actors. Every single non-player character on the island is a highly advanced artificial intelligence programmed to fit right into each scenario. The main characters are even organically based so that you can really believe that they're real – *they* certainly do."

Then a young woman appeared on the screen, looking relaxed on a velvet couch with her white hands resting casually in her lap. She had golden blonde hair, red lips and extremely pale skin, and wore a very tight black dress with a plunging neckline. She also had a distinctive mole to one side of her nose.

The narrator said, "Introducing Valentina, our resident vamp. Made of a mixture of synthetic and organic components, her brain is as intelligent and responsive as that of a human yet she can be programmed to be any character required. The first character she'll play is that of the villainous stepmother off the famous tale of Snow White and the Seven Dwarves."

"I don't remember this," I murmured worriedly.

The camera panned out and the girl – *me* – was sitting interview-style across from a smartly-dressed man with a shaved head. The man said to the camera, "I'm John Carver, and True Fantasies is my vision. I wanted a world where people could more than just act out their fantasies – I wanted one where they could *live* them. We have almost five hundred different characters, including a hundred highly advanced models. That's where Valentina comes into play. Valentina, why don't you tell us a little bit about yourself?"

"I've been married once, and engaged twice," the on-screen Valentina purred. "Each of my exes has tragically passed away before his time, but at least they were kind enough to leave me all their worldly goods. I've also taken very good care of myself, as you see, and my first husband coined the nickname 'Fairest of them all'."

"But you've met someone new. Someone who lives on Sweetheart Island."

The on-screen Valentina smiled as if she knew a secret. "I have indeed, John. Kingsley White owns the fabulous White Hotel, which is *the* place to stay when visiting Sweetheart, and he's fallen head over heels in love with me. Since he's richer than my last two exes put together, I've agreed to marry him. The hotel will be mine in no time." Her face hardened suddenly. "Unless his pain-in-the-neck daughter Snow gets in the way."

"You don't like your stepdaughter?"

"She's not my stepdaughter yet," the onscreen me said icily. "And she won't be for long."

The image merged back into scenes of what were presumably characters living out the various fantasies, and I recognised a few, although none of those around me. That was about as much as I could take.

"Turn it off." I turned away from the screen, feeling an inch away from vomiting up my lovely lunch. "These are lies, all of it. Except for Snow being a pain in the neck. That's true, but otherwise that's not me. Or if it is, then someone's just been taking advantage of my memory blanks to make me seem like some kind of…monster. Are you claiming that Kingsley's a cyborg too? Snow as well? She must be, because no real person would be so incredibly phoney and awful. And what about the two of you, huh?"

"Kingsley's a 'borg," Jafeer said cheerfully. "We're just actors. This is the test run, and Karey's afraid it'll get screwed up if it's just AI running the show. But Snow? She's the reason this all exists."

Caleb shot him a glare, then turned to me. "What he's saying in his very charming way," he said gently, "is that Snow is the paying guest. The *only* guest at the moment. That's why things have played out the way they have. This is her fantasy."

Snow's fantasy.

Now that, out of everything, actually made sense. Why Snow would have had so much attention. Why Tarquin would have fallen in love at first sight; why he would have distrusted me. But the idea that my whole life was just part of someone else's fantasy, that I wasn't even *human*...?

"No," I said emphatically, shaking my head. "I can believe that Snow's up to something, because *nothing* has made sense around her. But I'm human! I eat, I drink, I sweat. I have free will! I shouldn't even have to argue this."

"But I bet your hair and nails don't grow, do they?" Jafeer countered. "And have you wondered why your colouring is so perfect? So unusual? No one looks like that naturally."

"Some people do," I argued.

"Who? Besides you."

Snow, I would have said, but her colouring was as fake as Jafeer's beard. I looked down at my hands, at the white skin and perfect nails, and couldn't remember the last time I'd cut those nails. And my hands were always so cold... "I have bad circulation."

Jafeer let out a short laugh. "And super strength from all the enhancements. Hercules is still in a cast from the way you swung that shovel."

It had been a light shovel. Practically aluminium foil. Just like that metal sculpture...

And the wine glasses you cracked? They were just flimsy.

"I have free will," I said desperately. "Not programming. I *choose* what I do."

"Except for marrying the old man," Jafeer countered. "And hating Snow White."

"Stop helping, Jay!" Caleb snapped.

But I was shaking my head over and over. "I am human. I am, and I can prove it."

I pushed past them into the kitchen, quickly finding a paring knife in one of the drawers. I spun around to face the two of them – they both had the same horrified look on their faces.

"You don't need to kill us," Caleb burst out, and I stared at him in betrayed disgust.

"It's not for you!" Then I sliced the sharp point of the blade down my forearm, feeling the bite of pain and the warm liquid running down my skin as I did so. "See? Blood. I have blood, so I'm human."

My voice sounded a little frantic now, and their expressions didn't change. Caleb said very gently, "Valentina, would you please put down the knife? You're frightening us."

I dropped it with a clatter, but kept holding up my arm. "You've made a mistake, see? I am a person."

"You are a person," he replied softly, "but take a look at your arm."

Confused, I twisted so that I could see the cut. The sting was already fading, but the liquid running down my arm wasn't blood. It was purple-black and smelled a little oily, and through the thick sliced skin I could see very fine wiring and metal.

$\mathcal{9}$ Wretched

I dropped the knife, stumbling backwards until the wall hit my back, then fell with a bump to sit on the ragged carpet. The cut on my arm was already sealing together, the flow of blackish liquid had ceased, and it no longer hurt.

How could it have hurt at all? It was a robotic arm. It was *my* robotic arm.

I was a cyborg.

I couldn't think. I couldn't move. My head was just one big mess of…fear, panic, confusion. Disbelief.

"Valentina?" Caleb's voice was timid, quiet. "Are you OK?"

I turned to stare at him. "Should I be?"

He sat down on a chair opposite me, leaning forward so his arms draped over his knees. "Yes, actually. Or that's what they'd been trying to create. Someone who could be moulded into any character, who could live a thousand lives and never ask questions."

Jafeer scoffed. "They failed with that one. She's been asking questions from the start."

"Or succeeded brilliantly with what they came up with," Caleb challenged. "She's complex and intelligent, and has the ability to make choices outside of the programming. She didn't even want to marry old Kingsley. She wouldn't have, if they hadn't skipped that section."

"What?" I asked.

"Because you broke script so very badly, there was a whole section of the storyline skipped," he explained. "Your marriage and Kingsley's death. All the other AI had to have emergency programming to make them think it had happened." He smiled very faintly. "Look on the bright side. You're not a widow at all. Congratulations."

I put my head in my hands, the realisation dawning on me. *God help me,* I was a cyborg. I was some twisted blend of robotic and human parts, although apparently I had no real blood. But God help me, I'd never killed anyone. None of those nightmares, those ugly images that I'd tried to push away for so long – none of them were mine. Suddenly it all made sense.

"But I don't *feel* like I'm a week old," I said. My voice sounded like it was coming from a long way away. "I feel like I've lived a whole life. A long one."

"Implanted memories," Jafeer told me. "And what would you have to compare it to anyway?"

He was right, damn it. I frowned. "Then I really wish they'd given me happier memories." Caleb looked sympathetic, and I continued flatly, "So Kingsley's in some cupboard somewhere until he's needed again. And what about locals like Daniel Charmant and Tarquin Prince and…oh, Cindy Rayla? Who are they?"

"All cyborg characters too," Caleb replied. "There are no Sweetheart Island locals. Sorry."

He truly sounded like he meant that last part. I nodded slowly, beginning to make sense of the whole thing. Poor Tarquin – he had a nasty surprise coming his way. And while I didn't really believe it in my heart, I believed it enough. "Caleb…"

"Yes?"

"If you knew I wasn't human, why did you keep trying to talk to me? Trying to be my friend, to get me to ditch Kingsley? Surely it didn't matter."

He glanced away, his expression suddenly sad. "It's complicated."

"You're modelled after his dead girlfriend," Jafeer answered for him. "Although much hotter, of course, although you've still got that mole. He wanted to see if you were anything like her, although he really messed up with the way he tried to break your engagement. He could have been fired for that."

"Jay!" Caleb snapped. His face and neck reddened. "She is *not* hotter than Ruby. She's just…shinier."

"Ruby," I breathed in disbelief. "So it's not just that I look a bit like her. You're saying I was actually *modelled* after her?"

"Genetic donation," Caleb muttered. "So yes."

Modelled after Caleb's dead ex. Only unlike mine, his had actually existed. "And I'm just the shiny plastic version." The one with no personality except what 'they' tried to give me. Whoever 'they' were. And wow, did that hurt. Except a sudden, hopeful thought occurred… "But Caleb, you look like James Redwell. Or he looks like you, I mean. How would I have those thoughts if I hadn't known you before? Do you think…?" My voice petered out hopefully. *Please, please let it be possible.*

"What, that you somehow switched places with her?" He gave a twisted, disappointed smile. "I wish you had, but I saw her body. I saw her cremated. She's definitely dead, and while I am sorry that you've been given life in this twisted way, you are not her."

"But then why were you familiar to me?"

"It's the genes," Jafeer cut in. "Cyborgs are created as adults with adult brains. Their creators were worried that some of the donor's personality or memories would transfer across as well, so the programmers covered for that by implanting memories of people who might be familiar."

"*I* didn't know that," Caleb said. He looked away and I felt betrayed once again. He'd shown me so much kindness, so much attention, that I'd really felt special. Had felt wanted. But it had been worse even than I could have imagined.

Oh I wished, *wished* I'd been Ruby. That would have made this all bearable…maybe.

I turned away, looking at Jafeer who still studied me with

interest, his dark eyes bright. "And you, Jafeer, or Jay. Whoever you are. You knew I wasn't human, so why did you keep hitting on me?"

"I was just distracting you the other day," he countered. "It wasn't real."

"But before that," I persisted. "Outside that clothing boutique. Then before that, when I saw you and the others digging the first day. Someone said 'there's one. Check her out' or something like it."

For the first time Jafeer actually looked embarrassed, flushing a little under his tan. "Oh, come on. I didn't hit on a *cyborg*."

"Yes, you did," I shot back.

"I believe her," Caleb snapped. "And you knew she was modelled after Ruby! Family doesn't do that!"

Cyborg. I hated hearing that word in relation to me, but I watched the argument with interest.

"Who cares?" Jafeer retorted. "She's not Ruby, as you've said before. Besides, the guidebook said they were…" His voice faded into silence, and his neck went red. "You know. Anatomically correct."

My eyebrows shot up, but across from me Caleb's jaw had dropped. "You've got to be freakn' kidding me!" he shouted.

"I wasn't going to *do* anything," Jafeer argued. A moment later he amended, "She wasn't interested. It doesn't matter."

"It *does* matter!" Caleb shouted back. "Ruby was her donor, so she looks like Ruby! And if she is…*correct*, it's none of your damn business! Hell, I knew you were a tomcat, but this is just too much!"

"She's not Ruby!" Jafeer insisted. "It's not the same! It's like… her twin sister."

"He's right," I interrupted, fighting the urge to laugh hysterically. "I'm not Ruby, and I will not allow you to treat me as if I am and I'm not at the same time. Now I don't know what to do next, but I do know that it won't be with Jafeer." I shook my head in disbelief. "I just don't know what happens next."

"Anything you like," Caleb said. Jafeer glared at him, and he amended, "Within the realms of this island."

"So I can't leave, is that what you're saying?"

"Well…no."

"But can't you take me with you?" I persisted. "After this round? After Snow's got whatever she thinks she needs?"

Caleb looked stricken. "I can't take you, Valentina. I'd be arrested. It would be theft."

I looked away, my eyes pricking again with tears. "You're saying I'm a thing, not a person." There was a long, telling silence, broken by my shuddering sigh. "What about what you said before, about choosing differently? About doing what people didn't expect? I want to, Caleb, but now it seems you won't let me."

"It's not me…"

"But you're the one here now," I argued. "You're my only friend here." I looked up at Jafeer. "I'd trust this one as far as I could throw him. Not as far, even, since it seems I'm quite strong. But you…" I leaned into Caleb, meeting his eyes. "Please, please help me. Don't tell anyone we've spoken, and get me out of here as soon as it's safe to do so. I'll play along and do whatever I need to do here, but I can't bear to be reprogrammed again. It's terrifying and confusing and I don't know who I am, but I know that's not me. I'm not a villain. I'm not a murderer. Please."

There was a long silence, then Caleb finally replied, "This is my fault. I should have kept away from you, but I didn't. And I tried to see how far I could push you away from your programming, without caring what the result would be."

"Sure did," Jafeer scoffed.

Caleb ignored him, turning to me. He met my eyes with his warm brown ones, his expression earnest. "I know this is the complete opposite of what I said before, but I shouldn't have said it-"

"I'm glad you said it!" I cut in desperately. "I'm not sorry!"

"…but if you're to escape, then you'll need to play along perfectly. Finish the game perfectly so no one knows there was anything wrong." Caleb glanced sidelong at his cousin. "And Jay will have to keep his mouth shut."

Jafeer sighed, lifting his hands with palms outwards. "Just keep me out of it, and you can do what you like."

My heart rose. "Thank you so much!" I said eagerly. "Just tell me what I need to do and I'll do it."

The others exchanged glances, and Jafeer asked, "Don't you know? I would have thought they'd have programmed that in as well."

My eyebrows lowered. "All I know is that Snow White is a narcissistic pain in the neck. And yes, I understand the irony of *me* saying that. But I don't think it's programming. I think that's just her."

Jafeer barked out a laugh, and even Caleb smiled a little. "Maybe both. That's part of the story. It's a very old one, done many times. Ruby…she was a model, and she did a photo-shoot for some of the early True Fantasies tests." He smiled crookedly. "She played Snow White."

"You've got to be kidding me," I muttered. Even the sound of that name made me twitch with irritation. "I can't get away from the story. Well go on, what is it?"

Caleb cleared his throat awkwardly. "Um…the True Fantasies one is similar, but not quite the same as the traditional version. That starts with a widowed king who has a daughter called Snow White. It's one name, not two like she uses hers here, and she has white skin, black hair, red lips. That's why she has her name."

"Finally the chalky skin makes sense," I murmured. And if my hair had been black, I would have fit that description too.

He continued, "But the king remarries, and his new queen is really beautiful, but also really vain and evil. Sorry. After the wedding she kills the king so she can take control of his kingdom…and because she's just evil, I suppose. She has this magic mirror that can talk, and she's so vain that she asks it every day; 'Mirror, mirror, on the wall, who is the fairest one of all?' and then it would answer-"

"You are the fairest," I finished, chills running down my spine again. *You're Valentina, and you'll be happy.* "I thought that was my little peptalk, something I'd made up to encourage myself. For that matter, I thought *Fairest* was just a clever nickname.”

Caleb looked awkward. “Sorry. Shall I stop?”

“No. Go on, please.”

“So the evil queen was happy enough until one day she asked the mirror who was the fairest, and it said that Snow White was fairer than her. The girl had grown up, you see.”

I shut my eyes briefly, sighing in understanding. “Oh, that explains *so much!* Snow’s so competitive it was driving me mad…”

“Mad enough you’d try to kill her?” Caleb challenged. “Because that’s the next part of the story. You…*the queen* is supposed to try to kill her in all these different ways, but it fails. And then-”

“No no,” Jafeer cut in. “Snow runs away after the queen’s huntsman fails to kill her. She goes to live in some cottage with seven dwarves…”

“…and then the queen comes to kill her,” Caleb finished. “I remember now. She – you, I suppose – are supposed to try to choke her and poison her, but in the end you give her a-”

Parp parp parp. Parp parp parp. Parp parp-

Jafeer swore. “That’s my alarm. We have to go to meet Karey and the others. We have to finish up here.”

“But wait,” I pleaded desperately, “what about me? What do I do next?”

“Have you sent your loyal huntsman off to kill Snow?” Caleb asked frankly. He looked worried.

“I don’t have a loyal huntsman!”

“You’ve got Jorge,” Jafeer pointed out, tapping away at something on his wrist. “He’ll do.”

“But…” Then I realised the last thing that had happened today. I’d sent Jorge to get rid of Snow. I’d only meant for him to give her a talking to…or had I? “Oh.”

“We need to go,” Caleb said reluctantly. “Valentina, will you buy a few items to explain why you were in here? And remember, don’t tell a soul! We’ll all be in trouble if you do.”

Jafeer half-laughed. “She doesn’t care about *me*, cuz.”

In that moment I’d have disagreed. The two of them felt like lifelines. But I nodded, getting to my feet. The cut on my arm had entirely healed, leaving just a smear of blackish liquid that I studied with distaste before wiping on a nearby cloth. "Sorry."

"That's OK," Caleb said. "But you'd better go."

I nodded again, heading reluctantly for the door to the shop. Here in this ragged little home/shop I felt somewhat safe. No one was going to hurt me; they told me the truth. Out on the island...I was playing a game that I still didn't know the rules to. "I'll just pick a couple of things."

"Great. I'll be out in a moment."

I wandered out into the aisles, scanning my eyes over the piles of thick carpets while my mind ran a hundred miles an hour. There were so many more questions to ask, but so many had been answered. I thought about everything I'd experienced over these last few days…the only few days, if these three were right, and things made sense. From those guests saying I looked like an escort droid, to Kingsley's clueless behaviour and unreasonable preference for Snow…everyone's unreasonable preference for Snow. And me, with all those horrible thoughts? Programmed.

It occurred to me then that if this was all real, then whoever had created an 'enhanced' human-ish person had really messed up by adding murderous urges. How were they to know I wouldn't actually commit that murder, and to someone not really on the list?

The poison wouldn't be real poison, I realised a moment later. I would just think it was.

Hmm. "I probably should be more upset about all of this," I murmured to myself, "but maybe that's the programming too. Or perhaps the sedative still."

My gaze paused on a tall vase with a red rose motif, and I found myself catching the edge of a hushed conversation. Caleb and Jafeer's tones were quiet but just audible even from this side of the shop, and I wondered if they knew I could hear them. Maybe my hearing was better than average.

"Dane will go mad if he hears about this," Jafeer was saying. "It took enough to convince him to let us two in on it, let alone some bleach-blonde 'borg."

Or maybe they were just stupid. I mentally amended my 'lifeline' list to remove Jafeer.

"He doesn't need to know," Caleb whispered back. "And don't talk about her like that. She can't help what she is."

Caleb, of course, was still included on the list.

Jafeer laughed; I heard it even from here. "You're a bloody good liar, Cal. I didn't think she was going to believe you."

I froze, straining to hear the next words, but they were too hushed.

"You know we've got too much riding on this," Jafeer said next.

Caleb sighed. "I know," he said quietly. "And trust me, I'm not stupid. I'm not giving it all up for some meat puppet with Ruby's face. But she was so upset that I had to at least pretend to agree."

Meat puppet!? For a moment I couldn't breathe. The words hovered in my memory before breaking skin, slicing their way to my heart.

He'd lied. He wasn't my friend at all. He wasn't going to help me.

He didn't even think of me as human.

I gasped in a deep breath, bending over the rose-motifed vase, my eyes burning. I wanted to turn and scream at him. I wanted to smash something. I wanted to cry…

And the last glimmer of hope, of having aid to get out of this nightmare, vanished.

Bastard. *There's only one thing to do with betrayers.*

No, I told that ugly thought. No more killing, either real or imagined. I'd survived this far on my own. Now I was going to take control, and I was going to get myself out of here, and Caleb the Liar could just…be forgotten.

"But what about the map?" I heard Jafeer ask. "She was the last one to have it."

"I'll ask her," Caleb replied. A moment later I heard approaching footsteps. "Valentina? Have you decided what to order?"

I couldn't look at him at first. I couldn't hide my expression. I just waved a hand to my left. "That one."

"The turquoise vase? Or the jackal-headed one?"

Even with that chaos that was my mind, I'd never forget that last vase. The map that now sat inside it wasn't mine. It was clearly very valuable to these men. Jafeer had said Caleb wasn't a part of whatever they were doing, but he'd clearly lied too.

I took a deep breath through my nose, then swallowed. "Um…both."

"Sure. I'll have them sent up to the hotel." There was a silence, and out of my peripheral vision I saw him move closer, an expression of false-concern on his face. "Are you alright, Valentina? I can check on you later today…"

Meat puppet. "No!" I snapped. "I'm fine. I just need some time to come to terms with things."

"Oh. Good." He paused. "And ah…you wouldn't have seen an old paper document from the day before the wedding? It was misplaced near that little cottage you were staying in."

The map. "I did see it, but that was days ago. It must have blown away."

"Oh." The disappointment in Caleb's voice was palpable. "That's a shame."

"Was it important?" I asked lightly. *Yes, and I hope you suffer for its loss.*

"No, no. Just some plans, nothing that would interest you. We'd better be going now, and we'll have to shut the shop. You don't mind leaving, I hope?"

I shrugged as casually as I could manage, heading towards the door. "Of course not. I need to go too. Oh, and try not to be offended if I'm rude to you later on. I *am* staying in character."

I left, my full attention on walking down those cobbled streets without trembling or screaming aloud. It wasn't a town; it was a set. No, it was a zoo where people came to play with the animals, and I was *not* in the mood for being played with.

Breaking the glass slipper. I probably didn't have long before they came after me. If anyone tried to stab me with a needle, I decided viciously, I'd turn it back on them. I was not going to be their toy anymore. I did have a free will, and I was going to use it to be *free*. I would go to the ferry exit; swim off if I had to. I'd get some provisions…

Ah, but I wasn't the only one who was in danger, was I? I remembered Tarquin and his many questions. I didn't need to go alone, I decided. I should give him warning, take him with me. Maybe we could come back for the others…

I couldn't buy Caleb and Jafeer's story completely. Sure, I understood that something had been done to me. To my head, to my body. And when I thought about my childhood, about that spiel Caleb had rattled off that summarised all my memories; they seemed hollow. Incomplete, unlike the events of the last few days. Like a story I'd been told rather than a life I'd truly lived.

That was the whole point, I thought grimly. It was a story, and a stupid one at that. But how had I landed the villain's role? And where did the treasure map play into this? I'd add it to my escape bag if I could, I decided, as a last act of revenge. Besides, I'd need *something* to live off as I wasn't rich anymore – if I ever had been. Perhaps I could find it myself one day.

I passed the last of the shops and began to walk up the lane towards the hotel. Up ahead I could see the white-clad figures of hotel servers at the front doors. *Act normal, Valentina. Go inside, get some things, run for it.*

That was a stupid idea, I argued with myself. Karey was probably prowling around with a giant needle even now, and if she saw me I'd be done for.

That was why I found myself swerving away from the front entrance, heading around towards the forest at the back. I knew there was a beach over the other side, and all I could think was to get away.

But then something shining amongst the trees caught my eye. The greenhouse tower, I realised, but there was a patch of bright glass glowing like a torch from near its apex. Without meaning to I found my hand on the lock-pad, and two tired minutes after that, I was up in the tower room, warm from the exercise. You'd think that someone who created a perfectly programmable being – if that was true – would have made them fitter.

All the better so I couldn't run away, no doubt.

With that dark thought my mood plummeted further, but then I spotted the shining circle of glass. It was just about eye level, as though someone had taken a cloth and had rubbed a clean patch in the green mildew before losing enthusiasm. It was just enough for the sun to come streaming in, or to catch the light as it had before. It also provided a perfect view all the way down to the village. I could see the roofs of all the shops, as well as the long road leading down to a wharf, then the stretch of gentle sea before the mainland.

It was an excellent metaphor for my life, I thought miserably. Dark and confusing and small, and then someone shows me a hint of more: a hint of real life, just like this little circle of clean glass with its wonderful view. Just enough to make me desperate to leave…

And on a completely different note, I wondered, why did I have thumbprint access to all these rooms and buildings? I'd been able to get into the greenhouse, into my cottage after I'd moved out, and even into that hidden room inside the staff kitchen. Odd.

I pondered that mystery as I descended from the tower and made my way back into the forest, finally adding it to the pile of questions that probably would never get answered, unless I was *really* lucky. But then look at where I was. Surely things could only go up from here?

Minutes later I'd made it to the top of the hill, to the highest point of the island. Before me was a steep slope leading down to a small golden beach. Behind me was the hotel and the village, as well as the small, usually empty wharf that ferry passengers would disembark onto.

I frowned. On second thoughts, I hadn't ever seen the ferry there since I'd arrived. Not even once.

"Maybe I should just swim," I murmured under my breath. The gap between the island and the mainland was only a few hundred metres. How hard could it be?

A mosquito whined beside my ear, tickling my exposed neck, and I slapped at it absentmindedly. My hand touched something small and round, something sticking in my skin. I pulled it out. It was a tiny dart: its end round and black, and its tip so fine it wavered in my vision. Suddenly my neck was numb. It felt like rubber, and my body felt so very heavy. I could feel the effect rushing from my neck right down my body and my limbs.

"Oh *ches-*"

10 Distant

'They're not meant to escape. Ever.'
— from a police interview with Dane S

I was in darkness. My limbs were lead; my heart beating a rapid tattoo in my chest. Images flooded through my mind like an old film reel, almost too fast to take in. *My face in the mirror. The fairest of them all. I smile at my reflection.*

The townsfolk are in awe of me. Admiring. Respectful. Sweetheart Island is my kingdom and the White Hotel is my throne. I saw all of them, one after the other, from the lowest servant to the wealthiest local. *Mine. All mine.* This *is my home.*

I whimpered and shifted in place. Something tugged in the crook of my arm, and a moment later I felt a soft touch. Someone whispering in my ear. *"Who are you?"*

What a silly question. But the words were so very hard to form. "I'm Valentina."

"And what do you want?"

"What I've always wanted." I sighed, the images forming scenes of beauty. Safety. Comfort. "To be happy."

"And who do you despise?"

Only one face came to mind. Stylised, with the features indistinct, but the colouring unmistakeable. I frowned. "Snow White?"

"I think that'll do," the voice said. *"If three days doesn't do it then nothing will. Give me a hand, will you? She's heavy."*

I tried to raise my arm, but it felt glued down. I blinked, the grey light shooting little needles into my eyes. Where was I?

"Just sleep," the voice assured me. *"Everything will be just fine."*

Sleep. What a good idea. I closed my eyes, breathed in, and…

I was seated at a table. Colour and movement blurred all around me; sounds of conversation and footsteps and music. My hands rested on the table's edge in front of me: white skin, red nails. Just a handspan away was a half full wine glass. Red, of course. A smear of crimson marked the glass's pristine edge. I'd already been drinking.

"Your lunch, Mrs White. Beef heart Bourguignon."

A few moments later the plates were placed in front of me. I watched absently as my hands reached for the knife and fork then began cutting. *This is normal. This is your life.*

"Do you require anything else, Mrs White?"

"No," I heard myself say. "That will be all."

I began to eat methodically, pausing occasionally to sip at my wine.

"Are you alright?" someone said near my ear. Their voice was young, male, and low. "I haven't seen you in days."

I paused mid-cut, then turned to look at the speaker. My neck was stiff, my head heavy, my mind clouded. He was a server; a white-clad youth with black hair, a too-thick moustache and bright blue eyes. Handsome, except for the moustache. Poor. I turned back to my food.

"Valentina?"

Something bright broke through the mental fog, just for a moment. Some idea. Some knowledge. But then it was gone.

"Oh no," he breathed. "They've got you too."

The server left, and I finished my dinner. Good, but not perfect, I decided. It needed a little bite. Perhaps some gold dust?

"Ma'am, you called for me?"

It was Jorge. Good, faithful Jorge; his faded red hair almost vanishing into his tanned skin; his suit looking as perfect as always. "Yes," I said, feeling my lips form around unfamiliar words. "Tell me about Snow White."

There was a silence, and he leaned in beside me, right beside my ear. "She's been seen," he whispered. "Out in a little cottage in the forest. She's living with seven miners, although they appear to leave during the day."

Sweetheart Island had miners? But my curiosity didn't linger. "Who else knows she's there?"

"No one else, ma'am."

I looked back down at my plate. The stew was gone, but the sauce had left behind a reddish smear on the pure white china. *I do like heart. So very vital.* "Good."

"And the masquerade ball will take place tomorrow night as agreed," Jorge said. "White themed as you specified, in your late husband's honour."

"Good."

"Your costume is ready, ma'am. I've instructed the servers to leave it in your dressing room."

"Good."

"Will there be anything else, ma'am?"

Three seconds ticked by. "No, Jorge."

"Very good, ma'am."

I sat there at the table for some time after he left, breathing slowly in and out, people going about their lives around me. I was inside the hotel, in the smaller but fancier restaurant on the second floor. Occasionally someone would meet my eye. They'd either glance away quickly, or nod respectfully before going about their business.

They're afraid of me. Good.

Quickly on the heels of that thought came another one. *Are you freakin' kidding me? Not again!*

I went straight to my suite on the top floor. I had my finger on the lock-pad when I heard a voice from behind me. "Mrs White, that isn't your room anymore. You're now staying in the King suite, just down the hall."

Karey Godmother. I slowly turned to face her, my heartbeat

pounding in my head. She stood near the lifts, the 'down' button highlighted, and looked as professional as ever in her pink suit. But she was watching me oh so carefully.

"They're all my rooms," I said coolly, "and I'll take whichever I want."

One corner of her mouth quirked in a smile, and she glanced away. "My apologies, Mrs White. As you've been unwell these past few days, I thought you'd wish to know your belongings were moved this morning."

I turned away, blindly staring at the blank door. Unwell. Was that what I'd been? I resisted the urge to touch my neck. "That'll be all, Ms Godmother."

A moment later I heard her leave. With the greatest of control I turned and went to Kingsley's suite. The door unlocked for me, and as promised, my clothing was already inside the dressing room. My shoes. My makeup chest in the generous bathroom.

I closed the bathroom door and locked it, sitting down on the chair in front of the enormous mirror. Soft lights came to life all around its edge, shining on my reflected self. I was beautiful and golden today: my hair and makeup perfect; my lipstick a dark purple-red only a few shades lighter than my dress.

Who's the fairest of them all? You are.

I didn't even have the energy to counter the thought. But in the quietness of this space my thoughts were clearing, my memories returning in full brilliance. They'd never really gone; the confusion had just made them inaccessible. But along with those memories came others, uninvited ones that screamed their way into my mind, sharing space with the real ones. They told me a story much like the one Caleb had begun, but with myself as the main character, as the heroine trying to fend off all my enemies. But I knew it was just a story.

"I know who you are," I told my reflection very quietly. "I won't forget." The only question was, what did I do next?

Kill Snow White. An image of her smirking face came to mind, followed by one of those tiny jars and the sharp blades of a black and red jewelled comb. *You try to kill her,* Caleb had said. Out of jealousy, because I was vain and evil. Because they were trying to *make me* vain and evil.

I took in another deep breath, then let it out in a sob, leaning forward to rest my face in my hands.

"Are you feeling unwell, Mrs White? Do you require medication?"

The small voice came from somewhere near the mirror, and I froze in place. "What?"

"You appear to be in pain."

"I have…" *a headache*, I was about to say, then remembered what always came with headaches. Migraine injectors. What had I been putting into myself? "…I'm tired," I finished, spotting the speaker next to one of the lights. No doubt it also doubled as a camera. "It was a long day. And since when do I have observation in my own bathroom? Out of all the places in my home, this should be the most private."

"My apologies," the voice said. It was bland and neutral enough that it might have been an android. "Mr White requested such surveillance as he once suffered a heart attack while in the bath. He wished to avoid repeat incidents."

So that was their excuse. "I'm hardly likely to experience such a thing," I snapped. "I do not wish any form of surveillance while in my own home. Is that clear?"

"Yes, Mrs White."

The voice fell silent, but I was still shaken. I got to my feet, stepping out of sight of the mirror, my arms wrapped tightly around myself. Even through the haze still coating my mind, I had no confidence that my order would be obeyed. But even through that haze, I still knew what I was going to do. I would make a choice to reject my programming, and to live my own life. It probably wasn't going to be happily ever after, but hopefully it would be *mine*.

Every move that I made, I made carefully. I went to the dressing room and found on the back racks that ugly brown dress I'd spotted some time before. I emptied out the contents of a large gift basket, then put the dress inside, along with the long black wig, the flattest pair of shoes I owned, and some brown-toned sunglasses I'd found in the back of the dressing room. In went the most valuable jewellery I owned – most likely fakes, but still worth something – and the most energy-dense food I could find in the room. Chocolate. I finished off packing with a few cosmetics including bronzer and beige lipstick, then I was done.

I took the stairs to the lowest floor, detoured into one of the less used public bathrooms, and put on the disguise. In went the fairest of them all, out came a tanned brunette with terrible dress sense and a basket full of goodies to sell. Or at least that was the story if anyone asked. I took extra care covering that distinctive beauty mark, and wondered if that was why I'd been left with such a symbol of imperfection: it made it harder to disguise myself.

Still, I slipped outside without being accosted, forcing myself to walk casually away from the hotel and onto the less used side paths. Once I was sure I was alone I picked up my pace, heading off into the forested eastern side of the island, an area I'd rarely visited. I was hypersensitive to any sound, any movement; but there was just me. Whew, this forest really was bigger than I'd realised. I was right in the middle of it, and could only just make out the sea through the trees in front of me. I set my eyes on that slice of blue, lifted my chin, and walked boldly forward.

Suddenly the ground disappeared in front of me, and I tumbled head first into a grassy dip, shrieking in surprise. The basket went flying, sending its contents in every direction. I had fallen into a cobbled path dug into the hillside, and just five feet to my left was a little blue doorway, complete with bronze knocker. The house was built right into the hill, like a human version of a rabbit warren. It was completely hidden except from this angle. No wonder I'd stumbled across it.

"Chestnuts!" I sat up, scrambling to find my sunglasses. They were cracked. "Talk about the worst luck!" I shoved them back on my face anyway, then dusted off my brown skirts out of habit rather than necessity. They looked the same as before.

Just then I heard footsteps from inside the little house. I turned my back on the door, letting my black wig fall to cover my face, and concentrated on picking up my valuables, shoving them back in the basket even as I heard the door creak open. "Sorry," I called over my shoulder, pitching my voice high and breathy. "I didn't see your path. I'll be out of your way in a moment."

There was a pause, then a moment later small feet appeared in the edge of my peripheral vision. Tiny ankles, dark blue slippers. "What are you selling?"

Selling? But I knew that voice. I turned my head, my stomach twisting in dread. Yep, there she was. Snow White, in the flesh.

Kill her! The thoughts ordered. *Poison her! Kill kill kill kill kill!* A lovely image of Snow collapsed on the ground, her face grey, illustrated the instruction.

I gasped in a breath, choked on my own spit, then spent a few moments coughing hysterically.

Snow moved a couple of steps closer. Her expression was wary, but there was a small smile on her pale, perfectly made-up face. "Are you alright?" she asked sweetly. "Do I need to call for a medic?"

"No medic!"

She stepped back abruptly, scowling. "Fine. It was just an offer. So what are you selling here, jewellery?"

"Uh…"

"And chocolate. Odd combination."

"The two things girls like most," I said gaily, turning away from her. "But I'm sure you've got no interest in my old things. They're second-hand, you realise, except for the chocolates."

But Snow ignored my deflection, coming to crouch down next to me anyway. "I like antiques too. Let me see." She picked up a couple of bracelets, turning them over in her hands then putting them aside in the grass. "Ooh, a comb! Why's this one wrapped in plastic?"

It was an ornately decorated hair comb, the sort with sharp silver tines and black and red gems on display. I vaguely recalled adding it to the basket. "That one's very old," I said dismissively, quickly replacing the last few items into the basket. "It needs protecting. I'm sure you wouldn't like it."

"I'm sure I would," she retorted eagerly. "It would be perfect with my colouring. Red and black, see?" She tore the casing open, examined the comb briefly, then stuck it in her hair. It stood out sideways rather than flat, looking like an odd antenna. "Ouch. It's sharp."

I stood, grabbing the now-full basket and stepping away from her. "Mm, it looks really pretty. You should have it for free. Now if you'll excuse me...."

Snow made an odd whining noise and I glanced at her in surprise. She'd sat back on the cobbled path, the comb in her head and one hand half raised to it. Her eyes were glassy and her breathing rapid. As I watched, her hand slumped to the ground and slowly, slowly, she tipped over backwards.

"Snow?"

She didn't move. She just lay there, her eyes half open and her chest moving gently up and down. I crouched down next to her, checking her pulse. It *seemed* normal. Perhaps she'd just fainted. I moved around to her head, examining the comb but not touching it. As I did so an image flashed through my mind. *The comb, its tines so very sharp. Opening a little jar, using a clean makeup brush to smear its gel-like contents over the tips of those tines. 'Batrachotoxin,' I hear myself say with satisfaction. 'It'll work in moments.'*

I jerked back in shock, my mind a blank for several seconds. What was Batrachotoxin? It didn't sound friendly. Then the terrible realization dawned. *You'll try to kill her several times,* Caleb had said.

Even in my mind I wasn't free at all. No matter what I'd intended to do, I'd followed my programming.

I left Snow inside the house, still unconscious, and resisted the urge to call a medic. She'd *wanted* this, the little idiot, and she could enjoy every last stupid moment.

And now she is dead, life will go back to normal.

"Shut up!" She still had a pulse, stupid programming.

But how could you silence something inside your own head? I felt like I'd been injected with a parasite, one that I'd hoped to overcome but now realised had infected me right down to my movements. But I didn't give up. I walked around the edge of the island, my thoughts spinning in my head, fighting back tears. And then I finally reached the wharf. I hadn't even been intending to go there. The wharf was empty, not a sailboat in sight, and the smooth sealed road seemed to disappear right into the water's edge. In the other direction I could see all the way into the village.

At the beach's edge, where it met a fringe of greenery, was a shack. It was wooden and built in what looked like an intentionally rough manner, with one side propped open and a small doorway. It was also packed full of junk, reminding me of the props room back in the hotel. Anything and everything hung on the three walls, from umbrellas to broad-brimmed hats to bunches of fake flowers. A pink piggy bank sat on the bench, 'honesty box' scrawled on its round side.

I'd been studying the shop for at least a minute before I saw the old woman sitting in the corner, hidden by the partial darkness. I jolted in surprise, almost dropping my basket, then realised it wasn't a person at all. It was a full mask complete with grey hair, hanging on the wall.

"Ugh," I murmured, but I was fascinated. I picked it up off the wall and its edges immediately sealed to my hand. I pulled it away with a squelch, then let it reseal, wiggling my fingers and admiring how it looked like real flesh. Or like *my* flesh, I amended. This would be a really fantastic disguise. It was a shame I had no cash, and no one to buy it from anyway.

But it was *so* realistic. I bit my lip, glancing from the mask to my basket, then at the empty beach. A few seconds later I carefully hung one of my nicer necklaces over the piggy's nose, shoved the mask at the bottom of my basket, and was in the process of moving away when I noticed something about the piggy's eyes. They were small and black, but they didn't look painted. Something red moved inside them.

I gasped, turning it into a cough, then turned my back on the surveillance pig, trying to act casual. It would have an excellent view of the wharf from here, I realised, and there was no way I could exit here unnoticed. Even my idea of swimming seemed much harder than it had originally. I didn't even know if I *could* swim; my memories of resorts were more about lounging beside pools than doing laps. More than that, I'd been standing here long enough that my face would have been well and truly captured by the cameras.

Just then a trio of brightly dressed locals came down onto the beach, chattering all the way. They eyed me curiously and I nodded politely before quickly walking away.

Twenty minutes later I'd reached the hotel grounds again. It was as though I'd never left. I walked slowly back to the King suite and got into the shower, watching the tanner swirl away down the drain and leave behind the same old fairest Valentina.

Caleb had told me I had free will. That was before I'd known about the programming, but *he* had known. I'd believed him then, but now after my three-day 'illness' the evidence showed otherwise. *Sure, you had free will,* I imagined Karey saying. *But it was inconvenient, so we took it away.*

My hands clenched into fists so tightly that my nails cut into my skin. I studied the half-moon shapes for a few moments, watching the skin reseal, watching the oily not-blood wash away under the stream of water. Then I picked up one of the liquid soap dispensers in its hard metal canister, wrapped that same hand around its circumference, and squeezed. I stopped when the two ends broke in half.

Snow had been lucky she'd only got the comb in her head, I realised in horrified dismay. If I'd not been in my right mind, I could have snapped her little neck as easily as this canister. I dropped the pieces on the bathroom floor. Then I got into my robe, walked past the white angel costume hanging on the door, and went to bed.

When I woke it was completely dark. I had a few moments of panic, then realised it was simply night time. I was alone in the bed of the king suite of the White Hotel. Kingsley was dead, I was the new owner. The glowing digits of the clock read 12.15 – just after midnight.

No! A moment later I remembered the full story, right down to the comb sticking in Snow's head, and rolled over face-down into the pillow. Really, my waking life wasn't worth much. I should just lie here and refuse to get up. Then what would they do?

Tranquillise and reprogram you again?

I grunted into the pillow, then shoved myself into a sitting position. Through the dimmed glass of the windows there was a faint glow, one I hadn't noticed before. I moved right up close, cupping my hand against the glass to lessen the opacity, and then I could see it. Two double rows of spotted lights in the distance, looking just like a lit-up road.

How very odd.

I switched off the window's opacity entirely, leaving myself in darkness, and then I realised what I was looking at. It *was* a lit-up road, one that led from the wharf at the end of the island, right over to the light-speckled mainland.

A road off the island.

I sat on my private balcony early the next morning, sipping at my usual breakfast latte, and with a carefully bored expression on my face. Every now and then I'd steal a glance over to the flat blue stretch between the empty wharf and the mainland. I imagined I could see the faint signs of the hidden road beneath the water. The ferry hadn't brought the many cars onto the island. They'd just driven on.

Just wait until midnight, I told myself.

My wristpiece flashed red. *"Ma'am?"*

That was one of the first things I'd get rid of, I decided. "Yes, Jorge?"

"I bring urgent news. Are you alone?"

I checked in every direction. I was on the fourth storey of the hotel. There were balconies on either side of me as well as below, but they were vacant. "Yes, Jorge."

"It's Snow White, ma'am." Even through the slight interference of the wristpiece I could tell he'd lowered his voice. *"She was seen this morning near the cottage, alive and well."*

"Was she."

"Yes, ma'am. I've notified you at once, as per your instructions. It would be disastrous if she was to return, especially with the ball tonight."

'My' instructions.

The ball is tonight! She'll ruin it all! Kill her kill her kill her-

"Shut UP!"

"Pardon, ma'am?"

I let out a heavy sigh of both relief and frustration. Yay, Snow wasn't dead! But boo, I had to go fake-kill her again. "Nothing, Jorge. And thank you. That will be all."

The red light faded into its dormant state, and I slipped off the band, fighting the urge to hurl it forcefully into the nearby trees. It was almost certainly doubling as a tracker. But then 'they' would know that I knew, and…well, assuming I was able to sidestep the programming, I'd save the hurling for after midnight.

But until then, I had the whole day ahead of me. I took my time getting dressed, then when I came back into the main part of my suite I found it was occupied. There was an auburn-haired boy in his late teens crouching in front of my coffee table with a large camera in his hands, photographing a bowl of fruit that had been arranged on the table's dark, shining surface. He turned as I came in, an apologetic smile on his bespectacled face. "Good morning, Mrs White."

"Is it? And who might you be?"

The boy's smile faltered. "Jeremy Kricket, photographer. Nice to finally meet you, ma'am."

He looked to be a real person, judging by his expressions, but one without a reason to be here. "Mm. Mr Kricket, I might wonder exactly what you're doing in my private rooms."

His face fell. "Oh. But I asked- I'm so sorry. Your assistant told me that I could use this space for a few minutes as part of my portfolio." At my bemused expression, he elaborated, "I do the photography advertising for the White Hotel among other places, and I like to use little snippets like this." He pointed at the bowl of fruit. There were pears, apples and some kind of stone fruit: all looking as healthy and glossy as I'd ever seen. "See? A photo of these beauties would show the world that your food is as good as the service, but the lighting downstairs in the kitchen was no good. I needed something better, and…"

"Jorge sent you up here," I said in understanding.

"Jorge? No, it was a woman," Jeremy countered, clearly puzzled. "I didn't catch her name, but she was a nice-looking older lady in a pink suit. Have I done the wrong thing?"

Not Jorge… Karey. "Probably not," I replied dryly. "It's not as though I'm going to sit in here all day." Although that was exactly what I'd hoped to do. "Is this fruit from our kitchens? It's gorgeous. Those apples look delicious."

Snow loves apples. A big red shiny one…

I didn't even tell the thought to shut up this time.

"Oh, but you mustn't touch it!" he exclaimed fervently. "And definitely, definitely don't eat it! I only touch it with gloves, but to ingest the fruit means certain, immediate death. It's all been coated with photographer's fruit wax, which makes it look beautiful under the lights, but is highly toxic."

"Highly toxic," I repeated flatly, remembering that little tin from the props room downstairs. It was finally coming into play. "And it makes food beautiful. You didn't consider how this could backfire?"

Jeremy blinked in confusion. "Oh. I suppose it might, if one wasn't careful."

I sighed. "Then we ought to be very careful disposing of it."

"Yes, Mrs White."

I watched from a distance as he photographed the shining fruit from different angles for a few minutes, then he frowned. "I think I know what this needs. A banana. I'll just go and get one."

He left the room before I could say 'intercom', the same thing that Kingsley had once done, when he'd left Snow and I to have a snarky conversation. It had been only days ago, but it felt like an eternity had passed.

I watched the door to make sure he'd really gone, then retrieved a tea towel from the nearby kitchen. Wrapping it around my hand, I carefully picked up the biggest, reddest apple in the bowl, then bundled the whole thing up so none of the fruit was showing. "Certain, immediate death," I said aloud, studying the remaining fruit with a moue of distaste. "As good as an anvil to the head." Or a heart attack.

Alright, Snow White. This is what you want, and you're going to get it. Although not yet: it was barely nine o'clock. Time to scope out the island.

I hid the apple at the back of my closet along with the mask and my basket, then left before the photographer returned. He'd let himself in before, he could do it again.

Down in the hotel proper, the lower floors were being decked in rows and rows of sparkling white lights. I saw two servers carrying in an entire tree in an enormous pot, with every single leaf spray-painted shining white. It looked beautiful but lifeless, and I wondered if it would be able to grow again after being painted like this. For some reason that made me sad.

Jorge came up beside me, his expression as neutral as always. *Its* expression as neutral as always. Androids had no more freedom of expression than a vacuum cleaner. "Preparations for the ball tonight, ma'am. Was your costume to your liking?"

I'd barely looked at it. "Yes, Jorge. Thank you. What time does the ball start tonight?"

"Eight, ma'am, until two."

"Late night."

"Yes, ma'am."

Scintillating conversationalists, androids. "That'll be all, thank you. You go and…sort out the ball."

"Yes, ma'am."

I spotted a pink-clad figure at the other side of the foyer, deep in conversation with a server, and waving her arms like a composer. Karey was actually doing some work by the look of things. And while she was here, she wasn't somewhere else…

I excused myself from Jorge and took the back halls towards the staff kitchen. I passed a couple of servers on the way, but just lifted my chin and kept walking. They didn't question me, either because they were androids and couldn't, or because they were smarter and were too scared to.

The staff kitchen was empty, but when I let myself into the props room, it was occupied by a dark-haired youth, standing over by the far shelf with his blue-clad back to me.

I watched for a few seconds, waiting for him to turn around. Finally I coughed.

Tarquin leapt a foot into the air, then turned to face me, one hand held up in a martial arts pose. A moment later he lowered it sheepishly. "Valentina! Uh…do you know who I am?"

"Of course I know who you are. Why wouldn't I?" I studied him curiously. "You've lost the moustache and you're back to wearing colour, but that's what you wore when we first met."

He shrugged, his mouth downturned. "Yesterday you didn't even acknowledge me, and I didn't see you for three days before that. I didn't know what happened."

"Oh." I debated how to answer, then finally shrugged. "What happened to you, happened to me. We're not safe here."

"They did something to your head? I knew it!" he exploded. "Were there tubes? Did you wake up in a room like this? Are you injured?"

I smiled a little.

"What's so funny?"

"Nothing's funny. You're just the first person who's been genuinely concerned for me." Caleb had acted like he was, but really he'd just seen me as a…meat puppet. Not a real person. I wasn't going to poison him, but I wouldn't forget either. Ever. "It's nice."

"That's normal behaviour, Valentina." But he stepped backwards, closer to the shelf. One of his hands was partially hidden behind him. Had been the whole time, in fact.

"There's nothing normal about the two of us. Now what are you hiding from me?"

"What? Nothing!"

I set my hands on my hips. "You're clearly hiding something behind your back, something I can assume you stole from the shelves here. You can show me. After everything I've learned, there's nothing you could do that would shock me."

Tarquin shuffled his feet together, as visibly guilty as a schoolboy caught with vodka in his bag. "I don't know about that. What have you learned?"

"Don't try to distract me. I'll tell you later. Now show me, or I'll come over there and find out myself."

His lips tightened in a straight line, and then he sighed in resignation, pulling his hand from behind his back and showing me what he held. It was a small tin with a clear skull and crossbones symbol. *Photographer's fruit wax,* it read. *Highly toxic!*

"I'm going to take some photographs," he muttered, staring at his feet. "That's all."

I carefully removed the tin from his hand, replacing it on the shelf. That stuff really got around. "You're a terrible liar, Tarquin. Are you planning to kill yourself?"

His head shot up. "No! Why would you think that?"

"Because some of my programming is getting really nasty, and why should yours be any better? You're planning to kill someone. I know that. Who?" He still didn't answer, and my heart sank. "Oh. It's for me, isn't it. I should have known."

"It's not for you," he shot back.

"Then who?"

There were another three seconds of slow, painful non-reply. Then finally he took a deep breath, closed those sapphire blue eyes, and spoke. "It's for Snow White."

11 Startled

'Sometimes the most final solution feels like the best one.'
– from a conversation with Ezra B

For several moments I was shocked into silence. *Tarquin wants to kill Snow White.* Then I burst into laughter. I laughed so hard my chest hurt and my eyes ran, and I bent in half, my arms wrapped around myself.

"It's not funny! I mean it," he snapped, sounding very offended. He stomped past me to snatch the tin back off the shelf, pulling it into his chest with a mulish expression. "You can't stop me."

I composed myself, but could still feel the corners of my lips still twitching. "Why would I want to stop you, Tarquin? The more important question is why would you want to kill her? I thought she was your one true love."

He scowled. "That's what they *want* me to think. The thoughts going over and over in my head, of us kissing and sunsets and weddings and children – they're not my thoughts! And I won't be controlled by them. So I'm going to fix it once and for all."

Oh, oh, oh. I *so* wanted to laugh again, but he looked so very serious. I glanced away for a moment, letting myself grin the way I wanted to, then turned back to him with a carefully neutral expression. "Tarquin…that's the programming. I'm impressed that you're able to overcome it, but can I say that murder is not the answer?"

"But then what is?" He looked truly desolate in that moment. "I just want it all to go away. I want to go back to normal."

"It'll never go back to normal. Not while you're on the island." I checked the still-closed door behind me as though Karey Godmother was about to come storming through. "There are some things you really need to know, but the first one is that you don't have to marry Snow White. I swear it to you."

"You can't know that," Tarquin argued. "You don't understand how compelled I feel when I'm around her. I barely held myself back from proposing the last time I saw her."

"Which is exactly why you wouldn't make her best assassin," I said dryly. "I already have plans in that area, and you would mess them up if you did that, believe me. What you need to do is just act normal for the rest of the day, then come meet me at midnight tonight in the rose garden outside the hotel. If you can do that, I'll tell you everything you need to know."

"Like what?"

"I'll tell you *tonight*," I emphasized. "Right now we shouldn't even be in here, and if we get caught acting out of character, we're in trouble. They'll take us away. Do you understand that?"

"Is that what happened to you?"

I nodded, my lips downturned. "It's worse than last time. I don't know if I would survive through another session."

His eyes widened, and he nodded. "I'll be careful. But isn't midnight when everyone at the ball takes off their masks?"

"Ten past, then. Near the fountain in the centre of the rose garden. Don't be late, *definitely* don't let anyone see you. Alright?"

"I'll be there."

I moved for the door, checking that he was following behind, but one more thing had caught my eye. The air rifle. And not too far from it, those tacky shiny slippers. "Tarquin, do you have a car?"

"Sure, back at my house. Why?"

I picked up the air rifle, opened it, checked it was empty of pellets, then handed it to him. "Wrap this in your jacket. Hide it in the boot of your car, but don't let anyone see you."

"Are we going somewhere?"

"Hopefully." I tucked one slipper under each arm of my own jacket, which was as uncomfortable as it sounded. "But now we should get out of here."

The staff kitchen was still empty when we exited. I went to go back down the halls, Tarquin went to take the fire exit. Then he glanced back at me. "This is all real, isn't it?"

I knew what he meant. "Yes, it's all real."

"Then what are the slippers for?"

My lips curved into a smile. "Once we're out of here I'm going to smash them. I'm going to well and truly break the glass slipper."

"Er…OK."

He didn't get it, but I didn't care. I sneaked back up to the top level of the hotel, but instead of returning to my suite which was certainly full of cameras, I went down the other end of the hall to a room I'd never visited before. Snow's. And if she was the guest, I told myself, she'd not be watched. Probably.

The rooms were smaller than mine, almost rustic in style with quilted blankets, but nicely maintained. I poked around in the closet and drawers, noting the few items still in there. It looked like she'd taken a suitcase when Jorge had 'chased her off', but had left one or two items behind.

I opened the tall wardrobe and struck costume gold. There were half a dozen wigs ranging from short black curls to auburn to white blonde, as well as a sandy brown one that looked like it belonged on an old woman. I also found a tub of whitest-white foundation in one of the drawers, as well as a range of very strange clothes. There was a pair of very tight, very stretchy pants in fluoro pink, as well as a loose white shirt and what looked like an old-fashioned men's vest. It had darts for a woman's figure, though, so I wasn't sure what to make of that. Who would wear such a thing?

But at the very bottom of the drawer I found a few items that puzzled me even more. There was a small book full of scrawled writing which I at first took for a diary, but it seemed more like a list of odd things than a place to write deepest feelings. Not that I would be interested in the second, but it would have made more sense to me than what it said.

1-12-96. R.G.86, 40mg. 2ⁿᵈ d. Repeat weekly. 14ᵗʰ ATG...

The only thing I could understand in all of that was the date: presumably the first of December, 2096. The rest of it? Who knew. There was also a small box full of plastic vials. I picked one up, trying to work out what it was for, when suddenly a small electric shock made me drop it on the floor. I replaced it rather more carefully in its box, then studied the last item.

It was a wad of hair. Real hair, dark brown and fine textured, and tied in a bundle with a ribbon as though it was precious. I should have been disgusted, but instead I found myself reaching up to my own scalp, where my golden hair never grew so much as a millimetre. My eyes started to burn again, and I hurriedly shut the drawer. It was just hair.

I took the auburn wig and the plain brown one, as well as the stretchy tights, white shirt and vest. The latter would be definitely too small for me but I could wear it open. I had an inkling that it might be clothing from the outside: clothing which would help me to fit in on the mainland far better than my formal gowns and ornate jewellery. I bundled them up along with the glass slippers in a pillowcase and headed back towards my suite.

As I sauntered down the hall with my stolen prize, one of the servers came in the opposite direction. I acted as I normally would (I ignored him) but by turning my head away I noticed something not quite right in the wall panelling. There was a small knothole at just above eye level. Now that might seem normal in most places, but not here in the White Hotel. All the décor was fabulous and perfect and there were no knotholes, none.

Another secret room, maybe? Or just my imagination. Once the man had disappeared I sidled over, then gently pressed the back of the knothole where I could feel a slight bump. Nothing happened, so feeling rather silly, I did it again, harder. Again, nothing happened.

"Open!" I snapped at the hole. Still nothing happened, so I

naturally figured that it had been my imagination. It was just one lone, silly blemish in the piece of wood.

But that still didn't sit right with me. I tried one more time, shuffling all my 'borrowed' goods into my left arm, then pushing and holding the 'button' on the other side. "Come on," I hissed at it. "Don't leave me looking stupid. Open Sesame."

Right then there was an almost inaudible *creak* and I felt the emptiness behind me as the door swung inward. Huh. Of *course* it was 'open sesame'.

The darkness revealed a sizeable room, and it also had a presence to it that Karey's hidden room had lacked. There seemed to be a shelf right in the way, but then past that I couldn't see for lack of light.

Sticking the bundle of clothes in the door so that I wouldn't be shut in, I slipped inside to see if I could feel my way. Even with the faint light from the open door I could still barely make out more than vague shapes. The room was much larger than I'd first guessed, though, and it seemed to be filled with those same shelves, loads and loads of them, and some had large, long piles of…*something* stacked on them. I couldn't make out what.

Hand outstretched, I moved cautiously towards the closest object. Hmm. It was sort of pointy and hard, but squishy at the same time with knobbly bits. Cool in temperature, it almost felt like something organic…

I dropped the foot with a squeak and leapt backwards from the body, crashing loudly into the shelf behind me. It shook and I felt something flop off it and land on my shoulder. By now I could see what it was – a hand.

This time I couldn't stop the scream coming out, even as I realised that I must have found another 'storage room. That was when I saw that the door had closed.

I was trapped.

I scrambled over and grabbed for the bundle I'd dropped on the floor to hold the door open. Part of the auburn wig was stuck in the now closed door, and I pulled at it frantically but only succeeded in ripping a few strands of hair out.

Tempted to freak out completely, I pressed my back against the door and took deep, calming breaths. So I was shut in a room full of bodies. Even though I knew they'd just be androids, or others like me and Tarquin, here in the dark it felt like being trapped in a morgue.

Gathering my courage I walked back over to the closest shelf, then leaned closer and searched for some proof of life. But the body, a woman I saw now, was lying incredibly still and cold. Her hand was as chilled and stiff as a doll's, and I let it go with a shudder. "Just an android," I said under my breath. "Just like Jorge." But if she sat up I was going to pee my pants.

I would have left it at that if I hadn't seen the tubes stretching from the next figure to reach a machine sitting on the shelf below it. The android woman hadn't had that at all, instead lying all on her own. I moved closer to inspect the new figure and saw that it was an older man with a close-cropped beard. I couldn't see any colour in this semi-dark, but I still knew it was Kingsley, and he was breathing.

Hooray!

"I'm so glad I didn't kill you," I told him happily. It occurred to me then that if I felt short-changed being selected as 'the villain', then what about him? He'd been cast as the murdered husband… and if True Fantasies was as successful as that ad made it out to be, he could play that role over and over again.

I resolved then that after I'd escaped, I was going to find some way to free the others too, whether they wanted it or not. But I really ought to start with getting out of this room.

I went back over to the door, searching for a knothole or a lock-pad that would allow me to exit. When I couldn't find one, I gave the door a good shove. When that didn't work, I tried the shove in conjunction with 'open sesame', then along with a good deal of swearing. The door still didn't budge, but it made me feel very slightly better.After five minutes of trying I heard footsteps approach. I froze, unsure of whether to call out and try to get them to free me, or whether that would mean giving away my plan. I decided to be cautious and stayed silent, especially when

I heard the footsteps stop just outside the door. I ducked out of sight behind one of the shelves, grabbing my bundle of clothes and hair at the last moment just as the door slid open.

A figure was outlined in the bright light of the doorway. It was an unfamiliar man in his forties, plain-clothed, and with a belt full of technical-looking tools that I couldn't have named had my life depended on it. He paused in the doorway, staring at something. I realised in horror that he'd seen the few auburn hairs torn out from when the wig had got stuck in the door, and there were a few long, tension filled seconds before he bent down to pick them up, then shoved them in his pocket.

I shrank back into the gap as he flicked on a light, moving into the space right near where I was hidden. But his gaze was fixed on that same female android that I'd bumped into, and he moved over to it, cooing in the same way I'd heard women do with their lap dogs.

"Hello Miranda, my beauty," he crooned. "And what seems to be the problem here?" He switched to a falsetto: "*I don't know, Simon. My brain doesn't seem to be working.* Oh, that's alright, love. A lot of women have that problem."

'Simon' lost my sympathy with that last comment. He leaned over her prone body and abruptly peeled her hair back to display a silvery dashboard with a single glowing red light. I gasped in shock and the man spun around to confront me.

I panicked.

Holding the bundle over my face, I swung it hard and felt the crack when my padded fists hit the side of his head. He fell with a crash back onto Miranda's gurney and I didn't wait, I ran for the still open door and straight out into the empty hall, pulling the door shut after me. I didn't stop running until I was out of sight of that body-closet and back to my suite.

I wasn't even out of breath, but I was clutching that bundle of clothes and wigs to my chest like it was a lifeline. As long as they didn't realise it was *me* that was in that room. So much for there not being any humans at all except for the players, hmm? Talk about false advertising.

I stayed in my room until I'd recovered my composure, but I couldn't forget what I'd seen in that second storage room. It wasn't just one or two androids: there were people in there. Or sort of people, anyway. If Tarquin was like me, then who was to say that Kingsley might not have had the same potential had his programming been different? I vowed again that when I escaped I wouldn't forget the others. Somehow I would let the world know about them.

The clock was striking eleven when I made my way downstairs with a different basket, a different costume, and a fake-poisoned apple. The last thing I wanted to do was see Snow again, but I had to play along with the programming. The rest of my things, including my wristpiece, had been left in my bathroom. I detoured into the staff kitchen, stole half a dozen apples from the ever-full fruit bowl, then got changed in the nearest empty bathroom. On went the ugly mask and the short brown wig, on went a loose skirt and shirt over my clothes so I'd look rounder.

I studied my new self critically in the mirror. Chestnuts, I looked different with this mask on. It had hanging jowls and deep lines beside the eyes and nose, and it sealed right over my lips and to the edge of my green eyes. When I blinked or moved my lips, the mask moved with me. I checked the back view and grimaced. Fine, so I was an old lady with a nice figure. Some of those existed, right? Just look at Karey Godmother.

It was a lot easier to find the cottage this time. After fifteen minutes of wandering I stumbled across it – literally – but caught myself before my apples went flying. I checked the too-red 'poison' apple was still perched on the top of the pile as planned, took a deep breath, then knocked on the small blue front door.

Two minutes went by, and nobody came. I knocked again, beginning to grow nervous. Had I misunderstood the rules of the game? Or worse, had I *actually* killed Snow yesterday?

That thought had me swallowing back bile, but then finally a shadow appeared behind the small patch of foggy glass. "Who's there?" The voice was muffled by the door, but it was unmistakeably her.

I breathed a sigh of relief. "Apples for sale," I called back through in my impression of what a friendly old lady might sound like. "Organic and beautiful." Well, beautiful anyway.

A moment later the door opened a crack, and Snow peered suspiciously through the gap. Now this was a change from yesterday's attitude. "I didn't think you could get organic anything on Sweetheart Island." She watched my face with narrowed eyes, then glanced down at the basket.

"I grow them in my backyard," I replied, holding up the basket so it was filling her view. "You won't find a sweeter, crisper bite on the whole island."

She studied them briefly, her gaze fixing on the red one, then shrugged. "Sorry. I've got no cash." Then she closed the door in my face.

I stared at the blank wood for a few moments before knocking again furiously.

Snow opened the door again. "What?"

"If you've got no money, then that's fine, dearie," I said, my tone edging into irritated. "Have one on the house, as I've walked all the way out here. I wouldn't have it be for nothing."

Snow looked down again at the basket, then up again at my face. Then at the basket again. She shook her head. "I don't want it. Goodbye."

She went to shut the door again, but I slammed my foot in the gap. *Ouch.* "Seriously?"

Snow slammed the door several times on my foot, which was as painful as it sounded, but when she couldn't get me out she stepped backwards into the house. "You're trespassing!" Her eyes were so wide the whites were showing all around her irises. "You don't have any right to be in here!"

I just stood in the doorway staring at her in bemusement. "I'm sorry," I said finally. "I didn't mean to scare you."

"I'm not scared!"

"Really? 'Cos you sure look scared."

She lifted her chin defiantly. "And you've lost your accent, *Val.*"

Now I was the one stunned. I'd thought she would recognise me, but I had also thought she'd play along. Wasn't that the whole point? "I don't know what you're talking about."

"Yes you do. You might be wearing an ugly old mask, but I know exactly who you are. Now get out of here before I call security!"

Wow. I'd *really* misunderstood. I stood there for a few moments longer, the basket hanging at my side. *Kill her! Choke her! Force the apple in her mouth!* "I'm sorry," I said again. "I thought we were playing the same game." I stripped off the mask and wig, using it to remove the red apple from the basket, and set the lot down on the nearby table. "In case you change your mind."

I'd made it about twenty metres back into the surrounding forest when I heard Snow come huffing up behind me. "Wait!"

I turned to meet her. Her cheeks were pink, her chest heaving from the short run. "Wow," I said. "You are seriously unfit."

She glared at me, a moment later dissolving into a coughing fit. "Not everyone gets to be as perfect as you, Valentina."

Kill her! Kill her, kill- "Shut up!"

"No, you shut up," she snapped back. "I want to know why you said we were playing a game. You're not supposed to think this is a game! Did Karey tell you, huh? Did she tell you to play along instead of reprogramming you?"

I wasn't talking to you, I wanted to say, but hearing confirmation from her own lips made the whole thing so much more real to me. That last faint hope that it had all been a trick, that I'd misunderstood and I *was* just having a mental episode, was gone. "It turns out you can't entirely program away free will," I said quietly. "Even with someone like me. The more important questions is, why aren't *you* playing along? I thought this was your fantasy."

A flash of guilt passed over her face, then she looked around her warily. "If you're not going to kill me, you may as well come inside. We shouldn't talk about this out here."

I followed her back towards the house. "I was never going to kill you. I just wanted you to go away, and I don't get why you'd *want* death threats. Can't you see how it could go wrong?"

"Of course you weren't going to actually kill me," Snow replied snidely. "But the fun was in you trying. Now come inside before anyone sees."

I followed her inside, the door closing behind me, then stood a little awkwardly in the entryway while she collapsed on the couch. "You thought it was fun? *Why?*"

She shrugged a shoulder. "Not yesterday. That wasn't fun. That was scary. I meant before that; arguing with you. You're so easy to rile."

"So you were doing it on purpose!" I set my hands on my hips. "I knew no one could be that…that…"

"Incredibly annoying?" A smile curved the edge of Snow's mouth, and for a moment she almost looked pretty. "Heh. That first night – it was just about perfect."

I was struck speechless, thinking of my frustration and confusion over Kingsley's behaviour around Snow, about our romantic dinner being hijacked, about *everything*. "If you're trying to get me to like you more, this isn't the way."

She shrugged again. "At this point I don't care. The fantasy's almost over, and I don't want the last part. I told Karey that, but she said it might be too late, and I might have to go along with it anyway."

I took a seat opposite her. "What last part?"

"Of the story. Don't you know anything?" She smiled, which turned into a cough. "Of course not. You're a 'borg, and you hate fairytales."

She'd tried to tell me on the first night, I remembered. I'd cut her off. "So tell me what I'm missing, and what you're trying to do instead. I'd really rather not be tranquillised again like some kind of rabid animal. You said I was never going to kill you, but this programming they're giving me? It's a constant battle not to follow through."

Snow's eyes widened, and I waved a hand dismissively. "I'm not going to do it! But if you call breaking the glass slipper again, and I'm reprogrammed, I think it will be another story."

"Oh." She pulled away from me, tucking her legs up under her on the couch. "And if you tell on *me*, then I'll make sure you're reprogrammed. I'm not supposed to say any of this." I nodded, and she continued. "So the whole idea is that there's this huge competition between you and I. You hate me because I'm… um…"

"Beautiful?" I suggested dryly.

"Yes. And after my father dies you try to kill me. You have Jorge chase me away into the woods where I stay with seven dwarves…"

"Dwarves, seriously?"

"Yes, seriously," Snow snapped. "It's a fairytale, OK? So you find out I'm still alive, then come in disguise to try to kill me with a poisoned comb, and a corset, and a poisoned apple. Except we've skipped the corset part because you're not human and might accidently break my ribs."

"Good choice," I muttered. This was like what Caleb had said, but worse. *I* was the villain.

"And when I eat the apple I look like I'm dead, and there's the glass coffin, and Tarquin comes to wake me with a kiss, and we live happily ever after. That's all," Snow finished quickly, her eyes sliding away from mine. "Except I don't want to eat the apple. I didn't like fainting yesterday, it was scary. I want to skip to the last part."

"You could have skipped straight to it from the start," I said sharply. "Tarquin's programming was intense enough he would have married you if you'd agreed. But the way I was pulled into this mess, for competition, is unbelievable. You don't like fainting? I don't like killing, Snow, even fake killing."

Snow looked guilty and taken back at the same time. "You aren't supposed to be able to care."

"I guess my makers got a bit carried away with the realism," I replied bitterly. "I don't know what I am, exactly, but I have a sort of life, and I don't want to spend it playing the villain for rich girls' silly little games."

"It's not silly," she muttered, but she wouldn't meet my eyes.

"You're not supposed to care," she said again, clearly defensive.

"But I do care!" I cried. "Do you have any idea of the memories they programmed into me to make me like I was? I remember misery and heartbreak and committing murder four times over, but it never happened. But it's in my head! And here's you, young and healthy and rich enough to hire out a whole luxury resort, and you choose to play out a fantasy where you're adored for your *looks*. Your looks, Snow! Why? Why are you even doing this?"

"I'm not healthy," she replied in a small voice, brows furrowed.

"Pardon?"

"I'm not healthy," she repeated, finally looking at me. "And it's Jessie, not Snow. I have an illness that is very hard to treat. I've had it a long time, and…and I don't look lovely anymore. I used to be pretty, but now I just look sick. I'm too skinny and pale, and I've got no hair…"

"Oh," I breathed, suddenly understanding the wigs in her bottom draw, and perhaps even the diary. A medication schedule?

"You were wearing one of my wigs, weren't you?"

Now I was the one who felt guilty. "Yes. I'm so sorry. I didn't know…"

She waved a hand at me. "Of course you didn't know. You're a bloody robot, aren't you? And you can keep the damned wig for all I care."

I glanced over to where it sat on the table, looking rather like a long-haired guinea-pig. I didn't mention the auburn wig back in my suite. "So you're here, trying to what? Live your dream?"

Jessie/Snow shrugged desolately. "I suppose so. But it's not what I thought it would be."

I raised an eyebrow. "Really? But you did seem to enjoy arguing with me."

"Yeah, I did." The corner of her mouth curved slightly. "But it's all just a game, isn't it? It's not real. The adoration…everyone telling me how beautiful I was…it wasn't real. I may as well have just paid a paddy-boy to compliment me over dinner."

"What's a paddy-boy?"

"You know, an escort?"

Now I *was* shocked. "You hire prostitutes?"

"Not prostitutes!" she shot back, finally looking lively again. "Companions. Entertainers. They act like they're your friend, but of course they're just doing it for pay for a certain time. Everyone knows that."

Except me, of course. "I'm sorry this hasn't been what you'd expected," I told her. "It certainly hasn't been what *I* expected. But you need to finish out the story. We both do."

Jessie dropped her eyes, once again looking weary and perhaps a little scared. "I know. But don't make me eat that apple. I think…I think it might actually be poisoned."

"Why would you think that?" I asked cautiously.

"Karey and some others are doing something they shouldn't be," she admitted finally. "Something outside of True Fantasies. I don't know all the details, but I know more than I should."

"Like what?"

"I shouldn't say any more," she said mulishly. "They might be listening."

"Well, you shouldn't have said everything else in that case," I replied practically. "But if we agree that I won't make you eat the apple, you won't tell on me. So what do we do now?"

"The ball tonight," Jessie said pensively. "Tarquin's supposed to come find me right before midnight and take me back to the ball. We're supposed to surprise everyone, especially you. So you'd better play along."

Oh dear. "How much before midnight?"

"I don't know," she said a bit crankily. "Tarquin will come when he comes, and then we'll go." She sighed.

You do not *want Tarquin to come find you*, I wanted to say, but bit my tongue. "OK. I'll see you around midnight. Do we need to pinky swear or something?"

"I'll take your word for it if you'll take mine."

I didn't trust her. I thought she might have meant it, but just for the time being, and I didn't trust her to follow through long-term. But I had no other choice. "Good luck, then."

Jessie nodded, her expression serious. "And same to you."

I left her there in that hidden house, with the too-red apple resting on the nearby table.

I needed to find Tarquin.

Back at the hotel I barely remembered to slip out of the oversized 'old lady' costume in that same bathroom. I came out into the foyer, carefully checking each server I passed, then saw Caleb standing by the reception desk. Next to him was a wheeled trolley with two large vases strapped to it: one with a black dog-like head. I froze.

"I'm sorry, Mr Baba," the receptionist server told him politely. "Please take deliveries to the service entrance."

"But I'm already here," he argued. "I'm just looking for…" He looked up and saw me. "…Valentina."

I panicked. I looked one way, then the other, then realised he was still looking at me.

"You do know who I am?" he prompted.

Caleb the lying, betraying bastard. But that wasn't what he was asking. He wanted to know if I remembered him since being reprogrammed: if he could still entertain himself by befriending the Ruby-clone.

Not likely.

"You're the boy who sells rugs," I replied dismissively. "But I don't recall giving you leave to use my first name."

My tone was snootier than ever before, and his face fell. A touch of satisfaction shot through me at his pain, and then guilt, and irritation at that guilt. Taking revenge seemed to cut both ways.

"Sorry, Mrs White. I'm…Ali. Ali Baba."

I nodded coolly, moving towards him. "Mr Baba." To the receptionist I said, "See that those vases find a home, but for heaven's sake, not anywhere public. They hardly fit with the décor." Then I walked past him and out the front entrance.

I pushed Caleb from my mind and spent the afternoon searching for Tarquin. I looked all over the hotel, on the grounds themselves, in the village…I even went to his mansion only to be told he was away. I didn't push the request, since as the 'villain' I was pretty sure I wasn't supposed to be friendly with the heroine's love interest.

But Tarquin was nowhere to be found, and finally in desperation I returned to Snow's cottage just as the sun was setting. I found the door wide open, and the lights all on inside. "Hello?"

No one responded, and finally I stuck my head inside the door. "Snow? Anyone?"

In the entry/lounge room all the furniture had been pushed to the edges of the room, and in the very centre I could see a big, clear box. It was a coffin, and Snow was inside. Her hair and makeup was perfect; her hands folded over her chest with a single yellow rose clasped between them. She was wearing the velvet gown from the auction.

"Oh great," I muttered. "She changed her mind."

But the way she lay there so still in that coffin was just so eerie I just stood and watched for a few moments. I focused on her chest where it rose and fell oh-so-very faintly, and her slightly parted, red-painted lips. I tapped one finger on the plastic casing, my nail making a distinctive 'tink' sound, but she didn't move. Wow, she must be really out of it.

I'm sick, she'd said. *I haven't been beautiful for a long time.*

She just wanted to be admired, because it made her feel like she had worth. I could understand that, even though I didn't in any way agree with the choices she'd made. Besides, she hadn't created True Fantasies. Other people had done that, and if there was any justice in the world, one day they'd pay for what they'd done to me and the others.

"I hope you got what you wanted," I whispered to the still figure. And because Tarquin was still nowhere to be seen, I turned and left.

It was almost seven pm when I finally returned to the hotel, feeling dejected and weary. I ordered dinner from reception, then went to the King suite and began packing one of my largest handbags with what I thought might be useful for a girl on the run. I didn't have any cash, so in went the jewellery and chocolate again, as well as a few changes of underwear.

I still had a good five hours until I had to meet Tarquin tonight, and I didn't know what to do. If he gave in to the programming then he'd be storming in with Snow at midnight, accusing me of murder. Even though it was part of the game, it would be… awkward. It would also squelch my plans to leave tonight. But if I didn't go to the ball at all, the powers-that-be would know at once.

I studied my costume where it hung on the wall. It was mostly white as per the ball's theme, but true to character it was accented with bold red roses along the skirt and bodice. There was also a gem-studded mask and a pair of fluffy white wings rounding out the outfit. It would look fantastic with red lipstick, I mused regretfully, and the red edging would mean I'd stand out a mile away.

Sigh.

Chimes sounded at my door, announcing my meal had arrived. "Come in!" I called. If nothing else, at least I could eat.

A moment later the door opened. But it wasn't an android server bringing my food. It was that red-haired waitress, Cindy Rayla. She wore a White Hotel jacket over casual clothing – not usual staff attire. I gave her a querying glance and she blushed.

"The servers are all preparing for the ball, ma'am, and I was brought in at the last moment. I hope you don't mind."

I shrugged. "Not at all. But the ball is open invitation. All you need is a costume. Why aren't you attending?"

She began unloading the plates onto the dining table, her eyes studiously averted from me. "I don't have permission, ma'am."

"It's my hotel," I said dryly. At least for now. "And I said you could come. Are we really that short of servers?"

"It's not that." Cindy hesitated. "It's my stepmother. She specifically stated that I wasn't to go, that I was to work."

I raised an eyebrow. "How old are you?"

"Seventeen, ma'am. And she's still my guardian."

She looked older. But then she was a cyborg – she was

probably like me, and I didn't dare ponder how old I truly was. But I looked at her pretty, freckled face, her lanky figure, then at the costume hanging on the wall. Perhaps there was a way around this after all…

12 Determined

Half an hour later I was putting on the final touches of red lipstick. The figure in front of me was white-skinned with palest blonde hair, and the dress fit perfectly. Perhaps a little more space in the bodice, but I'd just call that leaving something to the imagination. "There," I said in satisfaction. "I knew the red would look amazing."

"I'm so excited," Cindy breathed, almost making me smear the lipstick on her teeth. "This is a dream come true. Are you sure no one will recognise me?"

I shook my head. "Not a chance, especially if you keep your mouth shut and keep the mask on." And thanks to Snow for inadvertently donating this blonde wig and heavy white face paint. It had been just the thing to cover Cindy's freckles. "Have you tried on the shoes?"

Cindy warily studied the red shoes with their six-inch stiletto heels. "They look a bit wobbly. A bit big, too. I have small feet, see?" She lifted the hem of gown to reveal that indeed, she did have small feet considering her height. Smaller than mine, anyway.

"All my shoes are the same size," I mused. "Or maybe …" No, Snow's feet were tiny. Even if I could find a pair suitable for a ball, Cindy would never fit them.

"What about those?"

I followed her pointed finger to where the stolen glass slippers were poking out from under the bed. Somehow they'd escaped their bundle. "Er…"

But she walked over to pick them up. "Oh, they're beautiful! They look the right size, too." She glanced up at me hopefully. "What do you think?"

"I don't know," I replied doubtfully. "I'm going to need those later."

"What time? Because I could give them back to you. I can't stay out all night anyway. My stepmother will be home straight after the unmasking at twelve, and I'll need to be back by then."

"That could work," I said thoughtfully. "Get them back to me at ten to, alright? We can meet at the edge of the rose garden, and you can go straight from there."

Cindy beamed, then slipped her feet into the shining shoes. "They're just about perfect! Maybe a touch too big still, but they're perfect with the costume. What are you going to do during the ball?"

I shrugged nonchalantly. "Oh, this and that. It's too soon after Kingsley's passing for me to hold a party, but I didn't want to disappoint everyone else." I studied her one more time, then realised what was missing. The silver wristpiece, because I was rarely seen without it. More importantly, if it was a tracker, it would immediately give away that I wasn't at the ball. "Here, put this on."

She looked curious, but didn't argue as I snapped it onto her wrist. "I suppose you'll want this back too."

"Oh, no," I said casually. "I'm going to replace it. Do what you want with it. Now you'd better get to the ball or you'll be late."

"I'm going to dance the night away!" she announced. "Or until midnight, anyway."

She swept out the door with a shiver of fluffy wings, leaving behind her white server's coat, and I got to work. Snatching up my travel bag, a bundle of clothing and the coat, I went down the hall to Snow's room. I put on the auburn wig, the tights and vest outfit I'd found the other day, and a good deal of bronzer, then finished it off with Cindy's coat. With the wig's heavy dark fringe coming all the way down to my eyebrows, it was quite a change.

"My eyes still stand out," I told my reflection in the small mirror, "and at some angles you can see the beauty mark. But it's not bad." I'd just have to make sure no one looked at me too closely.

I spent the next several hours looking for Tarquin, getting frustrated when I didn't find him, stealing supplies from various kitchens and storehouses, and hiding from passers-by. I finally settled in on one of the unused balconies overlooking the decorated ballroom. Through a screen I could see the whole of the ballroom as well as outside in the lit-up garden, and there was a nearby staircase that led to the garden while remaining out of sight of the ballroom. I'd 'borrowed' some white-chocolate dipped strawberries from the caterers, as well as a glass of sweet white wine. The ball's theme had carried over into the food.

As I sipped the wine I wondered absently if I really liked the taste, or if I was just programmed to think I liked it… Oh, who cared. It was my glass, and I was going to like it, programmed or not.

Just then I heard footsteps on the outside path below me. I shrank back into the deepest shadow and watched Karey Godmother walk briskly past with an enormous, full-skirted blue dress draped over one arm. She looked distinctly irritated. Nothing to do with me, I hoped. I wondered absently who the dress was for, since it didn't seem the sort that she would wear herself.

She disappeared around the corner, and I let out a sigh of relief. Snow had said something this morning about Karey and John Carver – Carver the island's co-owner from that article I'd read – being 'up to something'. Well, yeah. Of course they were. Even if the 'treasure hunters' were absolutely legitimate, the whole True Fantasies set up was terrible. A type of slavery, except they'd created their own slaves, supposedly without even free will to accept or decline an order.

If Snow – or Jessie, rather – had truly thought we were just things, just clever robots acting out our programming without true emotions, then I couldn't blame her too much for acting the way she had. Now I knew that she was ill, some of the things about her made sense. She hadn't exactly said she was dying, but if she was, I didn't understand why if she thought that she had limited time left, she would choose to waste it in such a way.

I pondered that thought for a while, still feeling unsettled by her choices. It seemed to me that a life like hers was a gift. And for me, even in the middle of this chaos that I found myself in, I was still happy to be alive. Even the others like Cindy or Kingsley who'd not known the truth of what they were, *they'd* seemed happy too. Or happy enough. I just needed to see how this all played out, to decide if I still felt that way.

Now I felt a bit grim, so turned my attention back to the ballroom. It was packed to the brim with white-clad island residents/actors, in costumes ranging from dull (white tux with half-mask) to surreal (a Tudor-style peacock costume). I gave the last a nine and a half simply for shock value. Alright, maybe a nine and three-quarters.

I spotted Cindy in the crowd, smiling and chatting and eating from the white-themed buffet. She obviously hadn't taken my advice to keep her mouth shut, but I found I couldn't begrudge her this time. While I'd been cast as the rich villain, she'd been cast as someone's dogsbody. It was odd, and I couldn't see that her story overlapped with Snow's at all.

Some time later, as the clock was ticking around to eleven, I saw Daniel Charmant make his way into the ballroom. "Late," I murmured, but watched him for a while. He was wearing a white half mask that did nothing to hide his identity, and his tux looked great with his tan and blond hair.

I saw Cindy notice him too, and from up here I watched as their eyes met. They stared at each other for a long moment, then he approached her, much in the same way Tarquin had walked up to Snow the night of the bachelor auction. Like it was love at first sight.

As long as he didn't think she was *me*.

Was there more going on here? I'd been certain Snow was the

only player. That's what Caleb and Jafeer had said, and I hadn't forgotten. So either they'd been wrong, or the programmers were entertaining themselves by making their characters fall in love. But there was more than one fairytale in action, wasn't there? Maybe they were tying up all the loose ends, I pondered. Maybe they were finishing out the other stories, whatever those might be.

My lips turned downward. Making false, temporary attachments was as cruel as what they'd done to me. Sure, Cindy and Daniel might forget it all later if they were reprogrammed. Or they might retain hints of those feelings and memories, and every time they'd see each other later, they'd wonder why they felt that connection.

That made me think of Caleb, and then I just felt grumpy and hurt all over again. I turned away from the scene, sat back in the shadowed corner, and closed my eyes.

What felt like two moments later I opened them again, disoriented. I stumbled up to the screen to spot Cindy in the crowd. I saw her look up towards the clock, then a moment later she picked up her skirts and quietly slipped from the room. Eleven fifty, I realised in dismay, suddenly alert. I'd almost slept through our meeting time. I carefully made my way down the long staircase, intending to cut her off, when suddenly she came racing out of the exit up ahead of me, as panicked as if the hounds of hell were on her tail.

But they weren't. It was just that damn Daniel Charmant.

"Wait, please!" he called out to her. "I just want to know your name!"

Cindy looked back over her shoulder, then stumbled at the base of the stairs. A moment later she caught herself, then took off into the rose garden like a champion sprinter.

She'd also left one of the glass slippers behind.

A moment later Daniel noticed it, and I saw his face light up. Well, they did say the man liked shoes, didn't they?

But this one was mine. As he reached for it I quickly walked over and gave him a good bump with my hip, knocking him aside. "Oops. Sorry." Then I snatched up the shoe and went to walk away as if nothing unusual had happened.

"Hey! You can't do that!" Daniel said in outrage. "That's mine!"

"Oh really?" I put one hand on my hip and looked at him sceptically. "I wouldn't have thought it was your size."

"Not mine! I mean, it belongs to – er, that girl. I need to get it back to her."

"That girl's name is Cindy Rayla, redheaded hotel server slash waitress. And I lent them to her, so it's mine," I said coolly. "Now leave it be, there's a good boy, and go back inside. You've got enough ladies' shoes already."

His handsome face flushed slightly, and he scowled. "Who do you think you are?"

"The person who's going to tell the world of your stranger proclivities if you don't go away right now," I snapped. "Now go away!"

"Not without that shoe. It's supposed to be mine!" He'd given up claiming he was going to give it back, obviously. He reached out and tried to grab the shoe out of my hand, but I was quicker. I pulled my knee up sharply into his crotch, and there was a stunned moment when we both realised that the hard blow hadn't bothered him at all.

That was when it turned into a real wrestling match. He tried to twist my arm to get the shoe, and I spun and whacked him into the side of the building, glad that my enhanced limbs made me his match. We grappled for a little longer and then a startled voice interrupted us. "What are you doing?"

We both froze with our hands on the glass slipper trapped between us. An elderly woman with a tall white feather in her hair stood in the doorway watching us, her hands on her hips.

"Uh – Grandma," Daniel said worriedly. "I was just…"

"I know what you were just," she snapped, "and it's completely inappropriate!"

"It's not like that! It was just the shoe-"

That gave me enough leeway to pull the shoe out and run away from him, crying, "You said you loved me, and you just wanted my shoe?"

He held up his hands in panic. "I swear it's not what it looked like-"

Yeah, because either he had a metal cup down there or he wasn't capable of that sort of shenanigans.

"Don't tell me what it was or wasn't!" his grandmother snapped. "I may be old, but I'm not stupid! Now come inside before you embarrass the family any further!"

Hiding my smirk, I ran for the garden, leaving the apologetic Daniel trying to sort things out with his grandmother. It was nearly twelve, almost the time when I was supposed to meet Tarquin.

Cindy was standing in the entrance to the rose garden, the second shoe in her hand and her pretty face creased with worry. "Mrs White, is that you?" she asked in surprise.

"It's me," I replied briskly, mentally cursing as I realised this girl was seeing me in disguise, and now knew who I was. "I'll have the shoe, thank you."

She held it back. "But if you take it, then Daniel won't be able to find me!"

I took it anyway. "Why would he need a shoe to find you? I told him your name."

"You told him?" Her eyes were wide and horrified.

"You should have told him yourself," I retorted. "Now go and leave the costume in the King suite, and… good luck."

Although she'd need more than luck. I left her there and ran for the centre of the rose garden. I arrived at the meeting point slightly short of breath, the shoes tucked under my jacket. At first the place seemed deserted, but then Tarquin stepped out of an alcove, wearing casual clothing and a hesitant expression. "Is that you, Valentina?"

"It's me," I replied, sighing in relief.

"You've got red hair! You look so different." He squinted at me. "Except for the mole."

"It's a beauty mark," I muttered under my breath. Clearly the makeup hadn't covered it. "And that's the point. But never mind me, I'm just glad that *you're* here. I thought you would have gone to find Snow."

"I did," he answered glumly. "I looked for a while but couldn't find her, and then I decided you were right. Murder's not the answer. So I locked myself in my mansion and played video games all day as a distraction." His hands were clenched in front of him, his thumbs nervously rubbing over his knuckles. "You said you know what's happening to us. Why we're like we are. So go on, tell me."

I thought of Snow lying in her glass coffin, waiting for a kiss that would never come. I didn't know whether to laugh or pity her. "The short story is that rich people are paying to act out fantasies, and we got dragged into it. We've got implants in our heads, just like people do when they've got prosthetic limbs, but we've been programmed to play out characters. Me the villain, you the love interest. Sweetheart Island isn't our real home, Tarquin. It's a giant set, and it's our prison."

For a moment his expression was completely blank, and I wondered if I'd misjudged by telling him. I hadn't even mentioned the part about being cyborgs. I didn't think he could deal with that and still leave tonight like we needed to. But then he asked slowly, "How do you know?"

I shook my head, turning away. "Besides the contrasting memories just popping into my head? Some of the paid actors on the island told me about it, and showed me an advertising video with me on it. I've no memory of ever saying the things I saw myself saying. And then Snow admitted the whole thing today."

"Snow? You saw her?" I didn't answer, and I saw understanding dawn. "She's the player, isn't she? She's the reason for all of this."

"Don't go blaming her for it," I said quickly. "She didn't set all this up. But I'll tell you about it later. If you don't want to be reprogrammed and stuck here indefinitely, you need to leave with me now."

"Now?"

I nodded. "Sorry about the short notice, but people are already suspicious of me since they know I've broken character. And I'm pretty sure that the stories are about to finish tonight, or shortly. If the next lot of programming works, we'd forget all about this."

"It's like being in hell," he breathed. "That's why I was in that closet."

More like a morgue, in my opinion. "Time's a wasting, Tarquin. Are you going or staying?" When he didn't answer straight away I added, "I have to go tonight. If I get caught, then they'll reprogram me and I'll forget this ever happened. I'll forget I ever could escape, and so will you."

There was only the briefest pause, and he nodded. "I'll come. You want to take my car, right?"

"That's the plan. Is it ready?"

He nodded again, eyes wide. "I left the rifle inside it like you said. The Jag's parked back at my house…the house."

"And you do know how to drive it?"

"Of course," he retorted, holding up the key. "I take it for a spin occasionally."

"Good, because I don't think I can." I looked down at his wrist where he wore a plain black band, a faint red light in its centre. "One last thing…"

We left his wristpiece in the centre of the rose garden, then walked over to his nearby mansion. Or whoever's mansion it was, anyway. The sleek black sports car sat unguarded and unlocked, and we got in and drove quietly down the main street to the wharf, headlights dimmed. The sea was flat and shimmered with the moon's reflection. Just over the other side, on the mainland, I could see a pair of headlights. It looked like a vehicle was waiting, but there was no bridge. I checked the clock. Twelve fifteen.

"How are we supposed to get out of here again?" Tarquin asked anxiously, his hands tight on the wheel. "There's no ferry."

"Just wait." I crossed my fingers.

But then the double row of lights appeared beneath the shallow water, and a moment later the bridge rose above the surface, water streaming through the many slats. The vehicle on the other side pulled onto the bridge, and less than a minute later it passed us where we sat quietly. It looked like a goods van. "Now go!" I ordered. "Before the bridge drops!"

Tarquin's eyes widened and the engine revved. We took off with a screech of tyres, but the bridge was already lowering. He accelerated and I closed my eyes, my fingers tight on the dashboard. I could hear the water splashing around the tyres, and a moment later the brakes slammed on, and the two of us went flying forward to jolt against our seatbelts.

"What happened?" I cried.

"I don't know," Tarquin replied in dismay. "The auto-driver's just switched off as I reached the bridge entrance. It's dead, see?"

I did see. "This isn't good. They must have known we were coming. Or maybe these cars are programmed so they can't just drive off the island." I scrubbed my hands over my face, my heartrate rising in panic. The bridge had gone again, right under the water. "Can you swim?"

"What?"

Just then a bright light filled the side window. Another vehicle was leaving, another van with dark glass. I looked over my shoulder to see it trundling up behind us, then it paused beside us while the bridge began to raise again. I could see inside its windscreen: empty. Autodrive. sI didn't wait. I jumped out of the seat, then ran straight for the nearest door, tugging at its handle.

"What are you doing?" Tarquin hissed.

"Getting us out of here. If we don't do it now, we won't ever do it." I tugged again at the handle, my heart pounding with panic, but it was no good. It was locked.

But when had that ever stopped me before? I pressed my artificial fingers against the handle's small lock, then leaned in and whispered, "Open sesame."

Nope. Still locked.

"Chestnuts!" I shouted, then remembered that wasn't a real swear word, so said something nastier that rhymed with 'skit'.

But Tarquin had climbed out of his dead vehicle, a bundle of something in his arms. "The roof!" he said urgently. Then he threw the bundle on top of the van. "Boost me up!"

After a few clumsy attempts I made a cradle with my hands.

He stepped into it, then I lifted with all my might.

"Argh!" Tarquin went sailing up onto the roof of the van, out of sight.

"Are you OK?" I cried. Even after everything, I'd forgotten I was so strong.

A moment later his head popped into view. "You didn't need to push so hard," he said crankily, stretching his hand down towards me.

"Sorry." I handed him my handbag, then took his hand, hiking up my skirt so I could brace a foot against the van's side mirror. Then suddenly I was flying through the air too. I came down hard on the van's roof, half landing on Tarquin. His knee was in my belly. 'Ow…"

"Sorry," he said, not sounding sorry at all. "You're lighter than I thought."

Or his arms were just prosthetic too, I thought irritably, moving myself into a more comfortable position.

But then the engine rumbled below us, and Tarquin just about squealed with excitement. "Hang on. We're going!"

Uh oh. Even as the van began to move, I shuffled my way around until I was lying next to him lengthways. The vehicle was the sort that had a raised rim on the roof so goods could be tied on, and we gripped onto that rim as the van picked up speed, my big handbag between my knees. I could hear the wheels splashing through the shallow water as we went along, and when I gathered my courage enough to look over the edge, I couldn't see the bridge at all. From my angle it looked like we were driving across the water – a true miracle.

I giggled to myself, half out of fear, half real humour, and Tarquin turned to me curiously. His eyes were wide with excitement, and his perfect teeth were bared in a grin. "What's so funny?"

I told him, and he let out a short laugh. "I'll tell you, Val, this is the most exciting thing I've ever done. I feel like I'm escaping from prison."

Same here. Except… "It's Valentina, Tarkers."

"What?" His attention was once again fixed on the road in front of us.

There was a slight jolt as the van drove up from the bridge onto the road – onto the mainland – and I sucked in a startled breath. Once I could finally breathe again, I sighed. "Never mind."

He took me at my word, and spent the next twenty minutes giving commentary on the scenery around us, where he thought we were going, and every time the van jolted or turned too sharply, and he thought we'd almost fallen off. Thanks, Tarkers. Greatly appreciated. It seemed that my makers had instilled within me the desire to survive, which also meant *not* enjoying near death experiences, which this seemed very much like.

We drove around the coast, with the flat sea to our left, and a high rocky cliff to our right. Then the road turned inland, and our surroundings became wilder, unfamiliar. In the headlights I caught glimpses of hilly fields and the occasional isolated house. There were few road signs, and the land seemed to stretch on forever.

It was cold up here, although not awful, but I said the thing that had been on my mind since before we'd left. "You know they'll come after us," I murmured. "They'll see how we left on the surveillance pig, then they'll figure out where this van is going, then they'll know where we must be. That's assuming they haven't tagged us in some other way."

"Surveillance pig?"

"By the wharf. They're watching that area."

"Oh." Tarquin paused thoughtfully. "We should jump off the next time the van slows down. We can walk from there."

Great, throwing myself off a moving vehicle! That sounded even better. "OK," I agreed reluctantly. "When?"

Just then the flashing lights showed up ahead, as well as the distinctive *ding ding ding* of siren. A train was passing up ahead. The van pulled to a stop, and Tarquin and I exchanged glances. "Now!" he said.

He threw his jacket and the rifle off, then catapulted himself off the roof, landing lightly on both feet. "Whew!" He grinned up at me. "Come on!"

I rolled my eyes but did so, my handbag hooked over one arm, grumbling the whole way. I still landed well, although I wobbled a little on my low heels. "I am *not* dressed for this kind of thing."

"Stop fussing, and walk!"

I looked at him curiously. Did he not realise that these kinds of stunts were beyond the average, non-ninja rich kid? Apparently not. "As long as we're walking towards a town," I said instead. "I saw some crossroads about two minutes back."

We walked back the way we'd come, finding the crossroads without difficulty. The moon was partially covered by cloud, but the signs were the solar kind that glowed in the dark. Hartford, which was the way the van had been driving; Sweetheart Island, which was the opposite direction, and Amber Springs, which was somewhere in the middle.

"Amber Springs it is," I announced.

Tarquin looked doubtful. "It says thirty ks."

Chestnuts. "Then we'll finish walking in the morning. It's late anyway. Shall we find somewhere to sleep?"

Not here, obviously. We were in the middle of a wide green valley with a train line running through the centre. There were a few trees scattered around, but apart from that it was desolate. Up ahead, the road to Amber Springs disappeared into winding hills with patches of forest visible even from this distance. "Maybe up there."

We walked for about half an hour before reaching the first sheltered area. At the side of the road was a narrow, grassy ravine that curved away out of sight. Something that might have been a stream ran down its centre, and trees grew in generous bunches on either side of the divide.

"I'm exhausted," I said flatly. "I need to sleep."

"In the grass?"

I shrugged. "It's not like we have any other options."

In the end we lay our jackets down on a flattish patch under some trees, out of sight of the road. My mood had gone from panicked exhilaration to a kind of tired depression. Perhaps being on the run sounded more glamourous than it actually felt. Tarquin had been quiet too, so maybe he felt the same.

But in spite of my tiredness I couldn't sleep. I lay awake for a while, eyes wide open, watching the play of moonlight onto the nearby trees.

"We were kidnapped, weren't we?"

I turned at Tarquin's quiet words. He lay on his back, his hands resting on his chest much like Snow's had in her fake coffin, and his eyes were fixed on the leaves above us.

"What do you mean?" I asked.

"I mean that the island isn't our real lives," he said. "All those memories, all those feelings, were made up. That wasn't my house, or my car, or my father, not that I ever saw him. So something else must be. I just want to know what."

I studied his profile, but didn't answer. I didn't know what to say, and I didn't want to lie.

He turned towards me. "Well?"

I took a deep breath. "The actors told me I was created for the role," I said very quietly. "They said I wasn't the only one."

Even in the semi-dark I saw his scowl of disbelief. "What, that you're a clone? That *we* are clones of some sort? Did you believe them?"

I shrugged and turned away. "Not clones. Sort of…enhanced human beings, with memory chips. And I don't have any memories besides being Valentina. So what else would I be?"

"I have memories," he said staunchly. "Of…a dog. A house on a city street, with no front yard. I'm going to find it."

Memories? I wanted to believe it was real, but it was just as likely to be something he saw once on the viewer. "OK," I said finally. "You go do that."

I closed my eyes, and I must have slept because next thing I was blinking in the bright morning sun through the sheltering leaves. I lay there for a few moments, disoriented, but then I remembered everything.

We'd escaped. *Yes.* And my memory lapses were becoming shorter. That had to be good.

I quietly got up from our pile of jackets and went hunting for a private spot. In the daylight I could see our location clearly. We weren't so far from the road after all, and what I'd taken for a stream was actually an old train track that ran down the centre of the narrow valley, partially covered in grass. I followed the track for a minute as it curved around the side of the hill and finally disappeared into a boarded-up tunnel.

I was out of sight of Tarquin's sleeping spot, so I took a moment to relieve myself and stretch. It was a pretty area, I decided, although too lonely for me to want to live anywhere like it. Even cyborgs needed company.

BANG. The sound of a weapon discharging echoed through the small valley, and I gasped. "Tarquin!" I'd left the air rifle back with him. Bad move.

I turned and sprinted back towards our 'beds', but I'd just turned the corner when I saw that we weren't alone. There was a vehicle parked in the shallow space at the road's edge, a large black one with tinted windows. Jafeer stood not far from the vehicle, aiming a pistol at Tarquin where he still lay in the shelter of the trees. His back was to me.

"Get up slowly, kid," I heard him say. "Hands above your head, and don't try anything. I wouldn't have any problem shooting you again and letting them put you back together."

Oh, dear. My heartrate jumped, and I quietly moved up behind Jafeer, my footsteps silent in the grass. I didn't have a weapon. I only had myself.

"You hurt me!" Tarquin was saying from his place on the ground. He sounded very unimpressed. "And how can I get up if I don't use my hands?"

"For heaven's sake, just get up!" Jafeer said irritably. He leaned over to grab Tarquin and gave me a very clear target.

I kicked him as hard as I could and he crumpled to the ground with a groan, showing that in one area, he was nothing like Daniel Charmant.

"Valentina!" Tarquin cried, sitting up awkwardly. "He shot me, for no reason! See?" He pointed at his shoulder where a small round hole seeped black fluid.

"I see," I said grimly. "You should put something on it to stop the bleeding." And maybe he'd notice that the fluid was black, not red.

I bent down to pick up the pistol from beside where Jafeer lay groaning, his knees pulled into his chest. It was far more modern in appearance than my antique air rifle, but the basic functions looked the same. I pointed it at his chest. "Hello, *Jay.*"

He turned his head to face me, grimacing in pain. "You've unmanned me. Are you going to kill me now?"

"Not unless I have to," I replied evenly. "Why don't you tell me how you found us so easily?"

Jafeer closed his eyes as if in pain, then focused back on me. "If I tell you anything else, they'll hurt me. I'm in enough trouble for what happened before. It's obvious the reprogramming didn't work properly. I don't know if it ever will." He smiled, a crooked half-grin. "And Caleb was so very disappointed when you didn't know him. Nice acting."

"You should choose your friends more carefully," I said coolly. "But you must realise that I'm the one here with a gun. Not anyone else. Tell me what I want to know."

"Shoot him!" Tarquin ordered from behind me. "That'll make him talk!"

I glanced at him in disbelief, and suddenly Jafeer reared up, grabbing for the pistol. I tried to pull it away and Tarquin grabbed it from behind, and there was another *BANG* and Jafeer went flying backwards.

He slapped one hand to his bloodied cheek where the bullet had skimmed, dark eyes wide in indignation. "You shot me!"

I was shaken, but I retorted, "It's not the first time I've shot at you. Don't sound so surprised."

"Anyway, we missed," Tarquin said darkly from behind me.

"He's a bloodthirsty thing," Jafeer muttered grimly, pushing himself into seated position. "Not really a candidate for Prince Charming."

"What's that supposed to mean?" Tarquin snapped.

"Never mind all that!" I shouted, pointing the pistol back at his chest. "How did you find us?"

"If I tell you, will you leave me alive? I didn't want to hurt you, you know. They're blackmailing me into it."

"Who's they?"

He slumped, taking his hand away from his cheek. It had already stopped bleeding. "Sinbad and Karey. They said I had to get you or else I would be in deep…trouble."

I gestured at the wound on his cheek. "Does it have anything to do with the way that's healing so quickly?"

He gave a half-hearted shrug, but didn't meet my eyes. Tarquin interrupted, "You didn't tell us how you found us so fast. Tell us, or she'll shoot you."

Jafeer looked at me, and I gave a casual shrug. "I've supposedly killed four men. What's one more who was trying to kill me anyway?"

"Trackers," he said quickly. "You've got trackers embedded behind your ears, that's how I found you so fast. Please don't kill me."

I swore, and he recoiled as if I would pull the trigger. "Tarquin. Would you give me a hand tying him up?"

"What?!"

"You'll be alright," I told Jafeer. "Stop complaining."

We left him tied up under the same trees, only partially hidden from the road. I figured he'd either escape eventually, or someone would come to get him. It was no longer my problem.

As for his car, the keys were still in the ignition, a map of the area glowed on the windscreen along with directions to the nearest town – Amber Springs – and there was plenty of fuel. That was as good as an offer to take it. Lucky us. Even luckier, Jafeer had a couple of hundred credits in cash in his wallet, more fool him. There was our breakfast sorted.

"The town's only twenty minutes from Sweetheart Island," Tarquin said uneasily.

"It's the closest one for miles," I replied. "We have to get to a doctor and get these trackers out ASAP, or else we'll be done for.

I'm not keen on digging them out myself."

Tarquin shuddered. "Fine. I just don't want to be caught."

"We won't be," I said with more confidence than I felt.

We drove in silence for a while, this time with me behind the wheel, until he asked suddenly, "Do you know why we healed so fast from those bullets? Both of us did. Me and that guy."

That was a question I didn't want to answer. I didn't know how he'd react to the truth, and I didn't want to deal with that while we were on the run. "Well…" I began slowly, "You know how when people lose an arm or something, it can be replaced by a robotic limb, and a chip is put in the brain to control it?"

He shrugged. "Sure. What about it?" Then a second later he burst out, "You think I've got a robotic limb? But it was in my shoulder!"

I didn't say anything, and he continued, "You think I've got a robotic shoulder?"

"I think a lot of you is robotic," I said gently. "And me too." Although I still wasn't sure what to make of Jafeer. "I did say that before."

There was a long silence, then Tarquin said slowly, "I understand."

"You do? I know it's a hard thing to take in-"

"I'm not a clone," he said sharply, glaring at me. "I clearly had an accident, and they rebuilt me. And then they made me forget my old memories and gave me new ones, so that they could use me like a puppet for their amusement. Bastards."

I blinked. "You remember an accident?"

"Of course not. They took my memory when they reprogrammed me. I just said that."

I turned my attention to the road. He'd chosen to believe the nicest possible explanation, and he obviously didn't want to hear anything different. He'd have to accept the truth one day, but it didn't have to be right now.

We drove into the town outskirts, and a minute later reached the small, busy centre. Rows of shops spread out in every direction;

with layers of grime and dust that spoke of years of use. It was no Sweetheart Island, that was for sure.

Tarquin pulled over into the nearest car park and looked around. I couldn't see a doctor, but there was a café right in front of us. "Wait here while I ask around. If they find me, you just leave, alright?"

He agreed and I headed into the café. It was busy and humming with conversation, and I looked around with interest. Just as the buildings were different, so were the people. Their clothing was more like what I'd borrowed from Snow/Jessie. So many tight trousers, and not always on people that it suited.

I sat at a table and after a moment a young waitress came over, a pleasant smile set on her face. *Not* an android, I noted, but then these small places probably couldn't afford AI. "How can I help you today?" she asked.

I ordered coffee and a couple of muffins to take away, and then when she brought them back she asked me if I was from the set. A moment later I realised she meant Sweetheart Island. "Ah...sure. Are there a lot of us around today?"

She shrugged a shoulder. "There's usually one or two. I can always tell, you know?"

I looked down at my unfamiliar clothing uncomfortably. "I'm surprised you know anything about it. We were told to keep it quiet."

Another shrug. "That's not what the guy at the corner table is saying. Jake, his name is, and he's been bragging for the last half hour to anyone who'd listen about what's going on there."

I followed her pointed finger to the young man drinking from an oversized mug, his dark blond hair flopping over his face. A half second later I recognised him – it was 'Aladdin'. He smirked at me, and I let out a sigh of relief. He didn't know who I was.

But a moment later I saw his eyes widened, and his lips form the words, "Hey, isn't that..."

Oh chestnuts. Acting on impulse, I quickly moved to sit down beside him, smiling pleasantly. "Hey, Jake. How's it going?"

"Uh…Mrs White?"

I laughed, flipping back my auburn hair. "Ches-um, heavens no. I'm, uh, Amber." Thank you, town sign. "I'm filling in after the cyborg flipped out and they couldn't get it to finish the fantasy."

His face creased in relief. "You're an actor? Wow, you really look like her. Your green eyes…"

"That's why they called me in," I said cheerfully. "The eyes are contacts."

"Of course." He nodded in agreement. "So that's some set up on the island, right? It's one of the craziest things I've ever done."

I nodded emphatically. "Me too. The only thing that spoils it is how they make us wear a tracker."

"You mean like a wristpiece?"

"No, an actual chip injected under the skin." I tapped the skin behind my ear. "They make all the actors wear them. They say it's for safety, but it makes me feel like someone's dog, you know? I've got another day or two on the set, but I want to get it removed now. I just hate it."

Jake was staring at me with his jaw dropped. "Ohh…I don't have one of those."

"Of course you do," I persisted, making it up as I went along. "Everyone does. Don't you remember them giving you a physical checkover before you were allowed to go on? There had to be at least one injection."

I waited with bated breath as his eyes narrowed. "Yeah. Yeah, I do remember. I don't want to have a tracker either! That's got to be illegal, or assault. I didn't give permission for that."

Yes. I smiled at him, bobbing my head. "My friend Tom's just outside. He's got the same thing, so maybe we can all go together to get ours removed. It shouldn't take long. There must be a doctor around here somewhere."

"Yeah, there's one just down the road. Miller went there after that crazy 'borg beat him up." He nodded at me confidentially. "You heard how she shot him, right? I'm glad they've taken her out of action. She's a stone-cold killer."

My smile froze in place. "I'll just go get Tom, shall I?"

Twenty minutes later Jake, Tom/Tarquin and I were all inside the surgery of 'Dr Lindquist, GP' while the doctor in question probed gently behind Tarquin's ear. She was a petite woman, silver-haired, with a non-nonsense manner. More importantly, she hadn't asked for ID. "I don't need the scanner to know there's definitely something here. And you say you never gave permission to have the device implanted?"

Tarquin gave me a brief glance from where he sat in the tall chair. "Definitely not."

Dr Lindquist clucked her tongue. "Some of these corporations think they're God, the way they act. I'll have it out in just a moment." She numbed the area behind his ear and carefully made a thin cut. A ribbon of scarlet trickled down his neck, and I said in surprise, "It's red."

"Blood is usually red," the doctor replied with a smile. "Unless you're an octopus."

"Of course," I murmured, but that very point had caught my attention. Where did the flesh end and the artificial begin? I knew that Tarquin's shoulder at least was artificial, as were my arms, but what about our brains, our hearts? *A cyborg is a mix of programmable mix of flesh and metal.* So maybe when I'd been slicing myself that other day, I'd picked the wrong place to cut.

Dr Lindquist fished out the tracker with tweezers then dropped it with a click into a small dish. It was the size of my fingernail and was almost paper thin, and had been barely hidden beneath the skin. A moment later she'd covered the cut with a plasti-skin bandage. "There. All done."

"I'll go next," Jake said. "I want this thing out of me."

'This thing' which was almost certainly his imagination, I thought wryly, trying to come up with a lie for why he wouldn't have one. But then to my surprise, the doctor said a moment later, "Ah, here it is. Just in the same place."

Tarquin and I exchanged shocked glances. My impromptu lie

had turned out to be the truth. But I kept my mouth shut as Jake's was also removed, and then it was my turn.

Oh, chestnuts. I still wore the wig.

"Can I have some privacy?" I asked. "I just need to have a chat with the doctor."

Once the two boys moved into the other room, I took off the wig. "I've been acting on the island," I said apologetically, "and the blond guy thinks I'm a natural redhead. It's kind of embarrassing to show I was wearing the wig the whole time."

"Nothing wrong with blonde hair," the doctor said briskly, running her fingers behind my ear. "Oh. It's a scalp implant, isn't it? I can feel the seam."

"Um…I was in a bad accident a few years back," I fudged. "But don't worry about that. Would you remove the chip?"

"Of course."

I winced as the needle went in for the anaesthetic, then I couldn't feel anything until she said, "Here. All sorted." And another circle of metal fell with a click onto the table. It was stained red.

I stared at it, fascinated, as the bandage went on. Red, just like my nails. Just like everyone else's blood…barring octopi, of course.

"So what kind of accident was it?"

"My accident?" I turned away from the tracker, replacing the wig over my pinned-back hair. "Um…a bad fall five years ago. Why?"

"Well, according to the scan, you've had some serious enhancements. I've never seen anything like it. I apologise if I'm intruding, but-"

"You scanned me? When did you do that?"

"When you sat down in the chair," she explained. "It's standard. We check for tumours, fractures, and anything else obvious that needs to be attended to. It also gives us an idea of your medical history." She moved over to a nearby table, bringing up an image on the large viewer screen. It was black and gold and white, vaguely in the shape of a human body, and looked to me like a jumble of bones and hardware. "See, here we have your body-shot, which I must say is absolutely fascinating. I'll need to have a chat with that other boy, Tom, as his scan looked similar. Not as much damage as you, though."

I closed my eyes briefly. She didn't seem to have made the connection between 'Sweetheart Island' and 'lots of enhancements', but it was probably only a matter of time. At least the trackers were out.

"Did you say my name?" Tarquin wandered back in to the room, Jake following closely behind.

They saw the screen, and Jake whistled. "Geez. How bad were you smashed up? That's a hell of a lot of metal."

"Do you mind?" I snapped. "This is kind of personal."

He grimaced, and both boys pulled back. "Sorry." Jake left again, but Tarquin just turned around to study one of the charts on the wall.

"See here," the doctor continued. "I've never seen such extensive enhancements. I hope you don't find me rude, but the truth is that such injuries as caused these should have killed you. Both your arms are robotic, and your whole left leg, and your right leg to the knee, and your pelvis and ribs are strengthened but I can see the breaks underneath, and I can see extensive scarring on your internal organs and the bowel has been replaced-"

"Wait," I interrupted. "Are you saying I look like I've been in an accident?"

"Of course," she said in surprise. "You just told me that you were."

I shook my head in confusion. "I- ah, I hit my head badly. Sometimes I get confused about things."

She nodded sympathetically. "That would explain why you have three chips in your brain instead of just the usual one to control movement of the prosthetics. I assume they're to help you remember basics?"

"Ah...yeah," I said slowly. "The chips are to help me remember normal life, because I've forgotten a lot from before the fall."

"Fascinating." Dr Lindquist shook her head, clucking her tongue in amazement. "You've been so rebuilt that if it wasn't for your clearly normal spine and brainstem, I would think you were a cyborg. You even have a scalp implant, and that's unusual, especially with how very regular your features are. The eyes are long-term contacts, are they not?"

"Would you really think me a cyborg?" I asked slowly, ignoring the last question. "But with this many enhancements, aren't I one really?"

She laughed. "There is a big difference between a human with major enhancements and an actual cyborg, and believe me I can tell. A cyborg is essentially a robot with biological components. They have the brainstem to control bodily movements, and the rest of it is programming. Anything more than that would be illegal, not to mention unethical. Of course that means that no matter how hard you try, you can never get them to seem quite human."

"What about the cyborgs on Sweetheart Island?" I asked. "You know how they advertised how lifelike they were."

"Lifelike in some ways, but they'll never be truly believable as humans," the doctor said confidently. "Not for a good fifty years even with our best technology."

I nodded slowly, my mind racing. Cyborgs, real cyborgs created in a lab, shouldn't be half as realistic as I was. And I looked like I had been in a terrible accident…maybe Tarquin's theory that we were actually human wasn't so far-fetched after all.

13 Excited

'Right then, my whole world opened up.'
— from an overheard conversation with R.A

Trying not to show my excitement, I asked carefully, "Would it be possible to get a copy of that image for myself?"

"Technically I'm not allowed to keep one at all," the doctor confided. "So even though I'd love to, unless you gave me permission I'd have to get rid of it anyway."

"Can you make two copies? Then we could have one each." It would be good to have proof in more than one place. Of what, I wasn't quite sure.

"Excellent. Now I will need your signature that I'm allowed to do this…"

"Of course." I signed the screen 'Amber Valentine', then handed it back.

She printed off two small images of the scan, then handed one to me. "And how were you going to pay for that?"

"Cash," I said cheerfully. Thanks, Jay.

As the doctor went to sort out the payment in the other room, Tarquin turned towards me from her desk, a large radio-box in his hand. His face was white. "Listen."

"…and recovery is uncertain. Suspect is described as a hundred and seventy-six centimetres tall, early twenties, attractive with very pale skin and blonde hair. If you see anyone fitting this description do not approach, she is armed and dangerous. Go straight to the police, or call this number…"

"You didn't hear the first part," Tarquin said worriedly. "They said that a player was in a coma because she'd been poisoned for real. Someone called Jessie Carver. They said she was the owner's niece."

"Snow," I breathed in dismay. I hadn't realised she was related to John Carver, who I'd seen in that advertisement days earlier. Surely he wouldn't want to kill his own niece? I hadn't seen him in person on Sweetheart Island - did he even know about it?

"Snow? Did you try to kill her?"

"What? No!"

"I guess I understand if you did, I mean I was going to, but that's not the same as actually doing it-"

I frowned, shaking my head. "No, no, I purposely left her be. I didn't hurt her, I promise."

"Then who did?"

"She said she had something on Karey Godmother and some others," I guessed. "I figure it's got something to do with those treasure hunters too, since Jay said Sinbad was in on it as well. Oh, chestnuts. We should get out of here." Paying the doctor had used up most of our stolen money, but maybe I could get more from Jake…

Just then we heard the door open and heavy footsteps in the other room, and a familiar male voice. An angry voice. "Where the hell are they?"

"Miller?" I heard Jake squeak. "What's the matter?"

"The bloody 'borgs, that's what. They're here, with you. Where are they?"

From what Jake had said in the café, I realised that 'Miller' must be Hercules – AKA the guy I shot then hit with a shovel – and he was blocking the only exit. Tarquin and I exchanged panicked glances then hid, him behind the supply bench and me less adequately behind the door between the two rooms. I shoved the precious body-scan into my pocket.

"Borgs?" Jake questioned. "They're actors, just like us."

Miller swore in reply, and I shrank back behind the door, my heart pounding in panic. We didn't even have a weapon.

"Excuse me, sir," I heard Dr Linquist say disapprovingly. "If you have a question, you may go to reception."

The rough footsteps moved closer.

"You can't go in there!" she snapped. "I have a client!"

The door next to me opened and Miller moved into sight, the much smaller doctor following him closely behind. He was moving stiffly and wearing a large jacket, but I could see the dull grey of the pistol showing through the gap in the pocket.

"You have no right to be in here!" the doctor snapped. "This is a confidential area, and unless you have permission from the patient, which you don't-"

"Where are they?" Miller cut in. Then his eyes lit on the other door.

"It's just a closet," Jake said.

Tarquin was still out of sight, but it was a miracle that Miller didn't turn around and see me standing there behind the door. I bet he would be as quick to fire as Jay had been this morning.

As he moved towards the closet his eyes lit on the doctor's copy of the body-scan where it lay on the nearby bench. He picked it up and studied it a mere moment before I saw understanding dawn on his face. "I see," he said softly. "That's not very good."

"That's confidential!" the doctor shouted. "If you don't leave right now, I'm going to call the police-"

Pop.

In one smooth movement Miller pulled that pistol out of his pocket and fired it at the doctor. She jolted backwards, a patch of red blossoming on her grey shirt, then slumped to the ground as bonelessly as a ragdoll. I was frozen in place, unbreathing. How had something so very quiet done so much harm?

"Holy #@*$!" Jake swore, blanching. "What did you *do?*"

"Don't get stupid about it," the other man retorted. "She would have told for certain."

"Told *what?!*"

Clearly Jake still didn't get it, I realized. But then Miller turned around and saw me standing behind the door. Our eyes met for one long, horrible second, then he smiled. "I've been looking for you," he said, malicious intent clear in his voice. "You'll be sorry you ever messed with me." He went to raise the pistol and I just stood there, panic making me stupid. Making me unable to move.

Crunch.

Tarquin stood behind Miller, the large radio-box in his hands, and his eyes wide. Miller swayed in place, his face blank, then collapsed face down. There was a dent in the back of his head.

I slapped a hand over my mouth, stifling the hysterical, inappropriate laughter that tried to emerge. *Has his skull always been that shape?*

"Oh no, you killed him too," Jake ground out, whimpering. He said a few choice words. "What are we going to do?"

"He was going to hurt Valentina," Tarquin pleaded. "What else was I supposed to do?"

"You did the right thing," I told him, my eyes still fixed on poor Dr Lindquist. I checked her pulse. It was still pumping, although weakly. There was a nasty wound high on her chest, and she was unconscious. "Call the medics," I said in a low voice. "She could still survive."

"But he shot her," Jake was saying. "I don't get why he did that. I mean, Amber's had an accident, right…"

Tarquin's hand lifted away from the call-alarm. "Amber? That's Valentina White," he said in disgust. "Haven't you figured it out?"

Jake's jaw dropped, and he looked at me in panic. "The crazy cyborg? But you said you were an actor like me!"

My lips tightened and I focused on pressing bandages onto the wound. There was a lot of blood, but maybe she still had a chance…if those medics got here in time.

"She lied, obviously," Tarquin retorted. He still held the receiver in one hand. "It's because the body-scan proves what they've been doing on Sweetheart Island. They've been kidnapping people, wiping their memories, then programming them to act as characters. We chose to leave, and they've come after us with guns."

"But…" Jake's eyes were wide, his face pale. "That's illegal."

"And that's why Dr Lindquist is bleeding on the floor," I snapped. "Tarquin, make that call, will you? Then we'd better get out of here, or we're just as dead as Miller."

"But I was just helping them look for the treasure," Jake whispered. "I didn't know about any of this."

"Treasure?" I finished strapping a bandage of the doctor's wound, then looked up at him. "So it really exists?"

Jake just shook his head. "I'm only nineteen! I don't want to die!"

"That's it," Tarquin said. "I've made the call. Are you coming?"

He was talking to me, but I saw the desperation in Jake's face. "You can come with us," I said quietly. "But if you give us up, you're dead too. You realise that?"

He nodded, lips tight, and I finally stood, leaving the doctor. There was ample evidence that we'd been here, but there was nothing I could do about that now. But my hands – they were stained red.

"Come on," Tarquin called from the front room. "We need to go!"

"Just a minute." I moved to the small sink, washing my hands quickly as the water ran pink over the white porcelain. There was a window right in front of me with a view of the surgery's parking lot, and I watched as a large black car pulled in. It was identical to the one we'd stolen from Jay.

I swore, then ran out to the empty reception room where the boys were poised on the doorway. "Tarquin! They're here!"

He froze with his hand on the clear exit door, Jake right behind him. "It's Sinbad and Jafeer," Jake gasped. "What do we do?!"

Tarquin slammed shut the emergency lock, and the door turned opaque. "There's another exit behind the reception," he said urgently. "Come on!"

Bang bang. Someone thumped on the locked door. "Miller. Are you there?"

We exchanged horrified glances, and Tarquin crept over to the back exit, trying to open it. "It's locked too!"

"It's an emergency exit," I hissed. "It won't be locked!"

"Let me do it," Jake said quickly.

He moved in to study the lock-pad, but behind us the thumping had become louder and more violent. The door frame shook. "I know you're in there!" Sinbad shouted, his voice muffled. "Open the door or I'll force it open!"

"The lock's not going to hold," I said in sudden realisation.

"Just a moment!" Jake snapped. "I've almost got it."

The door shook again, its material splintering away from the hinge. I ran over, pushing my back against it and bracing myself with all my strength. We just needed another few seconds…

"Got it!" Jake said triumphantly. The door swung open, and the boys turned back to me.

"Come on, Valentina!" Tarquin cried. "What are you doing?"

I felt another blow at my back, and I saw the open emergency doorway with our stolen vehicle just visible through it, and I shook my head. "We won't all make it if I let the door go. Maybe none of us will. You go."

Jake ran, but Tarquin hovered in the doorway, his expression a mask of agony. "I'm not leaving you behind!"

"They won't kill me!" I said urgently. "Not while I know where the treasure map is."

"What treasure?!"

"Never mind what treasure! We've got ten seconds till you lose your chance too. Someone has to tell the authorities what's been happening on the island. You go right now!"

He wavered, but finally he nodded, then he too was gone.

BANG. BANG.

Ow, my back!

I held out until I saw them climb into the vehicle, until I saw it pull away, then suddenly there was a great force behind me and I was sent sprawling onto the carpeted floor as the doors broke open behind me. I scrambled to turn over, pushing myself to my knees, but then I felt a cold, hard shape against the side of my head.

"Move and you're a paraplegic," Sinbad said coldly. "Again."

I froze in place, on my knees with my hands half raised. Execution-style. In my peripheral vision I saw him there, unsmiling and still wearing spectacles, just like when I'd last seen him. Just behind him stood Jay. He had a faint mark on one cheek where the bullet had grazed him earlier. It looked weeks old.

"What do you mean, again?" Jay asked.

"Go and check the other room," Sinbad snapped. "Miller hasn't responded. That's a problem."

Jay's figure retreated from sight and a few seconds later I heard him swear.

"What is it?"

"Miller's dead," Jay called back. "And some lady too, probably the doctor."

I hoped he was wrong about the doctor. But Sinbad moved around me so the gun was pointing right in my face, and his cold, cold blue eyes were right on mine. "Did you do that?"

I swallowed. "Self-defence."

A moment later Jay came back into sight. His cheek bore only a faint scratch, and his handsome face was twisted in disgust. "Someone cracked him in the back of the head. There's a dent the size of my fist."

"Self-defence?" Sinbad asked me softly. "Hitting someone from behind?"

I met his eyes steadily. "I wasn't behind him. I have very long arms."

Smack. Sinbad struck me across the head with the pistol, and I fell back, my head ringing.

"Was that really necessary?" Jay argued.

"You know she's a killer," Sinbad replied flatly. "She was made to be one. Now how are we going to get out of here without being seen?"

"Made to be one?" Jay retorted. "Yeah, I get that she's programmed, but that's failed, hasn't it? That's why we're here. But I want to know what you meant before when you said you'd make her 'a paraplegic again'. She's a cyborg, isn't she?"

"Jay," Sinbad warned. "Now isn't the time to ask questions.

It's time to go."

"But are you saying she's like me instead?" Jay persisted. "A human who's been enhanced, only she's been programmed too?"

"Yes," I said quickly, filing aside that information about Jay. Not purely human after all — maybe that handsome face wasn't the one he'd been born with. "The doctor told me so, and that's why Miller shot her."

"Shut up!" Sinbad ordered.

"Because she knew that I'd been in an accident," I babbled on, scrambling away from Sinbad. "Because she saw the memory chips in my head."

Jay stared at me wild-eyed for several moments, his hands loose at his sides. Then he turned on the other man. "You know I don't mind crossing the law," he hissed. "I don't mind shooting the occasional android or 'borg. It's practically a game. But coming after real people? You lied to me, Dane, and if *this* girl is like me, then I bloody well know who she is!"

Who I was? I'd made a guess at that too…

"She's not like you, because we don't have a contract with her," Sinbad snapped. "We fixed you after that rock climbing accident. You owe us service."

"Forget your damn contract, I don't want it. You can shove that right up-" and then Jay said something physically improbable and very impolite.

Sinbad's face hardened, and then the gun swung towards Jay. He squeezed the trigger. *Pop.*

I gasped, but then the gun had swung back towards me, faster than I could move. "You won't survive a shot in the head either," he told me. "Now get up. We're going for a ride."

I glanced at Jay's still figure down on the floor. Another headshot, but this one wasn't a graze. I squeezed my hands into fists to stop them trembling. "You're not going to kill me too?"

"Not yet. Not until you tell us what you did with that map."

The map. I knew they wouldn't have forgotten about it — but perhaps now my knowledge could save my life. I swallowed. "That's not much incentive to tell you, is it?"

"Let's try this," he said very softly. "Tell me where the map is, or I'll kill you."

"It's on Sweetheart Island. Hidden in the hotel."

"Where?"

"I don't know exactly where," I hedged. "But I could find it, if you took me there."

Sinbad stared at me a moment. "If you're lying to me, or if you try to escape, I will shoot you. No one will stop me, either. You're a murderous cyborg, remember?"

I nodded tightly. "I understand."

I walked out to the car, his hand tight on my arm and the pistol partially hidden, pressed right against my chest. "Open the back door," he ordered. "Sit."

I sat, and the doors locked on either side of me. He moved into the front compartment, which was separated from my seat by a thick clear barrier, then tapped at a few keys. The car began moving, but he didn't take his eyes off me.

"Aren't you going to steer?"

"It's a self-driving car," he replied, still staring at me. His eyes flicked over my body, my face, with a reptilian gaze that made me shudder inside. "You don't remember much outside the programming, do you?"

I shook my head.

"Interesting." He waved the pistol in my direction, a pointless gesture because of the barrier. "And yet you've caused so very much trouble."

"Surely it wasn't all me," I said in a low voice. "I didn't ask to be kidnapped and have these *fantasies* shoved into my brain. I didn't arrange for Snow or Jessie or whatever her name is to pay for such a stupid fantasy, or for her to fall into a coma…"

"Kidnapped?" Sinbad laughed. "You weren't kidnapped. You were *saved*. Your car drove right off a cliff, and there was barely anything left of you except for that pretty face. We took you from the morgue, gave you a new lease on life. And being queen of the White Hotel isn't so very bad, is it?"

Had they saved me, really? "But why?" I whispered. "Why

not just send me back to my family? Why not just create your own cyborgs, or use people like Jay-"

"Because the cyborgs were stupider than your average dog," he cut in. "Billions of dollars spent on creating them, and they were worthless for anything except to serve as waiters or receptionists. So we burned them all, but the insurance company wouldn't pay up. They thought the fire was suspicious. And then you, one of the original character models, just happened to have a terrible accident. Perfect timing." He smiled. It wasn't pretty. "Don't you think?"

I looked away, my mind working furiously. I'd been in a car accident. Ruby, Caleb's fiancée, had died in a car accident. And Caleb had been familiar to me from the moment I'd met him… "It's a clever idea," I said, and my voice was surprisingly even. "Except for the ethical issues of stealing someone's life and trying to change their character. I'm not the only one it didn't work on."

"It's been chaos from start to finish, with Karey trying to keep track of all those characters and no one doing what they were supposed to outside the first day or two. It's a good thing it was just a test run with no media present." He cocked his head to the side. "And with poor little Jessie Carver almost murdered by the evil stepmother? That's the best part."

I didn't argue with that last statement; there was no point. "Does Karey know about all of this? About Jessie?"

"Of course she knows. It was her idea."

"Oh." So it had been Karey and Sinbad who'd put 'Snow' in a coma. Not so timid and professional after all, was Karey? "Then why do you need the map?" I asked. "Does this have something to do with the flashing lights at night?"

Sinbad turned away for a moment, checking the screen in front of him. Around us the scenery had become more familiar, and we turned onto a coast road. "Why did you say that Snow White had the comm. unit?" he countered.

"Pardon?" I was startled by the sudden change of subject. "The comm. unit that was left in the foyer for one of our people to pick up, several days ago," he enunciated. "The one that you had a nice little conversation through, and finished by claiming you were Snow White. Why did you do that?"

I just stared at him. Out of all the things he could have brought up, the odd coin-thing had been last on my list. "Because I didn't like her, and I'd rather that she looked stupid than I did if it turned out to be someone's lost radio," I answered finally. "I suppose you must have had someone take it from my purse. Was it Karey? And what was the comm. unit for?"

"Never you mind," he replied, and his voice turned cold again. "Do what you're told, and you might just survive the day."

Which meant he never planned to answer my questions. That was OK; at least he wasn't shooting me yet. I turned away and watched the sea on my left. We turned a corner and the familiar silhouette of Sweetheart Island came into sight, lit by the midday sun. The White Hotel shone from the mid-point of the sloped hill, and my stomach twisted in fear.

"You know, you don't have to kill me," I said. "Or even reprogram me, because that clearly didn't work. Just tell me what you need and I'll do it. I can sign a contract like Jay did. I've got no memory of my life before this, so I don't need to go back."

He raised an eyebrow. "Not even to your long-lost love the carpet seller?"

So he knew about Caleb and…Ruby. "I don't remember him. I don't *like* him." Or I couldn't forgive him, anyway, and that felt a bit like hatred.

"What a generous offer. We'll see."

But then we turned towards the beach and the bridge rose through the water even as we drove towards it. A minute later we were across and back on the island. We drove through the empty main street, up towards the hotel, then pulled into one of the carparks. Sinbad climbed out first then opened my door, the gun still trained on my face. "We'll go in round the back."

All I needed was one moment, I decided. One single moment of distraction where I could grab the gun. "I need to go to reception. The map is hidden inside something, but the receptionist will know where it was put."

"Inside what?"

"I'll tell you once I see it."

He studied my face carefully and I did my best to look honest. Then he nodded once. "I'll be watching you. Go first."

It felt like the pistol left a brand in the middle of my back as we walked through those glass doors. Inside the reception area were two familiar figures. Daniel Charmant was checking in with Rhonda the receptionist, giving her his trademark grin. Wasting charm on an android; but she walked out to the back room, most likely in response to something he had requested. Next to him stood a taller, red-haired youth with spectacles: Jeremy Kricket, apparently next in the queue. I walked up beside them, keeping my head turned away, and waited for Rhonda to return.

"This better be necessary," Sinbad whispered in my ear. "Or you'll be sorry."

I was already sorry. "It's necessary."

Out of the corner of my eye I saw Daniel study me, first with generic interest, then with recognition. "Hey! You're the girl from the ball!"

"Ah…no?"

"Yes you are," he snapped. "You got me in the biggest trouble with my grandmother. And what did you do with that shoe?"

"I don't know what you're talking about," I answered hurriedly. "I didn't have any shoe."

"Don't give me that! I saw you take it. And then when I followed what you said about how to find the girl – and she doesn't exist! You lied to me!"

"What, Cindy the redheaded cleaner doesn't exist?"

His face fell. "I thought you said she was Candy the waitress. No wonder I didn't find her."

"Try again," I said desperately. "I'm sure she'll remember you."

But next to Daniel, Jeremy was watching me first with polite interest, then with narrowed eyes, and his eyebrows suddenly shot up. "Holy guacamole, that's Valentina White!" he exploded. "Don't you recognise her?"

"No, Mrs White has blonde hair," Daniel argued. "I don't know what you're thinking."

"She's changed her hair," Jeremy insisted. "But it's her. She's still got that mole!"

Apparently my makeup hadn't covered it for long. And I wasn't the only one to use stupid swear words…

"As amusing as this all is," Sinbad cut in flatly, "We have somewhere to be." The gun pressed in at the base of my spine.

"I need to speak to Rhonda," I told him over my shoulder. "I *must*."

Daniel's attention flicked between Sinbad and I, but the other man wasn't giving in so easily. "This is most important!" Jeremy persisted. "Don't you know she's a criminal? She killed Snow White!"

"I really didn't," I said, a little shaken by his vehemence. When we'd briefly met before, he'd seemed a pleasant guy, if a little naïve. But then perhaps his programming affected him much as it did me. "You're mistaken."

"We don't have time for this," Sinbad hissed in my ear. "You've got five seconds until I make you and them sorry. Where is the map?"

Just then Rhonda finally came back out to the reception desk. "Good afternoon, Mrs White. How may I help you today?"

Clearly this android was programmed to recognise me whether I was dark, light or polka dotted.

"Mrs White!" Daniel exclaimed from behind us. "What's going on here?"

"I told you, she killed Snow and Kingsley White!" Jeremy insisted.

"Actually I didn't," I repeated a little shakily. Then I took a big risk: "It was Sinbad here who set me up, and he has a gun on me right now."

"A gun?" Daniel echoed, and then Sinbad swung the pistol around to face him.

"Go away, boy, and stay away-"

I quickly swung my arm around to knock the gun away, and

a stray blast hit the ceiling. The other men stepped back with identical squeaks and the receptionist barely wavered. But Sinbad didn't let it go, and for a moment we struggled with the pistol, still gripped tight in his hand.

"I took voluntary enhancement on my limbs," he spat at me. "You might be stronger than Miller or Jay, but not me."

Uh oh. Although we were about the same size, it seemed like he was winning. But that was when Jeremy Kricket proved he had more than just misplaced zeal and ran over, trying to wrest the pistol away from both of us. I hit Sinbad hard in the gut with my knee, then the gun went flying and Jeremy and I both dashed for it.

He got there first, lifting it to point at me with shaking hands. "I don't care what he says," he told me, his eyes wide behind his spectacles. "I know that you're a murderer. You're a bad, wicked person, and you're going straight to jail where you belong."

The moment was so surreal compared to the day I'd had. I'd moved on from the daily chores of being Valentina White, Sweetheart Island's most ruthless widow, but it seemed that this boy hadn't. He was still very firmly stuck in the fantasy, and I didn't have the slightest idea what to say to make him believe the truth.

I held up one hand placatingly, one eye still fixed on Sinbad, who was crouched on the ground, clutching his belly. "There is far, far more to this than you know, Jeremy."

"You stole one of my apples, didn't you?"

"Um…"

"You did! You took one of the ones covered in fruit wax, and you killed two people!"

"Oh, for goodness sake. I'm not the danger here! *He* is!" I pointed at Sinbad. "He and Karey Godmother have some very underhand business going on, and they are far more likely to harm you than I would, do you understand that?"

"But they said you poisoned Snow White!"

Were we still on that topic? "I didn't poison anyone," I repeated wearily.

"She's telling the truth," came another voice from behind me. It was Caleb, and he looked very serious. "Trust me, if not her, Jeremy. That's not actually Valentina White. That's someone who's been secretly playing her character. She's a good person."

The gun wavered. "So you're saying that she's, like, undercover?"

"Exactly," Caleb agreed. Even as he said it he pulled out a small gun-like object from his pocket, shot it at Sinbad who was halfway to standing, and the man collapsed again and fell. A taser. He pulled out a pair of thin plastic cuffs, bending down to tie the man's hands behind his back where he lay. "We both are."

I hovered uncertainly, unsure why Caleb had claimed such a thing, but also not wanting to get shot in the face.

But it worked, because Jeremy finally lowered the gun. "Whoa. So you're both police officers? Can I see your badge?"

"Yes, we are," Caleb said shortly, pulling out a silvery disc from inside his shirt. I didn't recognise it, but it seemed to satisfy the others. Why was he carrying such a thing around with him? "You can do me a favour, though."

Daniel stepped forward to stand next to Jeremy, clearly having regained his courage. "What do you need?"

Caleb gestured at Sinbad. "Don't let this one go anywhere. He's a very dangerous man."

That, at least, was true.

Daniel's jaw had dropped. "Are you going to call for backup?"

"I already have," Caleb replied, but just then I saw a woman in pink approaching the glass doors from outside. Karey.

Was she his backup? Forgetting the gun, I turned and ran for the stairs. I heard a shout behind me and the *pop* of a weapon discharging as something skimmed past my calf, followed by a sharp streak of pain.

"Valentina!" Caleb shouted, but I just ran faster. I made it to the top of the stairs, then realised I'd run onto the mezzanine floor overlooking the foyer. There was no other way to get out except by the windows. I couldn't see Karey anywhere, but still I backed away into the wall.

He'd followed me up, and he stood at the top of the stairs, blocking my exit. "Jeremy is an idiot," he said. "Are you alright?"

We both looked down to where a streak of black liquid marred my lower leg. "You know I'll be fine," I said a little bitterly. "Why did you tell them you're a cop?"

"I *am* a cop."

I shook my head, my eyes fixed on the gun-thing now in his hand. It looked official, but the others had had them too. "No, you're up to something with Karey, and you're pretending to be a cop. You're too young to be one, anyway."

"I'm not pretending to be a cop, and I *am* a young one. Or a trainee, anyway. I was undercover as an actor, until about ten minutes ago." He took a step closer, his brown eyes warm on my face. "But the police know everything now. About the smuggling, about the way you and the others have been treated. I promise you that *everything* is going to be better now."

Smuggling? Who'd been smuggling? But I felt a surge of anger go through me at those last words. "Just like your promise that you wouldn't call breaking the glass slipper? Next thing I'm being shot in the neck with a tranquilliser and forced into three days of the most intense programming I ever had. I'm just lucky it didn't stick! You're a bloody liar, Caleb, and it's not the first time!"

He blanched. "I didn't tell. I swear."

"I heard you telling Jay after I'd left the room! You admitted you'd lied to me, and said it was because you didn't like to see me cry!" My hands clenched into fists at my sides, the memory of that time still hurting, still making me furious. "You called me a *meat puppet!*"

"Ohhh." Caleb's face turned ashen. "You heard that?"

"Yes! And now you're claiming to be some kind of good guy? I don't believe you!"

"I was lying to *Jay*," he said insistently, moving towards me. "I'm sorry I spoke about you like that, but I had to make him believe me! I couldn't let him think I...I *cared* for you, or that I fully planned to get you and the others out of here as soon as

I could. And I did! Try, I mean, and I sure as chestnuts didn't give you away. I didn't think they'd get to you so quickly." His expression was sincere, and he reached down to take my hands. "You've got to believe me, Valentina."

His hands were too warm on mine. Or mine were too cold – no real blood. I jerked them away, but I was feeling less hostile. Even after everything, I so wanted to believe him. I wanted to trust him – I always had. But what he'd said… "Hang on. Did you just say chestnuts? I thought that wasn't a real swear word."

His mouth curved into a crooked smile. "It's not, but we made it one, because you can use it around anyone without getting in trouble. Ruby and I…" His smile faltered. "I suppose that's a bit of her that was passed on, just like the mole."

"Beauty mark," I said automatically, but I was so caught by the sorrow in his expression. Maybe he didn't really care for Valentina. Maybe he *did* really think she was a sad, puppet-like replica of his old girlfriend. But he'd loved Ruby.

Me.

"You have to believe me," Caleb was repeating. "I swear it to you, on everything. On Ruby's memory. I've always tried to protect you."

And there it was. I believed him. Maybe I was stupid to do so, but I believed him. And this was the perfect time to tell the real truth…but I chickened out. "Then thank you." I folded my fake-bronze arms in front of my chest, turning away. The body-scan was still in my pocket. I didn't know what to say next.

"You look good with red hair," he offered. "It sets off your green eyes."

"It's a wig, and they're contacts," I replied shortly. "What did you mean about smuggling? And how did Jay and Karey come into it?"

"Oh." He leaned back against the nearby wall, folding his arms in a reflection of my posture. "I'm a trainee police officer over at Heartlands. That's the nearest city, and Sweetheart Island comes under its jurisdiction. We'd heard whispers that this place was more than just a luxury resort, and my bosses wanted to send someone in undercover, as an actor. I was new – I only started six months ago – but I'm young, and have the right look. And then there's my link with Ruby and Jay. I was one of many to apply for this job, but I was the only one who got in."

He smiled, and that little dimple appeared in one cheek. I watched his face as he spoke, for the first time with full awareness of who he was to me. "And you found smuggling."

Caleb nodded. "This place is perfect for it. Great location, isolated, very few people who'd know what to notice. Pretty much all the actors – me, Jay, Dane Sinbad – were actually here to keep that side of things moving. Jay's been in a bit of trouble before, and he's the one who let us know what was going on. He gave me an in. He told us what had happened to him, and then we figured out that True Fantasies were way bypassing the legal limits for organic matter in cyborgs, with the full knowledge of the owners. So while we don't agree about everything, he's on the right side. Mostly."

Except when he'd been shooting at me and Tarquin, that was. I also noticed Caleb was using the present tense for Jay. He didn't know what had happened less than an hour ago. I took a deep breath. "Actually, Caleb. I-"

And then the fire alarm went off. *'EVACUATE THE BUILDING. EVACUATE THE BUILDING. EVACUATE THE BUILDING...'*

"Great timing," Caleb muttered. "It might be just a distraction, but we'd better get out of here before the sprinklers go off."

I looked over the balcony to the foyer below. Several people were moving towards the exit doors, Daniel leading the way, but as he reached the doors, they stayed closed. He waved his arms at them. "Open." A moment later he tapped the manual lock-pad, then when they still didn't open, looked back in dismay. "They're locked!"

Caleb came up beside me. There were about a dozen people down below now, including Jeremy and several android servers. "I don't see Sinbad," he murmured. "That's not good."

But I smelled smoke, and that was worse. "He told me they

tried to claim insurance by setting a fire once before," I said in horror. "And why haven't the sprinklers gone off?"

Caleb's eyes widened and he grabbed my hand, pushing me towards the staircase. "You go and find another way out, alright? Even if you go out a window."

"Where are you going?"

"To check if there's anyone who's still in here."

I froze in place, remembering the secret cupboard that I'd found only the day before. "There are others," I said. "And there's no way they're going to be able to get themselves out."

"Tell me where."

I rolled my eyes. "I'll *show* you where they are. It's not easy to find." I set off at a run before he could argue, finding the nearest staircase that would lead me to the fourth level where the other hidden room was. I reached it within a few minutes, trying to remember exactly where the knothole had been. I'd been coming out of Snow's room…

And here it was. I pressed my finger against the little hole. "Open sesame."

Behind me Caleb looked bemused. "I thought that was my line."

"Pardon?"

"Never mind."

The door slid open, revealing the many racks of still figures. "Careful," I told him. "Last time I got shut in here. One of us has to hold the door."

"I'll hold it," he began, then changed his mind. "No, you hold it. I'll take a look."

A minute later he said, "I can only see five, and two of those don't have catheters. I think they're just androids." He moved over to the closest one, an older man with a beard. "Is that Kingsley White?"

"Yes," I replied tersely. "But I don't think we'll have time to wake them up. I think we'll need to carry them as they are."

It turned out that the shelves – gurneys, rather – had wheels, so we ended up piling them all onto the same one. There were two shelves per gurney, and we piled three onto one and two onto the other, with the cyborgs on top – which made it incredibly heavy, but we still managed to shuffle it down the hall to the stairs.

"Uh…is there a lift?" Caleb asked after it became apparent that the enormously heavy gurney wasn't going down those stairs.

"You're not supposed to use them during a fire," I said.

"It might have gone out. The sprinklers are off."

They were, but there was smoke trickling up the stairs. "I don't think so," I said worriedly. "We'll have to go another way."

There wasn't anywhere else to go. We came to a dead end at the other end of the hall since there were just more stairs, and the smoke had definitely got thicker from the other end. "There's no choice," Caleb said finally. "We'll have to go out the windows."

"We're four storeys up! You'll never survive it." I took a desperate look at the pile of limp bodies on the gurney, then at Caleb. "You take the stairs. I'll go to the window and throw them out; you find something to catch them with."

He hesitated a moment, then nodded. "Which window?"

I quickly checked. "Third from the right side of the north face."

Two minutes later he was gone and I was hanging out of that same window, thinking that four storeys really was a lot, and that he never would have left 'Ruby' behind. The smoke was getting thicker and thicker although I'd closed the door and stuffed a rag under it, and I knew we had no choice. Caleb was nowhere to be seen, but I picked up the first tube-free figure, a smallish woman, and hefted her over to the window. Maybe she'd break the others' fall, I thought grimly, because there was nothing to break hers except for tiles and a row of pot plants.

Just then Caleb came racing around the corner, followed by half a dozen others holding white parcels. They were bedsheets, I saw, and together they spread them out below. "Throw her down!" he shouted.

I glanced behind me. I could see flames licking around that rag I'd put under the door, and I knew I had only minutes if that. Without hesitating I threw down the first woman, then one after another, ripping out their tubes. Better a chance of survival than facing burning to death. They spun like dolls as they fell, then landed heavily in the sheet, one barely being pulled off before the next landed.

Kingsley was the last down, and boy he weighed a ton. If I had just been normal there was no way I could have carried him, even in a fireman's lift. As I hefted him over the ledge the flames were licking right around us, and I felt the scorching heat against my skin. A flame appeared on Kingsley's shirt, and I patted it out frantically then threw both of us over.

Riiip. Instead of falling, we jerked to a halt, me hanging onto his leg. His shirt had hooked on a break in the wooden windowsill, and he was stuck there like a bug pinned to a board as the fire grew ever closer. In horror I pulled at him, pushing my legs against the wall and swinging him repeatedly until all of our combined weight was hanging off that one notch of wood.

One swing, then two, then there was a sudden rip and a jolt and we were both falling. I barely had time to scream before we landed heavily on the sheet and then fell *through* it, Kingsley on top of me. Damn, he really was heavy, was my last thought before everything faded into grey.

14 Weary

'Most people don't have to prove they're human.'
— from an overheard conversation with Ruby Anderson

I could hear before I could see again. Sounds washing around me merged into distinct voices.

"She can't be dead," someone said. "She can't die."

"Sometimes they lose their personalities," another voice added. "Do you think her back is broken?"

My eyes opened a crack, and I saw a couple of unfamiliar faces surrounding me, one a middle-aged woman, the other a younger man with thick, hairy eyebrows like caterpillars on his face. They both wore light blue. "She's awake," the woman said.

Another face, a young, tanned one creased in lines of worry, came into sight. "Is she alright?"

"Let's see," the woman replied. She shone a bright light into first one eye and then the other, and as I blinked and tried to move away, she asked, "Valentina, do you understand me?"

"Of course," I replied, and my voice came out muzzy. "Who are you?"

"I'm Elizabeth, and this is Tony. We're medics."

The medics were leaning over me, and I could just see Caleb at the edge of my sight. 'Ali Baba' was really a cop, and was really my fiancé – although he didn't know that second part yet. I turned, trying to see him better, but the other two held me into place.

"You'll be better lying still," Tony said soothingly. "You might have spinal injuries."

"Again?" I muttered. "Lucky, lucky me."

"What's she talking about?" Caleb asked Tony.

"Probably delirious," Tony replied.

"I'm not delirious," I argued, again trying to sit up. Being held down felt quite awful. "Tell him, Ali?"

"Mm, she thinks your name is Ali," the woman commented. "That's not a good sign."

"My character's name is Ali," Caleb quickly corrected. Then he leaned over me, his expression serious. "I'm going to leave you with Elizabeth and Tony, alright? They're going to look after you and the others, make sure that you're treated right. But I have to go now. Police things."

"Oh." But I hadn't got to show him the body-scan. I *needed* to show him the body-scan. "When will I see you again?"

He paused, frowning. Then he smiled, but there was no dimple. "I don't know. Soon, I hope."

"Are you lying to me again because you don't want me to cry?" Irritated, I tried once more to sit up, this time managing to knock aside the restraining arms. "Oh, for goodness sake. I'm not paralysed, alright? Not this time. And I'm not going to cry." I fumbled inside my pockets, finding the body-scan that I'd taken from the doctor and handing it to Caleb. "See this? This is me. And if you lot haven't found out already, that's the reason that Sinbad shot Jay and Dr Lindquist out in Amber Springs. And I'm not the only one built like this."

"Jay's been shot?" He wasn't even looking at the image. "Is he alright?"

In the most recent chaos I'd forgotten he didn't know. My mouth was suddenly dry. I hadn't liked Jay, but I hadn't hated him either, most of the time. And he and Caleb were cousins… I finally shook my head, turning away.

"I see." Caleb stared blankly down at the body-scan in his hand. "And this is why he was killed?"

"He didn't know," I said quietly. "I didn't either. We all thought I was just a cyborg, but that shows…that shows that I'm not. Neither is Tarquin, and I'd bet a fortune that none of the others here are either."

Caleb's eyes narrowed on the picture, and he turned it sideways. Then he looked at me again, then at the picture. "Valentina…"

He didn't get it. But Tony had looked over his shoulder, his hairy eyebrows lifting with interest. "Who's this then?"

"Me," I said. "From earlier today."

Caleb handed him the picture. Much like Caleb had, Tony stared at the picture for a long time, then finally up at me. "Elizabeth, come have a look at this. It's our friend Valentina."

The other medic came to stand beside him for a few moments, then shook her head. "Can't be. Look at those rib fractures, at that brainstem. That's an accident victim, not a cyborg."

"It's me!" I said more loudly. "Why doesn't anyone get that? Sinbad admitted it! They couldn't make cyborgs that were smart enough, so they started scavenging from the hospitals. Having weird eyes and programming and- and prosthetic *everything* doesn't make me a cyborg!" My voice quietened as I realised what an audience I had. "At least that's what the doctor said."

"Well," Elizabeth said briskly. "That'll put a new slant on things, if it's true."

"It *is* true!"

"Then it'll be easy enough to prove," Tony cut in. He turned to Caleb, holding out the body-scan. "And you, lad. It'll be worth the weeks of wearing costume if this comes out. You'll be promoted for sure."

But Caleb didn't take the image. His face was bone-white and shocked as it searched my features. "Ruby?" he whispered.

I wanted to claim that I was, to see joy overtake his face, but I couldn't. I couldn't claim a name that felt so foreign to me, even though intellectually I knew the truth. I shrugged helplessly. "Apparently. But I don't even know who that is."

Caleb turned and walked away. He didn't come back when the medics helped me into the ambulance along with several others, saying I needed to be kept an eye on. He didn't come back when they took us first to the police station's medic quarters to take blood samples and skin samples and more body-scans, and then took over eighty of us to a very isolated building on the outskirts of town. An old hospital facility – but one with high iron gates and security guards. For our safety, they said. I privately thought it was for the safety of everyone around us. Who knew what these poor, enhanced souls were capable of doing?

Then they confirmed beyond the shadow of a doubt that I was Ruby Anderson, and I set myself to waiting patiently. There was a lot happening, and he'd come eventually.

He had to.

Two months later

I squinted at my reflection in the worn mirror, head cocked to the side. The image was flecked with age from the mirror itself, but under that my skin was perfect and pale under the old-fashioned white light, my hair and eyes dark. My clothing a matching light blue shirt and trousers as issued by the facility. I looked like a completely different person.

I looked like Snow White – if she'd been admitted to a mental institution.

But then I opened my eyes fully and stood up straight, and the patches of mould under the mirror's surface moved so they were once again just mould instead of dark hair and irises. And once again I was gold-haired, green-eyed Valentina, although regrettably still wearing that ugly blue clothing. No makeup. No jewellery. Just enough hardware and cosmetic surgery to buy three houses. Although my contacts had faded a little; the colour was now dark green rather than light, unnaturally bright green.

"Step one once I'm out of here," I told myself. "Get some hair dye, *not* mould-brown."

It would seem like the first step in reclaiming my identity. I still didn't really know who Ruby Anderson was, but I remembered that from my first day; that my colouring in the mirror hadn't felt right. I'd been clumsy too, although that must have been getting used to the prosthetic legs. Of course as the days had passed, those matters had been the least of my troubles. But even at the start, even when I'd thought I was Valentina Redwell, desperate for a happily-ever-after with Kingsley White, I'd still had the hope that things could be better for me. That no matter what had happened in my past, my future was full of potential.

I'd come full circle, because now I felt exactly the same way. Except for the part about Kingsley, of course.

Then there was nothing else to do, so I left the communal bathroom, went through the swinging door and into the cafeteria. The hum of quiet conversation faded as everyone looked up at me. Young faces and a few old ones too, all grown familiar in these past few weeks. I nodded, then most of them turned back to their conversation.

But one man beamed up at me from his seat by the door, his handsome face not marred by his neat salt-and-pepper beard. Ralph Kingston AKA Kingsley White might have had his brains scrambled by the programming, but he still reacted to me the exact same way. "Good gracious," he said enthusiastically. "You're simply the most beautiful girl I've ever seen. I *must* know your name."

"Hi, Ralph. It's Valentina, remember?" I smiled at him with some affection, wryly aware that my hair colour wasn't the only thing I needed to update. The name, now that was harder. "We just spoke ten minutes ago."

"We did?"

I heard the door open behind me, and turned to see a middle-aged woman in the same blue clothing as we all wore, but with her face carefully made up, and a heavy necklace around her throat. A gift from her family, perhaps. "Melaina," I said cheerfully. "Come say hello to Ralph."

"You should be calling me Anne," the woman scolded, but she smiled at him nonetheless. Cindy's fake-stepmother was a lot kinder in person than who she'd been programmed to be on the island. "Good morning, Ralph. You're looking well today."

As I turned to walk away, I heard him reply. "Good gracious, you're simply the most beautiful woman I've ever seen. Have we met?"

I found myself smiling as I took my regular seat on the circle of worn couches by the large window. The view was mediocre – grey gravel, grass, trees by the high walls – and marred by the shatter-proof wire built into the glass, but it was still the best view in the building.

As I sat, an auburn-haired boy stood and quickly shuffled away to another seat, mumbling what might have been apologies. I raised an eyebrow, but didn't respond.

"Don't you mind Jeremy," Cindy told me firmly from her seat opposite. "He'll get over it sooner or later."

Jeremy Kricket. Cindy Rayla. Not everyone was as comfortable using their real names as Anne was. Not everyone *knew* their real names.

"He's probably just nervous being so close to a window when I'm nearby," I said wryly. "He really does think I'm the character, not the person." And while 'Jeremy' *had* shot me in the leg back on the island, I wasn't holding my breath for an apology.

Cindy wrinkled her unfreckled nose; most of the spotted pigment had eventually washed off without continual reapplication. I wasn't the only one whose appearance had been messed with. "Well, Snow White's stepmother *was* very wicked, and so were most of the other characters they'd have had you play. Fairytales are so violent."

Just then Daniel (formerly known as Charmant) came to sit down beside her, setting a plastic tray on the low table in front of them. Even in the facility garb he still looked like a model. The stubble that had grown on his lower jaw didn't detract from that – unlike many of us, his handsome face was actually his own. "Two coffees," he announced. "Sorry, no cinnamon latte, Val."

I was tempted to roll my eyes at his use of the nickname, but instead waved a hand dismissively. "I don't even like them that much. I never did."

But Cindy was beaming at him in much the same way Ralph Kingston had looked at me. "Fairytales are violent," she repeated, "except for ours."

Daniel smiled back at her, and I rolled my eyes in earnest.

"You two. You know it's all programming, right? You didn't *actually* fall in love at first sight, at the white-themed ball."

"It might have started off that way," Cindy corrected, "but it's not anymore. Right, Danny?"

He smiled again, taking her hand and kissing the knuckles. "I'm just glad we both turned out to be single, otherwise I would have had to break some other girl's heart."

Blech. "I'm just glad Ralph hasn't been permanently scarred by everything that happened to him," I cut in. "He might have the memory span of a goldfish, but he looks happy enough."

We all looked across to where Ralph sat in his comfortable chair, both hands on Anne's. She was blushing and smiling.

"He's bloody lucky," Daniel said more darkly. "If he ever regains his memory he'll be tried for embezzlement, even if not for kidnapping and assault like Carver, Sinbad and Karey will be. Assuming they ever get caught."

I studied Ralph a little longer, unable to see the villain in those smiling, guileless features. He'd been one of the first identified — after me, of course — and I still found it so hard to believe the part he'd played.

See, John Carver *hadn't* been innocent after all, as I'd wondered. He might have been in the background while Karey and Sinbad did the actual dirty work, but it turned out he'd known about everything they were doing. It wasn't clear if he also knew about how they'd tried to kill Jessie, his own niece, when she'd found out about the smuggling side of the business. Either way, he was in big, big trouble…if he was ever found. He'd gone missing from his beachside mansion the moment the story had broken, his bank accounts emptied.

But as for Ralph? It was all over the news how he'd once been Carver's business partner, and when everything had gone wrong he'd tried to take the money and run. But the others had caught him and had had him remade, his punishment to be the duped and murdered husband over and over and over… but they'd never found the money, hence the 'treasure hunts'. I liked to think it had all burned up in that last fire. It would only be fair.

"They'll get caught," I said. "Bad guys always lose in the end, right?"

Daniel scoffed. "In a perfect world, sure."

"Ooh!" Cindy squealed suddenly. "I just remembered what I wanted to tell you! The doctor has given me the OK to leave! I'm going tomorrow."

"That's fantastic news," I said warmly. I glanced at the man next to her still holding her hand. "Daniel, you don't look surprised. Or…upset."

He shrugged, eyes dipping away from mine. "She told me this morning. But I was OK'd to go last week. I was just waiting on her."

"Oh. That's…good." And that left me here without my only real friends. My heart sank. "Fifty-five down, twenty-one to go," I joked.

But Cindy and Daniel exchanged worried glances. "We didn't say anything earlier because we know how strict they've been with you," Cindy explained. "We didn't want you to feel…"

"Like I'll always be the embodiment of evil?" I forced a smile. "The programming is fading every day. Sooner or later they'll see that." Although I still felt compelled to check my appearance in every mirror or reflective surface. But who knew? Maybe I'd always been like that.

I distracted myself by straightening the tray where it sat crooked on the coffee table, and after a moment Cindy said brightly, "So, how did your video contact go this morning? You got to talk to your dad and brother, right?"

"It was…good. Confusing, but better than the last time, I think." I looked out towards the distant wall, picturing Geoff Anderson's bearded face, his smile, the way he'd looked at me with so much hope, but with that same caution that I too felt. Like Caleb, he was a familiar stranger. "He reminds me of Kingsley. No wonder I never wanted to marry him."

"Ew!"

"I know, right? But my brother…" I shook my head, smiling a little. "He's got a little daughter, and she's just the cutest. She's only a baby, so it doesn't matter that I don't recognise her. I wouldn't have anyway."

"But you still don't recognise them?" Daniel prompted. "Any of them?"

I shrugged again helplessly. "Not really."

"The doctors say the memories will come back more easily once you're in familiar surroundings," Cindy said authoritatively. "And not to put pressure on. You were reprogrammed twice in one week!"

"I could hardly forget." Cindy had got off much more lightly than I, her mind less damaged. She'd remembered almost everything, right up to her kidnapping. She'd been one of the models for the cyborgs, just like me, but unlike me she didn't have a convenient car accident. But after everything that had come out, after Jessie woke from her coma and Jay showed up with a bullet-shaped dent in his metal-plated skull and told the police *everything*, even my 'accident' was being investigated. We might be isolated here at the facility, but they didn't keep the news from us. The point was to integrate us back in society, not keep us caged. The twenty-one of us still remaining…we were the difficult ones, the ones who'd had trouble remembering our past selves.

And then there was me… the only one programmed to be a murderer. There'd been other villains planned, I'd learned, but they'd wanted to see how it worked with only one at first. So they'd set me to play multiple roles. I'd spent days poring over the stories as soon as we were allowed the internet – finding out who I'd been playing, what fantasies people were choosing to act out. My interest in the greenhouse tower, the way I'd been able to access multiple rooms and buildings? I didn't know for sure, but I suspected that the story of Rapunzel might have come into play at some point. Unless we found Karey, or found some more information, we'd never know.

But I did know that I'd been right at the beginning. Fairytales *were* stupid. Good didn't automatically win, and the hero didn't come sweeping in to save the misunderstood heroine. No, he left her alone in a secure facility along with the other broken dolls, because things were…confusing, and because perhaps she wasn't ready to see him either.

I stood abruptly, the couch screeching backwards with the sudden force. "I'm going for a walk."

I sat under one of the larger trees, my back against its broad trunk, my eyes closed and my hands resting on the square reader I'd taken from the common room. Memories flickered through my head unhindered; snatches rather than whole scenes. *A picnic with plastic cutlery. Silver spoon dipping into scarlet soup, like a bowl full of blood. Arguing with a dark-haired child, my own voice equally childish. Dabbing makeup around deep brown eyes. Pushing a handsome teenager off a cliff, full of fury…*

"That last one I know is fake," I murmured aloud, my eyes still closed. "The file says so."

Both files were loaded onto the reader. I'd read the Valentina file only once during my time here. *A story is only as good as its villain,* it began. *Ms Redwell's character was shaped very carefully: Beautiful. Determined. Selfish. Ruthless.*

Ugh. Once had been enough.

I'd read the Ruby Anderson file five times. I now knew that I was twenty, turning twenty-one this December. I knew about where I'd been born, where I'd grown up, who my family and friends were. How my mother had died of cancer when I was ten. I'd had a flicker of memory at reading that: a smiling, kind face; a coffin covered in daisies. But that too felt like reading a story, just like Valentina's.

I knew about how Ruby had answered Caleb's ad for a flatmate for the house he rented from his parents, how they'd liked each other from the start but he'd thought that she had been dating someone else, which had turned out to be a misconception. And then they'd started dating, and with very little drama, that had turned into an engagement. They'd been engaged barely four months when her car had skidded off an icy road in an unseasonably cold patch in spring.

A story, someone else's life.

I heard a faint cough. "You've been reading up on yourself, huh?"

My eyes shot open and there Caleb was, standing ten feet away from me with his hands in his pockets. He wore grey trousers and a white shirt, the shirt's insignia reading 'Heartlands PF'.

My heart flipped, and I took a moment before I could answer. "Of course I read the file. Valentina's and Ruby's both the first chance I got. What's with the suit?"

He looked down at himself. "They wouldn't let me come in if I was just the boyfriend, so I played the police card." He smiled, and the dimple winked into place. "Now I've been promoted to officer instead of trainee, and I've actually got a card to play. Although I think the head nurse just likes me."

Of course she did.

A few seconds ticked by, then Caleb said, "You never responded to my video requests."

I shrugged, unable to meet his eye. "Sorry. I wasn't feeling up to it." I had wanted him to come in person, but now he was here I didn't know what to say.

"But you were OK to talk to your family, even though you don't remember them?"

I shot him a glance, and he added, "Yes, the head nurse told me everything." He sighed, then came to sit beside me on the grass. "It's strange that on Sweetheart Island you kept seeking me out. You knew me, even if you didn't know why. You even asked if it was possible you'd been switched with the real Valentina cyborg. You asked me to take you away. And now you don't want to see me."

"But I do," I said quietly. I glanced up at him. He was watching my face intently, and I knew he was seeing what I'd just seen in the mirror. Ruby, yet not Ruby. I looked away. "I'll admit I'm annoyed at the way you didn't even *try* to make contact for a good three weeks, and perhaps even at the things that happened on Sweetheart, but that's not really why I kept turning down those requests."

"I was being a coward in those first few weeks," Caleb

admitted bitterly. "And feeling guilty because of how I let you down so many times. I stared at you right in the face and didn't know you. I left you to get reprogrammed." He shrugged, shaking his head. "I understand if that's why you've kept me away. But if that's *not* it, then why?"

"Because you want Ruby! She's the one you love. And because even after everything, I still feel like Valentina." I glanced at him sidelong, feeling my cheeks heat. "I know that's the name they gave me, but if I try to use the other one, it feels like playing even more of a role. I'm too different now. No one else had as much reprogramming as I did, and I might never be what I was before." I sighed. "I'll let you down. Even when I dye my hair and my contacts fade, I can't change my eyebrows or my nose or my teeth to what they were before. More importantly, I might never change back on the inside." I did hope for the best, really I did, and I was going to make the best choices that I could. But I also had to be realistic.

Caleb was silent for a long time. Then, "I'm different too. My family, my friends, they all say that I'm more serious, angrier. Withdrawn. Focussed on work."

I studied him in surprise. "Then you must have been the life of the party before. You always seem so friendly to me."

"Do I?" He grinned crookedly. "Maybe it was just seeing you. Or maybe you're so grumpy that I seemed friendly in comparison."

Had he been joking? Suddenly I wanted to cry. "Maybe that's the programming. Ruby's – my file says that I was well-liked, but I'm definitely not that now. I'm not very friendly, Caleb. I don't know how to be."

Now he laughed. A real laugh, and I stared at him in shock. "What's so funny about that?"

"Because you said the exact same thing to me *before* the accident," he answered, still smiling. "Forget the programming. You're *not* unfriendly, but you're just reserved. Reserved, and well-liked."

"Oh." I found myself smiling back. "That's good news. Perhaps my personality hasn't changed that much after all."

"I don't think your personality has changed much at all. Just your memory."

My smile faltered. And there was the problem. How could I fit back into a life I couldn't remember?

"And," Caleb continued, "the doctor was saying this morning how far you've come. Your memory blanks have almost gone, and your behaviour has been very settled. They were saying that once you get back to a normal environment, perhaps even back to studying, you'll remember."

"Does that mean they're letting me out!?"

"Of course! You're under observation, not in prison. Especially now Jessie's woken up and testified that you had never harmed her, and that Sinbad and Karey forced her to take that poison that almost killed her because she'd found out what they were up to. The doctor said it could be as soon as this Saturday."

Three days away. I found myself suddenly short of breath. "No one told *me* that."

"Then maybe I get to give the good news. But Valentina… Ruby…" He set his hand on my arm. "Do you *want* to come back to live with me? Your room is still there, although most of your clothes are in storage, but if you weren't comfortable then you could go to your dad. He does live on the other side of the country, but-"

"As normal as possible," I cut in, hope and anxiety twisting my stomach. I distracted myself by turning the reader over and over in my hands, then finally set it on the grass, perfectly square in front of me. "Back to your place. If you want me."

Caleb was staring at the reader where I'd lain it in the grass. "Oh yes. Very much so."

Three days later I was sitting in the passenger seat of Caleb's car, beginning the long drive to his home. I was wearing some clothes he'd brought me: a loose T-shirt and comfortable black trousers. Very casual, and nothing like Valentina's usual clothing. Unlike our other meetings, this one felt stilted. We made careful small talk until finally Caleb switched on the car's built-in viewer where it sat between us.

"I'll set it on auto-drive," he said. "Let's catch up on the news."

LATEST ON THE SWEETHEART SAGA! the viewer screen screamed. *MASTERMINDS STILL ON THE RUN!*

Caleb glanced at me warily. "Do you want to watch this?"

"Yes, please. It's the main way I've been getting information."

A beautiful brunette appeared onscreen and began enthusiastically talking about the drama of human recycling, about the people who'd gone home, and about the island itself. The White Hotel hadn't been destroyed in the fire, I was disappointed to see, but apart from that there was nothing new. "You can turn it off if you want," I said after a while. "It's all the same stuff anyway."

"Were you waiting for something in particular?"

I shrugged. "Various things. Like, what happened to the android servers on the island. Rhonda the receptionist, or Jorge, for example. I know he's not a real person, but he felt real to me."

"Jorge? He's been impounded with the other androids, until we've got whatever information we need from them. After that, I suppose they'll be reprogrammed and sold off to pay debts." Caleb studied my face. "We could bid for him, if you like. Because you're used to him."

I considered it briefly. "I think not. I'll always look at him and think of…broomstick rifles and dead men. It doesn't make any difference to him, anyway."

"True enough," Caleb agreed. "Was there anything else you wanted to know?"

"Well… I wanted to see if Karey or Sinbad had been caught. I heard that John Carver is somewhere in South America, but still on the run too, and I still haven't heard from Tarquin. I wondered if one day he'd show up in an interview like Jessie did, but I haven't seen him."

"Sorry. I haven't heard anything. But speaking of interviews, did you know I've had over two dozen requests to show up on camera? I can't, of course, since I'm an officer." This last was said with some pride. "But you could if you wanted."

"No one's asked me."

He shot me a sidelong glance. "Then the doctors were keeping the requests away. *Everyone's* asked for you, especially after Jessie did her segment."

That one hadn't been entirely complimentary of me, but it had ended on a good note. "Oh."

"Some of the stations are offering big money," he continued. "It could pay for your study, if you don't mind doing an interview."

"Oh," I said again. It'd be like finding treasure on Sweetheart Island after all, but I'd have to give up the ugly details of my ordeal. "I'm not sure if I'm ready for that."

"That's OK. There's no pressure."

But there *was* pressure, and it didn't come from interview requests. It came from the gap between my real life and my fake one.

"There was one other thing I wanted to know," I said carefully. "Back on my first day, there was a sound like an explosion. They said it was a car backfiring, but I didn't know what that meant. I figured with everything..."

"They were probably lying about that too?" Caleb finished. "It's a reasonable question, but backfiring is just something very old cars do sometimes." He shrugged, smiling wryly. "Plenty of old cars on Sweetheart Island, you might have noticed."

"Oh." I was almost disappointed. I'd thought it was something that Karey and the evil masterminds had done, but perhaps not. Sometimes things *did* have reasonable explanations...and sometimes they turned out to be exactly as nefarious as you'd suspected. Take my clumsiness on that first day, when I'd almost knocked myself out on the marble steps while walking down to Kingsley's car. That had been because I was walking on fake legs, not that I'd known it at the time. The doctors had told me that was from my body becoming accustomed to my prosthetics, and that it wasn't at all unusual.

We sat in silence a little longer, and up in front of me the signed release slip sat in its envelope on the dashboard, shifting from the vibration of the vehicle. I absentmindedly reached up to straighten it until it lined up with the edge of the dash.

"Do you do that a lot?"

"Do what?"

"Straighten things like that."

I frowned, thinking about it. "Honestly, I have no idea. I barely even noticed I was doing it. Does it bother you?"

He let out a bark of laughter. "It drives me mad, but at the same time I'm so, so glad to see you doing it."

"Pardon?"

"Ruby always did that," he explained, and there was a small smile on his face. "When I saw you do it back at the facility I realised that there was still some Ruby in you, somewhere. More than just that mole they decided to leave on your face."

"It's a beauty mark," I said automatically. I slid my eyes across to look at him. "Do you not like it?"

"*Ruby* didn't like it," Caleb replied, his gaze flickering down to the mark in question. "She always talked about getting it removed, but I didn't want her to. I told her it was interesting." He paused. "I told you it was interesting."

I reached up to touch it again, then embarrassed, turned my attention back to the car. The envelope was now perfectly aligned with the dash, and then the car moved and it slid very slightly to one side. I itched to reach out again and straighten it, but I could tell he was watching me. A few long seconds ticked by as the envelope grew more and more crooked, and then I finally reached out and picked it up, tossing it in the back seat. "Drives you mad?" I muttered to myself. "Drives me mad, more like."

Caleb laughed again, and this time it was genuine. I smiled back, feeling warmer inside. I didn't know what the future held, but I hoped that in some way, this guy would be in it.

Caleb's house was at the edge of the city where it turned into suburbia, a smallish pale brick house set in a slightly neglected garden. He saw me staring at it and explained wryly, "Neither of us were really into gardening, but you'd always make more of an effort than me. Part of your neat personality, I supposed."

And when I'd gone it had fallen into disrepair. But who cared? Grass grew whether you cut it or not.

Inside was comfortable although not luxurious, and it was a bit of a shock compared to the suite at the White Hotel and even my small room at the facility. That had been sparsely decorated and although worn, perfectly neat. Familiar? Maybe.

Caleb gestured towards a worn couch with an ancient crocheted rug thrown over it. "Sit, if you want to. I'll go find us something to eat."

He left the room before I had a chance to decline so I just wandered the room, studying its contents. Beside a few well-worn pieces of furniture, there were one or two paintings and several scattered photographs. I could see Caleb in different stages of life accompanied by people who looked to be his parents, then another boy who seemed almost a carbon copy, presumably his brother.

There were also several images of some girl, pretty and pale-skinned with dark hair and dark brown eyes. It took a while to realise she was Ruby. Jay had been right; she wasn't as pretty as I was. Her eyebrows were a little lower and straighter, and her nose had the slightest bump to it. The mole looked less prominent with her dark hair.

But Caleb had been right too: she *wasn't* smiling in every picture. Good.

Caleb came back out with an apologetic expression. "Sorry, I didn't realise how empty the fridge was until I got home. I've placed an order, but it won't be here for an hour or two. Until then, do you want coffee?"

"Coffee is fine, as long as there's milk."

"Sorry, no milk."

"Oh. In that case, maybe one sugar?" I didn't like black coffee much, but I was thirsty. Besides, it seemed rude not to take anything. "What did Ruby drink?"

"Tea," he replied succinctly.

Well la-de-dah for her. I followed him into the kitchen, which looked rather more Spartan than I was used to. There was no stove to be seen, just a series of cupboards. "Hold on, did you say that you placed an order for groceries?"

"Yes, through the in-home system." He tapped on a seemingly ordinary cupboard door, and it lit up to reveal a screen. There was a series of food items listed there, as well as cleanser, and for some reason, socks. "Do you not remember this?"

I shook my head. I'd never needed to buy my own groceries on Sweetheart, and I didn't remember what I'd done before that.

"Well, if you need something, you can order it through there. Just remember we do have a weekly budget." He listed a small figure that made my eyebrows raise. I also hadn't had to think about the cost of things on Sweetheart.

Perhaps after he'd gone I'd look up the cost of an at-home hair dye, I mused. As long as it was cheap...

We drank in relative silence, and I realised that I really, *really* didn't like black coffee, although I did my very best to hide that. I got about halfway through the mug when Caleb said, "You don't have to drink that if you don't want to."

"It's fine," I replied politely.

He raised an eyebrow. "Your face suggested otherwise. Go on, toss it. There'll be more to drink soon enough."

I gave in, tossing the rest of the cup down the drain. "How could you tell? I thought I had a great poker face."

"Ah..." Another half-smile, then, "Your left eye twitches when you're lying."

"What?"

"It really does," he insisted. "Always has, and it's just the barest thing, but I do notice."

"Oh." I felt rather taken back, and a little annoyed. Was I so transparent? Perhaps only to him. "Well, I can tell when you're lying too. You're a terrible liar."

"Oh really? And what's my giveaway?"

"I'm not going to tell you," I said archly. "Else you'll stop doing it, and then I won't know." It was the pause, followed by the smile that didn't reach his eyes. Not exactly hard to work out.

Caleb just looked at me, and I felt a little foolish. It had been intended as a sort of joke, not that he had seemed to understand that. "Any chance I could have a shower?" I asked.

He stood abruptly. "Sure, I'll show you where it is. I have to…ah, go out." He paused, a fake smile on his face. "When the drone arrives with the groceries you'll need to sign. Just make sure you use the right name."

Ruby Anderson, not Valentina whatever. "Sure."

"Oh, and one more thing." He held up a small black and silver pistol. "This lives behind the toaster. Tap the top to switch on the green light," he demonstrated, "…and then you've got about six shots before the power dies."

"I won't need that," I said in dismay. "I'm in suburbia."

"Humour me. I've lost you once. I won't risk doing so again."

Warm pleasure spread through me, and I nodded. A picture flashed through my head – James Redwell and a rifle. "Caleb… did you teach me how to shoot?"

His eyes widened. "You came with me to the rifle range once. You remember that?"

I nodded again, smiling. "I do. I always did."

He smiled back. "Great. That's just great."

He still left, but we both seemed in better spirits after that. I showered, then spent some time wandering around the house, poking into cupboards and studying bookshelves. Perhaps I felt a twinge of recognition at some things, but it was hard to tell. It could have just been wishful thinking.

The doorbell sounded, and I went to answer it. But when I opened the door there was a girl there along with the box of groceries; fair-haired and pretty with a white-toothed smile. Kind of like Valentina if she'd been real and a bit older. "We've had a few issues with the drones," she said brightly. "You'll need to sign manually. Is Caleb Desmond there?"

"He's out, but I'm his…flatmate. I can sign."

"Great." She handed me a small black disk with a stylus attached. "Just scribble your name here, and I'll get the box inside the house. Where do you want it unloaded?"

It was on a hover-carrier, I realised. "Anywhere's fine, thanks." I stepped back to allow her inside, then carefully wrote my name on the disk. Ruby's name. I handed it back just as the box was mechanically unloaded on the floor.

The girl studied it for a moment, then frowned. "Ruby Anderson. I'm sorry, our records say you're deceased..." She looked up at me and her pale eyes widened. "Ohmygosh! You're the girl from Sweetheart Island! The evil stepmother!"

"Um..."

"You look *so* much younger in person," she gushed. "Without all that makeup and those fancy dresses. But don't worry about the order. I'll confirm it manually and get our records updated. Hey, I *so* admire what you did out there. Like, with escaping and hauling those androids out of a window – I heard you almost died!"

"Thanks," I said stiffly, taken back. "But they weren't all androids. Some of them were like me."

She waved a hand dismissively. "Yeah, sure. Hey, can I take a selfie? I *so* want to show the girls that I met you. It would be *amazing*."

The door slid shut behind her, and I stepped back a little. "No pictures please. But I can sign something, if you like."

"Oh. OK, why not?" The girl patted her pockets, then shrugged. "You got a pen and paper? We can do this the old-fashioned way."

I would have agreed to backflip over the couch if she'd just leave. "Sure. I'll go find one." I turned towards the kitchen bench where the stationery was stacked messily beside the appliances. There had to be a pen in there somewhere...

"And I heard that there's an amazing treasure hidden on the island," she chattered on behind me. "That Ralph Kingston – the one who got turned into Snow White's dad – hid it somewhere, just waiting to be found and make someone rich."

I finally found a pencil and a suitable piece of paper, only half-listening. "Hmm. OK."

"Where is it?"

I paused halfway through scrawling 'Anderson'. Her voice… it was familiar. I turned slowly to see the girl was now holding a gun in both hands.

It was pointed at my chest.

15 Triumphant

'She didn't see that coming, the idiot.'
— from an overheard conversation with K.W

"Where is the treasure, Valentina?" the girl said again. Her voice was no longer perky. No, it was cold and angry and so so familiar. "I know you know where it is."

I turned, my hands half-raised, with my pencil clutched in my fingers. I hadn't seen this coming. Not at all. "I have no idea what you're talking about."

"Don't give me that!" she snapped. "We found the map, but when we got to the location it was gone. We've got video of you in that hidden room with that idiot Tarquin, and we saw you coming out with something under your jacket. What did you do with it?"

I stared at her, at her classically attractive features now twisted in anger; at her curvy figure under that plain uniform, and finally I made the connection. "Karey?"

"Yes, Karey!" she snapped, rolling her eyes. "I would have thought you out of everyone would understand the difference clothing and colouring make. And you're about to have a hole in your head if you don't talk."

Uh oh. The toaster was so close. The weapon hidden behind it. *Distract her.* "But…is that *really* you?" I said again, my tone incredulous. "You look so different, so *young*. You look like…"

"Like you?" Karey's smile was mocking on her much younger face. "The fairest of them all was based on *me*. My colouring, my

254

figure. You've even got my fingerprints, almost. But then when it failed I was hardly going to reprogram myself, was I? You were supposed to be the generic heroine. But then we didn't need her after all… and I liked the idea of being the one to kill Ralph over and over. He was my fiancé, did you know that? And he robbed us, and he left us." She bared her teeth in what might have been a smile. "Or he tried to."

"I'm sorry." About the abandonment, anyway. It was clear that even someone like Karey could still be hurt. But I had her *hands* rather than Ruby's…? It would explain why I'd been able to access the same places she had.

"Don't be sorry. Just tell me where the treasure is."

"I don't know where it is. I swear it," I replied urgently. "I didn't even think there *was* real treasure. If you've read the map, then you're a step ahead of me. I never really looked at it."

I just needed her to look away, just for a moment. The toaster was so close…

Her lips tightened.

"I have a question," I blurted out. "What were the flashing lights on the island?"

She looked at me like I was crazy. "Morse code, of course. To say the shipments had arrived. Now where's the treasure?"

"I don't *know*…"

Just then there was a faint knock at the door, and I brightened. Caleb! But then Karey went to the door and tapped it open, and in came Dane Sinbad. His glasses were gone and he wore a low cap, but I recognised him immediately.

"You were taking too long," he said. "What's the problem?"

"She says she doesn't know where it is!"

Sinbad stared at me across the room. "Then she's not any use to us alive, is she?"

I shuddered, taking a chance to step backwards. Closer to the toaster. "Caleb will be coming home any time. You'll be caught."

"We know whose house this is," Sinbad said coolly. "And if you won't give us the treasure, then we'll have our pound of flesh instead." He glanced towards Karey. "What do you think, sister?"

Karey smiled, a wide, toothy smile, and for the first time I saw the resemblance between the two. And not to be rude, but she got all the looks in the family. "Black widow strikes again? Brilliant idea."

My hand closed over the cold handle of the weapon. I felt around for the on-switch, pressed it. A faint green glow showed in the reflected wall.

"I see what you're doing!" Karey snapped. "Drop that!"

No.

As if in slow motion I saw myself swing that black and silver weapon out to face the two of them. Karey pulled the trigger as I did. Something exploded behind me, and in a flash of white light her gun went flying from her hand. She screamed.

"We've been here before, haven't we Sinbad?" I asked, my heart pounding. "You know my aim is perfect."

He didn't answer.

"Don't hurt us," Karey begged.

She betrayed us. And really, there was no choice.

I pulled the trigger, and white light filled the air.

Five more shots, and my aim *was* perfect. They wouldn't be getting up again.

Suddenly I was exhausted. I stumbled back to lean against a dining room chair, dropping the weapon on the floor.

Just then the door opened. Caleb stepped inside, a square parcel tucked under one arm and his key in the other hand. His gaze lit on the bodies on the floor between us, and he froze. "What happened!?"

"I found the bad guys, as you see. They were going to kill me since I didn't know where the treasure was. But don't worry, I don't think they're dead."

"I wouldn't care if they were," he muttered, eyes wide. He quickly put down the parcel on the floor, then pulled out a similar black and silver weapon. He stepped closer to the fallen blonde figure, prodding her with one foot. "Who's this?"

"It's Karey Godmother, or whatever her real name is. She looks different, doesn't she?"

"I'll say."

Just then I saw Sinbad's hand reach out very slowly towards Karey's gun, lying at a distance where she'd dropped it. "Look out!" I cried, and Caleb moved faster than I'd seen him move: swinging his weapon towards the fallen man. There was a series of flashes and Sinbad jolted and fell still.

"He's enhanced," I said, ending on a sob. "I guess stunners don't work so well on him."

Caleb was staring down at Sinbad with a malevolence I'd never thought to see on his face. He still pointed his stunner towards them, the green light on. "Shame I'm a cop now," he said conversationally. "Otherwise I'd kick him in the face. Ruby, will you go to the draw beneath the toaster and get my restraints? There should be some rope in there too."

I moved to get them and he called the police. The other police, anyway. Then we hogtied Sinbad and Karey, shoved them into the corner of the room, and held the two remaining weapons on them. Caleb moved closer beside me, putting his spare arm around my shoulders, and I realised I'd been shaking. "Don't be scared," he said. "I'm not going to let you go. Not this time."

I didn't answer, but I leaned into his embrace. The shaking stopped.

Then the police arrived and took the two away. They stayed to talk with Caleb for a bit, to take my statement, but Caleb didn't move his arm from around my shoulders. Then they finally left us alone, and I slumped down again on that worn couch with a squeak of ancient springs. I felt exhausted, like I'd aged twenty years, and I commented on that to Caleb where he was messing around in the kitchen.

"It's the adrenaline wearing off," he said. "Now I've got something for you."

"As long as it's not black coffee," I replied tiredly. "Or an engagement ring."

The last part had been a joke – sort of – but when Caleb came into the room he wasn't smiling. He was carrying a square box, the sort with a lid you could lift off, and he set it down in front of me. "I already gave you a ring," he replied soberly, "and I don't recall ever breaking off our original engagement, do you?" I stared at him wide-eyed, and his mouth curved into a slight smile that didn't reach his eyes. "It was right before the accident, and for your information, you said yes." I still didn't answer, and he added, "I will renew the request when Valentina loves me as much as Ruby did."

I bit my lip, my eyes lowering. "Valentina is a confused cyborg," I replied quietly, "and Ruby is still out of reach. But I think it would be very easy to love you. The question is if you still want me, when I'm so…broken."

The mood had gone very quickly from light to serious. And I knew that Caleb was dead serious when he sat down beside me and took my hands in his. "You're not broken. Just cracked a little, and who isn't? I never stopped wanting you. Not when I thought you were dead. Not when you were a confused cyborg with gold hair and scary green eyes. And I definitely want you now, when things finally seem fixable."

My eyes pricked with tears. That could just be the adrenaline wearing off, but it sounded like the most romantic thing anyone had ever said to me. Better than fairest of them all, that was for sure. "Oh. Good."

"Yes, it is, isn't it?" He smiled again, and this time his eyes crinkled with warmth. "Now are you going to open this box? I've had it checked over at the centre, and I think you're going to like it."

I opened it, of course. Inside was the pair of tacky glass slippers, wrapped with packaging paper and seeming even gaudier in this setting. I laughed aloud. "Where did this come from?"

"Keep looking," he urged.

Underneath the shoes was a thin, square grey plate. When I touched it the screen came to life, showing a head and shoulder image of Tarquin Prince. But he looked different from when I'd last seen him. Younger, his hair messier. Happier.

The recorded Tarquin gave me an awkward wave. *Hi, Ruby.*

"This is incredible," I gasped, and tears pricked my eyes

again. "When did you get this?"

"Three days ago, but we had to check it was safe. Now shush, and listen."

I shushed.

'I've been watching your story on the news, and I'm so glad that you and the others are OK, that you got away from the island. I was also really glad that Dr Lindquist didn't die, because I really thought she would.'

Yeah, I'd thought that too. But then sometimes things did go right – and that had been one of them.

'I wanted you to know that I'm OK too,' the recording continued. *'I'm with my family. Jake helped me to find them, but I didn't want anyone else to find out what had happened to me because I'm still trying to forget it myself.'* Recorded-Tarquin's lips tightened, and I wondered if he was thinking of some of the darker things he'd done, or almost done.

'My real name is Ezra Bell, and I'm only sixteen years old. I went into hospital for an operation to replace my kidney and they said I died on the operating table, although of course I didn't. I was taken and remade like you, but I had only been missing four months. I think I can fit back into my old life eventually, and I hope you can as well. Maybe one day I'll come and visit and we can talk about Sweetheart Island, but not yet.' He paused, holding up the same shoes that even now sat in my lap. *'And I thought you'd want these. Break them, wear them, I don't know. Um… that's all. Bye.'*

The square faded to grey again. "Wow," I said. "Just…wow." Tarquin – Ezra – was alive. He was OK, and he'd found his family too. Forget the shoes; *that* was a happy ending. Or maybe not yet an ending, but a happy beginning.

"And there's one more thing in the box," Caleb told me. "You missed it."

I looked inside, and there was something small and blocky with a long handle. "What's this?"

"It's a mallet," he said proudly. "Designed to increase your natural strength so that you don't have to work too hard when smashing things." He nodded down at the shiny shoes on the table. "So…?"

I broke into a smile. "Let's do it!"

Clunk. The enhanced mallet came down heavily on the glass slipper for the second time, but just like before, the tacky gems refused to break.

"Seriously?" I exclaimed, feeling both annoyed and amused. "What are these things made of, diamond?"

I'd meant it as a joke, but Caleb didn't laugh it off. He put down the device he'd been using to record my attempted smashing, then came over to pick up the slipper with a frown on his face. "Wouldn't that be interesting."

"Oh, come on," I scoffed. "Look at them. Some of the gems are as big as my thumbnail. If they *were* diamond, then they'd be worth…"

"Billions?" Caleb met my eyes with his brown ones, showing a glint of excitement that I was beginning to feel as well.

"Don't you get my hopes up," I told him.

"I wouldn't dare. I just think we should have these checked before we go smashing them. Even if they're only cubic zirconia, they might be worth something."

So we had them checked at the local jewellers. And yes, they *were* diamonds. Natural diamonds, some of them, interspersed with a few big gaudy artificial ones to hide the treasure in plain sight. And yes, they were worth something. Quite a few somethings.

"Karey was right," I said in disbelief. "I *did* steal the treasure."

"Well, I can't believe it was in a pair of shoes," Caleb said again. His face was split in a wide grin, just like it had been since they'd told us. "*Shoes.* Who hides billions worth of jewels on *shoes?*"

"Someone running a fantasy-themed resort?" I suggested. It looked like Ralph Kingston hadn't *always* been a rather silly man. "I hope it gets back to Karey and Sinbad in jail."

"Oh, it will," Caleb assured me, still staring at the sparkling shoes with almost bugging eyes. "I bet this makes world news. Wait for it."

"I bet it all goes to taxes and creditors." I paused. "We still have to pay taxes, right?"

He laughed. "Yes, we still have to pay taxes. But surely you'd get some of it as compensation. You and the other survivors. Who knows, we might be able to go on holiday with this. Buy a new house. Pay for your studies."

"Buy a new couch?" I suggested. But in truth, whatever happened, I didn't care. I already had the most valuable thing in life right here with me.

Hint: it wasn't the shoes.

Almost The End

Dear Reader,

Caution: contains spoilers

I hope you enjoyed *Breaking the Glass Slipper*. I had a lot of fun writing it, and as always, the original idea came from a series of dreams. Back in 2012, I dreamed that I was Snow White's evil stepmother. In the dream I had pure white skin, red lips and very fake-looking gold hair, I was wandering around a large modern building rather like a hotel, and I was feeling guilty and confused over my past crimes. I also couldn't shake the thought that 'I should have been Snow White'.

Oh yes. The scene where Valentina walks past Sinbad, Hercules, Jake/Aladdin, and Jafeer was also from the same dream, right down to the odd names of the characters.

The story has gone through quite a few incarnations since, with extra effort spent making Valentina more likable in the first half of the book. Did I succeed? That's up to you to decide. Her name also used to be Teresa, but then I met an actual Teresa, and it felt weird.

Breaking the Glass Slipper is currently a standalone novel, but I've got ideas for a sequel that would show Valentina/Ruby getting back into real life and making use of her new strength and speed. It would also finish off the stories of Jake/Aladdin, Tarquin/Ezra, Jafeer/Jay, and of course the slightly evil John Carver, who in this book escaped justice. I could even see if Kingsley/Ralph Kingston gets his memory back…

Anyway, for up-to-date info please see my website **mmarinanbooks.com**.

Across time and space...and right into trouble.

Ash, George and Anne are unlikely companions, not least because they were born five hundred years apart. Taken from their own times for unknown purposes, they must find out where they are, how they got there, and more importantly, how to get away. The answers lie in the nearby village of Iversley, which hides a very BIG secret…

THE ETERNITY STONE

ACROSS TIME & SPACE BOOK 1

EXCERPT

The grounds of Renwick Castle, Iversley, Angland, 1556 AD

"My lady? My lady, where are you?" The maidservant's call echoed through the thicket edging the castle grounds, but Anne just pressed herself deeper into the greenery, sucking in her breath as though that would change the bell shape of her skirts, or make her unusual colouring somehow blend in better with the trees. She had no patience for Maura's ministrations, no matter how kindly meant. It had been that kind of morning.

"My lady!" The woman was starting to sound a bit frantic, and Anne pushed back a pang of guilt. Just because she was miserable didn't mean that she should share that misery with others. After all, 'twas only a marriage, and she a grown

265

woman of sixteen. A widow, even (the Eternal One rest poor Wilbert's soul) and she should be meek and obedient and accept the Queen's will that she marry yet another stranger, and not take it out on the servant who'd she'd known since childhood-

"Wicked, red-headed wretch," Maura muttered as she stomped by, fists curled and shoulders hunched with irritation. "Going to the garderobe indeed! 'Twas naught but an excuse for mischief, and when I get my hands on you, Anne of Covington, you'll be sorry you ever ran from me…"

But Anne was not at all sorry, and didn't intend to be found until she was good and ready. More so now she'd heard the woman's last words, which weren't at all as respectful as they ought to be. Maura had served Anne's own mother since childhood and then followed Anne to Renwick Castle upon her (ill-fated) marriage two years earlier, but usually guarded her mouth. Yet here, when Maura thought herself unheard, she spoke her true thoughts.

Rude, Anne thought. Red hair had naught to do with bad behaviour. She had *decided* to behave badly quite independently of her hair colour. As if in agreement, an orangey-red lock slipped out of her coif and into her mouth, and she shoved it back inside the cloth in annoyance, waiting for the woman's muttering to fade into silence as she finally gave up and headed back into the castle.

"Saints' eyeballs," Anne muttered at Maura's retreating figure. "One hour to think, 'twas all I wanted. You'd think I tried to run off with the gypsies, for all the fuss you made."

Sir Robert had given her the news of her new betrothal just one hour past, and she'd tried to take it well, she truly had. But then she'd had the sudden urge to be violently ill. She'd told Maura and the assembled others that she needed a moment of privacy, but when she'd arrived at the garderobe she'd found what she *really* wanted was some peace and quiet. True, these woods that bordered the castle might be filled with ghosts, fair folk and even a few bandits, but today she'd risk the bandits.

By the Rood, all she needed was one single, solitary hour of peace…

Mountbatten Manor, Iversley, Angland, 1818 AD

"Star's a fine mount, Mr Seymour," the stable boy said. "Steady, fast. But she gets spooked by squirrels."

George raised an eyebrow. "Squirrels in particular, or any small, furry creature?"

"Only squirrels, sir. She'll be fine with anythin' else, but if you see a squirrel, 'old onto your seat." He looked concerned. "I kin' change the saddle if you don't mind waitin', it's just the only other mount available is ten years old and we usually use 'er for teaching children."

So basically George had the choice between an ancient and incredibly slow horse, or one that was likely to try to throw him if they came across a squirrel suddenly. Not a rabbit, not a cat, just a squirrel. "I'll risk the squirrel," he said firmly. "I expect to be back within a couple of hours."

As promised, Star was a fine mount. Lively and obedient, and with no squirrels in sight, George rode her over the fields that bordered his neighbour's manor, heading for the woods. These were large grounds, and they also bordered George's own family estate.

Well, not *his*, his older brother's. As the second son of the late Viscount Morley, George was in line to inherit precisely nothing, not even a title – he was only an Honourable Mister. He was, however, free to go into the army, the navy, or possibly even the church…just not the occupation he'd chosen for himself. Before the Proserpine sank and took his savings and his self-respect along with it, that was. There was a reason that he was here at a neighbour's estate, borrowing a horse, rather than at his own home with his own mount.

It was a long, depressing story ending in the events of just a few months before, and one he didn't want to think about now.

"And I won't even think about Clarissa," he said aloud, but then realised that he was thinking of her right at that moment. By Jupiter, it had been over two years, he should have forgotten about it by now. She was off happily married to her solicitor in Cairnwall, and he didn't care about her. Truly.

Damn it.

Suddenly feeling very black again, George dug in his heels and set Star into a gallop past the ruins of the old castle that had sat between the two estates for a hundred and fifty years. He would see exactly how lively the horse was – barring any squirrels, of course.

❧❦❧

"Overseas adventure my ass," Ash muttered, pulling her well-used Cortina off to the side of the rutted country road. The sign by the small car park read, *scenic walk: 30 minutes return.* "I could have stayed at home for all the adventure I've had."

Home was the Southern Isles aka the Colonies; which like Angland were small, green and rainy, and where nineteen year old Ash O'Reilly had worked in administration. She'd set off for the other side of the world to have a grand adventure (since everyone else seemed to be doing the same thing), but so far, it seemed to be more of the same. Everyone just had a different accent.

To be fair, it might have been some of the choices she'd made coming over. She didn't like busy cities or high rents, so instead of moving to Lunden as most would, she'd gone for the more unusual option of renting a cottage in the small town of Whiteside, Leister County. She'd found a basic admin/secretary job in nearby Little Brimley, which paid just enough for her to rent her tiny two bedroom cottage. The landlord was a friend of her mother's who'd moved over twenty years ago, and they gave her a great price. Still, it wasn't enough to save for those European trips she'd imagined.

Generic, low paying job, tiny house, no solid friendships in the three months she'd been here…and now the highlight of her week; a quick walk around the 'forest' off this country road.

Her mother was right, Ash realised in dismay. It *wasn't* what she'd expected. And when she'd imagined the amazing things that adulthood would bring – this wasn't one of them. As of this moment, the most exciting thing she had to look forward to was last night's reheated lasagne.

"I need to be more spontaneous," she told herself. "Mix it up a little." Maybe she could think about getting a flatmate. She could afford the rent – just – but there was a spare room, and she could probably do with the company.

But she was still going for that walk. Although the air held the chill of early spring, this was the first day of sunshine in a week, and she wouldn't waste it. Locking her car, she set her warm woollen cap over her messy dark hair, zipped up her plain jacket, and set off.

The sign had promised a scenic thirty minute return walk, but two hours later, Ash was lost. Somehow the dirt path had disappeared without her even noticing – she'd stumbled over her own feet, then when she'd picked herself up she'd been lightheaded and didn't recognize a thing. She had tried retracing her steps, then retracing the retrace when that didn't work; and it didn't make sense, because the area wasn't even very big…

Ha, she could write a book when she got home, and call it 'How to get lost in a mile of forest; a guide'. That'd be a real money spinner, but she'd have to actually get home first. To add insult to injury, the walk hadn't even been that scenic. Angland was flat and boring compared to home, and Leister

County no exception. Green grass, brown mud…trees, and more trees.

Except…

Ash paused, looking around her with a frown. She still felt a little lightheaded from her earlier stumble, and it was long enough past her dinner that she felt very cranky, but the surrounding trees didn't look at all familiar. They were more jungle-ish than the forest she was used to. And now she was walking up a hill – that *certainly* hadn't been there before.

Oh, Deias. She was so lost.

After checking a large rock for bugs, Ash sat on it with her head in her hands. A small bird watched her from a nearby tree. She hadn't seen one like that before around here; it seemed far too bright for this part of the country with its pine green feathers, crested head and red chest. *A festively themed bird,* she thought, although it was the wrong time of year for it. The newly-named festive bird cocked its head to the side and stared at her with what she imagined was a smirk.

Ash glared at the bird, but it just kept staring with those beady black eyes as though there was something interesting to see. She waved a hand at it, but it didn't move, clearly aware of who had the upper hand. Hint: not her. She sighed; her mood must be foul if it felt like even the animals were against her today. "Don't you know staring is rude?"

"My apologies," the bird replied in a distinctly Anglish voice. "I thought perhaps you could direct me to Iversley?"

Ash jumped in surprise, almost falling off her rock. Behind her stood a boy in his late teens, to whom the voice had presumably belonged. About her age or a little older, he was fair-haired, slightly rumpled, and dressed like an extra for a Jean Austen film.

He smiled at her ruefully. "I didn't mean to startle you. I was thrown off my horse, and the blasted beast bolted. Squirrels, you know."

"Squirrels?"

"The horse," the boy explained. "She's easily started by

squirrels. But never mind that – I've lost my bearings, and the day is short. Would you be so good as to tell me in which direction I might find Iversley?"

He looked sane enough – more so considering he'd actually asked her for directions – but then so did plenty of serial killers. Ash stood, carefully taking a step back. "I don't know where that is, sorry. Is it a street name?"

He frowned. "No, it's the village near here, with the manor of the same name. It should be very close. I hadn't ridden for more than twenty minutes when I was thrown."

Deias, his voice was as posh as one of those films too, Ash thought. And what did he mean by manor? Was he playing a game? "There's no manor or village around here that I know of. The nearest town is Whiteside, and that's a fifteen minute drive north." She paused, debating how much to say, then added, "Perhaps you can help me, though. I came from the main road for a walk, but I've wandered off the path myself. Do you know which way that is? Or even where the road is? Then I can walk back to my car."

There was a long pause where the boy looked confused and irritated – perhaps those heavy eyebrows added to the impression of grouchiness – and then he said again, very slowly and clearly as if she was stupid; "Iversley. It's the village nearest here, just ten miles east of Markfield. Do you know where it is?"

"No...I...don't," Ash replied just as slowly. "Do...you... know...where...the...main...road...is? Or any road at all! I'll get a taxi."

He looked as disgruntled as she felt. "Ber'lody foreigners. Not making any sense at all."

"At least I'm not dressed like an escapee from a period drama," she snapped. "What are you, an actor?"

Mr Posh's jaw dropped, making an excellent impression of a stunned mullet. "You're a bold lad, to speak to your betters so," he snapped back. "What's your name?"

Lad? *Betters*? "None of your business," Ash retorted,

getting to her feet and backing away slowly. She carefully reached into the pocket of her bulky autumn jacket, feeling for her miniature can of pepper spray – just in case. "Now if you'll excuse me, Mr Darcy, I'm going back to my car." Wherever that might be.

But he stepped closer, now looking furious. "My name is not Darcy, and I do *not* excuse you. Whatever your game is-" And then he made the mistake of grabbing her arm.

Ash shot him full in the face with the pepper spray. He screamed, bent double and held his hands to his burning eyes. She didn't wait to see how well it worked. She ran.

The Eternity Stone is available
in print and ebook.
Go to **mmarinanbooks.com**
for retailer information.

www.ingramcontent.com/pod-product-compliance
Lightning Source LLC
Chambersburg PA
CBHW021112110726

47900CB00007B/2158